GRACE HOUSE

GRACE
HOUSE

LEE KAMMINGA

**REFORMED
FREE PUBLISHING
ASSOCIATION**
Jenison, Michigan

Reformed Free Publishing Association
1894 Georgetown Center Drive
Jenison, MI 49428
www.rfpa.org
mail@rfpa.org

Cover design by Kathleen DeJong
Interior design by Katherine Lloyd / theDESKonline.com

ISBN: 979-8-9871614-1-8
Ebook ISBN: 979-8-9871614-2-5
LCCN: 2025941223

To the home and children I love in India,
the PR Writers' Group,
my dear wife and three little blessings;
without whom this book would not be.

A NOTE TO THE READERS

This story is a work of fiction, yet it draws heavily on real events and circumstances based on personal interviews with foster children and social workers, as well as books and documentaries on social ills in India. None of the characters in this book are based on a single person or story; rather, I've woven multiple true accounts and fictional plot elements into a single narrative to foster a more intimate, personal connection to the struggles these children endure.

—*Lee Kamminga*

Warning:
*This book covers mature themes including abuse,
self-harm, and suicide.*

CHAPTER 1

"Kashvi, there goes Vishnu!" Asha giggled, watching the skinny older boy with bushy eyebrows. She picked up the ragged football she'd patched up from a dump. "You'll probably marry him someday."

I slapped her arm and glared at her, but a smile tugged at my lips.

My best friend and I sat in the shade of a coconut palm behind the make-shift goalposts in the dusty, open square. The boy, Vishnu, and my *thambi*, Sudhir, played football there against other boys from our village. They wouldn't let us girls play, so we entertained ourselves with Asha's patchwork ball on the outskirts.

Asha played with the jasmine flowers she'd woven into the looped braids of her dark hair. The calming jasmine scent mixed with the smoke of trash fires. She flashed her crooked teeth. "*I* wouldn't mind marrying him."

I groaned and pulled my faded turquoise shawl over my head, covering my flushed cheeks. But I peeked out just enough to watch Vishnu. He tore down the dirt field with the ball in our direction, clouds of dust trailing.

I probably will marry him one day, I thought to myself.

At twelve years old, I was the closest female cousin in age to his fourteen. As cousins, we were of the same *caste*, and only a little *dowry* would be required, so it was expected of me. Still, my cheeks grew warm whenever Asha brought it up. He was a handsome boy, after all.

Vishnu's agile legs carried him past all the other boys except one, who ran up alongside him to steal the ball. I could see Sudhir eyeing this last opponent between Vishnu and the goal, his eyebrows drawn together in that fierce furrow I knew too well. He slammed into the boy, and they both collapsed into the dirt.

Free from challengers, Vishnu sent the ball sailing past the goal-keeper's hands into the top corner of the palm goalposts.

I burst into a cheer. Asha giggled at me and joined in.

Vishnu grinned at us, flashing his cute dimples, sweat glistening in the midday sun. He wiped his face with his shirt as he caught his breath. The other boys gathered around him, cheering.

Behind him, a cloud of dust rose from Sudhir and the boy he had tackled. My scrappy ten-year-old *thambi* pinned the older boy to the ground.

Sudhir shoved his face into the dirt. "Say it!" he shouted. "Say you give up!"

The squirming boy mumbled some words, and Sudhir finally got up. With a triumphant smile, he ran up to Vishnu and the other boys, while his shamed opponent stumbled away.

"Where's the ball?" Sudhir panted, breathless.

"It rolled way over by the temple, I think." Asha pointed towards the ornate building beyond the palm goal.

"Can you go find it, Sudhir?" Vishnu asked.

"Why should I? We're the winners," Sudhir whined.

"I'll go find it," Asha gushed. "You can use my ball for now."

Sudhir curled his lip. "I'm not going to use a girl's ball."

Vishnu shook his head. "Grow up, Sudhir, it's fine."

I liked when he talked to my *thambi* like that.

Asha handed her ball to Vishnu, and I felt a sting of jealousy. "I'll get your ball!" I said, leaping towards the temple. I could hear Asha running after me, her plastic bangles clinking on her wrists. I grasped at my baggy *chudidhar* pants.

The rare wind shifted, and I choked in the thick smoky air mixed with earthen-sweet incense. The smell of the incense drew my eyes up towards the temple. Dozens of freakish gods watched me eerily with wild eyes, smiling.

Help me be the first to find the ball, I prayed to them. But they never seemed to care about me.

Behind the temple, Asha and I searched through thick brambles for the prized ball.

"Ahh!"

I heard Asha's chilling scream and scrambled towards her, confused. She writhed in the sunbaked dirt, clutching her ankle. Her face was twisted in agony.

Then I saw it. I stumbled back as my eye caught a glimpse of a gold-striped cobra slithering away, scales glistening as it passed the football and headed towards the temple. Terror washed over me.

Turning back to Asha and pulling her hand from her ankle, I saw two red stains marring her yellow pants. I rolled her pant leg up and found two harmless looking pinpricks...but I knew how serious they were. The venom was death.

"Help!" I screamed towards the boys.

Sudhir looked at me briefly, but his focus remained on his game with Asha's ball. When I screamed again, Vishnu came running.

"Amma!" Asha whimpered repeatedly.

I grasped Vishnu by the arm. "A cobra bit her! Get Asha's *amma*!"

His face paled, and he turned and ran.

"Your *amma* will be here soon. Everything will be fine." I squeezed Asha's hand. The tremor in my voice betrayed my lie.

I looked up at the gods atop the temple. Their once-bright colors had faded into muted pastels from the relentless sun. Their mocking eyes and smirks seemed amused by our suffering.

Help her! I prayed. *Save her!*

The temple shaded me from the sun, but it didn't feel refreshing; it felt dark. Beads of sweat poured off Asha's face. A puddle of vomit soaked into the parched dirt beside her braids. Finally, I heard the panicked voices of Asha's parents.

Asha's mother ran to her daughter and cradled her head in her hands. "My dear!" her voice cracked. "We need to take her to a hospital."

Asha's stricken *appa* took her in his arms, and we followed him around the front of the temple.

A raspy voice sounded from behind, "What's going on?"

The temple priest glided towards us from the front gate. The dark skin of his chest contrasted with the bright orange *lungi* draped around his waist. White ash was smeared across his forehead.

"She was bitten by a cobra," Asha's *appa* breathed out. "We're going to hospital."

"Don't you trust the gods?" The priest stroked the tip of the beard that hung down past his bare chest. "Bring her into the temple."

Asha's *appa* glanced at his wife with doubting eyes, but he followed the priest anyways. Asha's mother, Vishnu, and I trailed behind them.

My foot caught on something and I nearly tripped, but Vishnu caught my arm and held me up. I looked back and saw the golden bowl I had tipped over, spilling milk across the ground. My heart pounded. Milk was offered by the priest to lure the holy snakes in. I searched the ground around me. *Where has the cobra gone?*

I kept my eyes on the ground as we entered the shadowy, candlelit temple, watching for the snake. Asha's *appa* laid his daughter down on the floor in the corner where the priest had stopped.

The priest pulled a burlap sack off Dhanvantari, a blue-skinned god standing on a pedestal with four outstretched hands. I eyed the hand with the pot representing healing. Half of the pot was cracked off—broken for as long as I could remember. I prayed many times for my own healing when I was sick, but I never recovered immediately; maybe the gods were testing my faith. *Can they heal Asha immediately?*

"It is a great curse to be bitten by a snake. You or she has done something grave to bring such an evil." The priest waved a smoking stick of incense before Dhanvantari's nose. "Call out to him for mercy."

Shadowed figures of the gods danced on the walls in the candlelight as Asha's *appa* and *amma* dropped to the floor and wailed, slamming their foreheads on the ground.

"Please heal her!" I cried, joining in. *Don't let my only friend die.*

I repeated the same plea over and over. The smell of sweat, incense, and fear hung thickly in the air as I gasped for breath.

Asha groaned on the floor in front of me. I peeked up at her with hope. Her sickly face was covered in sweat. My stomach retched in fear, and I felt Vishnu's hand on my shoulder. I turned to him and saw a crowd of villagers joining us in the temple.

Asha's labored breathing turned into a horrid rattling. She turned to look at her *appa*, her *amma*, and finally me with lips trembling, then she couldn't keep her eyes open any longer.

Tears flooded out of my eyes, and I pounded my forehead on the concrete floor, thinking the more pain I felt, the more of a chance I had that one of the gods would grant my request. I had to show that I believed.

"Save her!" I pleaded. "Please, save her!"

"She needs to go to the hospital," Asha's mother cried, tugging on her husband's shirt. The blood of her effort dripped down from her forehead.

Asha's *appa* nodded, and he scooped his daughter's limp body up in his arms. Her chest was still heaving. She was still alive.

Asha's *appa* pushed his way through the crowd, all of whom had all fallen prostrate. As people realized what was happening, their groans and cries began to die away. The room fell silent, and the rest of the crowd parted to let Asha's *appa* and *amma* out.

As they approached the door, the priest called out snidely, "This is why the gods aren't answering." Asha's *appa* faced the priest, who pushed himself to his feet and slithered up to him. "You have no faith. If you take her away, she will die."

What about my faith? I thought. *I believe Asha can be healed. Does my faith not count?*

Asha's *appa* slumped down where he was, weeping. The room echoed again with chanting cries for healing.

I squirmed through the people to get up next to Asha as she lay in her *appa*'s arms. Her chest wasn't moving anymore. I shook her body. "Asha!"

Asha's *appa* pushed me back and looked down at her, then put his fingers to her neck, checking for a pulse. A moment later, he let out a blood-curdling scream.

Deafening cries reverberated through the cement walls of the temple. The chants for healing changed to chants for resurrection.

The priest crept through the people back over to the god of healing. "He has answered."

The room went quiet again, and everyone faced the priest.

"Now it is time for him to sleep." The priest grabbed the burlap sack from the floor and pulled it over Dhanvantari. He licked his fingers and began extinguishing the candles.

The weeping began again, but this time there were no chants for resurrection—just tears. Everyone shuffled outside as the room grew darker with every candle extinguished. There was no god to call out to anymore. No more hope. Just darkness.

The setting sun turned the sky a deep blood-red hue. The crowd gathered around Asha's parents, weeping with them.

"I didn't have faith! It's all my fault!" Asha's *amma* wailed over and over as she tore at her wiry hair.

My uncle Arjun—Vishnu's *appa*—stepped out of the crowd and put his hand on the shoulder of Asha's mourning *appa*. Uncle Arjun was as reliable as the turban wrapped around his head; our village knew to expect him at a time like this.

"Leave us." Asha's *appa* jerked away from my uncle. His eyes were glassy and hollow. He turned to his wife. "Come!"

Asha's *amma* followed, and we all watched them stumble down the path towards their empty home.

Behind us, a metal chain clinked across the cement floor of the temple as the priest dragged it behind him like a snake. The rusty gate of the temple screeched as he closed it, wrapped the chain around it, and locked it with a padlock.

A group of boys walked up from behind the temple. Sudhir was leading the group with a smile on his face. He stopped and looked around at all the somber, crying faces. "What's going on?"

"Asha's dead." My lips trembled, and I clenched my fists.

Sudhir stood with his mouth agape in shock and confusion.

I shoved him to the ground. "Do you even care? I called you for help, and you just kept playing." My whole body shook, and I fell to my knees and beat my head on the gravel.

Someone grabbed my shoulders and rolled me onto my back. It was Uncle Arjun. Vishnu stood beside him.

"Don't do this in front of the people, Kashvi." Uncle rested his calloused hand on my shoulder, but his touch wasn't calming to me like it seemed to be to others.

"Kashvi!" I heard my mother's voice.

I turned to see the person I loved most in the world hurrying towards me in her constrictive *sari*. Her eye was swollen, courtesy of my *appa*. The blues and purples around her eye matched her sari. I threw my arms around her. Tears squeezed through the swollen eye and dripped down her sun-spotted cheeks.

"Asha's dead," I croaked in a hoarse voice.

Amma pulled me tightly to herself and ran her fingers through my hair. "I heard, my dear. I'm so sorry."

"She was my best friend," I wailed. "She was just here playing with me."

"I know." *Amma* wiped the tears from my eyes with her shawl before wiping her own.

We sat in silence under the light of a flickering bulb outside the temple. I scowled at Sudhir as he crawled to the other side of our *amma*, using her as a shield between us. Uncle and Vishnu sat down beside us too.

I looked around; it seemed like the whole village had gathered here—except *Appa*. He was probably at home with a bottle in his hand.

Vishnu rolled his football back and forth on the ground between his hands.

Asha's ball… The sudden reminder overwhelmed me. *That's all that's left of my best friend. I need that ball.*

I craned my head around my *amma* to look at Sudhir. "Where's Asha's football?"

Sudhir looked down guiltily. "In the field…somewhere."

I shook my head at him in disgust. "Well, go get it."

"It's dark," Sudhir protested. "And what if that snake is still around?"

"*Now* you care?" I crawled over Amma to smack him.

"Stop fighting!" Amma pulled me back. "I'll get the ball."

"No!" I grabbed her arm. "What if the snake *is* back there?"

"I'll get it." Vishnu jumped up and ran off to the field before anyone could object.

I gritted my teeth at Sudhir. "If you weren't so lazy and had just gotten the ball yourself, this never would have happened! It's your fault she's dead!"

"Then I would've been bit!" Sudhir whined.

"Better you than her!" I shouted.

Sudhir's stunned face caused a twinge of regret to interrupt my anger.

"Kashvi," Uncle Arjun interrupted firmly, "this is not to be blamed on anyone here. This is the will of the gods."

"He's right, Kashvi." Amma gently rubbed my back. "Anger won't bring Asha back."

Vishnu ran back and handed me Asha's ragged ball.

"Thank you." I hugged the ball to my chest. Then I turned to Sudhir. "You better never touch this ball again!"

"Kashvi, enough!" Amma scolded. "You can keep the ball tonight, but you'll need to ask Asha's parents if they want it. We need to get home now. You know how *Appa* gets."

I nodded reluctantly, and we headed into the darkness for home, leaving the sleeping gods locked up in the temple behind us.

CHAPTER 2

Flames shot up from Asha's palm-shack home. I sprinted to it. Through choking smoke pouring out of the doorway, I saw Asha and both of her parents lying on a pyre engulfed in flames.

"They had no faith," a raspy voice hissed behind me.

I whipped my head around and came face-to-face with the temple priest. The flames were reflected in his eyes as he twirled the key to the temple between his fingers.

"Help!" Asha's voice cried through the flames.

I braced myself to run in and save her, but my appa *appeared at my side and held me back. I fought against him, trying to break free as I watched the flames consume Asha and her parents...*

I awoke in a panic, guarding my face reflexively as *Appa* tossed and mumbled in his sleep next to me. His mouth hung open, still wheezing out the sick scent of alcohol. The chill of the dirt floor stole my warmth through my tattered tunic and the straw mat beneath me.

It was just a nightmare, but part of it was true. I hugged Asha's football to my chest. My *amma* had suggested that I bring the ball back to her parents, so I went there three days ago. But all I had found was an ash pile. Their neighbors said the house had started burning in the middle of the night.

Asha's parents had set up a pyre inside their home and burned themselves on it beside their daughter.

I shuddered, the image of Asha crying out from the flames seared into my mind. Rubbing the crust of sleep from my eyes, I let go of the ball, pushed myself up, and stepped over Sudhir sprawled out next to me.

A ray of morning light shined through a rusted hole in our door. The light rested perfectly on our brass Kali god, who was perched on her shelf across the room. Her tongue wagged at me, and I trembled at her skirt of severed arms and her necklace of skulls.

My *appa* had stumbled upon her in a dump pile years ago. It was the only valuable thing in our house. He said Kali would protect us from evil forces, but only if we were truly devoted to her.

Maybe Asha's death is somehow my fault. Kali is the goddess of death; did I upset her in some way?

I didn't understand, and *Amma* didn't want to talk about Asha, her parents, or any of the surrounding circumstances. When I had told her about what happened with Asha's parents, she just nodded her head, stared at the ground, and never said a word.

But right now, I had more immediate concerns before me: the new school year.

I grabbed my blue and white checkered dress uniform from the shelf under Kali and shook the dust off it. Some students would get a new uniform every year, but we couldn't afford that. I squeezed into the same one I'd had for the past two years. Two raggedy *chudidhars* were left on the shelf, the tunics faded and a bit too small, and the elastic of the baggy, tapered pants all stretched out.

That was my entire wardrobe.

Creeping to the door, I eased it open. It squeaked, and terror gripped me as my *appa* groaned. I slid through and closed it as quietly as I could.

I breathed a sigh of relief, taking in the fresh morning air not yet tainted by the trash burning that would soon begin.

A thick-billed crow landed in front of me and ruffled its feathers

10

before scanning the area. Its gleaming eyes looked straight at me. It cawed before eating away at the carcass of a gray dove nearby.

"Good morning, Kashvi." *Amma's* voice startled me as she walked up from behind our house. The crow flew away, alarmed by the interruption. *Amma* saw it, and her face fell.

A bad omen to start the day. How could my life get any worse?

Amma kicked at an empty water bucket. "Help me refill the water," she murmured, weary before the day had even started.

"I need to relieve myself first." I grabbed the plastic cup lying in the water bucket and poured the last drips of water from the bucket into it.

Amma adjusted her *sari* around her midriff. "I'll go with you."

The cracked dirt felt cool under my feet, though it would soon be baked by the blistering June sun. We passed the gnarled, lifeless tree behind our home. Ever since Asha had been bitten, it seemed to me like a coiling cobra, poised to strike. A frayed rope dangled from one of the branches.

I'd seen my grandfather dangling from that rope. It was the earliest memory I could recall. I hadn't really understood what death was back then...but I knew now. After my grandfather died, my grandmother was driven out of our village. Just like crows, widows were bad omens.

Amma often told me that *Appa* was never the same since that day when Grandfather died.

"Why did Asha die?" I asked *Amma*.

She sighed. "I don't know. We are all part of the cycle of death and rebirth. Asha's soul has gone on to a new existence, hopefully a better one."

"But I want her here! Was it my fault? Did I not have faith?" I sniffled. "We were all praying for her; why wasn't she healed?"

"I'm sorry, Kashvi." *Amma* cradled my wet cheek. "I don't have all the answers. We accept our karmic fate and do good in the roles the gods have given; otherwise, there will be trouble."

How can I do better when I never know if the gods are pleased with me or not? The question burned in my mind, but I bit my tongue.

I hid behind some thick bushes as I relieved myself, then used the last of our water to wash with. We walked back home in gloomy silence.

Once we had returned, we each grabbed a water bucket and trod down the dirt path through the village. Every step kicked up dust, wearing the path down deeper. I wondered how long the path had been there, how long our village had been there. No one I knew seemed to know the history; it was as if it had always existed this way and always would.

"Why didn't the priest want Asha to go to the hospital?" I asked warily. "I remember reading about snakes in a textbook, and it said there is this anti-venom that hospitals have that can heal snake bites."

Amma's eyes narrowed in frustration. "I don't know."

"If it is all up to the gods to heal us," I probed, "why do we even have hospitals?"

Mother rubbed her forehead. "All these questions are not good, Kashvi. We cannot fight our fate. This is how society maintains order and balance."

Karma. *Fate. Order. Balance.* It always came back to that.

"Yuck!" I pinched my nose as an acrid scent assaulted me. Rotting cow placentas hung from the dangling vertical roots of a nearby *banyan* tree. Farmers had tied them there, as it was said to make their cows produce more milk.

Do the placentas matter if the farmers don't have faith? Some gods require sacrifices, others don't. So many rules for all the different gods, and nothing I do ever makes the gods give me what I ask for. Nothing ever goes right in my life. Why should I even try?

"What about Asha's parents? Why did they—"

"Enough questions, Kashvi," *Amma* scolded.

But her agitation didn't quell my unrest. "Were they hoping for rebirth to a better life?"

Amma stopped abruptly and looked at me with a piercing gaze. "No! There are no shortcuts to a better life!"

I shrunk away. Her tone sounded almost like *Appa* in that moment.

The bitterness in her voice made me wonder if she had once considered the very same escape as Asha's parents.

She regained her composure before speaking again in a quiet, trembling voice: "It may seem like there are shortcuts, but they all lead to a worse end. We can't take control of our lives and expect anything good to come of it. We must accept where the gods have placed us and do good. That is all we can do."

She turned her face from me to hide her tears and started walking again with hurried steps.

I followed in silence. *Amma's* tears assured me that her anger was not at me but at her own fate, which she couldn't change.

A group of women bickered around the short brick wall of the well ahead of us. The well was four meters wide and plunged down fifteen meters. The scraping of metal buckets echoed from the bricks of the well floor.

Amma pushed her way over to a woman who had just finished filling her bucket, tossing the metal bucket back into the well. *Amma* grabbed the rope before anyone else could and pulled it up, dragging the bucket across the thin layer of water at the bottom, then up the side.

The shallow water filled the bucket only halfway. She emptied the water into her plastic bucket, then threw the metal bucket back down and pulled up another half-bucket. By the third time, women who had lined up behind us began shouting. The next nearest well was about an hour walk and might not have water either.

Amma dumped the third haul into my plastic bucket and shoved the well bucket at an angry woman behind us. She then hoisted her bucket onto her head, resting it on her plaid head scarf.

"Mine's only half full," I protested.

"Pick it up," she snapped.

"But I can get another—"

"We're leaving."

I struggled to lift the bucket onto my head and keep it steady. As I turned to leave, I bumped a woman with my elbow.

She scowled. "You don't need two!" Then she pulled at the bucket on my head. Half of the precious water spilled out over me as I backed away, clutching my bucket. I ran after my *amma*, soaked and in tears.

"What's happened?" *Amma* frowned, looking over my drenched clothes.

I explained through soft sobs.

"I told you to hurry!" she scolded. "This is what happens when you ask too many questions and don't obey."

I bit my lip. It wasn't fair. Nothing was fair.

Neither of us spoke the rest of the way home.

My *appa* stood beside the house and stared at the cursed tree, a *beedi* hanging beneath his bushy, graying mustache. Sudhir was kicking around a football.

Asha's football.

"Sudhir, I told you never to touch that ball!" My blood boiled. The boy who didn't want to play with a girl's ball, who ignored my calls for help when Asha was bitten—now he was playing with it just to spite me.

Sudhir's face twisted into a mischievous grin, and he kicked the ball as hard as he could. It soared up over our house and out of sight.

Seething, I chased after Sudhir and hurled my bucket at him without thinking. It collided with his back and spilled the remaining water. We watched as the thirsty ground drank it all.

"Kashvi!" *Amma* shouted incredulously. "The water—"

"Get over here!" *Appa*'s voice thundered.

Sudhir and I froze, and my heart began to pound in my chest like a drum.

"I said *now!*" *Appa* screamed. We approached him, trembling.

Afraid to meet my *appa*'s piercing gaze, I stared at his stained toenails. *Smack!*

Appa slapped Sudhir across the face. Sudhir held his red glowing cheek, and his lips scrunched up. He ran into the house, trying to conceal his cries. He knew *Appa* would hit him again if he saw him crying. Boys weren't supposed to cry.

My *amma* stood by the door with her hand over mouth. She knew if she stepped in, she would only make things worse.

"He took my—" I tried defending myself with a quivering voice.

"Get the ball." *Appa* pointed his finger behind the house.

A knot tightened in my stomach. *What would he do with it?*

I stomped off behind the house and stopped in front of the twisted tree. The ball rested against the trunk. I was told never to touch or even go near the tree. It was cursed.

Is the ball cursed now? Will I be cursed if I touch the ball?

I crept towards it, and the hair on my arms stood up.

Could the curse be worse than coming back to Appa without the ball?

I grabbed the ball quickly, making sure not to touch the part that had touched the tree, and returned.

Appa ripped the ball away, touching the cursed spot. "If you can't play with this without fighting, then you don't get to have it."

My thoughts flashed to Asha dying on the temple floor. That ball was all I had left to remember her. I knew I couldn't let him take it away.

"No!" I grabbed the ball back without thinking and hugged it to my chest.

For a brief moment, *Appa* looked stunned. No one ever fought back against him. But his shock quickly twisted into rage, and he sprung at me.

Amma shrieked, knowing what was about to happen.

Smack!

Appa slapped the side of my chin as I turned away, sending a stinging pain through my jaw. I stumbled but stayed on my feet, still clutching the ball.

Amma ran up beside me, pleading, "Kashvi, give *Appa* the ball. Please."

I always give in, and the beatings still happen, I thought. *What if I don't give in?*

I took a deep breath and stared defiantly into *Appa's* fiery eyes.

Appa leapt at the ball. I twisted away and ran. He quickly caught up and shoved me forward, knocking me off my feet and sending me headfirst into the brick corner of our house.

Blood dripped down my nose onto my blue and white school dress— my only one. I touched my forehead and felt a warm, wet gash.

"What did you do?!" *Amma* screamed at *Appa*. She never talked to him that way.

"It was her own fault," *Appa* spat, scratching under his white turban. He grabbed a matchbox and *beedi* from the pocket of his faded plaid shirt. He struck a match, lit his *beedi*, and blew out a puff of smoke.

The football rested in my lap, stained with my blood. I tried to hold back the tears to show *Appa* I was strong, but the tears poured out, and I kept my gaze from *Appa*'s eyes.

Appa walked to his scooter and mounted it. I gave a quick glance at him before he left. His fierce eyes told me this wasn't over. He started the scooter and sped off down the dirt path to work.

I hurt, but something in me glowed with the feeling of power. I had won, at least for now.

Amma ran over and knelt beside me.

"Let me see it." She pulled my hand away from my forehead, and I winced in pain. "I'll be back in a minute, keep pressure on it."

I rested my throbbing head against our house, closing my eyes against the piercing sunlight. Hearing *Amma* return, I squinted to see her holding a small jar of turmeric paste and scraps of cloth. I closed my eyes just as quickly as I opened them. She wiped the blood away with a cloth, then tilted my head back and rubbed the turmeric paste into the gash. I ground my teeth at the pain.

She pressed a scrap of Sudhir's old shirt firmly over the wound. Eyes still closed, I sat back, biting my lip and trying not to focus on the pain. After a couple of minutes, she inspected the bleeding before tying the stained shirt cloth in place with another scrap.

Amma sank down, melting against me with a sigh. Her body sagged; her worn spirit weighed on me.

It's my fault she's so weary.

Sudhir crept out of hiding and stared, wide-eyed.

I glared at him, burning with anger. *No, it's all Sudhir's fault.*

"Kashvi," *Amma* sighed, "you need to learn to obey, and you need to stop fighting with Sudhir."

"But *Amma*, he—"

"It doesn't matter if he started it," she interrupted. "You are older than him. You need to take care of him. You know the consequences. You need to watch out for each other. Someday..." She trailed off.

Someday, what? I wondered, but she didn't continue.

"I'm sorry, *Amma*, it's just—"

"No, no, no! Stop the excuses!" She took a long breath. "Promise me: no more fighting, especially when *Appa* is around."

"I promise." I sighed. *Why am I the only one getting this lecture? It was Sudhir's fault.*

"How does your head feel now?" *Amma's* voice was so drained.

"Not so good." Remembering the first day of sixth grade ahead of me, I asked in a pitiful voice. "I don't have to go to school today, do I?"

I wondered what school would be like without Asha. I caressed her ball as my head pounded. She had been my only friend.

"Usually, Sudhir's the one trying to skip school." *Amma* gave a fleeting smile. "You don't have to go today."

How long has it been since I've seen her smile? I wondered. It almost seemed worth the gash to see that flicker of light on her face.

Amma looked up. "Sudhir, get ready for school."

"But—" Sudhir protested.

"No arguments. I need to catch the bus," *Amma* said, knowing she couldn't afford to miss a day of work. "Stay inside today, okay?" she said to me as she pushed herself to her feet, then offered me her hand.

I grabbed it and pulled myself up. "Okay."

Inside the house, Sudhir knelt before Kali to say his morning prayer. The waistband of his shorts, held together by a rusted safety pin, struggled to meet the bottom of his shirt.

I hadn't said my morning prayer yet. *Is that why my morning went so badly? Or was it for asking too many questions? For fighting with Sudhir? For rebelling against Appa?*

Sudhir grabbed his school bag and stuck his tongue out at me as he walked past.

Raising my hand, I stopped short, remembering my promise. I growled at him as he slipped out.

Sudhir would go one way to school. *Amma* would go the other way to catch a bus to the fields, where the sun would roast her bent-over body as she tended crops. But she never complained. Just like she never complained about *Appa*'s beatings. It was all part of her karmic fate.

There are no shortcuts to a better life! *Amma*'s words rang in my mind. I sank to my knees before the little Kali god. With my hands palm to palm in the namaste position, I prayed that my *appa* wouldn't drink today and that he wouldn't beat my *amma* or me today. I didn't pray that for Sudhir—he deserved a beating right now.

Could my good karma *ever outweigh the bad?* I thought, as I was supposed to be praying. *What difference does anything I do make?* I tried to fight off the thoughts, afraid Kali or some other being could hear them.

A small bowl near Kali held black powder. I dipped my finger to place a *bindi* on my forehead, but then I remembered the bandage there. I wiped the powder away, further dirtying my blood-stained dress.

Does it matter if I wear a bindi if I can't please the gods anyway? The doubts gnawed at me again. *How can I ever know what I'm supposed to do when I can't question anything?*

My stomach groaned. In the chaos of the morning, *Amma* hadn't made breakfast. I grabbed a handful of uncooked rice from the bag in the corner. It was the only food we had in the house aside from a few spices. Breakfast was usually plain rice or rice porridge. Supper was rice with a vegetable or two that *Amma* would buy on the way home.

I surveyed the tiny space where *Amma* asked me to stay all day. One room made up the entirety of our home. It felt like a prison. I doubted whether my decision to skip school was a good one, but going to school without Asha terrified me.

I'll work in a field like my amma *someday,* I thought. *What good is school for that anyways?*

Then I sighed. *What am I going to do in here all day?*

Stay inside. My *amma's* voice echoed in my head.

I looked outside, then down at Asha's football under my arm. Appa won't let this go, I thought. *He'll get the ball back from me.*

I shrugged off *Amma's* command to stay in the house and wandered behind it. The cursed, twisted tree loomed in front of me.

Appa won't dare go near that.

I circled the tree and found a nest of gnarled branches. If anyone was looking from the house, the ball would be hidden from view here.

Is it really cursed? I wondered. *Appa and I both touched the football after it touched the tree.* My fingers gently grazed the wound on my forehead. *If this was the curse, it was nothing out of the ordinary for me. My whole life is a curse.*

I lodged the ball between the branches, feeling a mix of defiance and fear.

CHAPTER 3

Kali glared at me as I knelt before her for my morning prayer the next day. She brought nothing but trouble into my life. Though I knelt before her, I didn't pray to her this time. There were so many gods—millions, I'd heard. Each had their own stories and powers, so surely one could help me get through the day, maybe even find a new friend at school.

I sent out my prayer to *anyone* who would listen and help.

Instantly, I panicked. *Will Kali send bad luck for not being devoted to her? Can any other gods even hear me if I'm not kneeling before them?*

Outside, the birds sang. As I opened the door, I prayed I wouldn't see another crow cawing. Yesterday had proved they really were a bad omen. Thankfully, the rest of yesterday had been quiet, but I remained tense, wondering when *Appa's* revenge would come.

I filled a bucket of water, set it on top of the school uniform resting on my head, and headed behind the house towards the tiny palm shack.

As I rounded the corner, I eyed the cursed tree. No one had found Asha's football yet. *Appa* never asked about it, but Sudhir had. He probably thought I was hiding it in the women's field. My foot caught on something, and I stumbled forward, spilling water over myself.

Sudhir laughed. He had tried to trip me.

"Are you *trying* to split my head open again?" I pointed at the cloth around my forehead.

Sudhir flashed his tongue. "You started it!"

"*Appa!*" I yelled.

Sudhir's amused expression dropped and he ran away.

Feeling victorious, I headed towards the women's field, but my smile faded as I remembered the conversation with my *amma* the day before. I had already broken my promise to her about not fighting with Sudhir… again.

I'm sorry, Amma.

Glancing around, I scanned the area to make sure no men were lurking around. I ducked past the tattered *sari* being reused as a curtain for the tiny palm shack. I removed my dress, stepped into the large empty basin that filled the floor space, and prepared to bathe.

Sighing as I thought again of the upcoming school day, I emptied a bucket over my head. Warm water soaked me, but my troubles remained.

Asha was my only friend. With her gone, who will talk to me? The rest of the girls my age are in a higher caste; they might not even acknowledge my existence.

I nervously scrubbed my skin raw.

In younger grades, we had played with whomever we chose. I had never felt bullied for the *caste* I was unchangeably born into. As each year had gone by, though, it was easy to see the other girls adopting the mindsets of their parents and the rest of their *caste*. But I suppose I had been conforming to the way of mine, too. The person I could marry, what or whom I could touch, and where I could go—this was all determined by my *caste*. Already at twelve, *caste* touched every part of life, and its reign was only going to terrorize me more as I aged.

Asha had been the only good part of school; we had each other, even as the others distanced themselves. This time, I was headed to school alone.

Reluctant to finish, I scooped up the used water and rinsed myself.

I climbed out of the basin and reached for my clothes. With just one look at that bloodstained school dress, I burst into tears. *Another reason for all the girls at school to mock me.*

For all the scrubbing in the world, the stains wouldn't come out, and we couldn't afford a new one. I put on the ugly dress. Crying wouldn't help anything now.

I scrubbed my other outfit in the cloudy water, peeling at the dirt with my fingernails, and threw it over the top of the shack to dry.

As I walked back to the house, the familiar scent of burning cow dung hung in the air. A cookpot rested on a platform of bricks atop the dung fire, filled with water boiling for rice.

I sat cross-legged in the dirt next to the cookpot. *Appa* sat across from me. We hadn't said a word to each other since the incident the day before, but that wasn't abnormal. He still terrified me, but a small feeling of control tingled inside me. I had stood up to him, and I still had the football. It was only a small victory, but a devilish pride welled inside me.

Amma served *Appa* first and then plopped a meager scoop of thick rice porridge onto my aluminum plate. I slid the slimy lump around my plate before shoveling it into my mouth with my fingers.

Appa finished eating and licked both his plate and his hand clean. He left his plate on the ground, and, acknowledging no one, he sped off to work on his scooter.

He worked as a bricklayer, a good job for men in our *caste*. Many were ragpickers, scavenging through garbage for anything that could be recycled or resold. My father got the job from Uncle Arjun, who had earned his way by offering to help for free until the company eventually hired him. Though my *appa* had a better job than most men in our village, our family wasn't any better off. He drank away the money.

Seeing *Appa* had left, Sudhir crept out of hiding and sat down. *Amma* plopped a heaping scoop of porridge on his plate.

"That's more than you gave me—" I protested, sizing up Sudhir's portion.

Amma's glare ended my objection. I'd let her down again. Like *Appa*, her looks were powerful. I feared *Appa*'s disapproval, but *Amma*'s disapproval broke my heart, because it meant I was adding to her pain.

"I'm leaving for work now." *Amma* wiped her sweating brow. "Please, children…" she trailed off wearily.

Sudhir and I looked down, ashamed.

"Do not cause trouble at home or school. I will see you tonight."

We nodded and waved goodbye.

She walked up the dusty path and out of sight.

After finishing my tasteless fare, I grabbed our tattered book bags from the corner of the house and thrust Sudhir's towards him, knocking some of the rice from his hand. He glared at me, shoveled the rest of his breakfast into his mouth, and got up.

"Wow, that was almost too much rice to finish," he said with a smirk.

I shoved Sudhir forward and thus began our trek to school. *Amma* wouldn't let us near the main roads alone because of kidnappings by local gangs happening nearby in broad daylight. So, we trudged on each day through roundabout fields and back paths—an hour there, an hour back.

Familiar eerie eyes peered over the homes ahead of us as the temple where Asha had died came into sight. It was my first time seeing the temple since that horrible day. My heart began to pound. Dread filled my chest, making it difficult to breathe. I tried to focus on the path as my ears rang. The gods hanging off the roof sneered at me as I struggled to regain control of myself.

My blurry vision focused on the priest outside the temple gate, standing in the Virabhadrasana yoga pose with his knee bent out in front of him and his arms stretching to the sky. The golden milk bowl sat near him. I spun in panic, scanning the ground for signs of a cobra.

I wanted to curl up into a ball, but I forced my feet to continue until the temple was out of view. I released the breath I'd been holding, and the tears erupted. Pain gripped my stomach as I dwelled on the thought that I would never talk with Asha again.

Sudhir furrowed his eyebrows. "Why are you crying?"

I sniveled, "Asha. The snake." *How can he be so oblivious?*

"Why are you scared? Snakes are only a curse to bad people," he said smugly.

I grabbed his patched shirt sleeve and screamed in his face, "Asha wasn't a bad person!"

Sudhir's face flashed a look of fear—the same one I saw on him when our *appa* was in a rage. I shuddered and released his sleeve.

"Maybe her parents did something really bad, then," he stammered.

Maybe, I thought. *Asha's parents seemed nice. How can anyone ever know where they stand with the gods?*

"I wonder what Asha will reincarnate as," Sudhir continued.

How can I even guess what she will become? I thought. *I thought she was good, yet look what happened to her.*

"Maybe the snake biting her means she'll turn into a snake."

"Stop talking about her! Maybe you will turn into a snake." I covered my ears, still sniffling, and ran ahead through the barren riverbed, where water hadn't flowed in years.

Beyond the riverbed sat another building that made me uneasy. Only twice the size of our house, the small structure held up a wooden cross. A man sitting on the front step brushed off the knees of his khaki pants as he stood.

The man turned to me, and I tried to avoid eye contact…unsuccessfully.

Half of his mouth turned upward warmly. "Good morning!"

Turning my eyes to my feet, I gave a nervous wave and walked a little faster. It wasn't a good morning. *Why is he always so happy? Every time I pass, he greets me joyfully—well, half-joyfully.*

"God is good!" The happy fellow lifted his arms up to the sky before he broke into a song: "Amazing grace! How sweet…"

I hurried away, the song fading.

God is good? I agree with Appa on one thing: that man is crazy. His god hasn't done anything more for him than my gods have for me.

Few people went to that church; most were widows, cursed and abandoned by their families but taken in there. Christians were already looked down on by most people, even those of us from the low *castes*. This gathering place of the cursed kept others away.

Sudhir ran up behind me and shoved me as he passed. "Tag, you're it!"

I stumbled sideways.

Squish!

I felt a warm mush ooze between my bare toes...cow dung!

Sudhir turned around and burst out laughing.

I kicked my foot at him, flinging bits of dung as he ran away. Gagging from the smell, I scraped my foot in the dirt and started crying again as I trudged along.

Soaked with sweat and tears, my school dress clung to my skin as I passed through the rusty metal gate into the dusty courtyard of the school. Six bare concrete buildings sat facing the bell pole in the center of the courtyard. Atop the bell pole, a faded Indian flag hung limp in the breezeless heat.

Sudhir was already wrestling with his fourth-grade friends. I searched the courtyard for any group I could join. I spotted Ishani with a group of other girls and walked up beside her nervously. Ishani wasn't really friends with Asha and me, but she would at least acknowledge us.

Ishani gave me a sideways glance, raising her eyebrows before looking away.

"Hey, ragpicker. I like your headband," the leader of the girls, Lalita, spoke with her chin up. "Did you find it digging through the trash on your way here?"

I felt the cloth wrapped around my head, hiding the gash. I had almost forgotten it was there.

"She smells like it," sneered another girl, looking to Lalita for approval.

The girls cackled.

Ragpicker? I thought. I had heard others in my village called that, but I had never heard anyone refer to me that way.

Ishani didn't laugh, but she wouldn't look at me.

My fears about school were all coming true. Hopelessness for the year ahead gripped me.

"Don't stand too close." Lalita smirked. "The lice will pounce on you."

I choked back a sob and ran behind one of the classrooms, releasing a muffled scream into my arm. My scalp itched, and I scratched at it as hard as I could.

It's probably true, I thought. *I probably do have lice; my head is always so itchy.*

Ding! Ding! Ding! Ding!

The school bell clanged. I wiped my tears away with my shawl, took a deep breath, and peeked out around the building. Lalita was walking to our classroom; the other girls were following her in a train. The bell stopped for a moment, but then the administrator spotted me hiding. Frowning, he obnoxiously slammed the clapper side to side until I rushed into my classroom.

I glanced around the room nervously as I entered. The girls were huddled together on the dusty concrete floor. Downfaced, I shuffled slowly towards them, sensing their glaring eyes on me. I sat a few feet away from any other girl, but not far enough, apparently. The closest girls scooted farther still, nearly piling on top of the others.

A mellow glow of light entered the dingy room through the iron-grated windows. There were no lights or electricity, except in the administrator's office. I watched a lizard flit in through the window and skitter across the ceiling.

I felt something tickle my arm and slapped it.

"Eww!" The girls grimaced.

An injured cockroach twitched on my lap, its insides smeared across my arm. I flicked the squirming insect away and wiped the remains on the hem of my dress.

"That roach came right out of her sleeve!" Lalita shrieked.

The girls groaned in disgust, and the boys began to laugh.

I hid my face in my knees.

Where is the teacher?

Minutes dragged by, and the classroom became increasingly chaotic as hope rose that the teacher wouldn't show up. Teachers often showed up late for class, or sometimes they didn't show up at all. Government teachers never got fired.

I lifted my head up as the laughter around me grew louder, and I saw paper airplanes, pencils, and erasers flying through the air. Something hit me straight in the eye.

"Ow!" I rubbed my eye and looked down at the eraser that had hit me resting in my lap. The girls all giggled at me.

That's it!

I grabbed the eraser and flung it at Lalita. She was laughing so hard that she barely even flinched as it flew a meter above her head. My horrible miss made her laugh even harder, and tears spilled down her face.

I turned my back to the mocking group and clenched my fists. A pair of scissors on our teacher's desk caught my eye. I grabbed the scissors by the sharp tip and turned around, winding up to throw them.

"Hey!" a voice yelled from the doorway.

I panicked and tossed the scissors towards the teacher's desk. They slid across the top then crashed to the floor.

The class leapt to their feet to show their respect to the teacher.

"Your hand…on my desk…now!" the red-faced man shouted.

I pointed at Lalita. "But she—"

"*Now!*"

I placed my trembling left hand on his desk.

"You don't look familiar," the teacher muttered. "You must be the one who skipped yesterday."

What a way to start off the relationship with my new teacher. I've only ever had my hand slapped a couple of times for giggling with Asha, but those were female teachers, and it wasn't something serious like this.

I closed my eyes so I wouldn't pull my hand away, which I knew would result in additional slaps.

Smack!

He slammed the thin edge of his meter stick on my knuckles.

"*Ahh!*" I grabbed my left hand with my right and massaged my burning knuckles. I slumped back to the ground, resting my back against the wall.

I hid my face in my lap again. I bit my lip and yanked at my pigtails. Pain shot through my scalp, and my body convulsed as I tried to suppress my cries. There I sat in my shell, closed off from the lessons and my classmates, waiting for the lunch bell to set me free.

When the bell finally rang, I darted to the secluded corner of the schoolyard, foregoing my free boiled egg lunch. I wasn't hungry. I sat against the rusted chain link fence. A *banyan* tree outside the fence created a small, shaded refuge from the heat.

It was where Asha and I used to sit.

The girls laughed and chatted animatedly in the courtyard. I watched them all double over as Lalita threw a crumpled piece of paper far above the head of another. I tore my eyes away and saw Sudhir playing football with a group of boys of all ages. As much as I hated him right now, I wanted to be him.

Nearby, a group of girls from Sudhir's class were hopping and chanting rhythmically as they jumped rope. I recognized some of them from our village.

I wonder if they would let me play with them.

Grabbing a notebook from my bag, I thumbed through the pages. My *amma* had found the notebook in a trash pile. Though each page was uniquely stained, all were unused. I began sketching with my pencil nub, little more than eraser and tip.

"What are you drawing?"

Clutching my notebook to my chest, I whipped my head up. Ravi, with his disheveled hair and hard-set jawline, strained to catch a glimpse of my drawing. Twine rope held his oversized shorts to his scrawny waist. Nobody in our class liked Ravi, either. Though he was from a higher *caste* than me, everyone mocked him for his rumpled appearance and for being unwanted because he lived in an orphanage. Despite that, Ravi was surprisingly friendly to everyone, shrugging their sneers off like he couldn't hear them.

I looked around nervously. It wasn't proper for boys to talk with girls at school.

Ravi shifted as I unconsciously relaxed my arms. "Is that our teacher?"

On my notebook was a sketch of an angry man with a bottle in his hand. I tore it from my notebook, crumpled it up, and shoved it into the pocket of my dress. "What do you want?"

"Sorry," Ravi said. "I just wanted to say sorry for hitting you with the eraser."

"That was *you?*"

"Yes, sorry. The person I was throwing it at ducked."

Lalita didn't even throw it. I laughed so I wouldn't cry.

"How is your hand?" Ravi inquired.

I looked down at my purple knuckles and rubbed them, laughing again. *Is this the answer to my morning prayer for a new friend?*

"And sorry for getting you in trouble. I should have been the one beaten." Ravi gave a toothy grin. "If it makes you feel better, I get plenty of beatings at the orphanage."

I felt sorry for him. Fate treated him worse than me, but he still kept a positive attitude. I looked at Ravi's big eyes and silly smile. He was kind of cute in his own way. I shook the thought away. I didn't need any more trouble.

"Yesterday, my warden beat me and sent me to bed without dinner just for smiling at him," Ravi said with a chuckle.

I gave him a half-hearted smile before looking around nervously. Ravi didn't seem concerned about *caste* or social rule, but if my teacher saw me talking to a boy alone, he would beat me again.

I saw Vishnu playing football with the other boys, and our eyes met. I quickly turned to my notebook again and pretended to write in it, ignoring Ravi. I didn't want Vishnu to think I was flirting with Ravi.

If Appa *thought I was flirting with a boy…* I wanted a friend, but Ravi wasn't worth the trouble. I needed to get away from him.

"I guess the gods were watching out for me though," Ravi continued. "All the other boys were throwing up last night from the bad rice they ate. You know, I've thought of running away and living on the streets, but I'm not sure which is worse—"

Yelling broke out across the yard, and students gathered around.

I took the escape from Ravi and ran over to see what was happening. I gritted my teeth as he followed me.

When I heard Sudhir's familiar grunts, I pushed my way to the center of the circle of students.

"Get off me, you dirty ragpicker!" shouted a stocky boy, pinned beneath Sudhir.

Sudhir was attacking the larger boy beneath him, punching him repeatedly as the boy tried to defend himself. He was larger, but Sudhir was a good fighter.

Ding! Ding! Ding! Ding!

The administrator rang the bell to signal the end of the lunch break, acting as if he didn't even see the fight.

Sudhir pushed himself up, brushed the dirt from his legs, and sauntered away, leaving the crying, struggling classmate in the dirt. Everyone hurried back to their classes to avoid a beating.

After sitting down separate from the other girls at the front of the classroom, I noticed that Ravi wasn't there.

Our teacher walked over to the doorway. "Ravi!"

Peering through the doorway, I saw Ravi in the courtyard helping Sudhir's victim. He didn't hurry at the admonition; he seemed unmotivated by fear and punishment. He ambled towards the angry teacher, who seized his arm.

"Late!" The teacher grabbed his well-worn meter stick and whapped Ravi in the rear multiple times. Though the teacher doled out what should have been great humiliation, Ravi wasn't humiliated. He looked at me and smirked.

I thought of Asha's hidden football—the small victory I had over my father.

Maybe Ravi and I weren't so different after all.

When the school day finally ended, I bolted out of the schoolyard as quickly as I could.

Sudhir and I dragged ourselves home, arriving after five o'clock. The sun was setting. I wasn't sad to see it go; it had drained our energy and even the moisture in our mouths. I dipped a cup into our water bucket and gulped it down, relieving my parched throat.

A few moments later, a man rode up on a motorcycle with a young boy behind him—the same boy Sudhir had fought with at school.

Sudhir took off running.

The man jumped off his motorcycle and chased after him. He caught Sudhir's shirt, ripping it up the side as he pulled him back. Then he slapped him across the face, launching into a tirade of curses and threats of what would happen if Sudhir ever touched his son again.

The son stood by the motorcycle with a smug grin across his face.

Just then, *Appa* came down the path on his scooter. He drove it right up to Sudhir and began barking furiously at the man. Beating Sudhir was *his* right—no one else's. Turning to *Appa*, the man released Sudhir, who fled into the house while covering his face to hide his tears.

The men began shouting at each other, their voices growing louder, cutting through the thick air. A crowd of neighbors grew around them and began to join in.

"He has every right to defend his boy from that bully son of yours!" said one man to my *appa*.

"If his boy can't handle himself in a fight, it's his fault!" another shot back, defending *Appa*.

"Like father, like son!" someone muttered.

Appa's face darkened. "You want to settle this between us?"

Before anything more could happen, Uncle Arjun arrived and stepped between the fuming men. "Let's not turn this into something bigger," he urged. His calm presence managed to dial down the rage. As night fell, tempers cooled, and slowly, the crowd began to drift away.

My *appa* lit a *beedi* and passed one to Uncle. Then, he reached under his scooter seat and pulled out a bottle.

One problem done; another just beginning.

Vishnu wandered up from the path. I tensed, expecting him to say something about Ravi.

If Appa *hears a boy was talking to me alone at school…*

"Looks like I missed all the action." Vishnu sounded amused.

"I'm sure there'll be more action tonight," I muttered, glancing at the bottle rising to Father's lips.

"For you and me, both," Vishnu sighed.

I shook my head. Uncle Arjun was so compassionate and caring to us and the rest of the village, and I used to wish he was my *appa*. But Vishnu told Sudhir and me the horrible things that happened behind closed doors. My aunt rarely left their home; he wouldn't let her.

I still could hardly believe the deception of my uncle. My *appa* was a brute, but at least he wasn't a masked brute.

My mind flipped back to Ravi. "I tried ignoring Ravi, but he just wouldn't go away."

Vishnu squinted his eyes, confused. "What are you talking about?"

Ugh! Why did you say something?

"It's just…" I stammered. "Ravi came up and talked to me today at lunch and I tried to get him to leave but he wouldn't, and I thought you saw us and I just didn't want you to think anything was going on there or say anything to *Appa*."

Vishnu chuckled. "Your secret's safe with me."

Oh no, what does he mean by that? Does he think I like Ravi? I couldn't defend myself more or it would seem like I really did like him.

We sat in silence for a few minutes before our *appas* parted ways, prompting us to say goodnight. I wondered if Vishnu's steps were as heavy as mine as we both walked to houses that offered no shelter for us.

I entered the house and quietly pushed the door closed, trying to be invisible. My stomach betrayed me, growling in disappointment at its missed lunch.

Sudhir lay curled in a ball in the corner, his torn shirt exposing deep fingernail scratches. *Amma* sat with her arm around him, comforting him. A few moments passed, then she got up and went outside to finish cooking dinner. I took her place next to Sudhir.

"You've angered *Appa* again," I sighed.

A small fire lit in his eyes, and his face scrunched. "Last time, it was *your*—"

A shadow looming in the doorway cut him off. My chest tightened. *Appa* stomped inside, the familiar sweet smell of alcohol and pungent *beedi* smoke thick around him. He knelt over Sudhir, their faces nearly touching.

"You get nothing to eat tonight," *Appa* breathed out heavily through bared teeth. "If you ever bring this kind of shame on me again, I will beat you ten times worse than he did!"

Sudhir curled tighter, turning away like a wounded street dog. *Appa* grabbed a fistful of Sudhir's hair and yanked his head around.

"Look at me!" *Appa* thundered, shaking the house. "You will not dishonor me! Do I make myself clear?"

Sudhir nodded frantically, tears streaming down his face.

"Stop crying!" *Appa* growled, shoving Sudhir's head into the floor.

"Stop! Please!" *Amma*'s voice wavered from the doorway.

My heart sank. *No, Amma! Why did you say something?*

Appa turned his fight to the doorway, cursing at *Amma*. I closed my eyes and covered my ears, trying to take myself to another place in my imagination. Howls about honor and respect slipped through my fingers, and then I heard the sharp crack of a backhand to the face. I curled myself up against Sudhir.

After a few minutes, the quiet coaxed me to open up. I saw *Amma* bringing in the cookpot, the red mark on her cheek bright and angry. *Appa* followed behind her and sat by the food as if nothing had happened. *Amma* motioned me to sit by her as she dished out the rice speckled with onions and bright red tomatoes—first to *Appa*, then to me. She'd feed herself with whatever was left over.

We ate in silence as Sudhir remained in the corner.

*He deserves it, doesn't he?…Still…*I glanced at Sudhir, his back facing us. I could hear his shaky, uneven breathing.

I formed a ball of rice in my hand and slipped it into my pocket. After we finished eating, I laid down on the straw mat beside Sudhir. When *Appa* stepped out to smoke, I pulled the sticky ball of rice from my pocket.

"Sudhir," I whispered.

He turned his head towards me, and I put the ball of rice to his lips.

Sudhir smiled weakly. "Thank you, *Akka*."

He slurped the rice from my hand and turned back to face the wall, chewing slowly.

As much as I hated him sometimes, I loved him. No one understood my life better than Sudhir. No one else knew what it was like inside these walls.

"You're welcome, *Thambi*."

CHAPTER 4

May had finally arrived: a month of freedom from school. Scorching heat blazed—May was the most oppressive month—but it was still better than school.

My thirteenth birthday was days away, but I felt indifferent. We never celebrated it.

The past school year had started miserably, but it had gotten a little better over time. No girls in my class talked to me, except to mock me. However, I ended up making friends with the younger girls from Sudhir's class, including one named Neeta. Neeta and the others were from our village and *caste* and looked up to me simply because I was older.

It was nice having other friends so I was never alone with Ravi, who was always following me. The girls joked about us getting married one day, which was both amusing and annoying. I worried what Vishnu thought of Ravi always being around. He had promised never to say anything to Father, but Sudhir might say something if he were upset with me.

Secretly, I had grown to like Ravi. He understood rejection and mockery, just as I did, and he bore his own scars from life at home— or in his case, at the orphanage. Still, I couldn't let anyone know my feelings. I walked a line between feigning annoyance and making him think I cared.

At home, Father's rage escalated, and he unleashed more frequent outbursts and beatings against *Amma*, Sudhir, and me. I felt helpless;

obedience seemed pointless. Regardless of how we acted, our very presence seemed to anger him. Like the gods, he did whatever he wanted, indifferent to our behavior.

A couple of nights ago, after a particularly violent outburst, *Amma* had slipped out of the house after Father passed out. She had told Sudhir and me that she was going to the women's field, but I saw her go the opposite way. For a moment, I had panicked, thinking that she had finally given up and was going off to end her life. I had started thinking through my own plans to run away if she didn't come back.

My racing mind had calmed when she came back a while later. When I had asked where she'd gone, she had simply looked away, offering no explanation.

After finishing breakfast, I knelt before Kali. My strategy for the last year had been to kneel before Kali but call out to all the gods, pleading for help from any who would listen.

I stepped outside and walked around the house towards the cursed tree, hoping to sneak Asha's ball away again to play with it today. Instead, I nearly jumped out of my skin when I saw *Appa* watching me from the other side of the house. He stared at the cursed tree, a puff of smoke trailing from his mouth. From my position, I couldn't see the ball, but I swallowed hard, wondering if he could spot it from his higher vantage point.

Appa fixed his eyes ahead. "We're going to the temple, so don't wander off."

Dread slithered up my spine like a snake. I hadn't been inside the temple since Asha died, and I never wanted to again. Whenever I passed it, I felt like the gods perched atop it were watching, waiting to devour me if I entered. I'd somehow avoided going during several major festivals by lying to *Appa*. I had told him I had gone with my friends or cousins, or I had even feigned illness, but I felt *Appa* was growing suspicious.

I considered in that moment that *Appa's* increased outbursts were punishments from the gods on me for avoiding the temple, or perhaps they were Kali's revenge for not praying to her.

How can I get out of it this time?

"I really need to go to the women's field," I said.

Appa grunted, flicking his *beedi* away. "Go quick."

I ran off to the field and disappeared behind the bushes, trying to think of a way out.

What if I just hide all day? Appa would certainly beat me when I came back, but he'll probably find another reason to beat me by then anyway.

Peeking from behind the foliage to ensure no one was watching, I snuck from bush to bush, aiming for Neeta's house. Just as I sprinted to hide behind a neighbor's wall, I collided with Sudhir, sending us both tumbling.

"You little snake," Sudhir scoffed. "I saw you sneaking away."

"Did you tell *Appa?*"

"No." He smirked. "This looked like too much fun. So where are we going?"

"We? Go play by yourself."

"I don't like playing by myself."

"You don't like playing with me either." I glanced around the corner of the house, then sprinted across the path.

Sudhir followed. "So how will we explain this to *Appa?*"

"Ugh!" I kept walking, ignoring him.

As we passed a small liquor stand, I noticed a boy Sudhir's age was handing over *rupees* for a bottle. I hoped it was for his father, but the smile on his face as he ran away with the bottle suggested otherwise.

I looked down at Sudhir at my side. "You're never going to drink that stuff, are you?"

His face scrunched in disgust as he shook his head. Then his expression changed.

"Hey, Kashvi, it's your boyfriend," he teased.

My heart jumped. I looked around for Ravi but saw Vishnu approaching. I felt the heat on my cheeks when I realized my mind had gone to Ravi.

What a crazy idea. Ravi wasn't from my *caste*. People could be stoned for mixed-*caste* marriages. Plus, in our tradition, I was basically promised to Vishnu unless his parents chose someone else for him.

"Want to gather some boys to play football?" Vishnu suggested.

"Of course!" Sudhir dashed off.

Vishnu smiled at me and I blushed, averting my eyes until he went to follow Sudhir.

I walked on until I found my young friends seated in a circle playing *pacheta*.

Neeta tossed a stone high into the air and skillfully scooped up the other stones scattered on the ground. She giggled with delight, catching the thrown stone as it fell.

I clapped my hands for her as I sat down.

"Hi, Kashvi. How are you?" Neeta scattered the stones on the ground and offered one to me.

I fingered the smooth stone, wondering if my parents were searching for us or if they had gone to the temple without us. "I'm fine. How are you?"

"Glad to be away from home," Neeta said, her voice shifting in tone. "My *akka*'s boyfriend broke off their relationship, and now she feels like a failure. And my parents didn't even know she *had* a boyfriend, so now they are angry at her." She sighed heavily. Her voice dropped to a whisper. "Yesterday, she left, muttering about going to drink pesticide. *Appa* dragged her to the temple, insisting she must have a demon in her." She rubbed her forehead, her face full of distress.

I shuddered at the mention of pesticide, remembering my fears about my mother the other night.

"I'm glad to be away from home, too," was all I could say.

"Where's Ravi?" another friend chimed in, lightening the mood. "I thought maybe he'd follow you here."

Neeta giggled. "We all know that you like him."

"I don't!" I blushed.

"Come on, Kashvi," Neeta said. "We've all dreamed of love marriages instead of arranged ones."

"That's just it: dreams, not reality," I replied firmly. "And no, even in dreams, I don't love Ravi."

The afternoon flew by with games and giggling. I knew what awaited me at home, but I pushed it aside, savoring the joy of the moment, of laughter and carefree play. Eventually, my stomach began to growl. I hadn't eaten any lunch, and the sun was close to setting. I said goodbye to my friends and walked off to find Sudhir. I spotted him with a group of boys, intently watching a cricket match.

The bowler wound up and hurled the ball. The batsman connected with a fluid swing, sending it soaring. A fielder locked eyes on the ball, sprinting backward and leaping to snatch it before tumbling to the ground. Jumping to his feet, he held the ball in the air, igniting cheers from his teammates and the crowd of boys.

When the cheers died down, I yelled across the field, "Sudhir!" He looked up with disappointment and dragged his feet over to me.

"Why do we have to go home now?" Sudhir whined.

"Do you want to stumble home in the dark?"

"Okay, okay. Fine." Sudhir sighed, and we began our walk home.

"I have an idea of what to tell *Appa*," Sudhir said deviously as we neared our home. "We both were sick from the food last night, so we were in the fields all day with cramps."

"*Appa* was waiting for me to come back from the fields, so I'm sure that's the first place they looked for us, stupid," I shot back, anxiety tightening in my chest.

Our house loomed ahead, a silhouette blocking out the remainder of the sun. Wails echoed from inside, chilling my blood.

Appa burst from the door, clutching a handful of *rupees*, his expression blank. We ducked into the bushes on the side of the road. A thorn tore into the flesh on my arm, and I grimaced. He passed us, eyes focused ahead of him. I held the cut on my arm.

As soon as *Appa* disappeared from view, we rushed into the house.

Amma was cowering in the corner, tears streaming down her cheeks, mingling with her blood.

I wrapped my arms around her, squeezing tightly, and her tears soaked my shoulder. Guilt gnawed at me—her beating was my fault. *Appa*'s rage over my running away had found its target in her.

I bit down on my lip; the pain offered a momentary distraction.

"I tried to stop him…" *Amma* choked out, looking down beside her.

I turned to see Asha's football lying there, a knife plunged into it. *Appa* must have found the ball while searching for me. His anger at me must have been greater than his fear of the cursed tree.

"W-what happened?" I stammered, feeling weak.

"We need to leave before he gets back," *Amma* mumbled, eyes glued to the ball. The knife gleamed in the dim light.

I looked back and forth from *Amma* to the ball, realization hitting me. This time, it was my treasured possession. Next time, it would be…

"Let's go," *Amma* whispered, little strength left. She struggled to stand, her legs shaking from *Appa*'s blows. Sudhir and I supported her, helping her limp through the doorway.

I stole one last glimpse at the ball with the knife in it, then Kali, the goddess of darkness, caught my eye. Her piercing eyes were fixed on me.

I stumbled out the doorway and slammed the door shut behind me.

"Quiet!" *Amma* whispered. She led us behind the house, avoiding the main path, fearful of *Appa*'s return. Sudhir and I clung to her.

I didn't know where we were going, but at least we were together.

CHAPTER 5

P anic gripped me as Sudhir, *Amma*, and I passed the shadow of the temple; the white fangs of the gods flashed as the lamppost flickered. We finally turned onto the main path, near the rubble and ashes of Asha's house. My mind flashed to Asha's parents burning there beside their daughter.

"Where are we going?" I asked anxiously.

"This has gone on too long," *Amma* mumbled. "The time has come."

Her words sent a shiver through me. Maybe she'd finally had enough. Maybe she was ready to take the shortcut—even if it meant a worse life in the next birth.

But what about Sudhir and me?

A cold sweat broke out over my body. I gasped for breath, but the moist, hot air didn't satisfy. Everything went black.

I opened my eyes in a blur.

A man was carrying me into a dark building. The air smelled like moldy schoolbooks. The shadow of a cross flickered on the wall beside me in the candlelight. I started to thrash in an attempt to flee, but I heard *Amma* and Sudhir muttering nearby. The man set me down on the cold, hard floor next to them, and I crawled into *Amma*'s lap.

The man who carried me sat down across from us. I blinked and realized he was the half-smile man I saw praying outside the church on our way to school every day.

We must be in that church.

Amma wrapped her arms around me. "You're okay."

"Water?" the man offered, handing me a chipped ceramic mug. "I think you fainted from dehydration."

I eyed the man warily.

"Sorry, let me introduce myself," the man said. "I'm Pastor Kurumuni. I'm certain we've seen each other during your walks to school!"

I nodded suspiciously and looked at my *amma* again before taking the mug of water and gulping it down.

The door creaked, and we all jumped.

A little girl, no older than five, came in with a big smile. "*Appa!*"

The left side of the man's face lit up as he opened his arms, and she climbed into his lap. He hugged her tightly.

Something was wrong with the right side of his face. Despite that, his obvious love for his daughter shone in his half-smile.

Did my appa ever hold me on his lap like that? Ever hug me at all?

The man glanced from Sudhir to me, then to *Amma*. "Are you ready?"

Amma's head dropped. "Yes, Pastor," she confirmed mournfully.

'Pastor'? Wait…this must be where Amma had snuck off to the other night. But what are we 'ready' to do?

The pastor nodded solemnly before rising to his feet. "It will be dark soon. I will take you there."

He lifted his daughter back onto the floor and kissed her tenderly on her forehead. "Run home, sweetie," he whispered, sending her off.

He blew out the candles, and we followed him out to the road in silence. Strangely, I felt less nervous now, despite knowing nothing about the man who was leading us away from everything familiar. The way he treated his daughter almost made me feel secure, like he might not be such a bad person.

The roar of traffic grew as we neared the main paved road. Horns blared—deep lorry blasts and the quick beeps of *tuk-tuks* and scooters. The vehicles wove dangerously around a lumbering ox cart.

The pastor watched up the road intently while Sudhir and I clutched Mother nervously. When a public bus approached, he stepped into the road and waved his hands. The bus creaked and groaned to a halt in front of us.

We followed the pastor, squeezing past the men hanging in the doorway, up the tall steps and into a cramped sea of sweaty bodies. We were packed so tightly, there was no need to hold onto anything as the bus lurched forward.

A few minutes later, the bus stopped at a busy intersection. Without the air moving, the heat quickly rose, and everyone panted, sweat trickling down their faces. Through the window, I caught a glimpse of a little boy and girl at the bus stop in stained T-shirts that hung down to their knees, holding out paper cups.

Home was awful, but at least we had food and shelter. Panic welled in me as a thought crept in: *Am I about to become one of them?* I shook the idea away. *Why would the pastor bring us somewhere just to beg?*

A couple of ladies got off at the stop, leaving the seat they were sharing. The pastor quickly slid into the open seat.

How selfish of him.

"Come, sit," the pastor said, motioning us over to him. He rose again, blocking the seat from others as *Amma*, Sudhir, and I sat down, then he stood beside us in the aisle.

I looked up at the pastor, and he smiled with half his face. I felt bad for assuming he was so selfish.

A unified sigh of relief came when the bus screeched into motion again, and the breeze through the windows provided relief from the stifling heat of all the smelly bodies packed tightly in the bus.

Sudhir laid his head on *Amma's* thigh and dozed off.

How can he sleep at a time like this?

I rested my head on *Amma's* shoulder, hoping her touch would calm me. Warm shivers ran down my head as she stroked my hair with her hand. I looked into her eyes. Normally, at the end of the day, those eyes would glaze over, her mind elsewhere. But tonight, she was fully present, her gaze soft as if nothing else mattered but me. I wished the bus would go on forever so I could stay in this moment.

"This is our stop," the pastor interrupted, as the bus slowed at a bend in the road.

Amma shook Sudhir awake. "Time to go."

Sudhir rubbed his eyes in a daze. "Where are we?"

We pushed our way through the stinky crowd and jumped off the bus. A single streetlight above us cast a dim glow, illuminating nothing but a few coconut trees.

I turned around and watched the bus rumble away, revealing three buildings with flood lights shining bright behind a high wall on the other side of the street. Jagged glass shards lined the top of the wall to prevent anyone from climbing over.

Is this a prison?

A towering *banyan* tree with gnarled roots loomed beside a foreboding metal gate. I squeezed my *amma*'s hand, lagging behind her as she followed the pastor up to the gate. He banged on it with his fist.

Inside, children squealed. I closed my eyes, clinging with both hands to my *amma*'s side as the gate's latch screeched open and the hinges screamed.

I peeked through slit eyes, muscles tensed in fearful anticipation.

CHAPTER 6

A girl around my age was waiting in the open gate. A long satin braid cascaded down her back, and she wore a smile that was wide and carefree.

"Pastor Kurumuni!" she chirped. "Where's your daughter?"

"Sorry, Sarina. It was too late to bring her with me." He gestured towards us. "I brought some others with me, though."

I glanced around the confinement. Inside the gate stood three buildings, two floors tall. The floodlights from each building—left, center, and right—shone into a central courtyard, casting shadows of children in every direction.

A young boy sprinted through the courtyard behind Sarina, and a towering young man chased after him, shouting, "Give it back!"

"Ameer!" A frowning woman in a turquoise *chudidhar* stormed out of the central building. Her gold earrings dangled, catching the light, but her tightly pulled-back black hair reminded me of the feathers of a crow—dark and shiny, bearing bad omens.

Ameer, the boy being chased, held out a wrench. "I was just keeping it safe for you, Dhiren."

Dhiren, the broad-shouldered young man who had been chasing him, didn't take the wrench. Instead, he grabbed Ameer and held him upside down from his ankles.

I flinched and closed my eyes. But instead of the expected thuds of a beating accompanied by screams, I heard giggling.

Dhiren was tickling Ameer's stomach as he giggled uncontrollably and dropped the wrench. He set Ameer down, retrieved the wrench, and walked towards a white SUV with its hood open, a small lantern illuminating the engine.

I blinked slowly, struggling to make sense of the scene.

The crow woman continued towards Ameer with stern eyes, but she caught sight of us at the gate and her face softened into a smile.

Turning to Ameer, she patted him on the head gently. "Wait for me in the office, Ameer."

What will happen to him in the office?

The woman approached us, casting a long shadow from the flood-lights behind her. Her sandals clapped loudly with each step.

I scanned the courtyard, trying to evaluate what this place was. A couple dozen boys bustled about. Some swept the ground, others gathered clothes from sagging lines. A sharp, pungent smell hit my nose—onions. Another young man, hands purple from chopping onions, looked up at us. His eyes widened, and he bolted into a nearby building, abandoning his work.

Who is this woman? Why are there so many childr—

Terror gripped me.

This isn't a prison, but it's the next worse thing—an orphanage. Amma *couldn't leave us here. She wouldn't. Right?*

Spinning, I looked into *Amma's* eyes. Her face crumbled with shame, and she looked away.

She's leaving us. She brought us here to abandon us.

I could feel bile rising in my throat as Ravi's words from school echoed in my head—stories of beatings, of hungry nights, of cruel punishments.

I grabbed *Amma's* arm so hard she winced. But I couldn't let go. My world was unraveling.

The Crow stopped before us. "Good evening, Pastor Kurumuni!"

The woman's smile was sickly sweet. "So good to see you, *Sagotharan*."

"You too, *Sagothari*." Pastor Kurumuni shook her hand. "Sorry for coming so late. These are the children I mentioned, from my village."

"Welcome to Karunai House. I'm Vasantha." She turned to *Amma*, offering both hands this time.

Amma reached out her own hands, and the Crow clasped them, wrapping *Amma* in false comfort, her eyes soft behind her wire-frame glasses, her expression too familiar, too understanding.

I can see through her act. Just like Uncle Arjun, who smiles at everyone, hiding the bruises his family bears. I have no doubt the Crow is the same, putting on a show to trick Amma into leaving us here.

Just then, a man approached, wearing a grey button-up shirt and purple striped tie. His beard was neatly trimmed, with grey streaks that made him look distinguished. He held a well-worn, leather-bound book in a hand at his side.

He smiled wide, shaking Pastor Kurumuni's hand. "Great to see you, *Sagotharan*! Praise the Lord!"

"Praise the Lord, Pastor Pradhan!"

The Crow looped her arm through his. "This is my husband, Pastor Pradhan. We are the wardens here."

Wardens. I stared at them. Wardens weren't supposed to be nice. I didn't trust them. *Don't fall for it,* Amma.

I diverted my eyes as the Crow turned to me. "What is your name?"

I looked to *Amma*. She gave a soft nod. I swallowed the growing lump in my throat.

"Kashvi." My voice wavered.

"Nice to meet you." She stretched out her hand towards me. I flinched instinctively.

"Don't be shy," *Amma* nudged.

Shy? This woman is putting on a show so you will abandon us here.

I gave her my limp hand, and she cupped it in hers. She peered into my eyes like she could read my thoughts. Feeling uneasy, I jerked my hand away.

She moved on to Sudhir, who shook her hand without fear. He didn't understand what was coming.

"Let's have tea and talk upstairs. It will be more comfortable up there." Pastor Pradhan motioned for us to follow him.

"I'll be right up," the Crow said. "I need to have another talk with Ameer in the office first."

Talk? Surely she means a beating.

❦

We followed Pastor Pradhan to the center building straight across from the gate, climbing a flight of stairs before continuing through an open hallway that overlooked the courtyard.

I glanced down and saw more children—busy, pretending everything was fine.

We stepped into a room larger than our entire house, with a high ceiling, bright lights that filled the whole room, and two fans roaring above. Two couches faced each other with a small table between them. Everything here was too comfortable, too clean. It made me uneasy.

Amma, Sudhir, and I sat down on one of the couches, and Pastor Pradhan and Pastor Kurumuni sat on the couch across from us.

The young man I'd seen cutting up onions earlier shuffled into the room, carrying a tray of steaming milk tea. He set a cup on the table for each of us.

"Thank you, Mahiyu," said Pastor Pradhan to the young man.

He nodded with a grin and retreated shyly out of the room. I watched him go, wondering if he had rushed to make tea to avoid trouble—maybe a beating.

I tightened my arms around myself, trying not to imagine what might happen here.

The Crow entered the room and sat by Pastor Pradhan, her expression serious. "Sorry about that," she said. "Now, please, tell us about the current situation in your home."

Amma's voice trembled as she spoke. She explained how *Appa* would

48

drink and beat us, how it had only gotten worse lately, and how she feared for our lives. Tears streamed down her face.

I avoided everyone's eyes, instead staring at the teacup in front of me, its steam curling upward. Their questions blurred in my ears—questions aimed at *Amma*, at Sudhir, at me. I heard myself answer, but my voice sounded far away, as though someone else was speaking for me.

The strangers moved on to discuss the process of admitting children, and I tried to focus, but my head was heavy, my thoughts pulling me elsewhere.

The Crow slid a document across the table to *Amma*, placing a pen beside it. The paper looked so official, so final. I watched *Amma's* fingers tremble as she reached for the pen, her eyes scanning the page that I knew she couldn't read. Anxiety twisted deep in my stomach—she was about to sign something she didn't understand. What if she was signing away more than she thought?

"If you sign this," the Crow said, "we can keep your children temporarily—"

I pulled on *Amma's* arm desperately as she picked up the pen. "You aren't going to leave us here, are you?"

Sudhir gasped, eyes wild, as he finally realized what was happening.

Amma tried to hold back her emotions, but her voice cracked. "It's not safe for you to come home, not after..."

"So it's all my fault," I moaned. "If I had gone to the temple this morning—"

Amma wrapped her arms around me. "No, my dear. It's really my fault. I was hiding money from your *appa* to hopefully buy you new clothes. I have not been accepting my place."

The Crow cleared her throat. "No one is responsible for his anger and violence except himself. Neither of you should blame yourselves for that."

"It is my fault," *Amma* sobbed. "I've been a curse on the family since the day I married."

Walking around the table, the Crow knelt in front of my weeping mother, placing a hand on her knee. "Our society looks down on women and blames them for everything, but it is a lie. Every person is responsible for their own sins against the living God. We all deserve far worse, but—"

"No, it is my fault. I need to bring balance. I need to put an end to this curse," *Amma* insisted, wailing.

She is going to end her life, isn't she? That's how she'll try to bring balance. And it will all be my fault.

Angrily, I turned towards her. "What are you saying?"

Amma realized my concern and quickly assured me. "I need to go back. Make things right with *Appa*."

"But—"

"We know of a women's shelter you can stay in." The Crow stood and stepped back. "They provide counseling and skills training to help women in your situation."

"No, no. I'll go and make things right." *Amma* pulled her arm away from me and signed the document.

The Crow smoothed back her hair. "What I was about to say earlier is that ultimately it will be up to the government to place your children. Sadly, they haven't been allowing us to admit girls here, so—"

"I'll be separated from Sudhir?!"

I panicked. Most of my life I had wanted to be away from Sudhir and his annoying teasing, but not now. *Amma* was leaving, and Sudhir and I would be all alone.

"I will do everything I can to try to keep you together," the Crow said. "I was separated from my *thambi* when I was young. I don't want that for anyone."

I want to believe her, but deep down, I know she doesn't really care about us. She probably just made that up about her thambi. She wants to convince Amma to leave us here so she will have more slaves to work for her. Just like all the other children in the courtyard.

I looked down as I felt something on my feet. A fat, stubby dachshund had waddled over and was settling on my toes, gazing up at me with sad eyes.

"Milo! Get off her," Pastor Pradhan said, making a shooing motion.

Milo reluctantly waddled away and lay at the end of the table, still casting glances my way.

Amma looked up at the clock on the wall, then handed the signed document to Vasantha. It was stained with her tears. She swallowed hard and pursed her lips. "This is your home for now." She squeezed Sudhir and me tight, then she stood to leave.

"We have a policy here," the Crow said, her tone professional. "A parent or guardian must visit at least once per month." She flipped through a stack of papers under the table, finally retrieving one and handing it to *Amma*. "We prefer if you visit on Sundays when we gather for church. It's in the city, so it's much easier to catch a bus there."

Amma nodded her head, her expression distant and resigned. She grabbed the paper but appeared completely uninterested.

Because she's never planning to visit.

I clung to *Amma*'s waist as she turned to leave. "Don't leave! *Amma*, please don't do it!"

Sudhir grabbed her from the other side. She tried to push us away like we were clingy dogs.

The Crow grabbed my arm. "Kashvi, I know it's—"

Who is she to pull me away from my amma?

I screamed and slapped her hand, then latched onto *Amma* again, nearly knocking her over.

"Kashvi, stop! I'll visit next Sunday."

"You promise?" I whimpered.

Her eyes struggled to hold onto mine. "I promise."

Sudhir and I released her, and the Crow ushered us towards the door.

"Would you like me go back with you?" Pastor Kurumuni asked.

"No," *Amma* said. "Without the children... If someone saw us..."

"I can go back with you," the Crow offered.

"No, thank you. I'll go back alone." *Amma* stepped out the door firmly.

Together, we walked solemnly down the steps, across the courtyard, and through the gate. We waited by the roadside; Sudhir and I clung once more to each of *Amma's* sides as she stared down the road with determination.

A bus came into view, and I began to sob uncontrollably. The Crow stepped into the road to stop the bus, and it screeched to a halt.

Amma wrapped Sudhir and me in her arms, weeping. "I love you."

"I love you, too." I squeezed her tight, not wanting to let go. I could hear Sudhir's muffled sobs.

Beep! Beep!

The bus honked, and people began to yell, "Hurry up!"

"Please don't hurt yourself," I whispered, panic surging through me.

Amma pulled away from us and stepped up onto the bus. I wasn't sure if she didn't hear me amid the chaos or if she was ignoring me, knowing what she was going to do.

Amma stared at us through the window, biting her bottom lip. She forced a small smile.

"Don't go," I whimpered, imagining that to be the last smile I would ever see from her.

The bus screeched forward, and I watched it until it disappeared, telling myself she wouldn't actually leave us. She would jump off and come back to get us. Soon she would be limping back down that road to us.

I felt a rough fabric on my cheek and looked up to see the Crow standing over me, wiping away my tears with her shawl. I pulled away from her.

Amma is gone, why is she still pretending to be kind? I thought. Then a new fear hit me: *I slapped her hand away! I'm going to receive a beating for that...*

Sudhir stared at the ground in shock. It was just us now. I remembered the conversation I had had with my *amma* a while back after fighting with Sudhir.

You need to watch out for each other. Someday...

Today was that day.

I wrapped my arms around Sudhir and held him close in silence.

CHAPTER 7

A smiling girl bounced up to the Crow. She was the girl we had seen at the gate when we arrived. Her big eyes contrasted beautifully with her dark skin.

"*Amma*! Mahiyu is calling you," the girl exclaimed.

"Thank you, Sarina, my dear," the Crow replied.

Amma? I thought. *She can't be Vasantha's daughter; she looks nothing like her.*

"Meet your new brother and sister." The Crow motioned to Sudhir and me, still wrapped in our embrace.

Brother and sister? I jerked away from Sudhir and wrinkled my nose.

"This is Kashvi and her *thambi* Sudhir."

Sarina's face lit up, and she threw her arms around me. "Welcome! I'm Sarina. I can't believe I'll finally have another girl here."

"Sarina, it's not certain—" the Crow started, but trailed off. "Never mind."

It's not certain I'll stay here, I remembered, anxiety pulling at my stomach.

"How old are you?" Sarina asked, eyes sparkling with curiosity.

"Um...twelve, I think," I said. "I don't know my actual birthday, just the one used on my school records."

"What date is it?"

"May 22."

"What?! That's tomorrow. You'll be thirteen tomorrow!" Sarina jumped with joy. "You'll be my age! We'll have to do something special for you."

"Special?" I exclaimed. I'd never done anything special for my birthday.

"Oh, we'll definitely do something special for you." She turned to look at the Crow. "Right, *Amma?*"

"Of course."

What's going on? Is this "special" thing some sort of trick? Amma is gone. There's no reason for them to act nice anymore.

"Let's go back in," the Crow said, turning towards the gate.

I grabbed Sudhir and followed the woman apprehensively into the courtyard. Sarina shut the creaking gate behind us. The bolt shrieked as she slid it down, locking us all in.

Sudhir scratched furiously at his scalp, reminding me my own scalp itched, and I scratched at mine too.

Beady eyes stared at us. "I think you'll be needing haircuts. Sarina, will you sit with them on the porch of the Common Hall while I grab my clippers?"

I took Sudhir's hand in mine and cautiously followed Sarina as she gleefully led us through the courtyard towards the Common Hall. I looked to the left and right. The two other buildings had iron bars fixed over all the windows, but they looked surprisingly clean—freshly painted white.

The Common Hall's windows were open, and it had multiple doors from the outside to what I assumed were different rooms. To the right of it was another small building with plates and pots sitting on racks outside it.

We sat on the porch steps under the glow of a hanging lamp, waiting for the Crow to return.

"How old are you, *Thambi?*" Sarina asked Sudhir.

Sudhir looked at me.

"He's ten," I answered abruptly.

Sarina shouted into the courtyard towards a group of boys. "Hey, Ameer! Come here!"

The wrench thief ran over. He had been pushing a wheelbarrow around, picking up the piles of leaves, branches, and trash that had been swept up.

Is that a punishment, or is this just what the children do here all day?

"Hey, Ameer, this is Sudhir," Sarina said. "He's your age! Can you show him around and help him fit in?"

Suddenly, the Crow returned with clippers in hand.

"Sure," Ameer agreed, glancing up at the returning woman sheepishly. "I...uh...just need to finish cleaning up first." He skidded back to the wheelbarrow.

"Making friends already." The Crow smirked at Sudhir.

"I guess so," Sudhir said, his voice uncertain.

The Crow settled on the step above Sudhir. "I'll shave you first."

She flipped the clippers on, and in a few quick swipes, he was nearly bald. His hair had been reduced to little more than stubble across his scalp.

The Crow leaned closer, inspecting his head. Her eyes narrowed, and she clicked her tongue. "Just as I thought—lice. The shaving will help, but we need to be thorough."

She left and came back with a plastic bin full of bottles, combs, and brushes. She pulled out a bottle and a fine-toothed comb. "We'll need to use this treatment on both of you." She squeezed a glob of thick cream into her palm. "This will get rid of that itch." She gently massaged it into Sudhir's scalp, the strong, medicinal scent filling the air. "Just sit for a few minutes so the shampoo can work."

Then she turned to me with an apologetic look. "I'm sorry, dear, but we'll have to cut off your hair too."

I spun towards Sarina, wide-eyed.

"I know, it's terrible!" Sarina twirled her hair around her finger. "I had mine cut off too. But trust me, it'll grow back even nicer."

Before I could protest, the clippers buzzed to life. I leaned forward instinctively, but the Crow grabbed my shoulder and pulled me back.

I felt the locks falling. I wanted to cry, but I swallowed the lump in my throat.

Once finished, she clicked the clippers off. "Sarina, could you fetch some water to rinse them?"

I ran my fingers over what was left of my hair—nothing but prickly stubble, just like Sudhir's.

The Crow began scrubbing the treatment into my scalp. I blinked away tears, feeling more exposed than ever.

Sarina returned with a bucket of water. The cold splash of it made Sudhir flinch, but he said nothing as the Crow rinsed the shampoo from his head. The soapy water ran down the steps, gray with grime and lice.

The Crow grabbed the comb she had taken from the bin and began working through his hair, scraping every centimeter of his scalp. I watched as she wiped tiny nits and lice onto a white cloth. "You'll feel better soon," she murmured, focusing on the task.

Sudhir was unusually quiet, his eyes closed, almost as if it were *Amma* combing his head, not this warden.

Then it was my turn. The water chilled me to the bone. I winced as the Crow scraped my tender scalp. The sight of the tiny lice eggs and bugs in the comb made my stomach churn and filled me with embarrassment.

"We have to get every last one or they could spread everywhere."

I hugged my arms tightly around myself, feeling small and vulnerable. When I looked over at Sudhir, I saw him give me a small, brave smile. Somehow, that made it easier.

"There." The Crow smirked at the two of us after she finished. "All done. You'll both feel better now."

I glanced at Sudhir again, and this time, I managed a small smile in return.

"Ameer!" the Crow called, disturbing the moment.

Ameer dashed over.

"Please take Sudhir with you to get washed up, and find a new pair of clothes that'll fit him. And tell everyone we're pushing supper back until nine-thirty tonight."

"Okay." Ameer nodded and grabbed Sudhir's hand. "Come with me."

Sudhir followed him towards the back of the building to our left but looked back at me with a twinge of fear in his eyes.

You need to watch out for each other. Amma's words rang in my head again.

I started to stand, but the Crow put a hand on my shoulder.

"Kashvi, you can't go back there; that's the boys' dorm."

Just as I was about to protest, a short, stocky boy jumped from behind the dorm and splashed a bucket of water on Sudhir and Ameer. He roared with laughter.

"Sudhir!" I shook the lingering hand off and ran over to Sudhir, who stood dripping. Ameer took off after the boy, chasing him in circles. I heard the Crow call my name.

"Are you okay, Sudhir?"

"I'm fine." Sudhir shook himself off.

"Kashvi!" Sarina grabbed my arm. "This is the boys' dorm; we can't be back here."

"They just humiliated my *thambi!*"

"Don't worry; that's just what boys do. It wasn't meant to be mean."

I looked around and saw a bunch of boys in their underwear, covered in soap suds, laughing and splashing buckets of water over each other. Ameer was grinning as he chased the boy who had drenched him.

"Ameer!" Sarina called. "You're supposed to be taking care of Sudhir. Don't leave his side."

Ameer rolled his eyes, but he stopped running and returned to Sudhir. "Follow me."

Sudhir glanced at me again, then followed Ameer onto the patio.

Sarina took my hand, gently leading me away. "Sorry, but we really can't be back here. The boys' dorm is off-limits for us. Sudhir will be fine."

"They're dumping the water all over the place," I said, brows furrowed. "What happens when the water runs out?"

"Runs out?" Sarina looked confused. "We have a very deep well here; the water never runs out."

My eyes widened. *A well that never goes dry?*

Sarina didn't share my wonder and started back towards the Crow. I followed, still unable to believe what I had just heard.

"Is Sudhir okay?" the Crow inquired as we walked up.

"Yes, ma'am," I muttered, looking down. I couldn't read this woman.

She stood, glancing at the room behind her as a phone rang inside. "I have to take that call. Sarina, please take Kashvi to get washed up, and get her some new clothes."

"Okay, *Amma*," Sarina agreed cheerfully.

I reached up and touched my scalp again—nothing there.

Sarina smiled at me. "You're still really pretty."

I couldn't hold in the tears anymore. "No, I'm not."

Sarina grabbed my shoulders and looked me in the eyes. "Yes, you are. Come on, let's get you washed up. That will help you feel better."

She led me behind the building opposite the boys' dorm. It also had a large cement patio, but this one was partially enclosed by sheet metal, giving a sense of privacy. Five metal doors stood open along the wall, each leading into a small, dark room.

Sarina guided me into the first one and bolted the door behind us. The door muffled the noise outside and enveloped us in darkness. I didn't dare move. Sarina shuffled behind me.

Click-click.

The room filled with dim light as Sarina pulled a chain hanging from the ceiling. "Sorry! Did I scare you?"

Her voice was cheery, but I didn't respond. I didn't know how to read *anyone* here.

I looked around the tiny room. A squat toilet was set into the floor next to a sink and mirror on one side, and there was a spigot with water buckets on the other side.

Sarina twisted the nozzle above the spigot, filling a bucket with ice cold water. She looked up at me. "You need to take a shower, Kashvi."

I hesitated, unsure of what to do. Did she want me to undress right here with her?

"It's okay," Sarina said in a reassuring tone. "In our home, we always help each other like sisters. Besides, it's better if someone helps with the water. I'll show you and make sure you're clean."

The thought of unlimited water to wash in coaxed me out of my *chudidhar*, but, still embarrassed, I kept my undergarments on.

"Here it comes!" Sarina giggled as I gasped, freezing water soaking me. My teeth chattered as she poured bucket after bucket over me, and I watched layers of grime wash away down the drain.

Sarina handed me a small white bottle.

I groaned, thinking of the acrid lice treatment.

"It's *nice* shampoo," Sarina said, giggling again. "Rub it through your hair. It smells good, not like lice shampoo. When your hair grows back, it'll make it soft and clean."

I squeezed the white cream into my hand and smeared it through what was left of my hair. The room was suddenly bursting with the scent of roses. Under different circumstances, it might have even been calming.

"Close your eyes," Sarina warned. "It will sting if it gets in them."

I closed my eyes reluctantly. Shivers ran from my head to my toes. As I listened to the squeak of the spigot and the sound of water splashing into the bucket, my thoughts raced.

Did I hear the door open and close? Or is it just the noise of the flowing water? Did Sarina leave me?

I opened my eyes, and instantly they stung.

"Ow!" I winced, rubbing them.

"I told you to keep your eyes closed!" Sarina said, still standing beside me. She picked up the bucket. "Now keep them closed for a second."

Icy water flowed down my head, washing away the suds.

"Here, rub this over your body." Sarina handed me a bar of soap.

I rubbed it all over, making foamy bubbles everywhere. The soap had a different smell, but it was also unexpectedly nice.

I handed the soap back to Sarina and she set it on the sink. She filled the bucket again and dumped it over me a few more times until my whole body was drenched and shivering. I hugged myself tightly, thinking of Sudhir, hoping he was alright.

Sarina wrapped a thick, soft towel around me. "Dry off. I'll be right back." She stepped out, shutting the door behind her. Then I heard a grinding noise that sounded like a bolt sliding into place.

Did she just lock me in? Panic surged, and I shoved the door. It swung open easily.

Sarina glanced back. "It's okay, I'll be right back."

I closed the door again and breathed a sigh of relief.

A few minutes later, Sarina returned, holding dry undergarments resting on top of a bright yellow dress. "Here, Kashvi. Put these on. I'll wait outside."

I looked at the dress, then at Sarina. She smiled before pulling the door shut again.

It was beautiful. Clean. I unfolded it. Emerald accents and intricate embroidery glimmered along the neckline and hem, catching the dim light. I tried to imagine the details in the actual sunlight. I put on the dry clothes and flung the emerald shawl over my shoulders.

I met my reflection in the mirror above the sink. The dress was beautiful, but not on me. I looked like an ugly boy in a dress with my buzzed hair. I ran my fingers over the jagged scar on my forehead, feeling its rough edge—no longer hidden by hair. I sighed, knowing this scar would forever identify me.

Is this some cruel joke? How could they give something so beautiful to someone like me, knowing I'd only make it ugly? Maybe I should run away and go home.

You fool! You didn't even pay attention to how you got here. You'll never find your way back.

Shifting my eyes from the image in the mirror, I wiped the tears from my face and picked up my dripping, shabby clothes that were resting in the sink.

❦

As I emerged from the stall, Sarina covered her agape mouth.

I was right, she's laughing at me.

Dropping her hand, she shocked me with a look of awe. "Wow! You look so beautiful!"

"I…" I stood in the doorway, frozen.

Sarina seems so genuine, but how can I be sure? No one would see beauty in someone like me.

I rubbed my hand nervously over my shaved head.

Sarina grabbed a bar of soap and a brush and pointed at my old clothes. "Let me help you wash those, Kash'i! Can I call you Kash'i? I'm going to call you Kash'i."

I wondered why she was giving me a nickname, as if we were best friends or something even though we had just met, but I was too overwhelmed to care what anyone called me. I just wanted to go home. I dropped my old *chudidhar* on the cement patio.

Sarina began humming a tune I didn't recognize as her hands skillfully scrubbed my old clothes, each swipe of the brush revealing the fabric beneath the grime. When finished, she hung the dripping clothes on a clothesline above the patio.

"Come here, Kash'i." Sarina motioned to me.

I followed her around to the front of the girls' dorm. She bounced along to the porch steps, and we sat watching the boys play football in the courtyard in front of us, their shadows dancing across the ground. Sudhir was playing with the other boys—nine of them—like he had known them for years.

Of course, he fits in right away. I'll need to watch out for both of us.

I felt something on my shoulder and flinched, shrinking away.

Sarina removed her hand and gazed at me. "Kash'i," she whispered, "no one will hurt you here."

I took a deep breath and allowed myself to relax—just a little—as she put her arm around me, though I didn't really believe her.

I focused my attention on the trees around the dorms and the Common Hall. They were covered in luscious fruits my family was never able to afford. Mangos, papayas, lemons, tamarind—and it looked like there were more in the darkness behind the Common Hall. Saliva rushed into my mouth, though I was sure it wasn't for us. The fruit would be for the wardens, and we would pick it for them.

My eyes turned to the Crow as she stepped into the courtyard. She smiled as she caught my eye.

I quickly shifted my gaze to the football. It reminded me of Asha's, which I had last seen with a knife in it.

It's all my fault for avoiding the temple. The gods have cursed me. Whether Amma ends her life or goes home to be beaten by Appa, it's because of me.

Sudhir darted after the football at full speed, oblivious to his surroundings, and slammed into the Crow.

I gasped. Sudhir rolled across the ground. The Crow remained standing, though she was rubbing her thigh and wincing in pain.

"Sorry! Sorry!" Sudhir pleaded from the ground, fear in his eyes.

"It's okay," the Crow said, "but try to watch where you're going next time so no one gets hurt."

Sudhir nodded and scrambled to his feet, still watching the woman warily, expecting a beating.

Surprisingly, she pointed at the ball and laughed. "Go get it!"

Sudhir ran after the ball, but he glanced nervously over his shoulder a few times.

Some of the other boys abandoned the game to talk with the Crow, each trying to be heard over the other with their questions and stories. Eventually, only Sudhir and Ameer remained playing. Ameer soon gave up and joined the others.

Sudhir came and sat next to me, the football resting on his lap. I wanted to warn him, to tell him to be cautious about *everything*, but Sarina's presence kept me quiet.

"Is Ameer taking care of you, *Thambi?*" Sarina asked.

Sudhir fidgeted with the collar of his pink and blue plaid button-up. "Yeah, he gave me this new shirt and jeans."

"They look great!" she exclaimed. "You know, Ameer loves to tease. He does it for fun, but sometimes he goes too far. If he ever bothers you, tell me. He's scared of me." Sarina winked playfully.

Sudhir giggled.

Eventually, the football game resumed, and Sudhir ran to join.

The Crow sat beside me. "Kashvi, that dress looks beautiful on you!" she cooed.

I forced a sheepish smile, distrusting her sincerity. A soft breeze brushed against my bare head, and I hugged myself, goosebumps rising on my arms.

"I'm sorry I had to leave you earlier. I had some government work to handle. I see Sarina is taking good care of you."

"Yes, ma'am."

She glanced at Sudhir, who passed the ball just as another boy tried to steal it. "Sudhir seems to be fitting in well."

"He always fits in," I murmured.

"And you don't?" she probed softly.

"No one likes me—" I blurted out, immediately regretting it.

Why did you say that? Why are you letting her know how you feel?

"I like you." Sarina wrapped her arms around my neck gently.

I tensed, pulling my shoulders up, bracing against her touch.

"You see all these children here?" The Crow waved her hand over the boys in front of us. "Many of them came from family situations like yours. They all had their first night here, their first week, their first month. I promise you, things will get better, and this will start to feel more like home."

"It's true," Sarina added. "You will love it here."

I don't want this to feel like home.

The Crow watched me, as if reading my mind. "God has done many miracles for us. He can surely make this your home. Sarina will care for you as a sister." She stood. "I better get ready for devotions."

"What is 'devotions'?" I asked Sarina as the Crow walked away.

"It's time we spend every morning and evening singing praises to God and reading the Bible," Sarina explained.

The Bible? I thought. *This must be a Christian home. That's why the pastor from our village brought us here.* Low thumping from a *dholak* drum reverberated from the Common Hall. The boys stopped their game immediately and followed the sound.

"Come, Kash'i. It's devotions time!"

CHAPTER 8

I trailed behind Sarina into a large open room in the Common Hall, where about thirty boys were already singing and clapping to the beat of the drum. Sudhir sat in the back, attempting to clap along. He smiled and waved at me.

Sarina sat beside the only other girl in the room, whose head towered over hers. I wanted to sit by Sudhir, but I didn't want to get in trouble for sitting by the boys. I sat on the floor beside Sarina and the tall girl, both singing along with the music.

"Kashvi, this is Nalayani." Sarina put her arm around the other girl. She looked to be around eighteen. "She is the assistant warden and head of the girls' dorm, which, until today, was just me."

"Nice to meet you, Kashvi!" Nalayani smiled warmly, throwing back a wayward curl. "*Amma* told me about you. We're so happy to have another girl here with us."

I stared at the two embracing girls like I was seeing a two-headed dog. *What kind of deception are they trying to pull off? What orphans embrace their wardens like this?*

Nalayani and Sarina joined in the singing again. I looked around the room, unsure of what to do. The singing stopped for a moment, then a new rhythm began.

The bull-like young man sitting on the drum was the mechanic who had chased Ameer for his tool when I first arrived. I tried to remember what Ameer had called him. *Dhiren,* I thought. Thick, wavy hair fell across his closed eyes, and teeth shone from his giant grin. His whole body danced along with the beat.

The singing resumed, and Sarina pointed to the words in a songbook she held on her lap. I couldn't read them all, and I didn't dare join in. The only songs I'd ever sung were silly rhymes with Asha. I glanced at Sudhir—he was clapping and pretending to mouth the words.

He doesn't know we'll probably never see Amma *again.*

I wished I could be like him, believing everything was going to be fine.

The Crow entered as the song ended and sat on a chair at the front. Voices faded, the drum stopped, and all eyes turned to her.

"Good evening, children!" she called out with enthusiasm.

"Good evening, *Amma!*" everyone shouted.

"*Appa* is meeting with Pastor Kurumuni, but he may join us later," she announced. "As you know, we have a new sister and brother who have joined us today. Please welcome them."

The room erupted in rhythmic clapping, ending with a chant, "Welcome! Welcome! Welcome!"

"Please make them feel at home." The Crow nodded to us. "Show them the love of God!"

Love of god? I thought of Kali on the shelf back home and the gods of our village temple smirking down at me as Asha died in front of them. *What love do the gods have for me?*

Biting my lip, I glanced around nervously as everyone smiled at me. I wanted to bolt from the room. All the talk of kindness, joy, and love… it couldn't be real. I almost wished the yelling and beatings would start. The anticipation and uncertainty were driving me crazy.

"I hope you all had a good day." The Crow opened a thick book on her lap. "I'll try to keep it short tonight since we are a little behind schedule. Tonight, we're reading from God's word in Colossians chapter 3."

It sounded like wind through leaves as everyone flipped through the thin pages of their small books. Each child had his or her own book in a zippered velvet case. *Those must be Bibles.*

Sarina rested hers on my lap. She tracked the words with her finger as the Crow read, but my mind was on our uncertain future.

"...Children, obey your parents in all things: for this is well pleasing unto the Lord."

I laughed to myself. *Obeying Appa in all things pleases the gods? I've tried that; it doesn't work.*

"Fathers, provoke not your children to anger, lest they be discouraged..."

That sounds better. The gods should punish Appa, not me.

"...But he that doeth wrong shall receive for the wrong which he hath done: and there is no respect of persons."

That sounds like karma. *Maybe Christianity isn't much different from Hinduism. But what have I done to deserve this? Appa is the one who should suffer.*

The Crow began explaining the passage, but my mind drifted back to my *amma*, fearing what was happening to her right now.

Suddenly, everyone shuffled to an upright kneeling position, eyes closed and hands folded. I mimicked the other children but kept my eyes open. I turned back to Sudhir; he smiled at me and waved in blissful ignorance. I heard my name and turned towards the Crow.

"...Comfort Kashvi and Sudhir, Father; protect them and their *amma*. We pray that you will use our family here and our church family to show them the love that you have shown to us. May they come to know and confess the glorious gospel of grace in Christ Jesus alone. May your will be done. In Jesus' name, Amen!"

Without warning, a chorus of voices recited: "Bless the LORD, O my soul: and all that is within me, bless his holy name. Bless the LORD, O my soul, and forget not all his benefits. Amen!"

Opening their eyes, everyone stood and beelined for the door, erupting in conversation and laughter. Nalayani jumped up and pushed ahead of everyone.

I tried to get Sudhir's attention, but he was in the middle of all the boys lining up out the back door. Instead, I waited with Sarina at the back of the line, wondering what would happen next.

We passed into an open patio area. Hints of spice from the room assaulted my nose, but as soon as we walked through the doorway, the warm scents of garlic and ginger mingled with freshly cooked flatbread.

Sarina grabbed two plates from a large rack and handed one to me.

"Go ahead." She nodded towards a metal table with three steel pots on it.

Nalayani stood behind the food, smiling as I approached. "I hope you like it," she remarked, pouring a generous ladle of steaming beef gravy on my plate.

I turned to leave, the fragrance making me salivate.

"Come back, *thangachi*; there's more!" Nalayani laughed, curls bouncing.

I turned back timidly, and she piled on more beef gravy and a mound of tomato rice, then placed two warm *chapatis* as big as the plate atop everything. My wrist sagged from the weight of the food, and my eyes widened. I'd never had so much food on my plate, and I had definitely never had meat before.

Meat was forbidden in my village, especially beef; only Christians and Muslims ate beef. If my life hadn't already been a curse, I may have thought twice about taking it.

But if the gods hate me anyway, what difference does it make?

My stomach groaned, begging for a taste of something more than plain rice. I started walking away again.

"Kash'i," Sarina said, "you should say 'thank you.'"

Ashamed, I turned around. "Uh…sorry…thank you."

"You are so welcome, *thangachi*," Nalayani replied. "There's plenty, and you could use it. Come back for more when you are done. We will make sure you are not hungry."

More? I wasn't sure I could eat everything she had given me. *This is nothing like the nasty food Ravi talked about at his orphan home. But I wonder if I'll get sick.*

I waited for Sarina to have her plate loaded up and followed her over to an empty space in the circle of boys next to Ameer and Sudhir.

My mouth watered as I breathed in the spicy aroma of the beef bathed in the thick brown gravy. Ripping a chunk off the *chapati*, I scooped up the beef, stuffing my greedy mouth. The tender meat dissolved into the sea of spice swimming in my mouth. Rich and savory: a world I never knew existed.

"Wait!" Sarina gasped. "We don't eat until everyone has their food. Then we pray together again before eating."

Looking around, I saw I was the only one who had touched the food. The others waited patiently with folded hands. I cowered and scanned the area for the Crow. She was looking directly at me while talking with Nalayani.

Is this an offense worthy of a beating? I stopped chewing, hoping she hadn't seen, but she just smiled at me. *Did her eyes twinkle? Is that anger gleaming, a coming punishment? Or something else?*

When she looked back at Nalayani, I gulped down the food, sweating. My mouth had a mild burn from the spice and salivated for more. It was the best thing I had ever tasted.

Sarina giggled. "Everyone does that when they first come here."

Out of the corner of my eye, I watched the Crow exit the common room and fly up a flight of stairs along the back side of the Common Hall.

I scowled. *Then why didn't you say anything to me first? Do you want to get me in trouble?*

Finally, Nalayani joined the circle on the cement patio. In one unified motion, everyone closed their eyes, dropped their heads over their plates, and chanted a short prayer in unison. Still hot from embarrassment and the single bite of food, I stared at my plate.

All at once, everyone opened their eyes and began devouring the food.

Eagerly, I shoveled another bite of the spicy food into my drooling mouth, sopping the gravy and grabbing the rice with my warm *chapati*. All too soon, my plate was empty.

Nalayani, stood up, taking long strides over to me. "How was the food, *thangachi?*"

"Delicious," I answered, with the first bit of enthusiasm of the day.

She smiled, satisfied. "Would you like more?"

Yes. That's what I wanted to say, but I was too nervous to admit it out loud. "No…thank you."

"I want more." Sudhir handed his plate to Nalayani.

I scowled at him, but Nalayani smiled.

She came back with another half-plate of food. Sudhir grabbed the plate from her and started eating greedily.

I punched Sudhir's shoulder. "Say 'thank you.'"

Sudhir rolled his eyes at me. "Uh…thank you."

Nalayani chuckled. "That's okay; you are very welcome."

The two girls showed Sudhir and me how to take care of our plates by rinsing them in a tub of water and returning them to the drying rack.

Sarina fought back a yawn, and I couldn't blame her; it must have been around ten-thirty.

"Time to brush our teeth!"

I stared blankly at her.

"You've never brushed your teeth, have you?"

"No." My cheeks burned with embarrassment.

"It's okay. I didn't either until I came here." Sarina smiled and skipped towards the stairs. "I'll get you both new toothbrushes."

"Meet me by the boys' dorm bathrooms once you have your toothbrush," Ameer said to Sudhir before heading out the door.

All the other boys filtered out of the room. Nalayani was cleaning up dinner in the kitchen. I was finally alone with Sudhir.

"Sudhir, don't trust—" I stopped short when I saw khaki pants coming down the stairs. Pastor Kurumuni came down and stood by us.

"Kashvi, Sudhir, you are in a very good place here. You are safe. And you must know that your *amma* loves you," Pastor Kurumuni said gently. "You know that, right? She didn't want to bring you here."

"It's all my fault," I muttered.

"No, don't burden yourself with that."

His voice is kind, but who can I believe?

"Is she really going home?" I asked, wondering what *Amma* had told him.

"Yes," he assured me. "But I told her if she ever needs help, she can always come to me. I know a place she can go if necessary."

Is he telling the truth?

"I need to get home now, but please don't blame your *amma* or doubt her love. It took courage to bring you here."

With a small half-smile, Pastor Kurumuni left.

I pulled Sudhir close, and he rested his head on my shoulder. *Just like he did with* Amma.

I gulped, missing her terribly.

"Sudhir," I whispered, "I know you like it here, but don't trust anyone. Understand?"

Sudhir frowned, confused. "Why not?"

"Just—"

He cut me off and declared firmly, "*Amma* will visit us next week..." He paused. "Right?"

"Yes," I replied, trying to sound confident.

"I like it here," Sudhir said, a little too eagerly. "Maybe *Amma* can come live here with us."

I sighed, forcing a smile.

"I'm glad you're here with me, *Akka*."

I smirked. "I never thought I would hear those words from you."

His presence was unexpectedly comforting, but a familiar wave of fear crept in. *What if the Crow is right, and they send me to a different home?*

Just then, Sarina came running back down the steps, braid flopping on her back.

"Time to brush away years of grime!" She gave a wide grin as she handed us each a toothbrush.

Sudhir grabbed the blue one. "What do I do with it?"

"Go find Ameer. He will help you."

"What are we doing after brushing our teeth?" I interjected.

"Sleeping."

I wrapped my arms around Sudhir. "Goodnight," I said. Then, pulling him closer, I whispered, "Be careful. Remember: don't trust anyone."

"Why—"

I hushed him, pressing a finger to my lips.

"Goodnight," he said, glancing back at me before sprinting behind the boys' dorm.

I followed Sarina, pausing for a moment to look up at the stars piercing the black sky.

If any god up there cares, protect us. Protect Amma.

Sarina led me to the bathroom and demonstrated how to brush my teeth. I scrubbed hard until my gums throbbed, foam spilling down my chin.

"I think that's enough." Sarina giggled, amused by my intensity.

I spit into the sink as Sarina did. It was tinged red. My tongue brushed over my gums, tasting blood. My eyes darted to Sarina in concern.

"It's bloody." Sarina nodded. "That's normal. It'll stop after the first few times. Let's go to bed."

I followed her to the front of the dorm.

"*Ahh!*" I screamed as four sighthounds, nearly as tall as me, charged towards us.

"Don't worry," Sarina assured me. "They're friendly!"

The dogs surrounded me, sniffing me from head to toe.

"She's our friend," Sarina said to the dogs, putting her arm around my shoulder.

The white and brown speckled dogs seemed to relax, their tails wagging furiously, dragging their slender hips with them. One of the dogs jumped up, placing its paws on my shoulders, trying to lick me. I pushed it back, overwhelmed.

"I think he likes you," Sarina teased. "We keep the dogs locked up during the day, so they are full of energy at night to stay awake and guard the campus."

Someone whistled in the courtyard, and the dogs ran to him. It was the grinning, shy boy who had served us tea.

At that moment, I realized that it had only been a few hours since I had my hair, my *amma*, my normal life. But that felt like forever ago, and now I was going to a new bed in a new place surrounded by strangers.

The white dog jumped up, disrupting my thoughts and pulling me back to the present. The shy boy grabbed the dog's front paws and began twisting in circles with it.

"Mahiyu loves dancing with them." Sarina laughed. "Follow me; I'll show you our room."

Sarina led me up a flight of stairs into a large bedroom with two double beds in it. Nalayani was in one of the beds reading a Bible.

"You can share my bed with me," Sarina offered warmly.

"You may regret that when she hits you in the middle of the night," Nalayani said with a chuckle.

Hits me? I thought of my father and wrapped my arms tightly around myself.

"Don't worry." Sarina rolled her eyes. "I'm not the crazy sleeper. Nalayani is the one who flops around at night; that's why I have my own bed."

Nalayani patted the mattress next to her. "Sit here."

I sat by Nalayani warily. "You're reading the Bible again?"

"Yeah, we always read and pray before bed," Sarina explained.

Nalayani handed the Bible to Sarina. "*Thangachi*, will you read tonight?"

"Sure, *Akka*," Sarina said.

I hope they won't expect me to read. I couldn't read well.

"Lord, how are they increased that trouble me! Many are they that rise up against me. Many there be which say of my soul, There is no help for him in God…"

There is no help for me from the gods.

I glanced at Nalayani as she stood, walked to the door, and slid two large bolts into place.

Who is she keeping out with those locks? Sudhir flashed through my mind. *Is he safe?*

"I will not be afraid…" Sarina read, her voice steady and calm.

I forced my thoughts to focus on her words.

"…Arise, O LORD; save me, O my God: for thou hast smitten all mine enemies upon the cheek bone; thou hast broken the teeth of the ungodly. Salvation belongeth unto the LORD: thy blessing is upon thy people."

Will any god ever strike my enemies?

"How can I pray for you, Kash'i?" Sarina asked.

I stared at her, speechless. No one had ever asked to pray for me before.

"When I first came here, I was afraid," she admitted.

"I was terrified," Nalayani added quietly. After a pause, she looked intently into my eyes. "Kashvi, I know you are scared, and I know we are strangers to you. I may be the assistant warden, but here at Karunai House, we are family. You've experienced many difficult things, but I promise to help and protect you as much as I am able." She waited, willing me to speak to her, but her words meant nothing to me. She sighed gently. "We just want to love you, *thangachi.*"

"Are you scared?" Sarina asked gently.

I nodded, unable to lie. To ignore their attempts to comfort me, I quickly changed the subject.

"This god you read about…how do you get him to strike your enemies and bless you?"

"Wow, there's a question." Sarina looked at Nalayani, stifling a giggle.

"Well," Nalayani began, her tone more serious, "There's too much to explain in one night, but you can be sure that God will bring justice for all wrong done. It's also important to know that you are one of your own worst enemies. We all sin against God, so there is no reason God

74

should bless anyone. But God is merciful to some and will bless them even though they don't deserve it."

So I can't do anything to please this god? That sounds about right.

Sarina slid off the bed onto her knees. "Let's pray."

Nalayani followed, and I hesitated before kneeling too.

"Father," Sarina began, "thank you for bringing another girl here. It is scary to be in a new home with lots of new people, so please keep her from fear. Protect her, keep her safe, and may she find joy here. Help her to know Jesus, the only one who can forgive our sins. Forgive us and bless us in Jesus' name, Amen." Sarina smiled at me and climbed into our bed.

For a brief moment, the prayer seemed to soothe my heart. I slid into bed next to Sarina. The bed had a cushioned pad on it and a fluffy pillow. It was my first time sleeping off the floor and using a pillow. The gentle comfort almost felt safe as I settled in.

"Goodnight," Sarina said softly.

"Goodnight," Nalayani said. "I'll turn off the light."

She flicked the switch, and the room was plunged into darkness. The warmth of the moment faded, swallowed by the cold grip of uncertainty lurking in the darkness. All my fears came rushing back into my mind.

I guess Sarina's prayer didn't work.

CHAPTER 9

M y eyes opened to darkness.
Where am I?
Something moved across my back.
An arm!

Instinctively, I shot away, falling on the hard floor. The cold tile shocked me into reality, and the sight of Sarina's long hair dangling over the bed brought relief. Sarina had sprawled across the whole bed as quickly as I fell out.

No one was trying to hurt me. Not yet.

My head felt strangely cool. I reached up and ran my hand over stubble.

The orphanage. The haircut. Amma.

Tears of reality silently washed down my face.

Cock-a-doodle-doo!

The crow of the rooster startled me in my grief for a moment, but I continued to weep.

I heard a rustle and then Sarina's hand patting around the bed. "Kashvi?"

"I'm here," I whispered, wiping my tears away and sniveling.

Sarina scooted to the edge of the bed. "What are you doing down there?"

"I...fell."

"Are you okay?"

"Yeah."

Sleepy-eyed, Sarina slid out of bed and offered her hand. "It's time to get up anyway. How did you sleep?"

I grabbed her hand, and she pulled me up. "Not good."

Every creak last night had made me panic. At least at home I knew where the danger was. I was surprised I'd slept at all.

Sarina navigated to the light switch and flicked it on. Piercing brightness flooded the room. Nalayani groaned from her bed.

I glanced around the bedroom, realizing just how large it really was. Pillows, mattresses, blankets, a ceiling fan, lights everywhere, unlimited water, unlimited food! Luxury surrounded me, but I wasn't at peace. *Amma* was gone, and soon I could be separated from Sudhir.

Even if I stay here, what are these comforts hiding?

"I remember my first night here. I was miserable." Sarina unbolted the door and opened it.

I followed her down the stairs to the courtyard. The sky was still dark, but a glow peeked over the horizon.

My eyes landed on Sudhir, and I exhaled in relief. He stood by the boys' dorm with Ameer and a couple of other boys, cheering as they knocked tamarind fruit down from a tree with long sticks. They all scrambled for the fruit as it fell.

He was safe. It hadn't taken him long to fit in. In some ways, I was happy for him. The fear that Mother had brought us here so she could take her own life never occurred to him.

I ran over and wrapped my arms around him. "How was your night, *Thambi?*"

Sudhir squirmed, embarrassed, as he glanced at the other boys. "It was great. We stayed up late tossing a ball around—"

Ameer nudged him and whispered, "*Shhh.* Sarina will tell on us."

Sudhir gave a sheepish grin.

Sarina rolled her eyes, grabbing my hand. "Let's go, Kash'i."

Sarina pulled me along to the bathrooms behind the girls' dorm where we brushed our teeth again. I felt ugly as I watched Sarina brush her long, clean hair.

When she finished, I followed her to the Common Hall, and she retrieved two brooms from a storage closet. Handing one to me, she bounded up the stairs of the girls' dorm, her braid flopping behind her, singing a song I'd never heard before. It repeated the name "Jesus" a lot.

I wonder if every song here is about Jesus.

When we reached the top of the stairs, I realized there was a lot more up there than just our bedroom. To the right of the room where we had just been sleeping was a small kitchen area. To the left was a hallway leading to three padlocked rooms. I wondered what was behind those doors.

Sarina began sweeping from the far end of the hallway as I swept from the near side.

We're just going to work all day, aren't we?

We met at the stairway, and Sarina swept her pile of dirt down the stairs with a flourish, her smile unfading.

I interrupted her singing and asked, "What are all these rooms for?"

"There used to be more girls here," Sarina explained. "But the government said no more girls can be admitted. So now there's thirty boys and me." She added, "And now you."

"Why don't they want girls here?" My stomach tightened with unease.

"The government doesn't like Christian homes." She frowned. "They make up new rules all the time, hoping to shut them down. First, they said the girls' dorm was too close to the boys', so *Appa* offered to build another farther away. Then they changed the rule to say boys and girls needed to be on separate properties altogether. They sent all—" Sarina stopped midsentence and swallowed hard. She squeezed her eyes shut but tears still snuck out. "They sent all the other girls away."

I wasn't sure what to do, so I awkwardly put my hand on her shoulder.

She sat on the step and wiped her tears with her shawl. "They took my best friend, Saachi. She was sent to one of the government homes that treats children like animals."

We both lost our best friends. I sank down to sit beside Sarina, silently grieving for both of us.

"Every day, I wonder if it's my last here. Most of the other girls were sent to relatives' homes, and Karunai House helps with their needs. Nalayani was almost eighteen, so she became staff. I was so glad she stayed. I almost lost all my friends." Sarina shook her downcast head. "Saachi didn't have any relatives, and I don't either. I'm only still here because there wasn't room for me in any other home in the district. I don't know if they're still looking or if they just forgot about me in the jumble of paperwork."

"I—I'm sorry," I murmured, my own fear deepening.

Sarina's eyes regained some of their usual sparkle. "This place isn't like other children's homes. This is my family. You're part of it now too. I'm glad you're here."

I managed a small smile. I liked Sarina, and I wanted to trust her, but I was still suspicious of this strange place.

"Why doesn't the government like Christian homes?"

"*Appa* says it's political," Sarina murmured, fingering the end of her braid. "Christians won't vote for the radical Hindu leaders."

"What will happen to me?" My voice wavered.

Sarina took a deep breath. "I don't know what will happen to either of us, Kash'i. We need to trust in God and pray to him. He is good, even when things feel bad."

Good, even when things feel bad?

"One thing I do know is that *Amma* will fight to keep us here," Sarina said. "She'll fight hard for you because your *thambi* is here, too."

"Why is that?"

"*Amma* was raised in a Christian boarding school, but her *thambi* wasn't. She doesn't want anyone else to feel the pain of being separated from their siblings. He's still Hindu. *Amma* is always praying that he will believe in Jesus someday."

Will they treat me differently for being Hindu?

Everything here seemed to center on being Christian. I'd have to be careful about what I said. And I'd need to warn Sudhir. He was already fitting in too easily.

"It's so nice having a girl my age to talk to again." Sarina stood. "But we better get back to work."

Or what?

Sarina began singing again as we finished sweeping the girls' dorm. When we finished, we moved towards the Common Hall. I took note of the layout so I could navigate myself. The ground floor housed the Crow's office, just off the side of the large common room where we had devotions. Of course, I remembered the patio where we had eaten the delicious food last night and the kitchen behind it. I breathed in deeply, trying to savor the meal again.

Around us, the boys watered plants, picked vegetables, gathered eggs from the random places in the yard where the chickens laid them, pulled clothes from the line, and tended a trash fire.

"You said the government homes treat children like animals," I interrupted Sarina's singing, again. "How is this place different?"

Sarina laughed, spreading her arms wide to gesture at everything. "There is joy here. There is love here. This is Karunai House—there's *karunai* here—there's grace here!"

I tried to imagine that what she said was true and took in my surroundings in a less-guarded light. The children *were* smiling, laughing, singing—working, but not under pressure. No one was yelling, no one was watching them with unblinking eyes.

At least that matched what she said.

"That's Dhiren." Sarina pointed towards the older teen drummer mechanic across the yard. "He makes sure we're safe and happy. He always makes everyone laugh, and he can fix anything."

Dhiren, sponge in hand, was scrubbing the old white SUV with his ox arms. Catching Sarina's eye, he flashed a huge smile. "Music?"

"Yes, *Anna*, please!" shouted Sarina.

Dhiren leaned into the SUV window, and moments later, the beat of a *tabla* drum thumped across the courtyard. Joyfully, he began to dance, and soon the others joined in as they worked. Even Sudhir was dancing, gathering groundnuts with Ameer and a few others in the field. I almost laughed watching someone as bulky as Dhiren acting like a child.

Sarina danced up the stairs of the Common Hall. I followed, allowing my body to sway a little. I'd never heard the song before, but when the voices came in, I knew it was another Jesus song.

On the second floor, I realized this must be where Pastor Pradhan and the Crow lived. Between songs, Sarina kept up a steady stream of chatter, telling stories about Dhiren's constant antics. We swept through Pastor Pradhan's office, a library room, three bedrooms, and a storage room.

Sarina changed subjects, mentioning how well Sudhir was fitting in, just as we turned into the living room.

"The boys really love Sudhir..."

I heard no more as we came upon the awful orange couch where I had sat with my mother just the night before. Eyes locked on it, I felt unsteady on my feet as all else faded from view.

How did Appa *react when* Amma *got home? If she actually went home—is she even alive?* I had to find her, had to know if she was okay.

Sarina shook me out of my trance. "What's wrong?"

My eyes were drawn back to the empty cushions. "*Amma.*"

Sarina guided me to the couch and rested her head on my shoulder. The chubby dachshund waddled in and sat on my feet again, his eyes full of concern.

"Milo always senses when someone's sad." Sarina patted his back.

I reached down, stroking the dog. I needed my mind off my *amma*. "How did you end up here?"

Sarina's voice turned solemn. "About seven years ago, my parents had a big fight, and my *appa* left. My *amma* tried to make me eat pesticide with her, but I knew what it was. I refused."

I flinched as she spoke, picturing my own *amma* with poison in some back alley. I looked back at Sarina's darkened face.

"She died right in front of me." Sarina's hand absentmindedly tugged at the end of her braid. "When *Appa* came home and saw her, he took the poison, too."

"That's…horrible." The words felt empty. I had no words of comfort to give. I had no comfort myself.

Sarina sighed, and her shoulders drooped. "I wandered to the bus station and begged for food for weeks before a social worker found me and brought me here."

I imagined she must have been remembering the last touches she felt from her parents, the fear she had endured as a tiny child watching her *amma* die.

Sarina's cheeks slowly lifted into her familiar smile again. "But God gave me new parents and a new home to live in."

I inspected her face, wondering how genuine that smile could be.

Sarina stood, moving on from the conversation. "Let's finish cleaning up before devotions."

We finished sweeping and left the orange couch behind.

Downstairs, we joined the others in the common room again for devotions. Dhiren's hair swayed over his forehead as he played the *dholak*.

The Crow explained that Pastor Pradhan had some house visits to do, so she led the devotions again, reading from the Bible and praying, just like the night before.

I found it strange how she thanked God for everything: food, clothing, health, shelter. In all my years of praying to the gods, I only ever asked for things. I never had a reason to say thanks, because I never got what I asked for. Simply surviving each day never seemed like a gift.

"Today is a special day," the Crow announced after her prayer. "It's Kashvi's thirteenth birthday today! Let's all sing 'Happy Birthday' together."

I had forgotten it was my birthday; it was never anything special at home. But now everyone sang to me and clapped. It felt strange to have this attention. I sat awkwardly, looking at the ground. When they finished singing, I saw Sudhir laughing at me. I wanted to whack him, but he was on the other side of the room.

"We'll have a special treat for you tonight," the Crow beamed, "but for now, go enjoy this beautiful day God has given."

Her face and tone were still disconcerting to me.

Everyone stood and wished me a happy birthday before lining up for breakfast. The smell of warm spices and frying oil filled the air as we ate potato curry with perfectly puffed, greasy, golden *puris*. Nalayani served me a huge portion like she had the night before. Once again, she vehemently encouraged me to eat my portion and more.

Remembering to wait for the prayer this time, I eagerly filled my belly with the delicious flavors.

After breakfast, I realized that our chores were done, and we were free for the rest of the day. We played games to pass the time; Sarina taught me how to play badminton and *carrom*. Later, everyone gathered to play volleyball.

Exhausted and sweating, we stopped for a snack of cool, red watermelon. Mahiyu walked around with a large tray, serving everyone. I had never tasted watermelon before. The juicy fruit slid down my throat, refreshing me and cooling my whole body.

Sarina led me to a giant jug with a tap in it. She filled the plastic cup on a string and drank first.

I filled it after her and stared at the water. It was clear—nothing floating, no tint. I smelled it, but it had no scent. I poured it into my mouth. It tasted like nothing but felt like purity itself—the best water I'd ever had.

Sarina and I played *carrom* under the tree in the middle of the large field behind the dorms as the boys organized a football game in the open area beside us. I watched Dhiren toss the football up in the air as they chose teams.

Once again, I was reminded of Asha and the knife in her ball. I couldn't go anywhere without those constant reminders of pain from my past.

I heard a motorcycle rumble into the courtyard and watched it pull up beside the Common Hall. The little windshield on it had a sticker of a cross on it. The man took his helmet off. It was Pastor Pradhan. He walked towards us, and I clenched my fists nervously.

Pastor Pradhan approached Dhiren with a big smile. "May I join?"

"Sure, *Appa*!" Dhiren grinned, and all the other boys surrounded him with joy, asking that he be on their team.

My jaw dropped seeing Pastor Pradhan, or *Appa* as the others called him, actually join the game. He played enthusiastically, and all the boys cheered him on. They clearly loved having him play with them.

I tried to imagine my *appa* playing football with Sudhir and me and laughed bitterly. He never played, never even watched us with interest. I forced those thoughts away, not wanting to dwell on home anymore.

Mahiyu walked onto the field with a tray of hot tea in hand. The boys dodged around him, nearly knocking him over. He tried to keep it steady, scowling at the close calls. By the time he reached Pastor Pradhan, half the tea had spilled onto the tray. But Pastor Pradhan graciously accepted what was left of it as he wiped sweat from his brow.

"Is Mahiyu a servant?" I asked inquisitively.

"No," Sarina laughed, "but he has a servant's heart. He's always looking for ways to help others."

"What's wrong with him?" I asked.

"Wrong with Mahiyu? Nothing's wrong with him." She shrugged, smiling. "God just made him different than a lot of us. He never passed sixth grade, but *Amma* hired him after he aged out to help with cooking and accounting. He's amazing with numbers. He remembers everyone's birthday and knows exactly how much of every ingredient we need to purchase each week."

"How did he come here?" I asked.

Pastor Pradhan walked over by us with his hot tea, seeking shade.

"His parents died from AIDS," Sarina said. "His uncle didn't want to care for him, so he brought him to us."

"Ah, Mahiyu. Such a special boy. We love him dearly. Once, we thought he was gone forever," Pastor Pradhan chimed in.

"Oh, yeah!" Sarina's eyes lit up. "One day, his uncle visited and then took him away without telling anyone. We didn't believe he had just run away. He loved this place so much."

"It took us two months to find him…" Pastor Pradhan took a large sip of tea, then held his mouth open awkwardly, breathing in and out to try and cool the scalding liquid.

"He was working at his uncle's restaurant over an hour away," Sarina continued the story, too excited to wait for Pastor Pradhan to recover. "When *Appa* and *Amma* showed up at the restaurant, Mahiyu dropped a serving tray full of food right on the floor and hugged them. His uncle had taken him to work for him without pay."

"Government homes would have just filed a police report," Pastor Pradhan added. "But we knew the police would never actively search for him. We had to find him. He's part of our family."

I closed my eyes, and a gentle warmth filled me as I imagined being a part of a real loving family. Smiles instead of smirks; laughter that wasn't mockery; hugs given for no reason at all, rather than only out of pity after a beating. I let myself bask in that dream for a moment.

I opened my eyes as Pastor Pradhan set his tea cup on the ground and stepped up to the tangled trunks of the tree we sat under.

"We call this the hugging tree."

I looked up. It wasn't just one tree—a *banyan* tree had spiraled around the trunk of a coconut tree.

Pastor Pradhan cleared his throat. When I looked back at him, I had to stop myself from giggling. Dribbles of tea sat in his neatly trimmed beard.

"The trees look like they're hugging each other," Pastor Pradhan remarked, stroking his beard and subsequently checking his damp hand. He saw that I noticed and grinned at me.

Sarina's arms closed around me. "And it's where I go when I'm sad and need a hug."

It felt strange, being hugged by this girl I barely knew. I rarely received affection, even from my *amma*. The warmth of Sarina's arms tried to comfort, but I put my guard up again.

Oh, how I wanted to believe Sarina about how great this place was, but how could an orphanage be a place of joy and love? That was just a dream.

My attention was pulled back to the football field. Sudhir and Ameer fought for the ball, shoving against each other. Sudhir tumbled forward, somersaulting, but quickly sprang to his feet.

Eyebrows scrunched; lips pursed—I knew that look. I wanted to stop the moment, but there was nothing I could do.

Sudhir darted around Ameer and kicked his legs out from under him. Ameer's chest and face hit the dirt with a thud.

"Sudhir!" Pastor Pradhan's voice boomed across the field as he pushed himself onto his feet. He started towards Sudhir.

Sudhir spun around, eyes wide with fear.

"Come here!" Pastor Pradhan commanded.

My body stiffened. *Now I'll see what it's really like here.*

Sudhir shuffled over, his gaze fixed on the ground. When Pastor Pradhan moved his arm forward, Sudhir flinched, shielding his face.

But the blow never came. Slowly, Sudhir lowered his hands to see Pastor Pradhan was simply motioning for him to sit. Sudhir sank to the ground beside a hanging root, and Pastor Pradhan sat down beside him. I strained to hear what the pastor was saying to him, but his voice was too low.

After they had talked for a few minutes, I noticed Pastor Pradhan's eyes were closed, hands folded.

Is he praying with Sudhir?

Sudhir stood up, and Pastor Pradhan extended his hand. Sudhir pulled him to his feet, and with a smile, Pastor Pradhan placed his hand on Sudhir's shoulder. He said a few more quiet words before they both laughed. Together, they jogged back into the field to rejoin the game.

Sudhir approached Ameer, said something, and Ameer clapped him on the shoulder with a grin.

The game carried on as if nothing had happened.

I looked at Sarina in disbelief. "Is that it?"

"What do you mean?"

"Sudhir's punishment. That's all?" I asked. "No beatings? No sending him to the dorms without food?"

Sarina chuckled. "Like I said, there is love here. Sometimes kids are sent to the dorms, but no one is ever beaten or starved."

I had expected something harsher, a terrible beating and starving like Father would have given. I thought he deserved at least a little beating for what he did.

"Why did they pray?" I asked.

"Because Sudhir sinned," Sarina explained, "and all our sins are ultimately against God. We need forgiveness from God, not just from those we sin against."

"How do you know if the gods forgive you?"

"Well, first of all, there is only one true God, not gods. So, the good news is you only have to worry about pleasing one God." Sarina laughed. "The bad news is, like Nalayani said last night, there is nothing you can do to make God forgive you, because everything we do is corrupted with sin."

"So…"

"So, that's where the best news comes in." Sarina smiled. "God came to earth as Jesus Christ, and he died to pay for the sins of his people. If you believe he paid for all your sins, God will forgive you because of what Jesus did."

"So, God will forgive, simply for me believing Jesus paid for my sins?"

"If you truly believe it, he will."

My head was spinning as I struggled to wrap my mind around this. All my life, I'd tried to do good so the gods would be happy with me. It didn't work. But this Christian God? Just one God? He forgives the bad things we do, just for believing? I didn't know what to think of it.

CHAPTER 10

Pastor Pradhan called off the football game and told everyone to wash up for devotions.

I followed Sarina to the girls' dorm and washed. The scented shampoo and soap reminded me of flowers and joyful celebrations, something that I knew barely anything about but that I longed for inside.

Sarina gave me a new turquoise *chudidhar* to wear. Peering into the dim mirror, I didn't feel quite as ugly today.

After washing, we gathered for evening devotions. Pastor Pradhan joined the Crow tonight. We sang to Dhiren's rhythm on the *dholak*, and then Pastor Pradhan opened his Bible.

"Today we are going to read from God's word in Psalm 115," Pastor began. "Not unto us, O LORD, not unto us, but unto thy name give glory...our God is in the heavens: he hath done whatsoever he hath pleased...Their idols are silver and gold, the work of men's hands. They have mouths, but they speak not: eyes have they, but they see not: They have ears, but they hear not...They that make them are like unto them; so is every one that trusteth in them."

I thought of the Kali idol in our house. I had never considered it before, but...someone had made her. I was afraid a chunk of metal controlled everything in my life, but there it just sat, lifeless, on the shelf. It wouldn't even exist if someone hadn't molded it.

When Pastor Pradhan finished, he looked up. I thought he was looking right at me.

"There are millions of Hindu gods, and each one was created in the minds of man, then shaped into an idol to be worshiped. But there is only one true, living God. He wasn't created by man; he created man and all things. He does what he pleases, and we cannot try to control him like the Hindu gods. But he is a good God."

Pastor Pradhan looked around the room. "Where do we learn about this one true God?"

A boy shouted, "The Bible!"

"Very good!" Pastor Pradhan smiled, silver flecks in his beard shining in the light. He held up his Bible. "This is a book of real events—from the beginning of time, when God created all things and man first sinned, until shortly after Jesus came to forgive sins, just as God promised."

Pastor Pradhan glanced around again. "How do we know the Bible is true?"

Sarina shouted, "Jesus fulfilled many prophecies written hundreds of years before him, including rising from the dead."

"Exactly, Sarina. The Bible contains fulfilled prophecies, and it also tells us the truth of the world as we know it. We are guilty sinners who need a Savior."

I stared at the ground, absorbing his words.

Could this really be true? One God, who is good? If he is real, how can he be good with everything that has happened in my life?

I sighed as Pastor Pradhan began to pray, not knowing what to think. Glancing around, I found Sudhir towards the back of the room. He grinned at me, fidgeting as everyone knelt, eyes closed, hands folded. None of these things seemed to concern him.

After the prayer, the Crow called to Sudhir and me, pulling us out of the crowd that was lining up for dinner.

"How are you doing here?" she asked, her tone gentle.

"Great, ma'am." Sudhir's smile stretched wide.

She turned to me.

"Fine, ma'am."

"I've never slept on something as soft as the bed I got. I feel rich!" Sudhir added.

The Crow put a hand gently to her mouth to hold back a laugh.

I stared at the ground but felt her eyes on me. When I looked up, she was watching me perceptively but didn't say anything. Instead, she turned and opened a cabinet under a bookshelf and pulled out two gift bags, handing one to each of us.

Sudhir couldn't contain himself. He immediately tipped his bag upside down, spilling three pairs of jeans, button-up shirts, T-shirts, and undergarments onto the floor. Bright patterns and buttons shone from the pile of tightly folded clothes, fresh from the store. On top lay new sandals, still tagged, and a velvet-cased Bible like all the other children had. The luxury before me sent a shiver through my body.

"Wow!" Sudhir's joyful expression warmed me.

I couldn't wait to open mine. I just hoped I wouldn't be disappointed.

The Crow's eyes shimmered as she smiled and turned to me. "Go ahead, Kashvi."

I knelt on the floor and carefully pulled out three new outfits, one by one. The soft fabric felt foreign beneath my fingers, too delicate for me. The first *chudidhar*: a soft pink with sun-shaped beadwork on the chest and with gold embroidery around the edges.

Just one outfit—one far less ornate than this—was the most I'd received in a whole year at home.

My breath caught, a familiar tightness building in my chest. I dropped the delicate pink fabric; its beauty mocked the chaos swirling inside me. The separation from *Amma*, the uncertainty of this new place, and even the kindness I didn't know how to accept pressed down on me.

A gentle weight settled on my shoulder. I looked up into the warden's calm eyes. Her hand was firm but kind, grounding me to this moment. My breathing slowed; the tightness loosened just enough.

"Hey, look! We'll match!" Sudhir's voice broke through my haze. He held out his own pink button-up shirt with a gold embroidered crest on the chest pocket. He grinned wide, his eyes encouraging me to keep going. "What else did you get, *Akka?*"

I blinked in surprise. His attention on me was so unexpected, so… caring?

Slowly, I pulled out the next *chudidhar*, fingering the smooth, silky fabric. My hands were steadier now, with Sudhir's smile and the Crow's touch anchoring me.

The golden fabric in my hands gave a slight rustle as it unfolded. Patterned with swirls, fabric flowers graced the neckline like a permanent garland.

Too excited to wait, Sudhir reached over and grabbed the last outfit, unfolding it with eager hands. I snatched it from him. The navy color popped with bright green embroidered patterns and rani pink beads from neck to hem.

At the bottom of the bag were undergarments, a pair of sparkling gold sandals, and fancy gold earrings, along with my own Bible.

I pulled at the plain steel stud in my ear as I looked at the woman before me, trying to find words. Unable to speak, I gently touched her hand that lingered on my shoulder, my gaze whispering gratitude. At that moment, I didn't see the beady, ominous gaze of a crow; I saw big, joyful eyes shimmering like stars in the night sky.

"You may have heard some of the other children talking about their sponsors," she explained. "Christian families from America send funds to support children staying here, and they write letters to you. They help us provide you with these gifts. You will have your own sponsors now."

Why would someone from another country help me when they've never even met me?

"Sudhir!" Ameer shouted from the door.

Sudhir left his stuffed bag and dashed over to his friend.

I packed my new clothes gently back into the gift bag.

"What's on your mind?" Soft eyes searched mine.

What isn't *on my mind?*

I asked the most immediate question. "Does this sponsor mean I get to stay here with Sudhir?"

"We have permission for the time being," the woman said, her voice gentle and cautious. "I promise I will do whatever I can to keep you and your *thambi* together."

I nodded, unassured.

"Is there anything else? You really may ask me anything."

I needed something to hold onto. "I just—I just want everything to be okay, and nothing is okay!" I shook as I started to weep. "It's not okay at home, and it's not okay here, and I don't know what to want or hope for."

Compassionate arms wrapped me tightly. I crumbled in them, not having the strength to fight.

"It's my fault," I whimpered. "I didn't go to the temple because I was scared—"

"No, Kashvi." She stroked my shaved head. "Your *appa's* anger is not your fault."

Opening blurry eyes, I realized Pastor Pradhan was standing next to us. I jerked away from the safety I felt in his wife's embrace and steeled my face, wondering when he had come back into the room. I braced for a rebuke for crying, but instead, his expression showed tender understanding, different from anything I was used to.

"I understand those feelings," the woman said, pulling my gaze back to her. "My *appa* drank liquor every day." Her voice was weighted with memories. "He was always fighting with my *amma*, and I often blamed myself for those fights. We lived in a dirt hut, barely surviving on meager portions of rice. You may not believe it, but I was just skin and bones then. *Appa* forced me to help him in his tailoring business instead of going to school."

I searched her convincingly sympathetic eyes, wondering if this was true. If it was, did she really understand?

She continued, "One day, I was rescued by a Christian schoolmaster who admitted me into his private boarding school for free. There I learned about Jesus. I didn't understand then, but God brought me through all those struggles so I would come to know him. He brought me through lots of pain, but he also blessed me in more ways than I can number. One of those blessings is being able to help children like you. Tragedy brought all of us here, but now I get to share with you the same love of God that I was shown."

How many government homes are run by wardens who came from the same place as the children they care for? How many wardens would say they were called by God to show love to hurting children?

Maybe all Sarina's smiles and talk about this being her family are true.

"Kashvi, we promise to show you the love of our good God here as best as we can."

The warden—Vasantha, I remembered—tucked a wayward strand of hair behind her ear. Loosened from the day, her pulled-back hair seemed softer, less sinister, less...birdlike. I thought of my own mother's hair, the way she would take off her scarf at the end of the day in the dim light of our little house. I knew I could no longer think of this woman as The Crow, even though I was still hesitant to trust her.

Pastor Pradhan cleared his throat. "The living God *is* a good God, Kashvi." He pointed in his Bible to one of the verses he had read earlier. "'He will bless them that fear the Lord, both the small and great...' You are small, but God can see and hear you; he is not a god made of stone. He is not like the Hindu gods. He loves his children, and he does what is best for them, though it may not always be what they want. 'Fearing the Lord' doesn't mean cowering before him. It means revering him as our creator and striving to live the way he wants us to. You will learn his laws in time, but your conscience already tells you many of them. Fear him, trust him, and you will see that he is good and does good."

I gave small nod.

"Kash'i!" Sarina's voice called from the doorway. The food line had cleared out of the room. "Are you going to eat?"

Vasantha smiled. "Go on. We can talk more later."

"Yes, ma'am." I grabbed my giftbag and Sudhir's.

"The other children call me '*Amma*,'" Vasantha said. "You may call me '*Amma*' if you'd like."

Would calling her 'Amma' *be a betrayal of my real* amma? Despite what Vasantha said, I still felt responsible for causing pain to my mother.

"We'll have another surprise for you after supper," Vasantha added with a warm smile.

"Thank you..." I hesitated, "Am—ma'am," I decided at the last moment.

With a quick glance at Pastor Pradhan, I rushed out of the room before he could suggest I call him *Appa*. I still didn't trust him. He could be like my uncle—kind to everyone in public, and anything but kind behind closed doors.

One day, he'll show his true face.

Sarina handed me a plate, and I noticed everyone's eyes on me. It dawned on me that they were waiting for me to start. I hurried over to Nalayani. The scent of rich spices and roasted chicken reached my nose—warm and savory.

"Happy birthday, *thangachi*!" Nalayani scooped a generous serving of chicken *biryani* onto my plate. "Normally, we only have meat once per week, but since it's your special day, we are having a special meal tonight!"

My face warmed, and I hurried to sit by Sarina.

As everyone prayed, my mouth watered at the incredible aroma all around me. It smelled like a spice cart, with more spices combined into this dish than I'd ever seen together in my life. This was the kind of meal served at weddings, and they were serving it for *my birthday*—something I'd never celebrated in my life.

After the "Amen," I grabbed a piece of marinated chicken, wondering what chicken even tasted like. It slid off the bone effortlessly. I placed it into my mouth with some of the spiced rice.

"Do you like it?" Nalayani watched my face carefully.

"It's…" There were so many flavors, layers of spice mingling with various textures. I didn't know how to describe it, but it was best thing I'd ever tasted, even better than yesterday's meal. "…Delicious."

I shoveled another fingerful into my mouth.

Nalayani interjected, "Watch out for—"

My furious eating halted when I cracked down on something hard. I pulled out a whole clove, and Nalayani laughed, curls bouncing.

"…the whole spices," she finished.

We laughed together as we ate, but after several minutes, I realized how suspiciously quiet it had become and glanced around. All the boys had finished, washed their plates, and left. Mahiyu appeared in the doorway. Nalayani jumped up and hurried over to him, and he whispered in her ear.

"Are you all finished, *thangachi?*" Nalayani asked.

I hesitated, wary of the change in tone. "Yes, thank you."

"Follow me." Her eyes danced. "We have a surprise for you."

I stood, looking at Sarina for assurance. She was smiling, too.

Mahiyu snatched the plate from my hand. "I'll wash it, *Thangachi*. You go."

I followed Nalayani, keeping some distance, until Sarina grabbed my arm and pulled me forward with a skip in her step. Nalayani opened the door to the common room, and a loud shout resounded.

"*Happy birthday!*"

Everyone stood around a small table with a chocolate birthday cake resting on it, thirteen glowing candles flickering on top.

I couldn't believe it—I'd never had a birthday cake in my life. Suddenly, I felt my throat tighten, tears threatening to overwhelm me. I wanted to run away, unable to handle the outpouring of attention.

Sarina pulled me along behind the table where Vasantha and Pastor Pradhan stood next to the cake.

Vasantha's gaze met mine, full of warmth. She patted my shoulder gently. "It's okay to enjoy this, Kashvi. You're worth celebrating."

Sudhir ran up to me with boyish excitement, practically drooling over the cake.

"Blow the candles out!" Dhiren shouted.

Looking from Sudhir to Vasantha to Sarina, I felt a flickering of safety. Turning with a smile, I blew the candles out and everyone clapped and shouted.

Mahiyu ran into the room, clapping, holding a plastic knife. He handed the knife to me and quickly removed all the candles.

"Let me help you," Vasantha offered, placing her hand around mine and guiding it to cut a small piece of cake. Picking it up, she brought it to my lips.

"Happy birthday, Kashvi. May God bless you with many more."

I opened my mouth and accepted the cake from her fingers. The chocolate flavor burst onto my tongue—smooth and sweet.

"Now you may feed it to the others," Vasantha instructed. She called Sudhir forward, and I cut a piece and fed it to him. Then I fed Sarina, Nalayani, Vasantha, and even Pastor Pradhan.

Dhiren stepped forward and waved his giant hand in front of me. "You're doing it wrong, *Thangachi*. You need to do it like this."

He grabbed the piece of cake from my hand and smashed it on Mahiyu's cheek. Laughter burst out from everyone.

"*Thangachi*, quick! Cut me a piece!" Mahiyu shouted, his face smeared with chocolate.

I sliced off a chunk and handed it to him. Dhiren darted out the door, and Mahiyu chased after him. I heard shouting from the boys as they ran through the campus.

"Those two." Vasantha chuckled.

I continued feeding the cake to the rest of the boys, until Sarina took the knife and cut another piece to feed me.

With a glint in her eye, Sarina giggled and remarked, "It's not just the boys who can have fun." She cut another piece and smeared it across Nalayani's face.

"*Thangachi*, it's in my hair!" Nalayani grabbed a chunk from the cake with her hand and chased Sarina outside as they both laughed.

The boys ran out to watch, leaving me alone with Vasantha and Pastor Pradhan again.

The joy of the moment faded as I thought again of *Amma*. Guilt pricked at me for forgetting her and having fun while she suffered.

Vasantha read my mind and put her hand on my shoulder. "I know the games, food, and cake can't replace your *amma*, but I hope you enjoyed at least some of your birthday today."

I had. No one had ever done anything special for my birthday before, but it was bittersweet.

Oh, Amma, I would trade it all to be back with you.

I knew my *amma* wished she could have given me this today and every other birthday of my life. I imagined that she would thank Vasantha for what she had done.

"Thank you, Vas—" I stopped and added quietly, "...*Amma*."

The gentle smile that spread across her face made something inside me soften. She was not my real mother, but I longed for this place to be the family it gave the illusion of being.

Nalayani and Sarina ran back in, laughter still ringing as they wiped cake off their cheeks. *Amma* and Pastor Pradhan joined in their laughter.

Could things really be so perfect here?

When the cake was gone and the laughter turned to yawns, I picked up Sudhir's and my gift bags and followed Sarina towards our dorm.

Sudhir was running around in the courtyard, playing tag with a rubber ball.

I ran to him and wrapped my arms around him. "Goodnight, *Thambi*."

Sudhir pushed me away and yelled, "Watch out!" as the ball came flying past us.

"Goodnight!" he called back to me as he ran to the other end of the courtyard.

I shook my head, smiling, and left Sudhir's bag in front of the boys' dorm as I headed to wash up and brush my teeth with Sarina. In our bedroom, I unpacked my new clothes, earrings, and Bible, carefully placing them in the chest at the end of the bed.

I hopped up on the bed next to Sarina as Nalayani opened her Bible to Psalm 4.

"Hear me when I call, O God of my righteousness…the LORD will hear when I call unto him…"

As Nalayani continued reading, I sent my first prayer to the supposed "only true God." *If it is true that you hear me, please protect my mother, and please protect Sudhir and me here.*

Whether it worked or not, praying for my mother was all I could do for her, and now that I'd done it, a tiny bit of peace settled over me.

"…be still." Nalayani paused.

My eyelids grew heavy from the long day and my poor night of sleep yesterday. My head felt heavy, too, and I let it slip down to rest on Sarina's shoulder.

"…I will both lay me down in peace, and sleep: for thou, LORD, only makest me dwell in safety."

CHAPTER 11

Excitement coursed through my veins as I got ready Sunday morning. I was going to see Mother again!

As the past week had gone by, I'd grown more hopeful that Mother would actually come to visit us. Maybe Sarina's persistent optimism was wearing off on me.

I put on my favorite new *chudidhar*—the yellow one with the flower garland—and fingered my dangling gold earrings. They made me feel more like a girl, despite my buzzed hair.

The days had passed surprisingly quickly. The routine at Karunai House was becoming familiar. We had devotions and chores in the morning. The chores consisted of cleaning, gathering laundry, collecting eggs, picking vegetables from the garden, and helping prepare food. At first, I expected to be treated like a slave doing work all day, but to my surprise, our afternoons were free to do whatever we wanted until evening devotions. Even the chores weren't that bad; they were actually a little fun with Sarina, Nalayani, and the boys always joking with each other.

My anxiety lessened each day, even though I still wasn't as carefree as Sudhir.

Sarina helped me with everything. Nalayani took great care of me, ensuring I was fed, comfortable, and felt as happy as I could be. After a couple of days of her hovering, I learned to appreciate the constant care. Vasantha—*Amma*—was always checking in, too, asking more questions whenever I gave short answers.

It didn't feel quite as strange to call her "*Amma*" now as it did the first time.

After slipping on my new sparkly strapped sandals, I skipped down the stairs with Sarina. Sandals still felt strange after so many years of being barefoot. We ran over to the Common Hall to see if Nalayani needed any help in the kitchen before breakfast.

"*Thangachi*! I hope you slept well. Breakfast is almost ready!" Nalayani smiled, handing me a tray with a beautifully painted teacup on it. "Mahiyu is busy now; can you bring *Appa* his morning tea?"

"Yes, *Akka*." I marveled at the cup's artwork—a peaceful scene of wooly sheep grazing in a grassy meadow.

"*Appa*'s mother painted it," she explained. "The cup is very special to him."

Taking the tea, I felt honored, but anxiety built in me with each step I took up to Pastor Pradhan's office on the second floor. Even after all the kindness I had seen from him, I lived in fear of the unpredictable moment that would finally set him off.

With anxiety clouding my focus, I missed the last step and tripped forward. I watched, horrified, as the beautiful cup flew off the tray and shattered into pieces on the floor. My heart raced as the door down the hallway flung open, and Pastor Pradhan looked out, taking in the scene.

This was it.

Tears blurred my vision as I watched the man pick up a jagged piece of the pottery and lunge for me. I blinked. Did he have a *beedi* in his mouth? I smelled the alcohol I'd been blissfully away from the last few days. Now I'd done it.

"Kashvi, are you—" The voice boomed, coming closer.

I collapsed into the fetal position on the ground, guarding my face with my hands. A *fool*. A *troublemaker*. *Clumsy*. *Worthless*. *Cursed*. *Yes, that's what I am*.

I heard howls swirling around me: *Appa's* familiar voice. I tried to be still, hoping to avoid the beating.

I felt a gentle touch on my arm. The roars in my head stopped.

"*Amma, Amma,*" I whimpered.

The touch was different, and the voice wasn't Mother's or *Appa's.*

"Kashvi, you don't have to be scared. I promise you: I won't hurt you," Pastor Pradhan said tenderly. "I was fond of that cup, but it's just a temporary thing. It's not worth getting upset over."

I laid still until I again felt fully present in this strange new place, away from the little one-room house and my *appa.* Slowly, I uncurled myself and looked up.

The compassion on the pastor's face unraveled me.

For the first time since arriving, I let myself imagine that he really was who he seemed to be.

He extended his hand out to me with quiet assurance. "I know you had a rough life at home, but you don't need to live in fear here."

I hesitated before grabbing his hand. He pulled me up gently. "Careful where you step."

He disappeared back into his office and returned with a broom and a rag. I put my hand out to take it.

"No, I'll sweep it up. Get your breakfast before we leave for church." He smiled as he began sweeping the shards. "I'm sure you're excited to see your *amma.*"

"Yes," I mumbled, in shock. He didn't get angry or punish me. I'd never even seen a man sweep before.

I was scared to leave, feeling like this could be some sort of test.

"What about your morning tea? I'll get you more."

He shook his head, still smiling. "I appreciate that, Kashvi, but don't worry about it. I'll have my tea at church."

I bowed my head and slowly walked away.

CHΛPTER 12

Λfter breakfast, I sat next to Sarina on the steps in front of the girls' dorm as Nalayani braided Sarina's hair. Amidst Nalayani's constant apologies for "pulling too tight," I couldn't stop thinking about how, in my mind, Pastor Pradhan had turned into my *appa* having one of his rages—it all felt so real. I finally got up the courage to ask about it.

"Nalayani," I said, hesitantly, "do Pastor Pradhan and *Amma* fight?"

Nalayani thought for a moment. "Sometimes they disagree, but I wouldn't say they fight."

"So…Pastor Pradhan never…hits *Amma?*"

"Oh, no. *Appa* would *never* hit *Amma,*" Nalayani said confidently. She stopped braiding and looked at me. "Does your *appa* hit your *amma?*"

"Yes."

Nalayani's face saddened. "I'm sorry. That's not the way things should be."

For so long, I thought every family had an angry *appa* like mine. I would see other *appas* in my village yelling at their wives and children, so I had imagined that was just the way things were. There were families that seemed happy together, but I always assumed that behind closed doors, they were no different than mine.

Pastor Pradhan sweeping up those shattered pieces of teacup and the kindness he and *Amma* had shown this past week…it all seemed too perfect. But everything I had seen—and everything everyone here said about *Amma* and Pastor Pradhan—pointed to something different. Maybe they really were just that loving.

Just then, Milo ran over and jumped up on the step beside me, laying his head in my lap. I scratched his head. *He really does sense when people are sad, doesn't he?*

"Do you have something else on your mind, *Thangachi*?" Nalayani probed gently.

"I just…" I stuttered. "When I broke the teacup, I thought Pastor Pradhan would be angry with me. He became my angry *appa* in my mind. I could actually hear my *appa*, even smell him."

"I'm sorry, *Thangachi*," Nalayani said softly. "That was a flashback. I get those too…from things that happened to me."

"Really?"

"Yes," Nalayani replied. "*Amma* taught me how to bring myself back to reality when that happens. Running my finger over my earrings, doing slow breathing exercises, and reciting scripture in my mind have helped me a lot. You should talk with *Amma* about it sometime."

I nodded slowly. "Thanks, *Akka*, maybe that would help."

Nalayani's eyes sparkled. "I'm happy to help however I can, *Thangachi*."

I wondered what things had happened to Nalayani, what memories she carried—but it didn't feel right to ask her outright. So instead, I asked, "Do you have parents?"

Nalayani resumed twisting Sarina's hair into a thick braid.

"I do, but my *appa*'s disabled…and they couldn't really care for me back home. Ah—sorry, Sarina."

Her face clouded as she spoke. I sensed there was more to her story that she didn't want to talk about.

A loud rumble drew my attention to the middle of the courtyard, where Dhiren waited in the white SUV, black smoke spitting from the muffler.

"We're leaving in one minute!" Dhiren shouted from the window as he sounded the obnoxiously loud horn. "Everybody in the *Qualis*!"

Nalayani quickly tied off the end of Sarina's braid, and we grabbed our Bibles. I giggled as I approached the SUV, wondering how the ten-seater would hold all twenty-one of us. I slid into the middle seat next to Nalayani, who had Sarina sitting on her lap. A group of boys shoved their way into the car, and Sudhir ended up on my lap.

"*Amma's* coming today!" Sudhir bounced with excitement.

I smiled back at him hopefully.

Dhiren sped off down the road, zipping by some of the older boys riding their bicycles to church. Pastor Pradhan drove by us on a motor-cycle with a large steel barrel of milk tea and Mahiyu riding behind him. Grinning ear to ear, Mahiyu hugged his precious cargo, determined to deliver the tea safely to church. The honk of the *Qualis* mixed with our playful laughter as we passed them, swerving back quickly to avoid an oncoming bus.

Dhiren slammed on the brakes at a train crossing, and the vehicle erupted in spirited shrieks. I watched out the window as the watchman at the crossing cranked the wheel, lowering the gate. The road quickly became a sea of cars, buses, and *tuk-tuks*. Motorcycles squeezed into every available gap, and a few even wove around the gate and over the tracks just before the train thundered past.

The ground rumbled beneath us. The faded carriages were streaked with once-vibrant paint, and limbs dangled out of the barred windows, grasping for fresh air. Men leaned out of open doors, their shirts billow-ing in the breeze. A few young boys clung to ladders on the sides or sat on top of the carriages, enjoying a free ride.

To our right, a Hindu temple stood just off the road. A towering, four-armed headless god sat cross-legged on a throne.

Dhiren laughed. "Looks like the thieves were out stealing the heads of the 'all-powerful' gods again."

A chorus of laughter echoed around me.

The noise died down as an old priest emerged from behind the temple, leading a cow. He was shirtless, white ash covered his body from head to torso, and yellow and red lines crossed his forehead. His tangled, gray-streaked hair snarled around bits of debris caught in its web. One hand held both the cow's rope and the priest's *lungi* to keep it from slipping down his slim hips. He reminded me of our village priest.

I shivered as thoughts of Asha flashed in my mind.

Colorful ribbons and jewelry decorated the cow's neck and horns, and a large bell clanged as it waddled along. With every step, its bloated belly looked ready to explode from the undigestible street garbage stewing inside. The cow's head leveled with Dhiren's window, and it stretched its nose through as if to kiss him.

We all burst into fits of giggles.

"Go away! Go away!" Dhiren cringed back from the snot-dripping nose and cranked the window up, pinching the cow's snout. The cow jerked its head back, and Dhiren turned to face us, his eyes wide. "That cow is crazy!"

The boys exploded with a series of exaggerated kissing noises, doubling over with laughter.

"Hey, Dhiren! That cow just kissed your wife!" someone shouted, sending the group into a frenzy of hooting and cackling.

Dhiren rolled his eyes, though a grin tugged at the corner of his mouth. His affection for the boxy white SUV—the way he babied it and kept it spotless—had earned it the title of his "wife" among the boys.

The cow ambled away, and Dhiren cautiously rolled his window back down. Into the window shot a hand, palm up, in front of Dhiren's face. The priest's rotten-onion scent wafted to the back of the *Qualis*.

"No," Dhiren waved the priest away.

The priest wanted money—a donation to the holy cow resting beside him. Refusing meant inviting a curse.

"Curse you all!" The priest stomped away, dragging the bedecked cow behind him.

Everyone laughed—except Sudhir and me.

The priest's words had sent a chill through my spine. *How can Dhiren and the others so easily shrug the curse off? What if the Christian God isn't the only one with power?*

Finally, the train passed, and the watchman cranked the gates back up. Chaos ensued as the masses of traffic on both sides of the tracks wove through one another in opposite directions. Goats inched across the tracks, adding to the confusion. We eased through the tangled mess, animals bleating and car horns blaring all around as we headed into the city.

We turned down a narrow alley between apartment buildings, pulled up to a two-story house, and piled out. Sarina led the way through a rusty gate into the house's small courtyard, an area surrounded by concrete walls. She explained that a Christian man lived on the ground floor, and the church rented the floor above his home.

Up the stairs, we entered an open porch with low walls. Two mounds of sandals framed the doorway in front of us. Following Sarina, I kicked my new sandals into one of the piles and walked into a large room.

"Here, help me." Sarina shoved a broom at me.

I set my Bible on the window ledge and got to sweeping, coughing on the thick city dust, a combination of exhaust, ash, and dirt kicked up from the sooty roads. The boys took plastic chairs from stacks along the back wall and set them up as we swept the floor clean ahead of them. Pastor Pradhan set up the microphone in front of a podium at the front of the room, while a young man played a short jingle on the keyboard beside him and adjusted the volume.

I nudged Sarina. "Who is playing the piano?"

"Oh, that's Jai. He used to stay at Karunai House, but he aged out. He went to college and got a job teaching music. Lots of the aged-out kids come back for church. You'll meet lots of new people here. See?" She turned me around.

Vasantha—Amma—stood by the door, greeting everyone who entered. Several older women came in together and stopped to talk with Amma. Since no men were with them, I imagined they were widows. If this church was like the church in my village, there would be many widows here. I shuddered; widows were supposed to be cursed, and now I was gathering with them. Amma didn't seem to mind; she welcomed them joyfully with hugs. While chatting, a couple of the women began crying, and *Amma* cried with them.

I leaned against the wall, my eyes fixed on the door, waiting for Mother. In walked elderly couples, younger couples with children, and more widows. As people arrived, I noticed there were a lot more women than men.

Across the room, Nalayani was holding the newborn baby of a young couple. She looked down at the infant, and tears glistened in her eyes.

"Nalayani really loves babies, huh?" I murmured to Sarina as she approached.

"She had a baby of her own once," Sarina whispered.

"Really?" I asked, surprised.

Sarina looked around, then leaned closer. "Her uncle was the father, but no one in her village believed that except her parents. The rest thought she was a bad girl. She was forced to have an abortion. Her parents brought her here because the village rejected her. She misses her baby a lot."

"Wow..." I had no words.

I watched Nalayani smile at the baby, tiny fingers wrapped around her own. Her story was hard to believe—she seemed so joyful. I remembered rumors of a similar story in my village, though the girl had taken pesticide so she wouldn't have to live as an outcast. *Would Nalayani have done the same if she weren't brought to Karunai House?*

"Nalayani seems so protective." I wondered how much the loss of her baby had to do with that.

Sarina giggled. "That's an understatement." Then, her face filled with compassion. "She never got to take care of her baby, couldn't protect it. I think that's why she's a little overbearing sometimes. But, Kash'i, no one will love you more than Nalayani, and she's the best *akka* and friend we could ask for."

I nodded, appreciating Nalayani in a whole new way.

Sarina pointed to an elderly woman wrapping her arms around *Amma*. "There's *Ammachi*."

"*Ammachi?*" I asked. "I thought you didn't have grandparents."

"No," Sarina laughed. "That's *Amma's* mother, but we all call her *Ammachi*."

"Is she a widow, too?"

Sarina nodded. "Her husband died a few years ago. He was a Hindu his whole life and he rejected *Amma* and *Ammachi* for becoming Christians, but he confessed Jesus as his Savior on his deathbed."

What a time to reject all the other gods. Just before death and reincarnation. He must have truly believed it to do that.

Three younger girls ran up to Sarina, wrapping their arms around her and excitedly sharing stories about their week. Sarina introduced me to them. They were all forced out of Karunai House by the government. Thankfully, they had guardians who could take them in with the financial support of Karunai House, rather than going to government homes. Their guardians brought them to church every Sunday, and some had even been baptized, joining the church.

As the church filled, I kept my eyes on the door, desperate for Mother.

"It's time to sit down," Sarina announced.

"But my *amma*..." I glanced back at the door where Dhiren was carrying an older man in. He set the man on a chair and sat beside him.

Sarina put her arm around me. "Mahiyu always sits at the back to welcome latecomers. He'll get you when your *amma* arrives."

We sat on the green felt mat in front of the pulpit, surrounded by the other girls I'd just met. The mat quickly filled with children, practically sitting on top of each other, while the adults settled in the plastic chairs—men on the left, and women on the right. The aisle behind us gave me a view of the doorway, so I kept checking for Mother.

Sarina covered her head with her shawl, folded her hands, and began to pray.

I took one more glance at the door. No Mother.

The room was packed; a few latecomers sat outside on the porch, enduring the scorching sun.

Pastor Pradhan stepped behind the podium.

"Welcome, everyone! We are blessed to be gathered together on this Lord's day."

He lifted his hands and spoke some type of blessing.

I followed everyone else and bowed my head.

"Please stand, and let's sing praises to our God," Pastor Pradhan exclaimed.

The room rustled as the man on the keyboard—Jai—played a piano melody overtop drum rhythms. As Pastor Pradhan led the singing, I watched Jai's hands, fascinated by the movements. I'd never seen someone play keyboard before. Still, I couldn't keep my eyes from drifting back to the door.

Sarina leaned in and whispered, "It'll be okay. Her bus is probably late."

I forced a smile back, not feeling as optimistic as she was.

After the songs, Pastor Pradhan began reciting a psalm, and everyone repeated after him. We sang once more, and then he started praying…and praying. It felt endless.

I kept checking the door. I caught Sudhir's eye—he looked at me expectantly, and I sighed, shaking my head. He frowned, disappointed.

When the prayer finally ended, Pastor Pradhan opened his Bible. I did the same, setting my new notebook and pen—gifts from *Amma*—on my lap. *Amma* had asked me to try to write down the main points of the teaching, as well as any questions I had.

"Our sermon today is based on Deuteronomy 1:31," Pastor Pradhan said. "This is the word of the living God: 'And in the wilderness, where thou hast seen how that the Lord thy God bare thee, as a man doth bear his son, in all the way that ye went, until ye came into this place.'"

As he spoke, I glanced at Sarina's notebook, copying down what she wrote. "Never fear! Trust in God. He cares for you."

I turned again; still no sign of Mother.

God, if you care for me, let my amma *be here.*

Pastor Pradhan caught my attention when he spoke to the fathers, telling them how they needed to be a father like God is a Father to us— compassionate, slow to anger, merciful, and loving. That description of a father was foreign to me, yet I thought of Pastor Pradhan's reaction to the shattered teacup that morning.

Is that what God is really like?

I started wondering how my *appa* had treated Mother in the last week. *If she even returned home.*

"...Maybe now you are thinking: 'I don't want God to be like my *appa*.'"

I looked up.

"Maybe your *appa* is violent..."

Yes.

"A drunkard... "

Yes.

"Unloving and distant?"

I felt like he was talking directly to me. Reading my thoughts.

With open ears, I listened.

"...A cruel father should not make you flee from this God. No, run from a cruel father into the arms of the perfect Father. God is not like this, even when we are rebellious and foolish. Why? Because God is not man. Man abandons...God does not."

I looked back over my shoulder again. No Mother.

Did she abandon me?

"OHM NAMAH SHIVAAYA!" Hindu mantras began blasting from a loudspeaker outside. The Hindu chants reverberated around the cement walls, competing with the roar of the ceiling fans at full speed.

Pastor Pradhan continued, unfazed. Jai walked over to the church speaker and turned up the volume.

I covered my ears, but no one else reacted. Their eyes stayed focused on the pastor. The chanting brought to mind the priest Dhiren had laughed at on the way to church. Maybe his curse had reached Mother.

Is that why she isn't here?

Turning back to check for my mother again, I glanced over at the widows who were huddled together in the back. *Or is it the curse of the widows keeping her away?*

Sarina's rapid writing caught my attention again, and I hurried to copy her words. Many of the words were new to me, and I had no idea what they meant. I copied them anyway, still fearful that some misstep, perhaps like missing a key point of the teaching, would trigger a beating someday.

Sniffling echoed behind me, and I turned to see several women wiping tears from their eyes as they knelt in the praying position. I turned back around and kneeled also.

After prayer, we sang another song as a man walked around holding a sack in front of everyone. I watched as people threw money into it. Was this like a temple offering, and God would be angry if I didn't give? Would Mother come if I gave?

My eyes searched the room uselessly for her again.

The moment the service ended, I pushed my way to the back and shuffled outside to where Mahiyu was serving tea and biscuits.

"Did she come?" I asked him.

"No, sorry." He shook his head, looking down sadly. "Would you like some tea?" He smiled. "It will help you feel a little better."

"No, thank you." I leaned over the wall to look down to the street below.

Sudhir came up next to me. "Do you see her?"

"No," I replied. "Maybe she couldn't find it. I'm going to look around the block."

Sudhir followed me down the stairs.

"You go that way." I pointed left. "I'll go this way. We'll meet on the other side of the block."

"Kashvi!" I heard a voice call from above. It was Pastor Pradhan.

I ignored him and ran forward, eyes scanning for Mother.

She has to be down here somewhere. She just has to be.

I ran halfway around the block, and Sudhir wasn't there.

Maybe he found her around the corner, I hoped.

Rounding the corner with anticipation, I found Sudhir kicking a football with another boy in the alley. He wasn't even looking for her.

I charged at Sudhir and shoved him down. "What are you doing?"

"I already looked! She's not here!" Sudhir uttered defensively.

I realized that the ball had rolled by my feet. I kicked it as hard as I could, pouring all my frustration into it. It smacked a mangy dog sleeping a few meters away.

The dog jumped up, growling and pacing towards us with bared teeth. Terrified, I froze. Sudhir jumped up and started to run, but the dog's gaze was locked on me.

Suddenly, I heard a shout, and Pastor Pradhan jumped in front of me, his arms high, rock in hand. The dog yelped and fled.

I fell to the ground, weeping. Everything was just too much. Too much fear. Too much disappointment.

"Are you okay?" Pastor Pradhan knelt beside me, his eyes filled with concern.

"*Amma* didn't come," I sobbed.

"I'm so sorry, Kashvi." He reached for my shoulder, but I pulled away.

"*Appa* killed her, or she killed herself. Maybe she just doesn't want us. Either way, she's never coming back."

Pastor Pradhan's eyes glistened. "When your *amma* dropped you off, I saw the pain in her eyes. She didn't want to leave you. She loves you."

I wiped the tears on my *chudidhar*, my chest tightening.

"Maybe she missed the bus, maybe she couldn't find the church," he said gently. "There are many reasons why she may not have come today."

"Or maybe I'm just cursed!" I fell to the ground, wailing again.

I looked up at Pastor Pradhan, and he shook his head. "You're not cursed, Kashvi. God is sovereign, which means everything happens for a good reason—one not rooted in curses. We will find out why she wasn't here. I'll ask Pastor Kurumuni if he can check in on her."

I closed my eyes tight, trying to be angry—at my father, at my mother, at this supposedly sovereign, good God who took me away from my mother.

I tried to muster up anger at this man standing in front of me, a representation of all I had lost, but when I opened my eyes, my shoulders slumped, and I gave up.

I saw someone who seemed to be everything a father should be. I'd spent the whole week doubting his intentions, but time and again, he had shown me compassion, patience, and kindness—just like the good Father he described in his sermon.

Is that who he really is?

Against my nature, as I looked at him now, I let myself believe it was.

He reached his hand out towards me, and I barreled into his arms. He held me gently, patting my back.

I couldn't remember ever hugging my father before. Tears poured down my cheeks, soaking his shoulder.

"Thank you...*Appa*."

CHAPTER 13

Birds chirped above as we stood under the *banyan* tree near the front gate. All of us children formed a circle, holding hands as we prayed before leaving for school. I wore my new school uniform and backpack. The thought of the fresh paper and pencils inside sent a quiet thrill through me.

A month had passed, and summer break was over. Mother still hadn't visited. At Pastor Pradhan's request, Pastor Kurumuni had passed by our house. He reported that he had seen her, but he didn't speak with her, in case anyone might have seen them talking and spread rumors of an affair or that she may have converted.

At least I knew she was alive, but fear gnawed at me. Why wasn't she visiting? Maybe Father had told her never to come, or perhaps she still planned to give up on this life but was waiting for the willpower to do it.

My doubts about the love at Karunai House had faded. Everyone really was as kind as they seemed. Every meal was better than anything I ever ate at home. The chores didn't feel like chores anymore; I talked and laughed with others while we worked. I even found myself volunteering to help, just like Sarina.

"Amen!" we declared in unison at the end of the prayer.

Sudhir and Ameer grabbed rocks and hurled them up into the tree. A hundred crows swarmed out, screeching.

I grabbed Sudhir's wrist. "*Amma* told you not to throw rocks over the wall. You could hit a car!"

Sudhir pulled away from my grip. "I would hear if a car was coming."

"Sudhir!" Nalayani called across the courtyard. She held a backpack above her head.

"How could you forget your bag?" I scolded.

Sudhir rolled his eyes and ran to retrieve it.

Despite everything feeling safer here, my patience with Sudhir had worn thin. He was the only one I didn't get along well with at Karunai House. I felt like he had become more of a bad influence on the other boys than they were a good influence on him.

Sarina and I walked along the roadside to school as the boys raced ahead. *Amma* had enrolled Sudhir and me in a private school with the other Karunai House kids, rather than a government school. Usually, only rich, high-*caste* children went to private schools because of the high tuition, but support from our sponsors gave us this unique opportunity.

I was nervous about starting at the new school, especially if everyone there was high *caste*. Sarina assured me it was a Christian school, and *caste* didn't matter. They weren't even allowed to talk about *caste* there.

It was the same at Karunai House. When I asked Sarina about the *caste* of others, she told me we were forbidden from discussing it at Karunai House. *Appa* and *Amma* taught that *caste* was a man-made concept, and that God treated all people equally.

I still felt nervous, but having Sarina with me helped. I never thought I'd have such a close friend again after Asha died, but Sarina had become just that. We laughed together and shared everything, and she filled a part of the hole Asha and Mother had left behind. I'd also grown close to *Amma* and Nalayani; in such a short time, they truly felt like family.

"Here we are," my new sister sang, turning towards the multistory school building. Balconies lined each floor. I wondered what the school was like inside all those doors and windows. I was positive I saw lights on, and excitement coursed through my veins at the thought of electricity inside the classrooms. But there was more: I glanced around the yard, and my breath caught. Swings and slides!

Maybe this would be better than I thought.

❦

I approached the gate of Karunai House with full heart and hands later that afternoon. Sarina had been right; everyone at school was so kind—all the girls I met, and even my teacher, Miss Pavithra. Each student had their own desk and chair, and there was even science equipment for experiments. And computers! Miss Pavithra took time to help each of us one by one, and Sarina also helped me whenever I needed.

I carried a basket full of delicious fruit that I couldn't wait to eat with my new family. As a first day surprise, Miss Pavithra held a competition for my favorite class of the day: art. Whoever created the best sketch of the basket would take it home.

My heart warmed at the memory of Miss Pavithra's compliments. Kind words from a teacher were foreign to me, but I liked the way it felt. One comment had stuck with me as I walked home with my prize: *Your art made me smile. I hope your drawings make you happy, too.*

Memories of my old drawings of Father shadowed me, and I made a silent promise never to draw him again. I would only draw things that made me happy. Like fruit, nature, and the many new people that I loved.

Nalayani opened the gate. "Where did that lovely basket come from?" she teased, eyebrows raised. "Don't tell me you've got an admirer already!"

I giggled. "No, I won it for my drawing."

"You won it for your drawing?" Nalayani's eyes lit up. She immediately reached out, gently pinching my cheek with pride. "Our Kashvi is an artist!"

I blushed, smiling at the affection that made my heart swell.

"How was the rest of your day?" she asked.

"Good," I replied in English, one of the only words I remembered from the day.

Immediately, Nalayani rattled off a string of English words I didn't recognize.

I swatted her arm playfully. "You can't say anything in English until you teach it to me first!"

I'd never felt this way about learning before. I wanted to know everything—everything Sarina knew, everything Nalayani knew, and more.

Inside the common room, I handed a bright green plantain to Sarina and grabbed one for myself. Just as I sat down, Sudhir came over and reached for the pomegranate in the basket.

I slapped his hand. "These are mine!"

He stuck out his tongue and stomped off to join Ameer and the boys on the other side of the room.

Sarina and I worked on homework together. She was patient, explaining each bit I didn't understand. She was the top student in her class last year, so with her guidance, school wasn't nearly as scary as I had feared.

Milo wandered in and settled by us. I scratched behind his ears as Sarina taught me more English words.

Mahiyu came in shortly after with a tray of water and a spicy groundnut snack mix for everyone. When he passed by us, I offered him the pomegranate that Sudhir had tried to steal from my basket as a thank you for always serving us. He hesitated, then shook his head with a smile, declining.

As he walked away, I glanced over my shoulder and saw Sudhir scowling at me.

After a couple of hours, *Amma* entered the room, missing her usual smile.

"Kashvi. Sudhir."

I glanced nervously across the room at Sudhir. He looked up from his game, and we both followed *Amma* outside.

"As you know, we require a guardian visit at least once per month," Amma said. "Since your *amma* hasn't visited yet, *Appa* and I would like to visit your home to check on her. Would you like to come with us?"

A thousand thoughts flooded my mind, each more overwhelming than the last.

How would Father react to seeing us? Did Mother tell him the truth?

As much as I longed to see Mother again, I wasn't sure I could handle the truth behind her absence. It could only mean she truly abandoned us—or Father had forbidden her to visit.

Sudhir's face lit up with excitement. "Let's go!"

Amma placed a hand on my shoulder, her gaze calm and reassuring. "I know you're scared, but we'll make sure you're safe…if you want to go."

Sudhir bounced on his toes, grinning. "I want to go!"

I knew he wasn't thinking of all the possibilities I dreaded; he just wanted to see Mother.

"I'm not worried about *my* safety…" I murmured, feeling the weight of my fears pressing down on me.

"God is in control, Kashvi," *Amma* reminded gently. "We can trust in him. I'm sure your *amma* would love to see you very much, and we can give her that chance today."

Her words wrapped around me like a warm embrace.

Maybe Amma is right. Maybe Mother wanted to come all along, but something kept stopping her.

"I'll go," I exhaled.

Sudhir and I climbed into the back of the *Qualis* with *Amma*. *Appa* sat in the passenger seat, while Dhiren slipped behind the wheel and stretched his thick arms out with an exaggerated yawn.

Before we pulled out, *Appa* cleared his throat and bowed his head, leading us in a quiet prayer for protection—for us and for our mother. I clasped Sudhir's hand tightly as we prayed, as if the tighter I squeezed, the louder our prayer would be before God.

As we drove off, *Amma* opened her Bible, reading verses from different places. Her calm, steady voice grounded me as my mind threatened to spiral. I listened quietly, trying to make sense of this God and his words. She read one verse about everything working for good for the people that love God, and about how it was all according to his purposes.

Who are the people the verse is meant for? They surely weren't poor, low-*caste* families like mine, who slept on dirt floors and worked themselves to exhaustion just to scrape by. If their mothers labored in the hot fields only for their fathers to squander the money on liquor and beat them, they wouldn't be claiming everything worked for good.

What kind of purpose could this God have for people like us? I scoffed.

"*Thangachi*," Dhiren's voice broke into my thoughts, "I know your village is somewhere around here. Point out the street where I need to turn."

"Uh, it's right there." I pointed at the cratered, dirt path, only a few meters in front of us.

Dhiren hit the brakes and yanked the steering wheel of the *Qualis* sharply left. We hit a deep rut, sending me bouncing off the seat. My stomach flipped as I floated momentarily in the air.

"Slow down!" *Appa* barked, adjusting his askew glasses. "We're not in a hurry."

"Sorry, '*pa*." Dhiren grinned. "It was fun, though, wasn't it?"

"It wasn't safe," *Appa* said firmly. "You'd better treat your real wife better than this someday."

Dhiren gave a sheepish grin and eased off the gas.

The road narrowed to a single lane. No cars ever came this way, just shuffling feet and the occasional scooter of those lucky enough to have one.

As the familiar outline of my home appeared in the distance, a knot tightened in my stomach. "There it is," I whispered.

Dhiren pulled to the side of the path, gravel scattering under the tires.

We climbed out of the SUV, but Dhiren stayed behind, reclining his seat and shutting his eyes.

Appa rapped on the window. "You're coming, too." His tone left no room for negotiation.

Dhiren groaned. "What do you need me for?"

Appa flexed his arms with a small grin. I realized he wanted Dhiren along just in case my father needed to be intimidated.

Dhiren sighed dramatically, dragging his large body out of the car. "I was really hoping for a nap—"

He straightened up immediately at the sound of Father's shouts slicing through the air.

I instinctively grabbed Sudhir's hand, gripping it tight as we approached the house.

Father stepped into view, lighting a *beedi*, its pungent smoke curling upward. Mother followed behind him, carrying a dented cooking pot in both hands. Sudhir broke free from me, racing ahead to throw himself into her arms.

"Sudhir!" Mother gasped, spilling water out of the pot as she set it down swiftly to wrap him in a hug. She looked up at me, her face full of guilt and sorrow. "I'm so sorry I never—"

"Why are you back?" Father cut in, sneering over her shoulder through a haze of smoke. "I thought you were off getting educated. Failed already?" His bloodshot eyes glinted with mockery.

My whole body tensed, heart pounding against my ribs. The month away had dulled my fear. Now it all came rushing back. The love I saw every day at Karunai House made him seem more monstrous than before.

Instinctively, I rubbed the scar on my forehead—the one he had given me—and rage simmered inside. I hated him. I hated that he was nothing like the father he should have been.

Father squinted at the group following us. His scowl mutated into an insincere grin as he shuffled forward. "Who are you?"

"I'm Pastor Pradhan," *Appa* replied warmly, shaking Father's hand. "This is my wife, Vasantha, and this young man is Dhiren. We're the ones taking care of your children."

I watched Father suspiciously as he masked himself. Fear clawed at me. *What if Appa and Amma believe his performance? What if they think we made everything up?*

"They in some kind of trouble?" Father spat to the side.

Mother stiffened and let go of Sudhir, her eyes darting nervously between us.

"They're not in any trouble," *Appa* said calmly. "They are doing well—well-behaved, respectful. But since it's been a month, and neither of you have visited, we wanted to check in. We require at least one parent to visit each month."

Mother opened her mouth to speak, but Father cut her off with fierce eyes. Then he turned to *Appa*, stroking his bushy mustache. "She never told me we had to visit."

Mother stared at the ground, wringing the edge of her *sari* between her fingers.

He's lying.

"Well," *Appa* said, unbothered by their reactions, "that is our rule. Your children would like to see you, and we would, too."

Father gave a dismissive harumph, clearly annoyed. "I guess I'll visit, then."

As he said the words, his eyes locked onto mine. My heart sank.

Is he so intent to continue terrorizing me that he'd take time to visit alone?

Mother broke the silence. "Have you eaten?"

Father's lips tightened.

"No need, but thank you," *Appa* politely declined. "We have food waiting back home."

"Tea, then. I will make some tea," Mother pushed, her voice panicked.

Appa nodded. "We can stay for tea."

Relief swept through me. I knew if they stayed for dinner, Mother would try to make something nice, using what little money they had. Father would beat her for it later, blaming her for wasting his money.

"You're back," Uncle Arjun's steady voice sounded as he approached from the road with Vishnu by his side. "How is your new school?"

"Good," I muttered cautiously. *What had Mother told them about us? That we were sent to a boarding school?*

"It's not just good," Sudhir exclaimed. "It's amazing. There's a playground with swings and slides, and they have a football field with real poles and nets. We even get a full meal for lunch."

Uncle chuckled. "The gods have favored you." His eyes shifted to me, scanning me up and down. "You look older with that short hair and those earrings."

Uncomfortable, I looked away and pulled at one of my new dangling earrings. I glanced at Vishnu, who quickly looked away from me. *Was he staring at my ugly hair?*

"It won't be long now," Uncle chuckled, "and you'll be ready for marriage."

I squirmed, not sure what to think of the assumed arrangement between Vishnu and me, considering my new circumstances.

Uncle turned to *Appa* with a cheerful smile. "Now, who might you be?"

Father clamped a hand on Uncle's shoulder, cutting him off. "Didn't you say you needed help moving something?"

Uncle nodded.

"Well, I'm ready now." Father steered him away, eager to escape.

Uncle waved over his shoulder as they left in a puff of smoke.

"Nice to meet you all," Father said as they walked off, throwing Mother one last warning glare.

Watch what you say.

I exhaled, feeling my muscles release their tension.

Mother crouched by the fire beside the house, setting a pot of water to boil.

"Want to play football?" Vishnu asked Sudhir.

"Sure!" Sudhir jumped to his feet.

I grabbed his shirt, pulling him close. "We're here to see *Amma*, not to play. Do you even care about her?"

Sudhir scowled, yanking free from my grip, and plopped down again, sulking.

Vishnu shrugged, then grinned at me before wandering off after our fathers.

I sat beside *Amma* as Mother passed out chipped teacups to *Appa*, *Amma*, and Dhiren, then poured steaming tea into each. As she poured the tea, I watched the calm kindness emanating from Vasantha and Pastor Pradhan...*Amma* and *Appa*. I was surprised at how quickly I'd come to call them that, but I wasn't ready to call them that in front of Mother. Guilt gnawed at me.

"Thank you," *Appa* said warmly.

When Mother settled down, Sudhir sidled up to her, curling against her side as she stroked his hair. A hot surge of jealousy flared in me. I wanted to slap him.

I stared at Mother, waiting for her to meet my eyes. When she finally did, I blurted out, "You promised you would visit."

Mother cast a nervous glance towards the road, then whispered, "He wouldn't let me. I have to work every day just to get by."

"We can help with food if you need it," *Amma* offered.

Mother shook her head. "That's kind of you, but—"

"*Appa* wants the money to buy booze," I interrupted bitterly.

"Kashvi!" Mother gasped. "Don't speak of *Appa* that way!"

He's not my appa *anymore.* I bit my tongue, seething. *Why did she always defend him?*

"It's not just the field work," Mother continued. "I need to cook, clean, wash. There just isn't any time left in the day."

"I'm sorry." *Amma* leaned towards Mother. "It must be very difficult."

Mother's eyes darted around once more, checking for Father, and then she broke. Tears spilled down her cheeks.

Amma wrapped her arm around Mother. "How have things been since you left Kashvi and Sudhir with us?"

"Fine." Mother tugged her shawl tight around her body—but not fast enough. Ugly bruises painted her arms. "I told my husband they are at a private boarding school for impoverished children. I'm not sure if he believed me, but he didn't ask any questions."

Because he likes having us gone.

"But you'll visit us now, right?" Sudhir smiled at her.

I clenched my jaw.

Now you care? Just moments ago, you were ready to ditch her for a football game.

"I hope so," Mother answered with a pained smile.

Appa had been careful with his words: the rule was clear—just one parent, once a month. What would Father want more: another day of wages from Mother, or the satisfaction of keeping us out of the house? Maybe he'd come himself—take off work for a chance to keep tormenting us.

"How are things going at Karunai House?" Mother shifted the conversation.

Sudhir launched excitedly into details about his new friends, games, clothes, and the delicious food. Hunger flickered in Mother's eyes as he described the smells and tastes of his favorite meals.

Turning to me, her gaze softened. "What happened to your hair?"

I dropped my head, embarrassed.

"It's a standard procedure for new children with lice," *Amma* explained. "We shave their heads to keep it from spreading."

Mother scratched her scalp awkwardly and nodded. "How have you been, Kashvi?"

"Um…" I stammered, unsure how much of the good I should share with my mother, who endured so much suffering. "I made a friend, Sarina, and got new clothes and earrings. I really like my new school… but…" My voice cracked, and the words caught in my throat. I crumbled against her. "I miss you, *'ma.*"

Mother's arms wrapped around me, drawing me close as I cried into her shoulder. "I miss you too, Kashvi."

In her embrace, my sobs soon quieted. We talked in soft voices about life at Karunai House, the little moments of our days. I watched, comforted, as Dhiren and *Appa* kept an eye out for any signs of Father returning.

But then Mother glanced up at the sky, where the orange hues of the setting sun signaled the end of the day. She jumped up. "I need to get dinner started. *Appa* will want it ready when he returns."

"We should head home, too," *Amma* said, standing to embrace her. "Remember our offer to help you into a woman's shelter…if things get too hard."

"This is where I belong," Mother said, resigned. "It is my fate."

Amma sighed deeply. "It's no woman's fate to accept abuse."

Mother stared ahead. She understood what *Amma* was saying, but she didn't agree.

I hugged her tightly. "You'll visit us Sunday?"

"I will try." Her words dripped of uncertainty.

"I love you, *Amma*."

"I love you, too, my dear," she whispered, her voice breaking.

Mother gave Sudhir one last hug before rushing into the house to prepare dinner.

As we turned to leave, I peeked into the doorway of our house. There stood Kali, her brass tongue forever protruding in silent mockery. I stuck my tongue out at her and walked to the *Qualis*.

On the drive home, my thoughts churned. *What will Father do when he returns?*

I saw *Amma*'s Bible on her lap and thought of the verse about all things working for good. My lip trembled and I burst into tears.

"How is any of this good?"

"Oh, my child." *Amma* held me close, her voice filled with compassion. "I'm so sorry for all the pain you've endured. There's nothing good in the way your father has treated you. That's not how God created the world to be. But good can come from it."

Her eyes showed understanding, as though she heard the weight of everything my words couldn't express. "Do you get scared at night, Kashvi? In the dark?"

I nodded *yes*, sniffling.

"The dark is scary because we can't see what lies beyond it," *Amma* said. "Our lives are like that. We see only what's in front of us, but

God sees everything clearly—our entire lives. If we could see what he sees, we'd know that even in the darkness, there's a purpose. One day, we'll understand—but until then, we must trust that God's plan for us is good."

Her words made some sense to me, but the ache in my chest remained. I forced a small smile.

I'd learned so much about God in the past month. I believed he was the one true God. But did I trust him? *Should* I trust him? God's way was only good for those who truly trusted him, right?

"How do I know if I really trust God?" I asked.

Amma's arms tightened around me. "Trusting can be scary, can't it?"

I nodded.

"I can't give you trust, Kashvi," *Amma* said compassionately. "Only God can. But you can pray for it, and, I promise, God will hear your prayers."

A flicker of hope stirred within me. Maybe she was right. I wanted to trust God, but my mind swirled with anxious thoughts of Mother.

"God has preserved your *amma's* life, hasn't he?" *Amma* prodded, reading my thoughts.

"Yes."

"He brought you to Karunai House, where you're with Sudhir instead of being sent to a government home, didn't he?"

I nodded.

Amma wiped my tears with her shawl. "He gave you a friendship with Sarina, new clothes, and a good education. Most importantly, he taught you about himself and his love in Jesus. I know none of this makes your *amma's* situation easier, but they are good gifts from God. Gifts we can be thankful for."

Her words settled over me like a warm blanket. I closed my eyes, taking her advice to pray.

Heavenly Father, please help me to trust that your plan is good, even when it's really painful. I don't understand, but I have seen your goodness to me at Karunai House. Help me to see it everywhere.

CHAPTER 14

"Come on, Kash'i! Let's play volleyball!" Sarina bounced a ball on the packed earth of the courtyard.

"I want to play, too!" Velu shouted, trailing behind me like a little shadow.

Three months ago, Velu had showed up at our gates with his uncle, a Hindu sorcerer half-dressed in an orange *lungi* and white turban. The six-year-old hadn't spoken for two weeks; he had been silent since the night that he had watched his father set his mother on fire and run away. His small hands carried scars from trying to save her. The horror of witnessing his mother screaming in pain as her life was burned out had stolen his voice. His uncle, unable or perhaps unwilling to care for him, had brought him to the nearest orphanage: Karunai House.

I had been the first person Velu had spoken to. I had tried to show him the same kindness I was shown when I arrived, though it felt like I was having little impact. Finally, we had connected through drawing.

The memory gave me shivers of joy. God had used my small gift of drawing to unlock something broken inside Velu.

It also stirred something new in me—something bigger than just the desire to survive. I didn't want to marry young and become a field worker like my mother. I dreamed of going to college, learning all I could, and one day helping hurting children just like this one.

Taking Velu's little hand, I followed Sarina to the volleyball net in the field. With no boys his age on campus, I'd taken Velu under my wing, drawing, reading, and playing games with him, and he clung to me. He was my *thambi*, and he adored me…unlike Sudhir.

As we crossed the courtyard, his joyful skipping filled my heart with a strange kind of comfort—a distraction from the painful turmoil inside me always threatening to overflow.

"No school! No school! Kashvi stays here!" Velu chanted happily as we made our way across the field. "It's '*poosam*! Kashvi—your earrings will protect us!"

Today was a public holiday for *Thaipoosam*, a Hindu festival. I smiled at my little friend. "No, Velu. Piercings don't protect us from evil; only Jesus does. Jesus was pierced so we don't have to be."

Velu grinned. "That's good. I don't like the piercings. They hurt!"

The thought of *Thaipoosam* stirred old memories: men staggering under the weight of hooks and spears piercing their flesh, ropes pulling against the wounds, their bodies weighed down with offerings. It was horrifying—even more so now that I knew all the suffering was meaningless.

A deep sense of relief settled over me. Months of devotions, sermons, and catechism lessons had shown me how different Christianity was. I saw the foolishness of lifeless, man-made idols, and the uselessness of trying to earn favor with any number of those man-made gods.

I now believed that Jesus died for my sins and trusted him for salvation. I saw God's hand in school: math worked because God was orderly; science showed the complexity of God's designed universe; even the confusing English language had purpose, attached to the story of Babel. Everything fit together in ways I had never imagined, all rooted in a person who really walked on earth and rose from the dead.

I wondered if Mother and Father were headed to the temple now, bringing offerings and seeking forgiveness and protection from useless idols.

Mother still hadn't visited us. We went to our village twice since the first visit. Once, Father wasn't there. During the next visit, he accused Mother of lying—saying she claimed to visit us but hadn't.

Every week, Pastor Kurumuni checked to see if Mother was home, reporting back to *Appa*. Some weeks she wasn't, and I lived in fear until the next update. I missed her, but I didn't long to go back anymore. Karunai House was home now, and these people felt like my family— *Appa*, *Amma*, my brothers and sisters.

"Here!" Sarina sent the blue and yellow volleyball soaring towards us, dragging me out of my thoughts.

I lunged for the ball, but it awkwardly grazed my hand and bounced away.

"I'll get it!" Velu shouted, running after it.

Sarina walked towards me, her brows furrowed as we sat in the dirt. "You look troubled."

"I'm just thinking about my parents and the festival today." I laughed bitterly. "I wonder what kind of penance my father thinks will erase all he's done. He'd need ten thousand hooks in his back, dragging a cartload of stones, to make up for how he's hurt us."

Sarina wrapped her arms around me. "I'm sorry for your pain, Kash'i. Truly."

Her deep compassion invited a rush of emotions, and anger overcame me. My body trembled, and before I could stop myself, I grabbed Sarina by the shoulders and shook her.

"I hate him! I wish God would strike him dead!"

Sarina's eyes widened in shock, her lips parting wordlessly.

A whimper drew my attention. I turned to see Velu standing frozen, terror etched into his young face.

Just then, *Amma* stepped out of the office and caught my eyes. She rushed over, concern written in every line of her expression.

"I—I'm sorry..." I stammered, guilt mixing with the anger still burning inside me.

Amma knelt beside Velu, whispering softly in his ear. His tense little shoulders relaxed, and before I could react, he bounded over and wrapped his arms around me. "It's okay, *Akka*! Jesus loves you."

Amma then turned to me, her expression soft but serious. "What's going on here?"

"I just...I'm so angry at my father sometimes!" I burst out. "*Appa* preached about God's justice for every sinner in the end, but...but why can't God bring his justice now?"

Amma studied me, looking past my words to the storm brewing beneath them. "Your father still has a part to play in God's plan," she said slowly, weighing each word. "And I think part of that plan is for you to pray that God changes his heart."

A scoff escaped before I could hold it back. I scrubbed at the hot tears on my cheeks. "His heart can't be changed."

Her eyes met mine. "My dear, God can change anyone's heart. He's changed the hearts of many angry people, even murderers, like the apostle Paul."

I gave a stiff nod, my mind already closing off. God may have changed the hearts of other bad people, but Father was different. I knew him too well. His heart was stone; no miracle could soften it.

Sarina and *Amma* exchanged a glance—one of those pitying looks adults give each other when they think a child doesn't understand.

Amma started to speak again, "Why don't we pr—"

She was cut off by Dhiren's booming voice, blaring like a loud-speaker across the courtyard. "*Amma! Amma!*"

Amma blinked, her brows furrowed. "What is that all about?"

Curious—and relieved to escape the heaviness of the conversation—I followed *Amma* towards the front gate. Rounding the corner, my stomach twisted.

Standing by the gate was Father's dusty old scooter, and, next to it, my parents.

A storm of emotions surged through me—shock, rage, joy, confusion.

By the *Qualis*, Dhiren stood wiping grease from his hands. He exchanged a glance with Mahiyu, who immediately darted off towards the kitchen—no doubt to fetch tea. Still half-covered in oil, Dhiren approached my parents just as *Amma* and I did, his eyes flicking between them and me.

"Where's Sudhir?" Father grunted at me.

No "*Hello.*" No "*How are you?*"

"I don't know." I turned away from him to give Mother a hug.

Father scowled, as if my not knowing was an offense.

"Sudhir!" Dhiren bellowed over the campus. He smiled down at Father, extending his hand.

Father looked at it, brows furrowed.

"Oops, I forgot my hands were greasy!" Dhiren laughed, pulling his thick hand back and pretending to shake the air instead.

Father shook his head in irritation.

Amma stepped closer, her smile warm despite the tension. "It's so good to see you here. Have you come for a visit?"

"Yes," Mother said quickly. "I feel bad for not visiting before, so since today is *Thaipoosam* and we aren't working, we want to take Kashvi and Sudhir to the city."

Amma's smile faltered ever so slightly, her lips pressing together in concern as she looked at me. "I see. Well, come with me. I'll need you to fill out some forms for their release."

Sudhir finally appeared, running up to give Mother a hug.

"Only your wife needs to sign the form," *Amma* said to Father. "You can sit at that table and spend time with your children."

I held back a bitter laugh.

Father nodded curtly, and we sat around the table outside the common room. Dhiren pulled a screwdriver out of his pocket and started fiddling with a shutter hanging crooked by the window.

The silence was thick and uncomfortable, broken only by Father cracking his knuckles as he glanced around, taking in the place.

I had once hoped Mother would feel guilty enough to visit us at church, but now I wished *Appa* had never brought up the rule about visits; Father was here to take us to the temple, to offer prayers and make sacrifices to gods I no longer believed in.

Is this Father's punishment for skipping out on the temple visit that led to us being brought to Karunai House? Will we be safe? Surely that's why Amma has taken Mother aside, to make sure we would be safe with Father. But how much can she do? Mother has every right to take us…and if Amma refuses to release us, the government might think we're being kept from a Hindu festival. There would be trouble for sure if that happened.

The only positive was that Father wasn't drinking or smoking today. *Thaipoosam* was his day of fasting, in hope for some special blessing from the gods.

Father broke the silence. "What do you do here?"

Sudhir jumped in, "We go to school during the week, then we do homework, chores, and play games when we're done. And we have devotions every morning and night—"

"Devotions?" Father interrupted, his tone suspicious. "What's that?"

"We learn about Jesus and—"

I kicked Sudhir's shin under the table.

"Ow, why—" Sudhir stopped mid-sentence at the look I gave him.

Father's scowl deepened, but before he could say anything, Mahiyu came up and placed a steaming cup of milk tea in front of him. *Amma* and Mother joined us, and Mahiyu served everyone. We all thanked him—except for Father.

As we got up to leave, *Amma* held Sudhir and me back for a moment. "God will watch over you today." She prayed quietly for our protection, then she watched us go regretfully.

I hugged Sudhir tightly on the tiny scooter seat as Mother climbed on behind us.

Velu ran up and grabbed my hand just as we were about to drive off. "Where are you going? Can I come?"

His sad, pleading eyes squeezed my heart. "Sorry, you can't come with us."

Velu's face crumpled, and he started to cry. Sarina quickly took him in her arms, holding him back as we pulled away. I waved at his tear-streaked face until we turned the corner.

Father parked the scooter in a mass of bikes and motorcycles lining the street, several blocks from the temple in the heart of the city. Mother lifted the seat and pulled out two teacup-sized metal pots filled with rice.

Sudhir looked up at me, waiting to see what I would do. The pots were for him and me to offer to the gods, and I knew we couldn't do that. It would break the first commandment, having no other gods before the true one.

But what would Father do if we refused to participate? Would he beat us? Would he refuse to take us back to Karunai House? Worse, would he complain to the government and get Karunai House shut down?

There's nothing wrong with simply holding a pot of rice, I told myself, trying to settle my nerves. I took a pot, feeling its weight in my hands.

Sudhir, still watching me, took one too. We clutched the pots to our chests, merging into the sea of barefooted pilgrims moving towards the temple.

The air was thick with incense and sweat. My own uncertainty and growing feelings of guilt also pressed on my chest, making each breath feel like work.

I tried to make myself small, avoiding eye contact with my parents and the devotees moving with me. Some staggered under the weight of heavy pots tied to both ends of a rod digging into their shoulders, their faces strained with effort. Bare-chested men shuffled by, with small pots hanging from hooks pierced through their skin swaying with each step.

I grabbed Sudhir's hand to steady myself in the cacophony. The deep, rhythmic beats of drums mingled with the high-pitched wail of bamboo flutes. Labored breaths and groans of the pot-carriers filled the space around me. Screams from above pierced through the music, and I looked up to see men dangling from a crane, hanging by metal hooks piercing their backs. Below, a line of men waited for their turn to endure the same torment, hoping for blessings in return for their physical suffering.

Clanging cymbals startled me, and I whipped around, bumping into a young man. My breath caught when I saw the thin spear piercing both his cheeks. His face looked like Velu's—and that probably would've been Velu someday if he hadn't been brought to Karunai House.

The mix of sights and sounds made my stomach churn. Growing up, I had accepted all these piercings and acts of self-inflicted pain as necessary, just the way things had to be for balance and order. Now, I knew the truth—these gods the people were trying to appease were nothing but stone and metal. All this pain was for nothing. Even worse: the true God hated it and would judge them for it.

I swallowed hard.

Will God hate me for being here? For holding this pot?

I didn't know what to do but keep going.

We arrived at the huge, gold temple gates, where the massive crowd converged around us, shouting mantras to the music. Drummers and pipers lined the wall surrounding the temple. Hundreds of gods sat on tiered platforms of the colorful pyramid that reached to the sky.

The towering city temple blocked out the sun, leaving us in its cold shadow. It was at least a hundred times larger than the tiny temple near our village. An orange-skirted priest stood at the entrance. He blessed the visitors by smearing white ash powder on their foreheads as they entered to signify purity and to ward off evil spirits.

When the priest wiped the ash on my forehead, I felt dirty, not pure. I spit into my hand and began wiping it off. Sudhir watched me and did the same.

Father wrenched my hand away from my head with an iron grip. "What are you doing?"

Panic shot through me.

"My…face is itchy," I stammered.

Father narrowed his eyes but released my hand.

We moved inside, the air thick with incense, the flicker of candles casting long shadows. A towering statue of Shiva loomed before us on a pedestal, its golden face gleaming, crowned with jewels and surrounded by a garland of white flowers.

My parents bowed their heads briefly before adding their pots to the sea of offerings surrounding the lifeless god—large and small pots, fruit, and jewelry.

Father's gaze bored into me. "Make your vow and offering."

I froze. Carrying the pot was one thing, but offering it was another.

Sudhir watched me, waiting again for my lead. I thought of Mother at home, bruised and beaten. I thought of police pulling up to Karunai House, taking all of us away to government-run homes.

I didn't buy the pot, and I don't believe in the idols. It's just rice, I reasoned. *It doesn't mean anything if I set it down.*

I vow to serve the living God, I thought, feeling clever. I stepped forward to put my pot down, but my trembling legs tripped, and I spilled the rice everywhere. My heart raced as I hurried to scoop the dirty grains back into the pot.

Father shook his head in disgust, but I didn't care about him at that moment. The guilt was heavy in my chest. My excuses hadn't eased my conscience.

I watched as Sudhir placed his pot down beside mine, and the weight of my guilt doubled. I'd led him into sin, too.

As we walked out of the temple, *Appa's* voice from morning devotions rang in my head: "'*We cannot pay for our sins with our good deeds. Even our good deeds are tainted with sin and add to our debt to God. Only Jesus, the sinless one, can pay for sins.*'"

My vow to serve the living God couldn't undo my sin of offering to the idol.

"What did you vow?" Sudhir asked as we passed through the temple gate.

"None of your business," I snapped, angry with myself.

"Did you vow to marry Vishnu?" Sudhir cackled.

I punched Sudhir's shoulder, and Father grabbed my arm. "What's going on here?"

"I just asked her what she vowed, and she hit me!" Sudhir whined.

Now I'd hit Sudhir; my sins kept stacking up, all because I was too scared to confront Father.

I felt the weight of guilt pressing down on me. I had to confess his name.

"I vowed to serve the true God!" I blurted out before my courage escaped me.

Father tightened his grip. "What do you mean by *true* god?"

I quickly considered lying again, but somehow, my boldness remained.

"Jesus," I said, trembling.

Father hissed in my ear, "Take that back!"

"No!" I jerked free from his grip and ran, pushing through the crowd. Panic set in as I realized I had no plan. I crawled under an ox cart blocking an empty alleyway and bolted.

"Kashvi, stop!" a voice called behind me—not Father's, but I didn't dare slow down.

Footsteps pounded closer. Strong arms grabbed me from behind.

I screamed and kicked until I heard a familiar voice. "Calm down! It's me—Dhiren."

Relief flooded me as I looked up at his exhausted but smiling face. *Dhiren? Amma must have sent him to follow us, to protect us.* My heart settled for a moment at the knowledge that I was protected and loved.

My relief vanished when Father appeared, wheezing and stumbling towards us. When he finally reached us, he bent over, hands on his knees, gasping for breath between fits of coughing.

"You okay?" Dhiren asked.

"Fine—" Father rasped.

Dhiren towered over Father. "I think it's best if I take Kashvi and Sudhir back to Karunai House."

Father, still gasping, waved us off. "They're cursed. They bring nothing but trouble."

Dhiren and I made our way back. Ducking under the ox cart again, we found Mother and Sudhir waiting.

Mother wrapped her arms around me, her tears spilling onto my shoulder. "Why did you do that, Kashvi? Why do you always fight?"

"I'm so sorry," I cried, guilt clawing at my heart. This had probably been her idea—an opportunity to finally visit with us—and I'd ruined it. Father would probably punish her for my behavior later.

What was I supposed to do? How can I serve Jesus and keep everyone I love safe?

Father stumbled up and clamped his hand onto Mother's arm. "We're leaving."

We said a hurried goodbye as he yanked her away from us.

My heart ached. *What's Father going to do to her tonight?*

"What happened?" Dhiren asked as we followed him to his motorcycle.

I told him everything—how I was too scared to refuse the offering, how I feared it could bring harm to Karunai House, and the guilt that was eating me.

"When you confess and repent, Jesus will take your guilt away," Dhiren said, looking at me intently.

"I know that," I said. "It just seems too easy. Like there's something more I need to do."

"Jesus came to call sinners, not the righteous, right, *Thangachi?*" Dhiren smiled, brushing his hair aside.

His smile brought my heart back to the safety of my new family and my new God.

"Right," I agreed. My confidence grew with every step we took further from the temple.

"As for the future of Karunai House, we must trust God," Dhiren said, untangling his motorcycle from the mass of other ones surrounding it. "*Appa* and *Amma* always remind me: the end doesn't justify the means. Sinning, even with good motivation, is still sinning. Obey your conscience and leave the results to God. The fact that Karunai House is

still operating after all the government inspections and interrogations…
that's a miracle. If God wants it to continue, nothing will stop it."

I let out a long breath, taking in Dhiren's words. Then I looked at
Sudhir.

"I'm sorry, *Thambi*."

"I forgive you." Sudhir grinned. "We shouldn't have given the rice
to the god, right?"

I nodded, still feeling guilty, before hopping onto Dhiren's motorcycle. As we sped down the road, I scrubbed the rest of the ash off my
forehead with my sweaty hand and prayed.

*Father in heaven, forgive me for my anger, my lies, and my offering to a
worthless idol. I'm sorry I feared my father more than I feared you. Give me
courage and boldness to keep my vow to serve you.*

I exhaled deeply as the familiar lights of Karunai House shone
brightly at the end of the long, dark road.

CHAPTER 15

"Why are you crying?" Sudhir, breathless from running over, asked as I climbed into the *Qualis* after Velu.

I scowled. If Sudhir paid any attention to what was happening around him, he would know.

"You should know why I'm crying," I shot a fiery look back at him.

My emotions churned inside. Velu, my faithful companion, my shadow, my source of joy for months, was leaving.

Sudhir shrugged carelessly and started back towards his game.

"I wish you were the one leaving instead!" Immediately, I clapped my hand over my mouth.

"*Thangachi…*" Dhiren scolded.

Sudhir turned back to me, his face twisted in a frown. I expected nasty words back, but he only stared at me, looking wounded, before running off.

Huffing, I tried to justify my words by Sudhir's behavior. He probably *didn't* know why I was crying. He thought only of himself—of playing and getting out of work. He contributed the bare minimum here, and he had barely passed the exams to remain in our private school. Everything about him was getting under my skin.

"That was not nice, *Akka!*" Velu piped up from my lap.

I realized I felt worse about snapping like that in front of Velu than I did about the words I'd said to Sudhir. I turned my attention back to the *thambi* I wished was staying. Velu was going to live with his uncle and his family now.

Ever since Velu had arrived, his uncle, Abhiraj—who currently sat in the front seat beside Dhiren—had been visiting Karunai House, meeting with *Appa*, hearing the gospel. Abhiraj had been a Hindu sorcerer; he had practiced black magic for a living, taking money to curse people's enemies. He went to all the death festivals, rubbed the ashes of burned bodies on himself, ate raw meat, and drank blood, all to try to gain the power of the gods in himself.

But he had since repented and confessed that he believed in Jesus. He had even recently been baptized. The man who once dealt in darkness was alive in the light of Christ. Now he believed it was his responsibility as a believer to take his nephew home and raise him with his own family.

Appa climbed into the back seat of the SUV with us. *Amma* and Sarina waved goodbye from within the front gate; they stayed back with everyone else to prep for supper, but I wouldn't leave Velu any sooner than I had to. *Amma* graciously let me off my chores to go with Velu to his uncle's home.

"Can't he stay with us, *Appa?*" I whispered as we drove off down the road.

"Remember, my child, this is a good thing," *Appa* whispered back. "God has transformed Abhiraj's heart. Caring for his family is his responsibility before God. Despite the financial burden, Abhiraj desires to obey God in this. That is something to rejoice in, though it is difficult for us."

I tried to feel joy in Abhiraj's changed life, but I was too stuck on losing Velu. I hugged him tightly, tickling his side to stop the tears from flowing. "I'm going to miss you, *Thambi*. Who's going to keep me in line now?"

Even though I'd see him at church every week, it wasn't the same. He wouldn't be there first thing in the morning, trailing after me during chores, asking me questions, or sitting beside me in the evenings to draw.

Velu wasn't just my companion; he'd become a constant presence of comfort in a world still full of uncertainty. Knowing I'd only see him on Sundays now felt like losing him forever, even if he wasn't really gone.

"Do you think there are tigers in the trees, *Akka?*" Velu asked me a million questions in the car about everything we passed, like he did every day at Karunai House.

My heart tugged as I remembered the first day he spoke to me, when drawing together had opened his heart. He'd inspired me to live to care for others, not just myself.

Dhiren and Abhiraj talked in the front seat as we drove to Abhiraj's home; *Appa* leaned forward to join the conversation. Abhiraj recounted the joy he felt last Sunday at his baptism and the baptism of his family. His voice held a new kind of energy, a freedom. Through his nephew's time at Karunai House, God had touched him, had saved him from the power of Satan.

"My soul is unburdened now, free from the devils I invited in," Abhiraj said, his words vibrant with hope. "The Holy Spirit is in me, the power of the living God. He is powerful to save even the worst of sinners."

I thought of my father.

If God changed the heart of a sorcerer like Abhiraj, could he change my father's heart?

I didn't *want* to consider it. I didn't want my father's heart to soften. I hated him, and I wanted him to get what he deserved. I could never forgive him.

Shaking off the thought, I pulled out a drawing I'd been sitting on.

"Velu, I made this for you." I handed him the picture. In simple black and white, I had drawn the two of us sitting under the hugging tree, with Milo between us.

"It's Milo! And us by the tree!" Velu beamed. "You're the best, *akka.*"

His smile was so big, so pure. I squeezed him tight, my heart aching.

All too soon, the *Qualis* pulled to a stop. Abhiraj opened his door, and the weight of the goodbye settled on me. I got out slowly, feeling the huge change ahead for all of us.

Tears slipped down my face. Velu wiped them away with his scarred little hands. "Don't cry, *Akka*. I will see you at church."

"You need to sit by me each week at church, okay? Promise?" I kept my voice light, but it cracked.

He nodded eagerly.

"I love you, *Thambi*." My voice trembled.

I climbed back into the SUV with a sad heart, and we headed back to Karunai House. It wouldn't be the same there without Velu, but still I hoped *I* would never have to leave. I imagined myself living at Karunai House forever. Safe from my father, safe from *caste*, safe from poverty, Karunai House was a refuge for me.

"Kashvi," *Appa* turned back to me, "how are you?"

My face twisted. "Why did God take Velu away from me?"

Appa took off his glasses. "God designed for us to live in families. This is good for Velu, and it's good for us, too, even though it's hard to lose him. God's ways are higher than our ways. His thoughts are higher than our thoughts. Isaiah 55 verse 8."

I sat there for a minute, thinking over what *Appa* said.

"I'm going to miss him."

"He was your *Thambi*," *Appa* said, wiping a tear from his eye. "I'm going to miss him, too."

The Qualis rumbled down the uneven road, and I stared out the window as the world blurred past— a rainbow of faded pastel buildings, small homes between smaller roadside shops, tangled electric wires hanging like vines between them.

"God brings many children to this home temporarily." *Appa* sighed as he spoke again. "Runaways and lost children. Some stay for only a few months or weeks, then we need to let them go. Often, they go back to families who will show them no love. It rips a hole in our hearts, especially *Amma's*."

"*Amma* is always so full of joy. I never see her sad," I said, somewhat shocked.

"She puts on a joyful smile every day for the children here. You all have enough sadness of your own to bear. *Amma* never wants you to bear hers. But at night when she often can't sleep, she is in tears on her knees before God."

Appa's eyes glistened, and he rubbed his chin until he regained composure.

"There have been days we felt we couldn't go on, but God always gives us strength to continue…he reminds us that Karunai House is not our home; it is his. He gives, and he takes away as he wills. Sometimes we see the good in it, and many times we don't."

Outside the SUV, a naked little boy chased a goat along the shoulder as a woman in a faded *sari* yelled after him while balancing a sack of rice on her head. A red-faced man stomped out of the nearby house and gripped the little boy's wrist violently. I turned away and looked at *Appa*, remembering the life I came from, the life Velu had come from.

"Faith trusts God's plan, Kashvi." *Appa* spoke confidently, "One big part of that plan is for you to trust him and pray to him. One day, you will look back over your life in awe of how he used every second of it to weave the most beautiful tapestry of his plan."

I was surprised to learn of weakness in *Appa* and *Amma*. They always seemed so strong. As I considered his words, I thought about how many things God must have worked in the lives of *Appa*, *Amma*, my father, my mother, and myself to bring me to Karunai House. I didn't understand why it had to be this way, but I was thankful that I was at Karunai House, even if Velu wasn't there anymore.

A peace settled over me as we drove the rest of the way home.

When Karunai House came into view, my peace instantly disappeared. Something was terribly wrong. Mahiyu stood at the gate, waving frantically. A few boys beside him signaled us to come quickly, their faces panicked. Dhiren accelerated and rolled down the windows. Everyone was shouting, but the only word I caught made my heart drop—*Sudhir*.

Appa's voice boomed. "Quiet! One person, tell me what's wrong."

Nalayani came running, her strides long and hurried. She climbed into the *Qualis* beside me. "Go; I'll explain on the way."

"Where are we going?" Dhiren asked, thoroughly confused.

"The hospital." Nalayani turned to me. "Sudhir had an accident."

My hand flew to my mouth, stifling a cry. "What kind of accident?"

Dhiren sped away, and Nalayani looked angry and afraid. "The powerlines."

"No…" Dhiren's steady strength wavered, and I felt the weight of their fear pressing down on me. "What happened?"

"You know the metal rods the boys use to knock down tamarind fruit? Sudhir took one to the roof of the boys' dorm to reach better, and…" She trailed off.

Dhiren slammed his fist into the steering wheel. "*Amma* has requested so many times for the government to move those lines, and they never listen! This was an accident waiting to happen!"

"Calm down, Dhiren," *Appa* placed a hand on his shoulder. "And slow down. We don't want another accident today."

A knot tightened in my stomach. I knew powerlines were dangerous, but I was unsure how afraid I should be.

"Is he okay? Will he be okay?"

Nalayani swallowed hard, silent.

I grabbed her shoulders and shook her in fear.

"Tell me, *Akka*!"

Nalayani closed her eyes. "He was in contact with the powerline for several seconds…He was alive when the ambulance took him, but he… he wasn't in good shape."

Letting go of her arms, I collapsed against her and sobbed uncontrollably. She stroked my arm. "The hospital here has the very best doctors. They'll do everything they can."

I couldn't stop the flood of guilt as I remembered my last words to Sudhir.

I wish you were the one leaving instead!

144

Would that be the last thing I ever said to him?

Appa was bent over in prayer, his knuckles rubbing hard across his forehead.

My mind was too overwhelmed to pray.

Would Karunai House be shut down? Would Mother and Father demand we come back? If I hadn't insisted on going with Velu, maybe I could have stopped Sudhir.

Dhiren pulled up to the hospital.

"They won't let more than two of us in there," *Appa* said. "I'll wait with Dhiren in the parking lot."

Nalayani guided me inside. The waiting room was chaos. Every bench was full, and the aisles were crowded with people lying on the floor, writhing in pain. Amid the noise and confusion, I spotted *Amma*, leaning serenely against a wall, her eyes closed in prayer.

We approached, and Nalayani gently touched her arm. "*Amma.*"

Opening her eyes, she wrapped us both in a hug. "He was alive when we arrived; I don't know anything else."

Nalayani nodded, tugging nervously at a curl by her ear. "I'll head back to get everyone settled. We'll all pray, *Thangachi*. I love you both very much."

Amma nodded. "Tell Dhiren and *Appa* to pick up Sudhir's parents." She exhaled deeply, gathering her strength, and said with resolve, "It's all in God's hands."

Nalayani left, and *Amma* turned her attention to me. "How are you holding up, *Thangachi?*"

I broke down in tears. "This is all my fault for being so mean to him this morning!"

"Oh, my sweet girl." *Amma* wrapped her arm around me. "We do not live under *karma*. God is in control of all things, even these painful things. He holds us tightly and will never let us go."

I tried to believe it, but the gnawing fear was winning the battle of my mind.

Amma clasped my hands and prayed earnestly, pleading for God's protection over Sudhir, for healing, for his glory, and for his love and power to be a witness to all around.

"Vasantha?" a doctor shouted from the door.

Amma ended her prayer, and we rushed over. The doctor informed us that Sudhir was stabilized and would likely survive.

"It's a miracle," the doctor said. "I've never known of anyone to survive that kind of contact with a powerline, especially for as long as he was."

As he led us through the winding hallways, he explained that if all went well, Sudhir would need months—maybe even years—of special care and skin grafts to fully heal. We took the elevator, marking my first time on one, and went to Sudhir's room.

He lay on a bed, his body mostly covered in gauze bandages, tubes snaking out from his arms. His eyes were closed, mouth slightly open.

If it weren't for the slow rise and fall of his chest, I would have thought he was dead.

A machine by his side beeped, wavy lines dancing on its screen.

The unfamiliar sights, sounds, and smells of the medical equipment overwhelmed me. I leaned against the bed, taking Sudhir's bandaged hand in mine.

"I'm sorry, *Thambi*," I whispered. "Please forgive me for how I treated you."

We sat there for hours, doctors and nurses coming and going—changing bandages, checking the machines, adjusting the tubes, putting strange necklaces into their ears and touching the metal ends to Sudhir's chest. Sudhir remained motionless through it all.

Amma left to get us some snacks.

I tried not to think about losing Sudhir. It terrified me. For all our fights and how much he annoyed me, he was still my *thambi* and the only one who knew what it was like to grow up with our father.

Will he go to heaven if he dies? He said he believes in Jesus, but was that just because everyone at Karunai House does?

And what about me? I thought. *Do I say I believe because everyone else does? When I told my father Jesus was the only true God, was it because I truly believe it, or because I wanted to defy him?*

Amma returned, handing me a glass bottle of *Thums Up* soda.

"Thank you, *Amma.*" I mustered a smile, taking the bottle. I took a sip, savoring the sweet, fizzy burn in my mouth. It was my first time drinking soda.

The momentary enjoyment didn't last long. I looked up at the doorway and saw Father standing there. His presence darkened the room, his expression hard as ever. He stepped in with Mother trailing behind him, Dhiren entering after her.

Mother greeted me with a somber hug, then joined me sitting at Sudhir's bedside, gently holding his hand. Father just stood near the door, silent. No greeting, no questions.

Amma began explaining the updates we had received from the doctors, but before she could finish, a nurse entered the room.

"Only two visitors at a time, please."

We left Father and Mother with Sudhir and waited in the hallway.

Half an hour later, Father walked past us without a word, his face hardened like stone. Mother lingered, watching Father leave before turning to speak with us.

"He thinks this happened because I sent you both away." Her voice trembled. "He's convinced it's the curse of the gods, that Sudhir needs to be brought to the temple for prayer."

"Like Asha!" I swallowed hard. "She would have survived if she'd been taken to a hospital."

Mother's shoulders drooped.

"Perhaps she would have; I don't know, Kashvi. Many things happen to keep the balance of life, and we just can't know." Mother looked weary. "We can't take Sudhir, even if we wanted to. He'd die if we removed him now. It's the law that he stays here." She glanced down the hallway where Father had disappeared, her voice hushed. "But he's not happy about it."

Her excuses didn't matter. I could only focus on one thing: *If this had happened in our village, Father would have brought Sudhir to the temple, and he would have died.*

We waited in silence for a while before *Amma* explained that she had worked in this hospital as a nurse before starting Karunai House. She explained the history, how it was one of the best hospitals in India, built by Christian missionaries, and all the lives that had been saved in it.

Amma placed a comforting arm around Mother.

"The doctors will tell you themselves—Sudhir surviving was a miracle. No one survives something like this." She paused. "This isn't a curse. God saved your son."

Mother's face crumpled, tears spilling from her eyes as she leaned into *Amma*'s embrace.

For the rest of the night, *Amma* and I took turns with Father and Mother sitting with Sudhir, rotating every couple of hours.

I told *Amma* all about Asha's death and what had happened in the temple. We prayed with thanks to God that Sudhir had been in a place where he could be brought to the hospital.

The next day was Sunday, and Dhiren picked up *Amma* and me from the hospital to go to church in the morning. *Amma* invited Father and Mother to come. Unsurprisingly, Father declined, but I was shocked when Mother accepted, especially with Father standing right beside her.

Father shook his head disapprovingly but didn't stop her.

As we drove to church, Mother broke the silence.

"I've been thinking all night...maybe this happened because we've neglected your god."

Amma turned towards her from the front seat, her voice calm but confident. "I know you believe in many gods, but we confess there is only one true God. He allowed this to happen for reasons we may never fully understand. But he is good, and whatever the reason, we can be sure it was for good."

We arrived just minutes before the service began. Mahiyu was picking up candles lying in front of the church door.

"Who put those here?" I asked Mahiyu as we passed.

"A Hindu woman comes here early some Sunday mornings and lights these candles," he explained. "She wants to make sure there isn't a god she doesn't pray to, in case our God is real."

Mother's eyes lit up at the story as she found herself relating to this unknown woman.

I nodded at Mahiyu and hurried in with Mother.

As we walked down the aisle, a few women in the front row moved to give us their seats, insisting *Amma* and Mother sit up front. I took my place amidst the throng of children next to Sarina, who immediately wrapped me in a warm hug.

Before beginning the service, *Appa* explained Sudhir's accident and gave an update on his condition, asking everyone to pray for him.

Appa preached on Acts 17, the passage that talked about people creating an altar to the "unknown god" because they were afraid they may have missed one and didn't want to offend it. It was like he had written the sermon for Mother.

When the offering was taken, Mother scrambled to find a few *rupees. Amma* tried to stop her, knowing she was only giving what little she had in an attempt to appease God. But Mother insisted and dropped the *rupees* in the bag.

After the service, *Amma* offered Mother bananas and onions that had been given away by some church members during collection instead of *rupees*.

"Take these as a gift, please," she urged.

"I would never take from this god!" Mother refused, appalled. "That would bring more anger and punishment from him. One accident is enough."

Amma nodded sadly at Mother before another member of church pulled her away to talk.

I stared at my mother, who seemed distant.

"What did you think of the service?"

She turned to me, focusing back on the present reality. "It was good to learn about this god. I never knew much. Hopefully he will heal Sudhir now."

I sighed. Mother clearly heard the gospel proclaimed in that sermon, but still, she saw Jesus as one of many gods, entirely missing the point. But I had the same idea when I first came, so maybe there was still hope.

"Will you come again?" I pleaded.

"I think…I will," she said hesitantly.

A little while later, *Amma* found us again and insisted that I rest at Karunai House, but I couldn't bear to think of Sudhir alone at the hospital. *Amma's* mother, *Ammachi*, joined our conversation and offered to take turns sitting with Sudhir.

Dhiren drove us all back to the hospital. After checking on Sudhir, *Amma* and *Appa* left to rest, and Father and Mother went home. *Ammachi* stayed with me through the night. She sat quietly beside me, providing peace in the chaos of the hospital.

I had never spoken much with *Ammachi*, aside from short exchanges at church. I still had to consciously fight against the fear instilled in me about the bad luck that would come in crossing a widows' path, but her gentle spirit drew me in.

Ammachi turned to me. "So, your *amma* came to church?"

I nodded. "She came, but she doesn't believe in Jesus. She thinks worshiping with us will keep him from hurting her."

Ammachi sighed. "I was just like her once. I was baptized only ten years ago. Before that, I wanted nothing to do with Jesus."

I'd heard *Amma* tell me bits of *Ammachi's* story before, but this was the first time I was hearing it from her. I knew Jesus had changed her life, and she was still very emotional about it. Whenever I heard a nose blowing behind me in church, it was usually *Ammachi*, crying over the sermon.

"I didn't deserve God's grace," *Ammachi* sniveled. "I rejected my own daughter for marrying a Christian man and shunned her for it. We lived in poverty, and I suffered the beatings of my husband. Still, I clung to the Hindu gods who never did anything for me."

She beamed with a joyful smile, a stark contrast to the sorrow in her words, continuing. "But Jesus…Jesus broke my hard heart and changed me."

"What made you finally become a Christian?" I asked, my heart yearning for a simple answer that could change my mother's mind, something I could use to bring her to follow Jesus with me.

"I don't know." She shrugged her shoulders. "God just…changed my heart."

I sighed in frustration. "But how?"

"I truly can't explain it," she said. "I heard the gospel many times over many years from Vasantha, but it didn't have any effect on me. Then, one day, as I was praying in a temple, I suddenly realized I didn't believe in the gods surrounding me. It just hit me—the living God, the one my daughter had been telling me about all along, was real. I prayed to him, asked for forgiveness, and wept for all the years I had rejected him—and my daughter. I knew I would be rejected by my husband, my son, and the whole village, but none of that mattered anymore."

I sat in silence, both awed and frustrated. *Appa* always said only God could work salvation in the heart, but I wanted there to be something I could say or do to convince my mother. There had to be something.

I wrestled with God all night. *Why did you change* Ammachi? *Why Abhiraj? Why not my amma?*

Out of my questioning, the words of God that *Appa* had spoken to me popped into my head: *My thoughts are not your thoughts, neither are your ways my ways.*

I don't think I like your ways, God, I thought bitterly, my tears blurring the dim light in the room.

Suddenly, a soft rustling came from beside me. I turned to see Sudhir's fingers twitch beneath his bandages. His eyelids fluttered weakly, and then his eyes opened, blinking slowly. He looked at me with his half-bandaged head, and his lips parted just enough to let out a faint, scratchy whisper.

"*Akka…*"

His weak smile renewed hope in me. *Thank you, Jesus.*

CHAPTER 16

"*Ahh!*" I shot up in bed, gasping for air, my heart pounding in my ears. Sarina sat up next to me and Nalayani stirred in her bed.

"What's wrong?" Sarina mumbled groggily.

"A nightmare," I huffed. "My *appa* killed my *amma*, and then he came and burned this place to the ground. It's just a nightmare…" I buried my head in my knees and cried. "But it felt so real."

Sarina wrapped her arms around me. "Take no thought for tomorrow, Kash'i. God holds you, your *amma*, and Karunai House in his hands."

The nightmare still lingered, and I worried about it all. Karunai House had survived Sudhir's accident—*Amma* called it a miracle—but ever since, officials started making weekly inspections, showing up unannounced and exhausting us with the extra work and constant questioning.

And how could I not worry about Mother? She had come to church a few times over the last three months since Sudhir's accident. She never stayed long, and I watched fear cloud her eyes as she left each time. I knew she wasn't coming to learn about Jesus; she was just trying to keep us safe by offering money to appease any god who might be angry. She was playing the game of the gods, even enduring Father's wrath for wasting what little money they had.

Sarina began softly reciting Psalm 23. "…Yea, though I walk through the valley of the shadow of death, I will fear no evil: for thou art with me; thy rod and thy staff they comfort me…"

"How can I not fear?" I whispered.

Sarina's voice was steady. "He can harm you—but only in this life. He can't take away your dwelling in the house of the Lord forever."

"And what about my *amma*?" I asked, my voice trembling.

"She's coming to church," Sarina encouraged. "She's hearing the gospel. We just have to keep praying."

"I wish the answers were easier," I sighed.

"We all do," Sarina replied.

I looked at Sarina in the dark and thought of all she had suffered. She had watched her parents take poison right in front of her as a little girl, yet here she was, the most joyful girl I'd ever known.

Will I ever get there?

"I'm so glad you're here with me," I said.

"Me, too." Sarina squeezed my hand before lying back down.

I flopped back onto my pillow, but sleep wouldn't come. My thoughts whirled, my heart heavy with the weight of everything—fear for Mother, Father's rage, the never-ending inspections. And what if God didn't give *Appa* and *Amma* the strength to continue? I had a gnawing worry that Karunai House would one day be crushed under it all.

I clung to the verses *Amma* always encouraged me to meditate on, trying to "take my thoughts captive," as she said, but it felt like fighting a losing battle. I turned my head and cried into the pillow, dwelling on my fears. I made myself miserable missing Velu, Mother, Asha, and even the simplicity of my old life, despite all the pain.

Eventually the rooster crowed.

Rubbing my eyes, I dragged myself out of bed, disappointed for not trusting God like I knew I should. I felt like a failure.

"Are you okay?" Nalayani asked, her sleepy eyes full of concern.

I hesitated, wondering if I should admit how weak I felt. "It's just the nightmare I had last night."

She gave me a sympathetic look. "Let's go do our chores. It'll take your mind off things."

I kept to myself throughout chores and devotions, but breakfast made me feel a lot better. My mood lifted as I ate, easing some of the weight pressing down on my heart.

Finding a smile, I bounced over to Sarina, who was washing her plate. "Want to play *carrom*?"

"Do you still want me to help you with homework today?" she asked.

"Oh…" I sighed. I had spent two months with Sudhir in the hospital, until last month, when he was able to return to Karunai House. He needed constant care to prevent infection. Between school and caring for Sudhir, I struggled to finish my homework and had fallen behind. Sarina had begun tutoring me to help me catch up.

I thought of Velu and my dreams to help children. It was important to me, and I didn't want to lose sight of it.

"Yes, please help me."

"Well, it's been a long week for you. Let's play one game, then we can start!" Sarina smiled.

Sitting to play, I was excited to finally relax, but almost immediately, a knock came at the gate. Mahiyu ran to open it. I watched, curious, as the gate creaked open.

My mother walked into the courtyard, and Mahiyu closed the gate behind her. No sign of my father. Mother must have come by bus. A mix of excitement and dread knotted in my stomach.

I hurried towards her, fighting the surge of emotions rising in me. *Why would she be here alone? Maybe she finally decided to leave and live at the women's shelter.*

Her eyes appeared calm, and she offered a generous smile as I approached.

I wrapped my arms around her. "I'm so glad to see you."

It was rare to have her all to myself without the rush of church or the weight of Father's presence looming.

She pulled away from the embrace and smoothed her head scarf.

"Today is your *appa*'s fortieth birthday. Uncle Arjun is having a celebration for him, and he wants you and Sudhir to be there."

The knot in my stomach tightened. I hadn't seen Father since he visited Sudhir that first night in the hospital. I didn't even know it was his birthday. I felt sick and fought the urge to run up and lock myself in my room.

Amma and Dhiren came out of the office to greet Mother. Mother explained the situation to *Amma*, who kept glancing at me with concern in her eyes.

Amma nodded. "Dhiren, why don't you see if Sudhir is up to it, and then you can bring them all there?"

"Yes, *Amma*," Dhiren said, striding off to the boys' dorm.

The thought of seeing Father made my skin crawl, but the thought of Dhiren's towering figure overshadowing Father made me smile.

Dhiren came out holding Sudhir's hand, who hobbled down the steps from the dorm.

He had only just started to walk again after being in bed for three months. His weak legs had a hard time holding up his skinny frame, which looked even skinnier due to his clothes, loose-fitting to prevent friction. The skin on his legs and arms was a patchwork of scars and skin grafts. His recovery had been slow and painful, full of surgeries and constant checkups. Most of the major work was done, but there was still more to come. Every slow step he took reminded me of all he had been through.

Dhiren left Sudhir by us and pulled up the *Qualis*. I gently helped boost Sudhir up into the middle bench, then I got in after Mother. Sudhir shifted in the seat.

"Are you comfortable?" I asked, concerned with his wiggling.

He smiled at me, that familiar big grin brightening his face. "It's as good as it's going to get, *Akka*. But it's not too bad."

Our relationship had transformed since his accident. Knowing how close he came to death made me realize how much I truly loved him. We had spent countless hours together as I attended to him, and it created a bond I never thought we'd have.

Sudhir had changed, too. Before the accident, he had been carefree and mischievous, but now, he spent hours reading the Bible and praying, filled with gratitude for the God who saved him. His knowledge of Scripture and his excitement for God were contagious, encouraging everyone at Karunai House to rejoice in God's goodness.

As we drove down the narrow, bumpy roads to our village, we passed familiar sights—a patchwork of dusty fields filled with wandering goats, decorated cows standing outside temples, and mangy dogs curled up by the roadside shops and tea stands.

We talked to Mother about school. Sudhir was relieved to be back. He had missed the first term of our second year, and his teacher had given him a special curriculum to help him catch up. He spoke excitedly about what he was learning, showing such a change from the *thambi* I knew before.

"How is your English coming along?" Mother asked Sudhir.

"It's hard to learn, but I've come a long way. I can't wait to learn more so I can go to university!"

I watched Mother beam with pride, a look I never remembered seeing from her before.

Dhiren jumped into the conversation.

"God brought your children to Karunai House. He is a good God. He saved your son for a reason."

"Yes, I'm sure," Mother murmured. Looking at Dhiren, she asked, "How did *you* end up at Karunai House?"

"When I was ten, my *amma* died. My *appa* was a drunk, and eventually, he just abandoned me," Dhiren said somberly. "I found odd jobs here and there to earn money. Eventually, a social worker found me and brought me to Karunai House."

I listened eagerly. I knew Dhiren's father from church and had heard a little of Dhiren's story from Sarina before, but never from Dhiren himself.

Dhiren continued. "Years later, my *appa* showed up at Karunai House, paralyzed from an accident. Someone from church knew a Christian factory owner who hires disabled people and helped him get a job. He started coming to church, and soon, he believed and was baptized."

Mother looked engaged in the story until the part about the conversion.

"That's nice," she responded dismissively.

Dhiren persevered. "Actually, I hated my *appa* when he first came back. I thought he deserved to be paralyzed for abandoning me and only coming back when he needed help. But now I praise God for it. He used my *appa's* abandoning me and his accident to bring both of us to know him. God is so good!"

Dhiren's face shined with his faith. I knew that should be my attitude towards my father—praying for God to change his heart and for Jesus to forgive his sins—but it just wasn't. My hatred ran so deep.

"I'm happy for you," Mother said, staring out the window as we turned down the path to our house.

That's it? Can't she see how amazing God is?

Once, at church, I had introduced her to Abhiraj, who, as always, shared his story of what God had done in his life. It was the same reaction. Mother refused to rejoice in God's goodness for fear of angering other gods, not wanting to "upset the balance of life."

I wondered at how she could live her life in such slavery to dumb idols, convincing myself that I would have realized on my own how silly it was to worship idols when I grew out of childhood.

I turned to look out the window in frustration. In the village, I saw wilting flower garlands strewn around.

"Did someone get married recently?"

A smile graced Mother's face. "Yes, your friend Neeta's sister was married yesterday."

"Esha?" I murmured, remember Neeta sharing her fears with me about her sister's hopes for a love marriage and about her threatening to hurt herself.

Mother shook her head. "No, the middle daughter, Ilani, was married."

She paused. "Esha…Esha upset the balance of life and caused many problems. Her desire for a love marriage led her to her death."

My jaw dropped. "What happened?"

"She tried to pursue the boy she had been with, and his *appa* threw acid on her for coming back to find his son. Then she refused to live with the shameful scars she had brought upon herself."

Mother eyed me intently. "Let us just learn from the misfortunes of others and not bring them upon ourselves."

Her words felt like a warning, and I wondered how much I would disappoint her in my new life as a Christian. My head dropped as I felt the tug in my heart between making God and my mother happy.

After a moment, I looked up at her. "Isn't Ilani only sixteen?"

"Yes, Kashvi."

She was a couple of years older than me. Parents often bribed schoolmasters into signing graduation certificates for their daughters so they could marry early. Early marriage meant lower dowries to pay, one fewer mouth to feed, and less chance of the girl earning a bad reputation. It was normal growing up, but that all seemed so far away now that I was at Karunai House.

I planned to finish school, go to college, and help others.

But what were my parents' plans for me?

Dhiren turned the *Qualis*, and we bumped down the familiar cratered dirt road, pulling off to the side by Uncle's house.

Anxiety rushed in. How would Father act today? I was sure Sudhir's and my being here was Uncle's idea, or maybe Mother's, but not Father's.

Getting out of the *Qualis*, I spotted Father, laughing with Uncle and some neighbors.

Then my eyes fell on Vishnu. He had gotten older. I noticed that he was taller and broader than the last time I had seen him, and a shadow covered his upper lip. However, the childish attraction I had once felt had disappeared. So much had changed for me. I didn't want to think about any plans our families once had. I hoped the plans had vanished altogether, somehow.

Beyond the group, I saw my aunt squatting near a cookpot by the house. It had been over a year since I'd seen her. Her eyes stared lifelessly into the pot as she stirred.

Uncle had a bottle in his hand, and he flailed his arms around in wild gestures before bursting into a fit of laughter. Father was laughing, too, but the moment he turned and saw us, his smile faded.

Uncle yelled, "Hey, everyone's here! Cheers!" and clinked his bottle against Father's. Father forced a smile and took a long drink.

"Kashvi, you get prettier every time I see you!" Uncle patted my head, glancing at Vishnu with a smile.

With the nutritious meals at Karunai House, I'd grown a lot, surpassing my mother. And my hair had grown back quickly since being cut. It was just past my shoulders now.

Uncle turned to Sudhir and glanced over his scarred skin. He let out a whistle. "I can't say the same for you, Sudhir! Your father said you were electrocuted?"

Sudhir nodded and went on to explain his accident and recovery in detail.

Uncle's eyes were wide. "And you're here to tell the story."

"God saved me," Sudhir said.

"Indeed, they did," Uncle nodded. "You better make it up to them. Speaking of that, we were just about to go to the temple to get a blessing for your *appa*'s birthday. Come on, everyone!"

Sudhir looked at me to see what I would do, but I was just as unsure as he was. I looked up at Dhiren, hoping for an escape, but he only gave me a small smile. I sighed. He couldn't tell me what to do, especially here in front of all these people.

Not knowing what to do, I simply followed the small crowd—Mother, cousins, neighbors—down the road towards the temple. Sudhir trailed after me with his arm around Dhiren for support.

I felt ashamed. I was such a coward. My mind raced with excuses to get us out of this without sending Father into a fury. Meanwhile, Father beckoned Mother over. They whispered to each other in low voices, and I saw Father glancing back at Dhiren, his brow furrowed.

I knew I needed to stand up to Father and refuse to take part in any rituals, but I was terrified. Even with Dhiren's towering presence, I knew my choices wouldn't just affect me. If Father couldn't take out his rage on me, he would take it out on Mother.

When we reached the temple entrance, memories of Asha flooded my mind. The gods perched on the temple roof still sneered at me. As the group continued in, Sudhir and Dhiren stopped and turned to me. We shared a look of anxious understanding.

Vishnu turned. "What are you waiting for? Come on."

Father and Uncle heard him and turned, too, their eyes narrowing.

"We're not going in," I said, my voice shaking but resolute.

"What?" Father grunted, stepping forward, his shadow falling over me like a storm cloud.

My confidence faded in that shadow, and I blurted out, "Asha died in there!"

Mother's eyes softened, and she gently laid a hand on Father's arm. "We can't expect them to go back in there after what happened to Asha."

"She's been to the temple with her friends." Father's eyes bored into me.

"No, I haven't been there since Asha…" I felt small in my web of deceit. "I lied about going with friends before. I just couldn't go."

Father's glare pierced me, but his gaze shifted upwards, meeting Dhiren's eyes. After a moment, Uncle slapped Father on the back, laughing. "Let them stay. Don't let this ruin your day."

Father turned in disgust, following Uncle into the flickering shadows of the temple. I breathed a sigh of relief, but shame immediately followed, twisting in my gut. I'd used Asha's death as my excuse instead of standing firm in my faith.

Jesus, forgive me, I prayed silently.

Sudhir, Dhiren, and I walked the familiar path Sudhir and I used to take to school. It was hard to believe over two years had passed since we had last walked it. Nothing seemed to have changed. Things rarely did here.

A rotten stench filled the air, making me look up. We were passing Asha's old house. What was once a home was now only charred walls, and a huge pile of garbage spilled out from the crumbling doorway. A cow, its ribs protruding from its thin frame, stuck its nose through the refuse, searching for scraps. My stomach turned at the sight.

Unable to look any longer, I spun around. "Let's go back." I bit my lip hard, trying to keep myself composed. The physical pain in my lip felt more bearable than the emotional pain that had been rocking my soul for years.

I dragged my feet towards the temple, and Dhiren and Sudhir followed behind. I heard Sudhir explaining to Dhiren the significance of the house we had just seen. I pressed on, not wanting to engage in the conversation.

The birthday crowd was just starting to leave the temple when we arrived.

I spotted Mother and made my way to her.

"What happened to Asha's house?"

Mother sighed. "Villagers throw waste there to keep the evil spirits away."

"But…" I started to protest but didn't know what to say. It seemed so wrong, but this was the way here.

Mother shut down any further conversation. "We are not talking about this again. This is all a part of—"

"—*Karma*. Fate. Order. Balance. I know." I rolled my eyes, finishing her sentence and turning away from her.

As we walked back to Uncle's house, I slid to the back of the group. I didn't want to talk to anyone. I felt alone. A growing nausea twisted my stomach.

Asha had died without knowing Jesus. Her parents did too…and

Neeta's sister, Esha. They died without hope. They took their own lives, wishing for a better, or at least a different, one. Were they so hopeless that they didn't even care that their next life could be worse?

I thought of my sweet friend and wondered if she was really in hell. *Appa* and *Amma* taught me that the Bible said anyone without salvation in Jesus would perish in hell. That didn't seem fair. Asha didn't really have a chance, and she was the nicest girl I knew—*way* nicer than me.

Why should I go to heaven and not her?

I kicked the dirt with my gold-strapped sandals, and the strap broke from the bottom. I kicked off my other sandal, then grabbed them both and threw them towards a burning trash pile.

Uncle's loud, boisterous laughter snapped me back to the present. Everyone around him was grinning as he spoke. It made me furious.

How can they be so happy, surrounded by death and misery?

I drifted away from the path, wandering behind Uncle's house. Turning back to see if anyone was watching, I caught Dhiren's concerned eyes watching me. I kept walking and soon heard his footsteps behind me.

"Where are you going, *Thangachi?*"

"Please, I need some time alone," I said.

"Don't go far, *Thangachi.*" Dhiren's eyes pleaded with me.

"I won't," I promised, and sank down against the wall of the house. I tried to pray.

Father, I'm confused. Everything seems black and white at Karunai House, but when I'm here, it's all so muddy.

After several minutes, Uncle's voice drifted through the open window above me. The pungent *beedi* smoke wafted through the air, and I thought I heard Father's voice, too. I strained to hear.

"You need to get her away from those Christians before it's too late," Uncle said.

"You still want her for Vishnu?" Father's raspy voice asked.

"Yes," Uncle replied. "Once she's back here, we'll drive all those Christian ideas out of her one way or another."

163

I shivered.

Father coughed intensely.

"Ever since your kids left, you've been sicker, weaker. And then what happened with Sudhir…and your wife sneaking off to that church. It's a curse from the gods," Uncle said. "Vishnu will be eighteen soon. We should consult an astrologer to find a *muhoortam* day for the marriage."

My heart pounded. I had to get away. I tiptoed around the side of the house and walked right into someone.

"Sorry," I mumbled. Looking up, I froze. It was Vishnu.

"No problem." He laughed, steadying me with his hand and letting it linger. "Are you okay?"

"No, I'm…sick," I said, my voice barely audible.

"I can get you some water, or maybe my *amma* can make you some rice porridge," Vishnu offered, still holding my arm.

Squirming away, I shook my head and brushed past him. My chest felt tight, and I could barely breathe. Dhiren, standing near Sudhir and Mother, looked towards us with concern.

I hurried over to Dhiren's safety and whispered, "We need to leave."

"What's wrong?" Mother asked as she felt my forehead. "You look ill."

"I just need to go back to Karunai House and rest," I said, trying to hold back tears.

"You can lie down here," Mother suggested. "You just arrived. We haven't even spent any time together."

I saw Father and Uncle emerge from the house, and I began to panic. "We need to go now."

I gave Mother a quick hug and pulled Dhiren and Sudhir towards the *Qualis*.

Mother spoke behind us, but her words were lost in the fog of my mind as I considered my future.

I helped Sudhir into the SUV and sat beside him, looking out the window as we drove away. Father was glaring at me. Vishnu was waving, his expression a mix of confusion and disappointment.

As soon as they were out of sight, I broke down in tears.

"What's really wrong, *Akka?*" Sudhir asked.

"Everything," I sobbed.

I thought of Neeta's sister Ilani, married off at sixteen. That would soon be me. What would happen if I refused? Would Father beat me until I agreed? Or would he hurt Mother to make me do it? Would Uncle or Vishnu throw acid on me for defying them? Becoming a Christian and refusing Hindu worship was already unthinkable, but to add the shame of refusing a marriage would heap trouble upon trouble. It was the ultimate upsetting of the balance and order Mother always spoke of.

Before Karunai House, I would have accepted marrying Vishnu without hesitation. He was familiar, kind enough, and seemed to understand me—and I could have finally left my father's house. I hadn't known a better life was possible.

Now, though, I knew better. I had hopes and dreams.

But in this moment, I almost wished I hadn't come to Karunai House. Life might have been easier if I had stayed ignorant.

CHAPTER 17

When we drove up to Karunai House from our village, Mahiyu opened the gate, his face tense. As we pulled in, he whispered to Dhiren through the window, "Inspection."

My heart thumped at the word. All I wanted was to cry alone in my room or maybe talk with *Amma* or Sarina or Nalayani. That wasn't possible now. The future of Karunai House was always on the line during inspections, and the threat of being sent back to my old life loomed with every visit from officials. Or worse—ending up in a government home.

Inspections demanded everyone's focus and energy. Sometimes they scoured every room, or they interviewed us, or they scrutinized stacks of daily logs. Everything down to a pencil or stick of gum handed out was logged somewhere. Sometimes, they did all of it in one long, draining visit.

In the courtyard sat two silver SUVs from the Child Welfare Department. I prayed the officers were friendly ones. Some saw the love and care at Karunai House and respected it, despite it being Christian-run. Others tried to find any reason to shut us down, despising anything Christian.

Dhiren parked, and we climbed out. I hit the ground with my bare feet.

Mahiyu turned to me, his face unusually strained. "*Thangachi*, make sure the girls' dorm is inspection-ready."

I wasn't prepared for this right now. Anxiety swelled in my chest, and I felt like I was going to explode.

"*Thambi*, you just sit on the steps and rest." Mahiyu said.

"But I can help," Sudhir replied, limping towards the boys' dorm.

Mahiyu put an arm around him instinctively.

"I can do it on my own," Sudhir pushed Mahiyu away gently and Mahiyu watched him carefully, waiting to jump in if Sudhir made the slightest misstep.

Raised voices echoed from the office; one of the voices sounded like *Appa*'s, and that sent a shiver down my spine. Mahiyu, visibly shaken, walked with Dhiren towards the office, where *Amma* and the other staff were meeting the officials.

The inspections were getting more invasive and frequent. The last inspection had lasted seven hours.

Sudhir looked at me grimly. "I wish we could just bribe them and send them away like the other homes do."

I shuddered, remembering what I had heard about the Wish House, a nearby girls' home run by a wealthy businessman, where donations were pocketed by staff, and the girls were thin and sickly. *Amma* had told me a sad story about a girl who had been abused and died there, but no one was prosecuted, and the home still operated, passing inspections every time.

"Me too."

"But *Appa* and *Amma* will never bribe them," Sudhir muttered, his voice carrying a mix of frustration and admiration. "They trust God's will for the home."

I sighed. Some of the officials seemed bent on proving that the children here were coerced to convert to Christianity, trying to find any reason to shut us down like the thousands of other Christian charities the government closed in the last year. I knew only the grace of God kept us open.

"Why do they keep wasting time here? They know we follow the rules better than anyone. We aren't hiding anything."

"Except for the Bibles." Sudhir smiled.

I tried to laugh, but my chest felt tight. I had to keep myself busy so I wouldn't collapse under the weight of everything on my mind.

"I'd better go." I left Sudhir and ran over to the girls' dorm.

I hurried up the stairs to my bedroom and wrapped the Bibles in a *chudidhar*, hiding the bundle at the bottom of the chest beneath my other clothes. I ran around the room, tucking in bedsheets, straightening backpacks along the walls, wiping cobwebs from corners.

All the while, I wondered where Sarina was and why she hadn't been cleaning in here already. Were they interviewing her?

I glanced out the window and saw Sarina step out of the office, tears streaming down her puffy face. She walked towards our dorm, her shoulders shaking.

I met her at the top of the stairs as she stumbled her way up. When she saw me, she collapsed where she was, weeping. I wrapped my arms around her. I didn't know what she was crying over, but finally together with my best friend, I let my pent-up tears flow with hers. Her closeness gave me a small sense of security.

Sarina looked at me, barely able to get the words out. "They're taking me—"

"What?!" I gasped, panic setting in.

"They're taking me to another girls' home—" Sarina broke down, weeping again.

I stared at her, unable to move, unable to process what I heard.

"No…" I gripped her arms tightly, as if I could keep her from being taken. "How can they do that? Why now? You can't go!"

Sarina wiped her face. Taking some deep breaths, she found her voice. "They want to separate me from *Amma* and *Appa* and put me up for adoption."

"Adoption? But you've said before you'd never want to be adopted. You said Karunai House is your home."

"They don't believe me. They think *Amma* and *Appa* are coercing me to say that I don't want to be adopted," Sarina said bitterly. "They can't understand why an orphan wouldn't *want* to be adopted. They don't understand this place." She wept again.

Sarina was a true orphan. No relatives, no guardians—no one to speak up for her. The government was her guardian; they could take her wherever they wanted. If *Amma* could have stopped them, she would have.

"I need to pack my things," she whispered, picking herself up and walking into our bedroom.

Gripping my hair in my hands, I yanked it down, clenching my teeth until my jaw hurt. It took everything in me to hold back screams. *Why, God?*

In shock, I stared at Sarina through the doorway as she stuffed her clothes from the chest into her school backpack. With no warning, my best friend was being taken, and I might never see her again.

When Sarina's backpack was full, she packed the rest in a plastic bag, including her Bible, hidden under clothes.

I wanted to say something, anything. My mind raced and swirled with panicked thoughts.

What can you say to a best friend you'll never see again?

Sarina walked over to me with her bags and wrapped her arms around me. "You're the best friend I've ever had, Kash'i."

We stood there, holding each other, weeping for all we were losing. The noise of voices and crying from the courtyard drifted through the window, and we slumped down the stairs together. Everyone crowded around Sarina, crying and saying their goodbyes.

Nalayani stood nearby, looking paralyzed.

Appa and *Amma* stood by one of the silver SUVs, pleading with the Child Welfare officers one last time. The officers watched the scene, their stern faces softening as they took in the crowd's tears. Still, their minds were made up.

Sarina threw her arms around *Amma*. *Amma* was so strong. I knew she was weeping inside, but she didn't let it show. She wiped away a single tear from her eye as she held Sarina.

"Don't be afraid, my dear," *Amma* said with a steady voice. "God is always with you, and we'll do everything we can to bring you back."

Sarina's voice shook, but she tried to match *Amma's* strength. "I won't accept any adoption. You are my parents. I love you, *Amma*."

"I love you, too, my dear." *Amma's* weak voice betrayed her strong façade.

Sarina turned to *Appa* and embraced him. "I love you, *Appa*."

"I love you, my child," *Appa* whispered, letting his tears fall. "Do you have your Bible?"

"Yes," Sarina whispered.

"Seek the Lord every day in the word and prayer," *Appa* said, his voice thick. "The Lord is your strength. Whatever happens, he will never leave nor forsake you. Wait on him."

An officer cleared his throat. "We need to leave soon."

Appa turned. "One last thing." He placed a hand on Sarina's head and prayed over her, his voice unwavering despite the officers watching, frowning but silent. Everyone finished the prayer in unison with *Appa* and Sarina, "Bless the Lord, O my soul: and all that is within me, bless his holy name. Bless the Lord, O my soul, and forget not all his benefits. Amen."

I didn't feel any benefits at that moment. The joy and hope I had for a couple of short years felt elusive. Velu had already been taken from me; now my best friend was being taken, too.

But does that even matter anymore? Soon, I would be taken back to my village, forced to marry Vishnu and suffer the same fate as my mother. I would never finish school, never go to college, and never help children like I had once dreamed was possible.

Sarina turned to me, and I gave her one last hug.

"I'll never forget you," I stammered. "I'll pray for you every day. I love you."

Sarina climbed into the back of the SUV and shut the door. Milo barked, running between us and the vehicle, clearly sensing something was wrong. He looked between us and the car, and he seemed to be wondering why no one was stopping Sarina from leaving.

Amma's arm wrapped around me as they drove away. "I'll do everything I can to get her back."

We waved goodbye, tears flowing down all our faces as Mahiyu opened the gate and let the SUVs through.

I stared at the gate, numb, like that day my mother had left me at Karunai House. Everyone was in the courtyard, but I'd never felt so alone. The boys began drifting back to chores or study, but I didn't understand how life could just...go on.

Appa, *Amma*, Nalayani, and Sudhir stood by me, but I didn't want to be around anyone. I turned and bolted for the girls' dorm.

"Kashvi!" *Amma* called after me, but I didn't look back. I ran up the stairs and into my bedroom, where the emptiness of the chest at the end of the bed mocked the missing piece of my aching heart.

I kicked the chest barefoot with all my might.

"*Ahh!*" Pain shot through my toes, and the chest top slammed down with a noise of finality.

I collapsed to the floor, clutching my throbbing foot before I let loose scream after scream, punching the chest until my knuckles felt like my heart.

Nalayani and *Amma* hurried into the room, dropping down beside me and holding me in their arms as we sobbed together.

CHAPTER 18

"Kashvi!" *Amma* called as she got out of the SUV. I packed up my pencils and glanced over the half-done sketch of Sarina, Velu, and me under the hugging tree, before closing my sketch pad.

Hungry for a scrap of good news, I hurried to *Amma*, who had returned from visiting yet another children's home in her search for Sarina.

"Did you find her?" My heart battled between hope and fear.

"There's always hope, Kashvi." *Amma* offered a soft smile, but I caught the pain masked behind it.

Nearly a year had passed since Sarina had been taken, and *Amma* had scoured every orphanage within a couple of hours' drive away. Government officials refused to reveal Sarina's location, and many of the orphanages refused to let her know if Sarina was there.

"Grab your Bible and come into my office for our meeting. My visit took longer than expected."

My shoulders slumped as I turned towards the girls' dorm.

Amma had started meeting with me a couple of months after Sarina left. At first, I'd struggled just to get out of bed, do my chores, finish homework, even eat. I was doing better now with the day-to-day tasks, but *Amma's* weekly check-in was still a lifeline, especially for my faith.

Bible and journal in hand, I strolled past Nalayani outside the common room, her head buried in her books. She didn't even look up as I passed. Everything had been different since Sarina had left. Now, busy with an intense course of study at college, she had little time for me or anyone.

Irritation welled up in me at her lack of acknowledgment, but I didn't feel like making a one-sided effort.

I knocked on *Amma*'s door and was welcomed with her warm embrace. As cold as I tried to stay, her hug melted my resolve. I wrapped my arms tightly around her neck, my face pressed into her beautiful, ebony hair. It was always pulled back and neat. I remembered how her hair reminded me of a crow when had I first arrived, how much things had changed. Now she was *Amma* to me.

I pictured her finally letting her hair down late at night, in a rare few moments when dozens of children weren't vying for her attention, no officials were visiting, no more paperwork had to be completed between constant interrupting phone calls. But even then, she probably couldn't lay aside the burdens she carried for all of us; they surely lingered even in her sleep.

Tears poured as I let my emotions run freely.

"Where is she, *Amma*? And when will Nalayani be finished with school? I've lost everyone."

"I'm so sorry, my dear," *Amma* said sympathetically. She slowly separated from me, glancing up at the large sign on her office wall. I followed her gaze and swallowed hard as I read it.

When my father and my mother forsake me, then the LORD *will take me up. Psalm 27:10.*

I knew she was right. God had taken me in. But after Sarina was taken away, I struggled to read my Bible or pray alone, at church, or in devotions; my mind lingered on my wounds.

Still, *Amma*'s counseling helped, bit by bit.

Amma began in prayer. Then we discussed my latest schoolwork and how I was handling my chores again. She noted I was managing better than I had been, even with my new share of some of Nalayani's responsibilities.

After a brief moment, *Amma* sighed. "Kashvi, it's been months since your *amma* visited church. We may have to make a visit to your village soon."

My stomach dropped. I couldn't go back. I wouldn't.

Panicking, I blurted out, "I'm sure she will come again soon. Can we just wait a couple more weeks before doing anything?"

I had never told *Amma* what I'd overheard Father and Uncle planning; I did whatever I could to force the thought out of my mind, as if ignoring it would mean it would never happen.

Amma's eyes searched me.

"She was coming every month for a while. We'll see what happens this week. Your *amma* mentioned your *appa* had some health issues; perhaps that is keeping her."

I felt *Amma* watching my reaction. A mixture of emotions flooded through me. Worry…guilt…anger.

I didn't care if my father was sick. I wanted him gone. I knew I shouldn't, and justifying my hatred was getting harder to do. I was never truly remorseful over it, though I did feel guilty at times.

"Kashvi? Did you hear me?" *Amma's* voice broke my spiral of thoughts. "I asked what God has been teaching you in your personal devotions."

I opened my journal, reading over notes about my recent readings in 1 Peter about the suffering church. My heart softened. I read my notes about an eternal inheritance, the joy yet to come, the price Jesus paid for my soul, being chosen by and precious to God.

"Yesterday, I wrote this about 1 Peter 4:19: *He is my faithful Creator. Always has been. Always will be. Even when I am suffering, I can entrust my soul to him. He will keep my soul because he redeemed me from Satan, at the cost of his own life. He suffered so that when I suffer, I can be absolutely certain he will hold and keep me.*"

Amma smiled. "Remind yourself of that often, Kashvi. One day, we will see how perfectly he kept us."

We talked for a few minutes more, and I felt my heart lifting. After months of wandering through spiritual darkness, even small glimpses of light felt amazing. *Amma* prayed to end our meeting and dismissed me.

But as I walked out of her office, she stopped me.

"*Ammachi* has a pile of clothes to mend. Would you help her, Kashvi?"

I nodded, grinning. *Ammachi* had become a new source of joy for me since that night in the hospital with Sudhir. She had moved into a spare room to the left of the common room at Karunai House to help when Sudhir came home, even though her own health was fragile.

With *Amma* and Nalayani so busy, *Amma* asked *Ammachi* to teach me sewing, mostly so I would have someone to talk to instead of isolating myself. I cherished my time with her.

I walked across the common room porch and entered the spare room where *Ammachi* had been staying. She looked up at me from behind her sewing machine with the same warm smile as *Amma*'s. I stepped across the room and sat down on the wooden bench beside her. Milo lay under the bench, his tail thumping as he rolled over. I gave his belly a quick rub and then looked at *Ammachi* for instructions.

"The last person I taught to sew was *Amma*, when she was five years old." *Ammachi* grabbed a pair of torn jeans from the pile next to her with her shaky hands.

"Really?" I took the pants from her.

"Yes," *Ammachi* said. "Back before any of us knew the Lord. Praise his name!"

Ammachi couldn't go a few minutes without blessing God's name. Some days it made me feel guilty for my weak faith. It was hard to believe that she came from Hinduism like my mother, that she was once so hardened that she'd even rejected her own daughter for marrying a Christian.

I threaded the machine like *Ammachi* had taught me to, then began to pump the large pedal, slowly feeding the torn fabric under the needle.

When I finished, *Ammachi* held up the patched jeans and looked at me with pride. "You're doing very well. Lots of practice has helped you improve."

I giggled, remembering the first jeans I had mended. The poor work had caused the jeans to twist, and the patch had shown clearly through the material. Sudhir had worn them for a few hours just to make me feel good, then never again.

As I lined up the next pair, an unfamiliar horn honked outside the gate. Milo sprang up and ran to the doorway barking. I followed after him, peeking my head out. I watched Dhiren running to open the gate.

When the gate opened, a police cruiser pulled in, and Dhiren called for *Amma*.

My heart thudded. Were they here to take me away like they took Sarina? Or was this the end for Karunai House?

"*Ammachi*, it's the police!" I said, my eyes wide with fear.

Ammachi slowly lowered herself off the bench onto her shaky knees, closing her eyes as she began to pray.

I peeked my head back out the door again. Two policemen stepped out of the cruiser, and one opened the back door. A skinny boy with a hard-set jawline stepped out, his face marked by faint scars.

Something about him looked familiar.

While glancing around, his eyes met mine and I jerked my head inside. I heard voices and strained my ear to hear *Amma*'s voice inviting them into the office.

"I need to get some water," I murmured to *Ammachi*, who was still deep in prayer. I couldn't just sit there—I had to know what was going on.

I stepped out onto the porch and filled a steel cup with water at the tap just outside *Amma*'s office door, listening closely to the voices inside.

"We don't admit boys over thirteen," *Amma* said. "Bad habits have often already formed, and we don't want those bad influences on the younger children."

"We understand," said one of the officers. "But there's a court order. Unless it's contested, the boy will stay here for his parole…"

My mind was turning over old memories, indexing faces from the past, trying to place the young man. I gulped the water down and went to fill the cup again, but I fumbled in my nervousness and dropped it. The steel cup clanged on the concrete, and I dashed back into *Ammachi*'s room.

Ammachi was still kneeling when I came rushing back into her room. She looked up with a smile.

"You couldn't just pray?"

"I had to know."

Ammachi sighed. "Is there anything you could do to change it?"

"No," I admitted.

"Then prayer is the only thing to do."

I nodded.

"So," *Ammachi* asked, "why are they here?"

I laughed. She had to know, too.

"It's a boy," I said. "There's a court order for him to stay here on parole." She nodded. "Let's pray for him."

I joined *Ammachi* as she folded her hands around mine. We knelt for what felt like hours, *Ammachi* praying steadily.

Car doors slammed, and I opened my eyes and ran to the door in time to see the police cruiser pulling away. The boy wasn't in the car.

Ammachi said, "Amen."

I needed to see the boy again. He looked so familiar.

"I'm going to welcome him. I'll be back soon to finish sewing." I hurried out before *Ammachi* could respond.

In the courtyard, I spotted the boy trailing behind Dhiren. When he saw me, he walked over.

"You look familiar," he said, his eyes flicking to the scar on my forehead.

I looked into his big, round eyes…

"Ravi?"

He looked surprised that I knew his name. Then recognition filled his eyes.

"Kashvi! It's you! How did you end up here?"

I grinned. "I could ask you the same question, given the police escort."

He smirked.

"Hey!" Dhiren called, noticing Ravi had wandered off. He ran over to us protectively. "What's going on here?"

"We know each other from elementary school," I explained. "I was just curious about, well…the police escort." Glancing at Ravi, I saw hesitation. "Of course, you don't have to tell us if you don't want to."

Dhiren nodded, but the curiosity on our faces betrayed us.

Ravi shrugged. "I had to eat but had no money. Begging got me nowhere, so I stole."

I studied his face, searching for pride, remorse, guilt. But all I saw was a weary boy who looked like he hadn't had a chance to rest or eat a decent meal in a long time. I felt sorry for him.

"Well, you are here now, so I will give you the tour, " Dhiren said dutifully.

"I better get back to *Ammachi*." I smiled. "And welcome, Ravi, it's so good to see you again."

"You, too," he replied, smiling back at me before following Dhiren.

I watched them walk away, feeling a forgotten warmth inside as I returned to the guest room.

Ammachi was just pulling herself up on the bench when I returned, clearly having stopped to pray again. I wondered what she had prayed for this time.

My mind refused to focus on any conversations with *Ammachi* as we finished up mending the last few items. My thoughts drifted to Ravi, the few positive memories of him from my old life comforting me.

All afternoon, I felt my spirit lifting, higher than it had in a long, long time. Filling my day once again were small prayers of thanksgiving.

Thank you, Father.

When devotions time came, I ran into the common room, more excited than I'd been since Sarina left.

Ravi sat by the drums with Dhiren, who was teaching him the rhythm to one of *Appa's* psalms. His bony figure and closely shaved hair contrasted with Dhiren's broad shoulders and loose hair hanging to his eyes.

Ravi waved at me with a grin. His angular jaw looked better turned upward. Smiling back, I settled near him and watched with admiration as he picked up the rhythm quickly.

When Nalayani came in, I glanced at the window where we normally sat together and patted the floor beside me near the boys. She squinted her eyes at me and sat alone by the window.

Appa and *Amma* took their seats at the head of the room, introducing Ravi to everyone. We gave our warm welcome chant, and *Appa* led our devotions from Psalm 115, explaining the futility of idols and the goodness of God.

Ravi seemed intrigued, soaking in the gospel, and I tried to match his interest, listening carefully to the beautiful explanation by *Appa*.

Afterward, *Appa* prayed and dismissed us for dinner.

I sat close to Ravi at dinner, feeling as though he and I had a shared bond. Sudhir and the other boys sat around Ravi, excited to hear from the boy who'd been to prison, but Ravi didn't say much about it. *Appa* and *Amma* got their food and settled down by Ravi as he told everyone how he and I had become friends after he hit me with an eraser in class.

"You were the only one from our class who talked to me when everyone else was mocking me," I said, smiling. "I remember that same day when you helped Pugal after Sudhir beat him up. You were always kind."

I wanted to put Ravi in a good light for *Appa* and *Amma*. I knew they had objections to admitting older boys and worried they might try to have him placed elsewhere.

Sudhir moved closer, also enjoying the connection to years past. The three of us reminisced about our school days, our strict teachers, and their brutal punishments. Dhiren, *Appa*, and *Amma* joined our laughter. Milo joined, too, introducing himself with some friendly licks to Ravi's face.

When Ravi finished his plate, Nalayani walked over, offering him more.

"No, but thank you," he replied with surprising politeness for his first meal here.

"You can wash your plate and store it there," Nalayani gestured to the rack.

I reached for his plate. "I'll wash it for you!"

Sudhir raised his eyebrows.

"I can take yours, too, *Thambi*," I said quickly, grabbing his licked-clean plate.

Amma sent Dhiren to help get Ravi set up for the night, and she left to take a phone call in her office. *Appa*, Nalayani, Sudhir, and I lingered.

I felt strange looks resting on me occasionally, but I couldn't piece together what the people around me were feeling.

Sudhir rose to leave but surprised me by giving me a quick hug first.

"It's good to see you smile, *Akka*. We've missed your joy."

Appa nodded in agreement. "Your face tonight during devotions was different, Kashvi. It looked closer to the Kashvi we used to know. Is God the one touching your heart?"

The wording of his question seemed strange to me.

"I feel a joy that has been missing a long time. God is so good! It's been a good day."

I looked at Nalayani, expecting a smile, but I saw a hurt look in her eyes. She tried to cover it with a smile, but it was a poor effort.

Her attitude confused and irritated me, but my feelings were interrupted as *Amma* burst from the office, her face shining.

"I found her! I found Sarina!"

We all jumped to our feet with joy, peppering her with questions.

"Hush, everyone!" she motioned with her palm down. "That was an off-the-record call from a kind official. She gave me the name and address of the home where she is."

We hugged each other, exclaiming praise to God. *Amma* continued, "The official doubted whether that home warden would let us visit; however, I will try my best."

Thank you, Father, for finding us when we are lost, I prayed.

Later, as I lay in bed, I said goodnight to a quiet Nalayani, and my heart filled with grateful reflection. I ended the day with one last prayer.

I'm so glad I can entrust my soul to you, Father. You are faithful. Thank you.

CHAPTER 19

All my excitement over *Amma* finding Sarina's orphanage came crashing down in a wave of disappointment.

We had visited the orphanage, but the guard at the gate refused to let us in or give any information on whether Sarina was there. The warden was called out, and she threatened to call the police if we didn't leave immediately.

Seeing Ravi was the only thing that gave me any life and joy these days.

I met Ravi's eyes across the courtyard as he began to set off down the road for school with the other boys. I grabbed my schoolbag and jogged to catch up to him with a spring in my step.

Ravi wasn't accepted into the private school I attended because of his past and the fact that he hadn't been to school for years. *Amma* had enrolled him in a standard government school further up the road.

I strolled up beside Ravi, trying to look casual.

"I liked your drum playing this morning," I said. "Where did you learn to play so well?"

"From a homeless man," Ravi explained. "I was hooked after he taught me. I played with his drum for hours every day until I...stole my own drum."

"Is that how you got arrested?" I asked quietly, finally daring to touch the subject after avoiding it for weeks.

"Not for the drum. I stole a lot of things. At first, I stole to survive, but then I started taking whatever I wanted," Ravi's shoulders slumped as he walked. "I was a lookout for my friend robbing a shop. The others ran, but I stayed. We both got caught."

Ravi's honesty surprised me. He had been quiet and guarded since arriving at Karunai House. Though he talked with *Appa* and *Amma*, I knew little about his past.

I pressed further.

"How did you end up on the streets? Weren't you in an orphanage when we went to school? What happened to your parents?" The questions tumbled out.

"Okay, sure. I'll give you my life story." Ravi chuckled, a hint of bitterness in his voice. "When I was three, my *amma* was hit and killed by a bus—possibly because my *appa* pushed her. He disappeared afterward, and my uncle and aunt took me in."

"I'm sorry, Ravi." I reached for his hand but stopped, pretending to itch my leg instead.

He shrugged. "I stayed with them and their daughter for years. When my aunt got pregnant again and they found out it was another girl, my uncle forced her to have an abortion. It broke her, and she committed suicide."

I stopped, stunned and unsure of how to comfort him. I wanted to hug him but knew it wouldn't be appropriate.

Ravi gave me a half-smile and continued as we started walking again. "My uncle said he couldn't care for me with my aunt gone and sent me to an orphanage."

"I'm so sorry, Ravi." I couldn't imagine it. His life seemed almost worse than mine.

"Don't be." Ravi laughed, though his eyes betrayed him. "It doesn't hurt anymore."

I hardly wanted him to go on, but it seemed like he was aching to finally tell someone.

"I learned to laugh at pain. I had to. The wardens didn't enjoy beating me when I laughed." His jaw tensed.

"I remember some of your stories," I said. "I was terrified when I came to Karunai House because of them."

"It got worse." His humor disappeared. "A new warden came. He was…evil. I ran away."

I recognized the vengeful look in Ravi's eyes—it mirrored how I felt about my father.

"Anyway, I spent the past year in juvenile detention. The judge let me out on good behavior, with the condition that I stay here for my parole."

Amma had told me that a Christian judge sent Ravi here, convinced that Karunai House was the best place for him to change.

"Do you feel guilty for stealing?" I asked.

"I didn't back then. But now? Yes. I know it was sin."

I saw shame cross his face and marveled at how quickly God could work in someone. Ravi was full of questions and eager to read the Bible. He had been reserved at first, but after only a few weeks, he was becoming part of our family. I hoped it was real, not just an act.

"I rebelled, too." I touched my forehead. "One day, instead of curling up, I looked into my father's eyes in defiance. He gave me this scar."

"I'll add him to the list of men I need to beat someday." Ravi's eyes flashed.

The thought thrilled me, but I suppressed it. "Revenge isn't ours to take."

"Right," Ravi nodded, "hell is for men like that."

"Hell is for all of us," I countered, knowing the truth but not always being convinced of it. "We all deserve it."

Ravi sighed. "That's hard to accept when you've suffered so much. Why do I deserve the same as them?"

"I wonder that, too." I kicked a stone. "Maybe we just don't see how bad we really are or how holy God really is."

"I guess not," Ravi said. "I don't get why God let me go through all I did if he loves me."

"If you'd had a loving Hindu family, you wouldn't be here now," I offered. "God brings us to himself through pain."

Where are these answers coming from? They were easy to give, but not easy to believe.

I knew how Ravi felt, questioning God's ways. Especially after everything that had happened with Sarina. God had taken so much from me.

Do I really believe the answers I'm giving?

"Why couldn't I have been born into a loving Christian family?" Ravi asked.

I sighed. "I don't know, Ravi. God's ways are not our ways."

Ravi frowned, unsatisfied.

A memory surfaced in my mind.

"*Amma* explained to me once how our lives are like walking around in the dark. We can only see a little distance, but God sees everything in perfect light. We have to trust that he knows what he's doing."

My heart stirred at my own words.

God, I want to trust you fully. I don't want to be left hopeless in the darkness. I want to trust that you see and plan everything perfectly. Help me and Ravi to understand.

I wished Ravi a good day as we approached my school, and he continued on to his own.

After the long day ended, I waited for Ravi to walk by before starting my journey home.

At first, I tried to make it look like a coincidence, but soon, I realized I wasn't fooling anyone. This pattern continued for weeks.

Though I was trying to make up for my poor school performance last year, my days became a battle with daydreaming, mostly of Ravi. He had been increasingly filling the hole in my heart left by Sarina's absence.

Everyone else at Karunai House noticed how Ravi grew in faith and character. He went out of his way to help everyone, took turns playing the drum with Dhiren during devotions, and always had questions when the Bible was opened.

For the first time in my life, the thought of having a "love marriage" instead of one arranged by my parents seemed like more than just a fanciful dream, though I wouldn't admit it to anyone…and could barely admit it to myself.

I was growing to love Ravi.

☙

As *Appa* wrapped up the church service on Sunday morning, I glanced at Ravi, wondering what questions he might have today.

My first priority, though, was Mother. I had seen her through the back doorway while checking for her during the service. Seeing her made me glad, not just to see her safe, but also because we wouldn't have to make a visit to our village. I didn't ever want to go back there after what happened last time.

I pushed my way out to the porch, where she sat among others. More than a hundred people now worshiped with us on Sundays, so someone always sat outside. Mother chose the porch on the rare occasions she visited.

"*Amma*," I greeted warmly, pulling her into an embrace. "How are you? Where have you been?"

I looked her over, taking in the gray strands peeking from her headscarf and the worry lines marking her face. Just thirty-three, yet she had lived and seen so much.

"Kashvi," she whispered, melting into my arms.

I held her, wondering when I had become the stronger one.

She pulled back. "I'm sorry for not visiting. Your *appa* has been weak lately and is not always able to work full days, so I've had to work more to make up for it. How are you doing? How is Sudhir?"

I squirmed a little. "I'm doing well. Sudhir's around here somewhere."

I glanced back to see Sudhir approaching with Ravi. I thought of the story of Esha and her attempt at a non-arranged relationship and Mother's warning to me. Panic surged.

"I need to use the toilet. I'll be back."

Away from Mother, I tried to compose myself.

Act calm. Nothing is happening; she can't read your thoughts about Ravi.

I willed myself to return, wanting to spend more time with her before she left. Also, I feared what Ravi or Sudhir might say while I was absent.

I stepped up to Mother, shocked to find Ravi engaged in a spiritual discussion with her.

"...how can there be true and false statements at the same time?" Ravi pressed her.

Mother rubbed her forehead. "The Bible has many wise sayings, but life is more complex than that. There's a balance we need to keep."

"It's hot out here," I interrupted, careful to avoid the slightest look at Ravi, knowing how disastrous it would be if Mother suspected I even thought about a boy. "Want to step inside, *'ma?*"

"No, I'm used to the sun," Mother said. "Did you know Vishnu is doing a carpentry apprenticeship?"

My heart trembled at Vishnu's name. "That's...good for him."

I swallowed hard, unable to stomach the thought of going back to life in our village with Vishnu. I knew that was what she was hinting at. Mother couldn't begin to imagine more for me than what she knew for herself. I wanted to run before she could say anything else of Vishnu.

God, protect me from this!

Mother continued to make small talk with Sudhir and didn't mention Vishnu again. Eventually she hugged Sudhir and me and left.

Ravi and Sudhir wandered off, and Mahiyu, noticing I was without tea, remedied that. "Cup number eighty-four," he informed with a huge grin. I smiled and thanked him before he scurried off for number eighty-five.

After a few sips, Nalayani came over by me, a baby in her arms. "What's wrong?"

Nothing I can tell anyone.

"Nothing, really. Just thinking about stuff," I responded dismissively.

She frowned. "*Thangachi,* I am here to help you, but I can't help you if you don't let me."

"I don't need a lot of help right now," I snapped, tiffed at her role switch from friend to staff. "I'm even doing some of your work since you've been so busy. And I'm doing a lot better now."

Her eyes clouded. "Yeah, you do seem to be doing better." Frowning, she swung the cooing boy to her other hip and walked off.

Confused, I watched her hand the baby back to his mother. I had my own worries, so I didn't dwell on the situation with Nalayani.

Instead, I sipped my tea, mulling over when the day would come for me to face my parents about Vishnu. Anxiety brewed as I clung to a sliver of peace, reminding myself God was in control.

He'd protected me…today, at least.

That night was restless.

The next morning, I felt somewhat refreshed by devotions and a hearty breakfast. Grabbing my school bag, I stepped outside, hoping to see Ravi. I spotted Dhiren laughing with him.

Despite Ravi's progress, Dhiren always shadowed him. *Amma*, I guessed, wasn't fully convinced by his rapid change.

They grinned when I approached. "What's so funny, *Anna?*"

"You missed it," Dhiren teased. "Don't take so long getting ready."

"I wasn't long!" I protested, joining their playful banter. "Tell me!"

Ravi leaned in. "If you really want to know…"

Dhiren smacked him, but Ravi combed his fingers through his short hair. Then he leaned close to whisper in my ear.

His cupped hand lightly touched the skin on my ear as he whispered, "Did you really think I would tell you my secrets?"

The boys cackled at their antics, but a shiver ran down my spine.

When Ravi had leaned in, out of nowhere, I smelled my father, coated in the smoke of his *beedi*. I heard his voice as he lifted his hand to hit me.

I crumpled to the ground, shielding my head.

The blow never came.

I peeked through the gaps between my fingers, but it wasn't Father's face I saw. It was Vishnu's. He smiled at me and bent down, resting his hand on my back.

This isn't real, I cried as I fingered the hem of my beautiful *chudidhar*, trying to remind myself where I really was.

I became aware of a hand resting tenderly on my back. As my ears stopped ringing, I heard, "Kashvi, can you hear me? It's okay. You're okay. It's me, Ravi."

I looked up.

"Dhiren went to get *Amma*," Ravi said, his eyes fully of worry.

I sat up and rubbed my head, sighing. "The flashbacks don't happen so much anymore. But they're so real when they do."

Ravi sat back and stared at the ground. "If they're anything like my nightmares, I know how real they can be."

I watch him smile, trying to cover pain-filled eyes, as he assured me, "But you're here now. You're safe."

In that moment, I felt like my life was going to change for the better. Like everything God had done in my life had brought me to this moment, to the safety of Ravi.

Amma ran to me and wrapped me in a hug. She looked from me to Ravi, and Ravi jumped up.

"Go on to school, Ravi," she said. "I can take over from here."

I smiled at Ravi as he set off, then looked to *Amma*.

"I am exhausted. May I stay back from school today?"

"Yes, of course," she replied, helping me up and leading me towards her office. "Tell me. What happened?"

I shared about Dhiren and Ravi joking around and how the flashback came out of nowhere. I left out the part about Ravi's hand brushing my ear. Though the flashback quickly overtook any other feeling, I distinctly remembered the brief feeling of my heart jumping out of my chest as his hand brushed my cheek and his breath tickled my ear.

"Did anything particular set it off this time?" *Amma* prodded as we sat down in her office.

I ran my fingers along the hem of my *chudidhar* to keep myself grounded and shook my head.

"It felt so real. I could actually smell my *appa* smoking."

Amma frowned. "How were you able to deal with it?"

Nalayani and *Amma* had helped me figure out ways to remind myself of what was real during flashbacks. Feeling the edges of the beautiful clothes I was given here was one of the methods I had found most comforting.

After I explained, *Amma* began to read reassuring passages from the Bible. The beauty and grace of the words wrapped me in a warm embrace, helping me to fight against the lingering fear.

I spent my day reading my Bible, thanking God, battling anxieties, and letting hope grow in my heart.

Ravi gave me hope. Hope that I wouldn't end up like my mother. Hope even that maybe I could dream of more than an arranged marriage.

CHAPTER 20

"One! Two! Three!"
I leaned over the wall on the roof of the girls' dorm and plugged a jumbled string of Christmas lights into the extension cord. Thirty boys erupted in cheers from below at the mix of red, green, and blue illuminating the courtyard. Christmas was a couple of weeks away, and the air buzzed with excitement.

Ravi smiled at me from across the courtyard atop the boys' dorm, admiring the strings of light hanging around the building. He gave me a thumbs-up before Mahiyu shouted at him from below to adjust some of the strands that were hanging unevenly. I laughed at Mahiyu's meticulousness and playfully gave Ravi a thumbs-down. He shook his head as he went about adjusting the strands.

When Ravi finished, I ran down the steps into the courtyard to join him in admiring our work from below.

"They're beautiful, aren't they?" I said to Ravi.

"Yeah…" he said, looking at me with wonder in his eyes. "Beautiful."

A blush crept up my cheeks.

"Nice job, you two." *Amma* stepped over to Ravi and me. "Kashvi, can I talk with you in my office for a moment?"

"Sure." I shrugged my shoulders at Ravi and followed *Amma*.

We both sat down, and *Amma* looked at me with her eyes that could see straight through me.

"I've been hearing that you are spending a lot of time with Ravi recently."

I twisted my hands in my lap.

"Ravi and I were friends before we came here. It's just been nice to have a good friend again. That's all, really."

Some of the boys on campus had been teasing Ravi and me about liking each other. We both denied it, but I knew I was lying when I said no. I wasn't sure if Ravi was.

"Did Sudhir say something to you?" I asked, defending myself. "He's just overprotective."

Sudhir had been casting disapproving glances at Ravi and me whenever we were near each other. He'd made it clear he didn't approve of us being around each other, even though he was friendly to Ravi when I wasn't around.

Amma smiled. "I've just been noticing you two together frequently. I'm glad you've reconnected with an old friend." She paused, as if she was waiting for the right words to say. "Friendships can become…complicated between boys and girls at your age, and I want you to know that I'm here to help. Do you really have no feelings for him?"

I forced myself to meet her eyes, trying to mask the lie.

"None."

"Okay," *Amma* said. Her voice carried a weight that made my chest tighten. "I just want you to know that I love you, and you can talk to me about anything."

"I know," I mumbled, lowering my eyes to the floor. "Is there anything else?"

"No, go on. Enjoy your free evening." She smiled, then added, "My dear, guard your heart. Do you know Proverbs 4:23? I'd like you to read it today and think about what it means for your life."

I feared she had seen right through me. But she and *Appa* had a love marriage. Why was she so concerned? Ravi had learned so much about Christianity, and he was taking one-on-one lessons with *Appa*. Always asking questions, always growing. Sometimes I felt he knew more than I did.

Ravi was even considering becoming a pastor. What harm could there be in our friendship? Ravi was my encouragement to study the Bible more, if only to answer his questions and have deeper discussions.

Yet, I had to admit that sometimes it seemed I studied more to impress Ravi than to fellowship with God.

"Okay, *Amma*. I'll go do that now. Thank you," I said, hoping for a quick exit. I had overheard the boys planning a football game, and I wanted to watch.

Amma nodded, and I ran up to my room to grab my Bible. Milo was sprawled in the doorway, tail thumping as I approached. I stepped over him, and he nipped at my heels and barked.

"What's wrong with you, Milo?" I scolded.

Milo darted to a pile of clothes thrown in the corner and kept glancing from me to the clothes, barking insistently.

I grabbed my Bible, sat on my bed, and flipped to Proverbs 4:23. *Keep thy heart with all diligence; for out of it are the issues of life*, it read. I read it a couple of times but couldn't really meditate on it with Milo barking non-stop.

"What are you doing, Milo? Be quiet!"

He growled at the pile of clothes again.

I rolled my eyes. *Whatever*.

I hurried back down the stairs, excitement bubbling at the thought of watching the game—mostly to watch Ravi.

The boys were just heading into the field behind the Common Hall to play. I followed after them, through the courtyard and around the building. Sudhir was walking just in front of me, and when he turned his head back and saw me, he stopped and stood with his arms crossed, blocking my way.

Sudhir wasn't very intimidating. It had been over a year since his accident. Most of his skin grafts were complete and he was able to be active again. But even though he was putting on a little weight and muscle, he was also growing taller, so he had the frame of a baby monkey.

A frown tugged at his mouth. "We need to talk."

"Sure, what's up?" I huffed.

Sudhir glanced at Ravi, who was laughing with Ameer in the field as they stretched, then looked back at me. "You're always with Ravi. It's…I don't know, it feels weird."

My guard went up at this second confrontation of the day. I crossed my arms.

"He's just a friend, Sudhir. Why does everyone have such a problem with me having a new friend?"

"Maybe he's just a friend," he scuffed the dirt with his sandal, "but the boys are always talking, saying he likes you. And you act all…different when he's around. You're going to get yourself into trouble, and you know it."

A flush of irritation shot through me. "Since when did you become my protector, Sudhir? Stop acting like you're older than me."

His eyes narrowed. "Someone has to. He's a boy, *Akka*, and that means trouble. *Amma* will be upset, and you're just—ugh, you're not thinking. And what if Father or Mother found out?"

I let out a sharp breath. "You don't know anything, Sudhir. I just need a friend to talk to, someone who understands."

"I'm sorry there was no one here for you before Ravi showed up," he spat bitterly, before jogging into the football field.

I spun around to stomp off but saw Nalayani standing in the kitchen doorway looking wounded.

"Really, *Thangachi*? No one else you can talk to? No one who understands?"

"I…" I stammered.

Nalayani's eyes blazed, but then they began to glisten with tears. "Whose fault is that? You shut me out after Sarina left. She was your best friend, but she was mine, too. It hurt me, too, and it still does. A lot."

Shame welled up, washing over my anger.

Her voice shook. "I tried to help you while you stayed in bed, skipped chores, didn't study—even when my classes got busy. I tried to love and care for you. There was no thanks, no acknowledgment.

Now, suddenly, this boy—who's on parole—shows up, and you're back to being happy and helpful."

"Ravi and I were friends before," I stuttered.

"Am *I* not your friend?"

The words stung. "I'm sorry—"

"I'm sorry for getting so emotional about this. I'm just so worried about you," Nalayani interrupted. "You don't know him like you think you do. He's trying to make a good impression, but you don't know what he's really like."

My guilt spun back to anger. "He stole because he had no choice. And weren't you listening during devotions? God can change anyone. We're supposed to treat each other like family here."

Nalayani's eyes narrowed. "Family? Brothers and sisters don't flirt."

Anger flared in my chest. "If you were really my friend, you'd be happy for me. Ravi makes me feel like there's hope again. Doesn't that matter to you?"

Silence hung between us. Finally, she whispered, "I'm not happy for you if your hope is rooted in someone other than Jesus, Kashvi."

Her words struck a nerve, but stubbornly, I held my ground. "It's not. And you *should* be happy for me, Nalayani."

Without waiting for a response, I ran to our room, boiling over with anger.

Why can't anyone just let me be happy?

Still huffing, I stepped into our bedroom and found Milo lying stiffly on his side, his tongue lolling out.

"Milo," I whimpered. But he didn't move. "Milo!"

I stepped closer, my eyes catching the swollen mark on his side, two tiny dots of blood punctuating the wound. I knew those marks too well…

Memories rushed in—the temple, the desperate pleas before the idols, Asha's lifeless body.

My knees buckled.

Why, God?

My mind raced back to my scolding words. I'd left Milo in the room while I ran to see Ravi. Milo had been trying to protect me, and I ignored him.

Protect me…

The realization jolted me to my feet and my eyes darted around the floor, searching wildly before I dashed out of the room and into the courtyard, nearly colliding with Ravi.

"Hey, Ameer got angry and kicked the ball up onto your dorm, can you…" Ravi trailed off and his hand found my shoulder, steadying me. "What's wrong, Kashvi?"

"Milo is dead!" I choked out. "A snake bit him. I think it's still in there."

Ravi's eyes narrowed. "I'll kill it." He grabbed a broken broomstick from a pile of junk waiting to be burned.

"Ravi, please," I clung to his arm desperately. "We can call a snake handler. I've lost enough friends."

"I'll kill it." Ravi pulled away and raced upstairs.

"*Amma!*" I shouted, running to the office.

By the time *Amma* and I reached my room, Ravi stood in the doorway, a triumphant smile on his face and a cobra impaled on the end of the stick.

Relief filled me briefly, but that was quickly replaced with grief when I turned to Milo's lifeless body. I sank to the floor, sobs tearing through me.

It was my fault. Milo was gone because I'd ignored his warnings, too distracted in my rush to see Ravi playing football.

Ravi and Dhiren dug a grave under the hugging tree as *Amma* gathered everyone around the hole. I stood beside Ravi, my throat tight and eyes burning. Dhiren gently laid Milo's body into the ground. The four white sighthounds, our night guard dogs, paced around us anxiously, whimpering into the pit.

Appa's voice broke the silence, recalling stories of Milo's loyal, comforting presence, how he'd sensed when people needed him most.

Others shared their memories, voices trembling, some even smiling through their tears.

Ravi and Dhiren started filling in the grave, shovelfuls of earth hiding Milo's body one by one. I stared, taking one last look at the friend who had died to protect me.

"The Lord gives, and the Lord takes away," *Appa* breathed deeply. "Blessed be the name of the Lord. Let's pray together."

We joined hands in a circle, my sweaty palm clasped around Ravi's. I felt a pang of guilt at the warmth I drew from his touch. My pulse thudded in my ears as I forced my mind to focus on *Appa's* prayer.

"Father, we give thanks for the gift of this dear friend, Milo," *Appa* prayed, his voice catching. "We are grateful for the comfort and joy Milo brought us in his life and for the protection that Milo gave to our dear daughter. We know that this death happened by your will, but we also know death is a consequence of man's sin. We look forward to the day when all things will be made new, and death and crying will be no more. Forgive us of our sins against you. Amen."

Together, we echoed, "Bless the LORD, O my soul, and all that is within me, bless his holy name. Bless the LORD, O my soul, and forget not all his benefits."

I let go of Ravi's hand, wiping mine on my *chudidhar*. He seemed unmoved, staring at the fresh mound of dirt, lost in thought.

Appa turned to Ravi. "Still want to have our lesson?"

"Yes, *Appa*," Ravi replied. He had taken to calling him *Appa* quickly. Like me, he had never known what it was like to have a loving, caring father.

As *Appa* and Ravi walked, Ravi's voice floated back to the tree. "Will Milo be in heaven?"

"Well," *Appa* said gently, "only humans have souls…"

Everyone dispersed, leaving me alone by Milo's grave. My tears fell unchecked.

Why did you take Milo, God? Haven't I lost enough?

The question lingered like an accusation. Was God taking all these things away from me because he was angry with me? Was Nalayani right? Was I putting hope in Ravi? I tried convincing myself that wasn't true, but I wasn't so sure.

I dropped my head into my hands, despairing for my weak faith. Every time I felt like I was close to God again, I failed. Did he even love me?

Anger replaced the tears as *Amma's* words came back: *Guard my heart.*

A bitter thought echoed: *I have to guard it myself because no one else will—not even you, God.*

I sat by Milo's grave, lost in my doubts. Could I be a Christian with all this anger and confusion? If that cobra had bitten me and I had died, what would have happened to me? I truly didn't know.

CHAPTER 21

I woke to the barking of our sighthounds slicing through the night's silence. The full moon was casting a ghostly glow of eerie blue through the curtains in our room.

The hounds probably saw a mouse, I thought, but the memory of Milo and the cobra tightened my chest. I slipped out of bed, rubbed my eyes, and peered out the window.

My heart lurched. A shadowy figure crept away from the boys' dorm towards the field.

A drunk from the forest?

Maddened barking echoed in the courtyard as the dogs raced from behind the boys' dorm and charged towards the intruder. The figure knelt, whispering to the dogs and patting them as they jumped up at him. They fell silent. He glanced around, his movements quick and deliberate. I gasped when I saw his face.

It was Ravi.

What is he doing? Is he running away?

Through Christmas and our New Years' celebrations, Ravi had really grown in his knowledge of God, and he was always working hard and helping others. He was good young man, and I refused to stop being friendly to him even though Nalayani, Sudhir, and others questioned how close he and I were. They doubted how genuine his faith and kindness were, but I didn't.

I watched Ravi send the dogs away and walk to the back of the field, towards the dark edge of the forest.

What are you doing Kashvi? I thought, as I found myself quietly unbolting the door, careful not to wake Nalayani. I didn't need this straining our relationship any further. I'd never hear the end of it. Right now, I saw her as staff and nothing else. Nights were uncomfortable, but as long as she refused to see the good in Ravi, I wasn't budging.

My pulse quickened, and I crept down the stairs and crossed the courtyard, the cool earth beneath my bare feet stinging in the chilly air. The sighthounds, still restless, barked once at my approach but quieted as they sniffed me. They paced anxiously around me as I made my way to the chain-link fence at the back of the property.

Amma had been asking for permits to extend the tall concrete wall along the back of the property for years, but the officials never gave her clear answers about when it would be reviewed for approval, likely waiting for a bribe. In the meantime, the fence was all we had.

The hounds whimpered as I climbed over it, their concerned eyes wide in the moonlight.

Riiiip!

My breath caught as I glanced down—a jagged tear in my *chudidhar* pants ran from my hip to my knee, goosebumps crawling down my leg as the chilly air intruded. I clutched the fabric together at my thigh and cautiously followed the trail into the forest, leaving the dogs pacing and whimpering behind.

With every step, leaves crackled underfoot, the sound piercing the stillness like a drumbeat. The damp, dewy ground numbed my feet, but I continued following the path away from Karunai House deep into the woods.

Shadows tangled and danced around me.

I should turn back before I get lost, I told myself.

I paused, straining to catch any sound. A faint, low laugh drifted through the trees.

Curiosity overcame reason, pushing me towards the muffled voices.

I crept closer, my breath shallow, and stopped behind a thick tree trunk.

A flickering flame snapped in the dark, casting a wavering light over Ravi's face and that of a weathered man with tangled hair and bloodshot eyes. A glowing red ember brightened as the stranger drew on a *beedi*.

"Keep that away from me," Ravi muttered. "I can't bring that smell back."

The sharp, musky scent floated through the crisp night air, making my stomach twist.

That's it. That's the smell that set off my flashback when Ravi whispered to me.

Their easy chatter told me this wasn't Ravi's first time here. *Amma's* voice echoed in my mind—her worries about the drunks and dealers who haunted the forest.

Is that where Ravi got this idea?

The haggard man handed Ravi a glass bottle. The moonlight glinted off it as Ravi raised it and took a swig.

I crept forward, breath held tight in my chest, straining to catch their words.

Snap!

A branch cracked under my foot. Ravi and the man looked up.

"Did you hear something?" the man slurred. Squinting into the dark, he stepped towards me.

"Probably just a rabbit or something," Ravi said.

But the man continued forward, and his red, beady eyes swept closer.

My heart pounded as, moments later, he loomed over me with a smirk.

"What are you doing here, pretty girl?

Ravi stepped forward, eyes wide when he saw me.

"Get away from her!"

He shoved the man, who stumbled and fell, laughing.

"Whoa, calm down," the haggard man chuckled. "Is this your girlfriend?"

Fear of the man morphed into anger. Turning to Ravi, I spat, "What are you doing?"

"I just needed some fresh air." Ravi's hands quivered, and he looked up. "It's a beautiful night."

His breath smelled sour and familiar…like my father's.

Smack!

I slapped him. His head turned, eyes misting with shame.

I can't believe I did that.

Then the realization slapped me.

I'm acting like Father.

"Feisty girl, huh?"

The man staggered up. He pointed at the torn fabric on my thigh. "What happened there?"

Shame flushed through me as I clutched the two halves of the tear and ran, Ravi's shouts behind me fading into the rustle of leaves.

I didn't stop until I reached the fence, scrambling over and landing hard on the other side. The sighthounds pounced on me, licking my tear-streaked face.

Then, Ravi landed beside me, breathless.

I pushed the dogs away and glared at him, rage and betrayal burning in my chest.

He's just like my father. Just another liar and drunk.

"Kashvi, let me explain," Ravi pleaded.

"I'm not talking to you!" I stood, shaking with fury, and stomped towards the dorms.

"I haven't been able to sleep," Ravi's voice cracked. "The nightmares…this is the only thing that makes them stop."

I hid my face in my hands, but I stopped walking.

"Kashvi, I'll never do it again. I promise. Please don't tell anyone. If I'm kicked out of here, I'll go back to jail. I can't go to another orphanage. And this is the first place that's ever felt like home."

My heart wavered, torn between anger, pity, and responsibility. The shame and desperation in his voice were real.

Plus, I wasn't ready for Ravi to be taken away, even if I was furious at him right now.

Suddenly, one of the sighthounds barked sharply, darting out of *Ammachi's* room into the courtyard. He nipped at my heels, barking urgently. The dog ran to the door and back, trying to get our attention.

Fear prickled my skin. *Another snake?*

"Ravi, come on!" I yelled as I rushed to *Ammachi's* room.

Ammachi lay on the floor, clutching her chest and gasping for air.

"Help," she barely wheezed out.

"Get *Amma*!" I shouted.

Ravi bolted out of the room as I knelt beside *Ammachi*, searching her face in panic. "*Ammachi*, what's wrong?"

She didn't answer. I didn't know what to do, but I knew what she would do.

I held her hand and prayed.

God help her!

After a few minutes, *Amma* and *Appa* burst in, Ravi and Dhiren behind them. *Appa* scooped *Ammachi* into his arms, and *Amma* climbed into the back of the SUV as he laid her down.

"Kashvi, get the car keys. Ravi, get the gate," *Appa* barked.

I snatched the keys from the office and threw them at Dhiren. Ravi swung the gate wide and the *Qualis* roared away, dust and headlights cutting through the dark.

Ravi stepped back slowly, his face shadowed and unreadable as I wiped my tears.

"Should we pray for her?" Ravi whispered.

I trembled, struggling to find words. *How could I pray with you? After everything…?*

"If we hadn't been here, who knows how long she would've waited for help," Ravi said softly.

I looked at him, disbelief knotting my gut. *Was he justifying what he did?*

I turned away without a word and trudged to my room.

What would Nalayani say if she found out what Ravi had done?

I collapsed to my knees beside my bed and clutched my hands together, tears falling fast. I saw my folly in the trust I had been placing in Ravi. Nalayani had been right. He had failed me like everyone else. I felt despair rising again. Doubts swirled as I wept, questioning everything and everyone, even God.

God, will you take Ammachi, too? Will you continue to punish me for not trusting you?

CHAPTER 22

"How is *Ammachi* doing today?"

Ravi's voice startled me awake, and I launched my English book off my lap.

The drooping branches of the hugging tree surrounded me, leaves swaying in the early evening breeze. Ravi stood above me, smirking with a half-apologetic look.

"Sorry, I thought you were closing your eyes to concentrate."

I sighed, glancing out at the mingling wisps of orange and pink in the sky.

Ammachi was back at Karunai House. She was on medication for her heart condition, and over the past month since her heart attack, it had kept her stable. Still, she was very weak and stayed in bed most of the day.

The doctors said if we hadn't gotten to her so quickly, she would have died. Ravi had been right about us being there that night, and I hated admitting it. Why would God use such a horrible reason for us to be awake to save *Ammachi*'s life?

Amma had asked me how I knew something was wrong with *Ammachi*. I'd lied, saying I heard the dogs barking. I'd made up a story about the dogs ripping my pants to alert me. *Amma* believed it and even bought me a new *chudidhar* to replace them, but I felt too guilty to wear it.

"You're still not going to talk to me?" Ravi asked, hesitantly.

I grabbed my schoolbook from the dirt beside me, pretending to read. I hadn't spoken to Ravi since that horrid night. Though he poured himself into studying the Bible and grew close to *Appa*, I didn't know if it was genuine or just an act.

As Ravi seemed to draw closer to God, I felt farther away. A heavy darkness settled around me, and I withdrew from everyone. My devotion readings were hollow, my prayers repetitive and cold. I had begun making efforts to initiate conversation with Nalayani, but my secret kept me at a distance, so talks never went deep. I was afraid of Nalayani finding out about Ravi's misbehavior, purely because she had been right, though I knew she would never hold that over me. I missed having my *akka* close but didn't know what to do. I felt lost with everyone.

Amma noticed the change in me and tried to get me to talk, but I couldn't tell her the truth, so our relationship suffered, too, despite our weekly meetings.

Ravi broke the silence. "I'm a new person, Kashvi."

I wanted to believe him, but years of watching my father succumb to the bottle hardened my heart.

How could I trust that? But why do I still want to believe him?

"I know I messed up. I know I don't deserve—"

"No! You don't deserve anything!" I snapped, shooting him a sideways glance.

"Hey, you spoke to me." Ravi's chuckle was tinged with sadness.

I shook my head and gazed back at the papaya sunset, searching for figures in the pink clouds, like I had the first day Ravi talked to me at my old school three years earlier.

He sat down in the sand next to me with a deep sigh. "Will you give me a chance to explain?"

I nodded and closed my eyes, breathing deeply as I waited.

Silence.

I opened my eyes to find Ravi's face tense, his thumb and forefinger moving across his chin in a nervous rhythm.

"That orphan home I ran away from…that warden…he did things

to me I can't even…" His body trembled, and his hollow eyes stared into the distance, holding back a torrent of painful emotion.

I remembered stories I'd overheard from *Amma* about the horrors in other foster homes, and bile rose in my throat.

"I started drinking after I ran away." Ravi rubbed his eyes hard, and I noticed a wet glisten on his hands. "It helped me forget."

His vulnerability relaxed my anger. To my surprise, I wanted to reach out, to offer comfort.

"In prison, the guards made us walk around without clothes sometimes. It was meant to humiliate us, but I was terrified it would turn into something worse. I was lucky; for stealing, they just broke my finger." He held up his hand, and now I noticed how one finger was awkwardly disjointed. "Others…well, you don't need the details."

I shivered, imagining the torments.

"Drinking was my relief," Ravi whispered. "It kept the nightmares from playing behind my eyelids when I closed them to sleep. I overheard *Amma* talking about drunks gathering in the forest, so one night when I couldn't sleep, I snuck back there to find relief from the bottle. I've only done it a couple of times, but I'm never doing it again."

He paused, looking truly remorseful and I couldn't resist the urge to console him.

I wiped my own tears on my shoulder and scooted closer, glancing around to make sure no one was watching. A nervous, forbidden shiver coursed through me as I put an arm around him.

Ravi looked at my arm nervously, like he was unsure whether to pull away, but then offered me a fragile smile.

"I watched my *appa* drink my whole life," I said, sniffling. "He beat my whole family. I hate him, Ravi, and I don't want you to end up like him."

"I won't, Kashvi," he said, his eyes earnest. "God changed my heart. I want to live for him now. He's greater than my nightmares, a better comfort than anything else."

Could someone really change so quickly?

I thought of *Ammachi*, who had turned from her old beliefs in a moment, willing to be rejected by her village and family for following Jesus.

"I've been talking to *Appa* about being baptized," Ravi said, hope glimmering in his eyes. "And about going to a Bible college next year."

Maybe God really is working in him, I considered.

Or maybe he will disappoint me like everyone else I've loved.

"Hey!" Sudhir's voice cut across the field.

I jerked my arm back, scooting away from Ravi and grabbing my book as Sudhir marched over, scowling.

"What were you doing?" he demanded, his arms crossed.

"Just trying to study." I rolled my eyes. Ravi stood up, looking uncomfortable, and began to walk away.

"Yeah," Sudhir threw him a hard look, "go away."

"Sudhir!" I snapped.

"You've been ignoring him for a month," Sudhir shouted, "but now you have your arm around him?"

I clutched my book. "I don't know what you're talking about."

"Oh, sure you don't," Sudhir retorted, kicking at the ground. "I'm telling *Amma* about this!"

"No, you're not!" I jumped up, grabbing his shirt.

He smirked. "If it's 'nothing,' then why do you care?"

My heart sank. "You're not really going to tell *Amma*, are you?"

"Maybe I will." He eyed me deviously. "First, you can't be away from him. Then you stop talking to him, and now this."

"He's just a friend," I muttered, defensively. "A brother, really."

Sudhir laughed. "Right. I'm your brother, and I've never seen you look at me like that.""Sudhir, please," I pleaded.

He gave me a long look, then shrugged. "Fine. I won't tell *Amma*… if…you stop hanging around him."

"Fine," I agreed, my frustration boiling over.

Sudhir walked away with a smug look of satisfaction.

Feeling tears pricking my eyes, I remained under the hugging tree until I felt composed enough to head back towards the courtyard.

Once I stepped into the courtyard, I saw Ravi and *Amma* coming down the stairs. Ravi gave me a warm smile, and I blushed, looking away, furious with Sudhir for his threat and the promise he had forced me to make.

"Good evening, my dear," *Amma* greeted me, her gaze knowing. "How was your day?"

"Fine," I mumbled, but *Amma* didn't seem convinced. She glanced at Ravi's retreating figure and then back at me.

When Ravi was out of earshot, she addressed me gently. "Kashvi, what's going on with Ravi?"

My heart pounded. "Sudhir told you?"

"Who told me what?" *Amma* raised an eyebrow.

I bit my lip, feeling trapped.

"Why did you ask about Ravi?"

Amma placed a calming hand on my shoulder. "Dear, I'm not blind. I can see that you like him…" She paused. "So, what is it you were worried about me knowing?"

The dam broke, and tears spilled over. "Oh, *Amma*, can we talk upstairs?"

She nodded, leading me to the orange couches—the same place where, three years ago, my mother had once sat with us.

I collapsed on the couch and confessed, "I was talking with Ravi by the tree, and he started telling me about…terrible things that happened to him. I felt so bad, I put my arm around him. I know I shouldn't have…"

Amma's expression softened, and she pulled me into a hug.

"Thank you for sharing this, Kashvi."

I blinked back tears, thinking of how differently my father would have reacted. He would have beaten Ravi, maybe more. What would he have done to me?

"Sin can't be repented of if it's never confessed," *Amma* said gently. "That's why I want you to know you can come to me with anything, no matter what."

"Was it a sin to put my arm around him?" I asked.

"Only you can answer that," *Amma* replied tenderly. "The Bible tells us if we think something is wrong and do it anyway, that is a sin for us. Being close with a boy can easily lead to temptation. Did anything happen beyond that?"

"No," I said quickly.

Amma nodded. "Ravi is a hardworking young man. We hope and pray his desire for God is genuine, but he hasn't been here long, and he lived a long, hard life before coming here. We have not had enough time to know his true character."

I nodded, feeling the sting of truth.

"You're young, Kashvi," *Amma* said. "The next few years will change you and those around you. For now, focus on your studies and trust that God will guide you. He'll bring the right person when you're ready."

I swallowed hard. "*Amma*...I do like Ravi, but..."

Amma waited, then asked gently, "You stopped speaking to him, didn't you?"

I nodded. "I promised I wouldn't say anything, but I can't hold it in anymore. The night *Ammachi* went to the hospital, I...caught Ravi drinking in the forest."

Amma sighed, her face unreadable.

"He told me he used to drink a lot...to forget things that happened to him. He promised it would never happen again, but..." Tears slipped down my cheeks. "Please don't say anything, *Amma*. I promised I wouldn't tell."

"I'll have *Appa* find a way to bring it up in conversation. If Ravi is truly repentant, he'll confess. He doesn't have to know you told me."

"Thank you, *Amma*. I don't want him to...to become like my *appa*."

My throat was choked up with a mix of worry and shame; I was unsure if my concern was for Ravi's soul or for the future I had imagined with him.

"I've seen in my own *thambi* firsthand what drinking can do." *Amma*'s eyes softened. "Let's pray that Ravi's heart is truly changed."

What will happen to him? Will he confess? Will he be sent back to jail? I had no idea, but I knew it was out of my control now.

"Thank you, *Amma*…for listening…for everything," I whispered.

"It's difficult, Kashvi," *Amma* said. "When we see sin, our instinct is to cover it up, but sometimes it needs to be brought into the light, so it can be dealt with properly. Sin festering in our hearts only leads to greater pain and trouble. Confession brings peace, and that peace is better for all of us."

I nodded, wondering what my own heart was full of now. Certainly not peace.

Nalayani closed the Bible, and I hopped up to turn off the light.

"*Thangachi*, can we talk?" She played with a curl nervously. "I over-heard some of your conversation with *Amma* today about Ravi and the night of *Ammachi*'s heart attack."

Horror flooded my body; followed immediately by relief, knowing my secret wasn't hidden anymore.

I turned around, nervous, but I wanted to have this conversation. I wanted my *akka* back, and this is where it had to start.

But before I could start my apology, Nalayani began.

"I'm sorry for the way I have treated you in the last year. In my own pain, I wanted you to be a close friend and was angry when you grieved a different way. I'm overprotective of everyone, according to *Amma*. I wanted to protect you from more hurt, and I wanted to control how that would happen." Her voice cracked. "There have been people I loved very much that I could not protect." She struggled to go on.

"I know, *Akka*, I know," I assured Nalayani. I didn't want her to relive the pain of having her own child murdered and torn from her womb. "And I'm so incredibly sorry."

She offered a barely audible, "Thank you." With a tear escaping down her cheek, she continued. "With all the circumstances, I became angry and acted immaturely as a staff member and as a friend. Will you please forgive me?"

I nodded and reached over to hug her.

When she released me, I gave my own confession.

"I'm sorry for pushing you away. You were—you were right about Ravi, I guess. And I never thanked you for all you did for me when I was struggling after Sarina left."

"I forgive you," Nalayani embraced me again. "I'm just thankful to have my *thangachi* back."

I pushed away slightly, still wondering. "*Akka*, you and Sudhir seem to get upset with me when I speak to Ravi. *Amma* said he must confess his sin if he is truly repentant. I don't know what to think of him right now, but if he is repentant, will you still be upset if I talk with him? He told me he wanted to be baptized and go to Bible college." I quickly added, "Of course, I don't know if that's true."

Nalayani sighed, looking contemplative. Finally, she spoke carefully. "I'm not going to try to tell you what to do, *Thangachi*. I'm only going to ask you to trust *Amma* and *Appa* with decisions concerning boys and marriage."

I cut in, "I'm not thinking about marriage. He's only a friend I enjoy talking to…sometimes."

Nalayani gave me a small smile. "Not much, lately, right?"

"Well…"

"I know. Just let me tell you a story." She readjusted on the bed. "A while before you came, one of the girls here aged out and went back to live with her mother. Her mother arranged a marriage for her with a much older man. *Appa* and *Amma* were very opposed because he was Hindu, and they encouraged her to reject the marriage. But she was so enamored by the man that she married him."

I shifted in my seat but stayed quiet.

"Kashvi, the man she married promised that he would come to church with her, but he never did. Instead, he forbade her from coming to church, and now he forces her to go to the temples with him and follow all the Hindu practices."

I became defensive. "Ravi's not like that! I mean, I'm assuming that's why you're telling me this story."

Nalayani put her hand out quickly. "No, no. All I'm saying is that it is sometimes difficult to see things for what they are when it involves a boy. *Appa* and *Amma* can help you with that. I'm only asking you to trust. Please don't be mad at me. I love you, *Thangachi*. I promise to stop trying to control everything, but please promise me you will consider this."

Her tenderness calmed me. I could promise to think about it. Anyway, I didn't even know how I felt about Ravi. I took a deep breath and looked at Nalayani. "I promise…and…*Akka*, may I sleep in your bed tonight?"

She gave a huge smile, and we hugged once more.

CHAPTER 23

As I sat in church listening to the sermon, I kept glancing over at Ravi sitting at the front with his *dholak*, accompanying the music. He looked perfect. Handsome, carefree, brave, and kind.

The night I had confessed to *Amma*, Ravi had spoken with *Appa* during their private Bible study. Unable to bear the weight on his conscience, Ravi had confessed to his drinking before *Amma* even had the chance to tell *Appa* about it. *Appa* had prayed with him, and he had even arranged for Dhiren to sleep in front of the bedroom door, ensuring that Ravi wouldn't be tempted to sneak out again.

Three months had passed since that night. *Appa* still had regular Bible studies with Ravi and planned to send him to a Bible college in the fall.

God is powerful to change hearts.

Then I thought of Father.

Father can't be changed. But Ravi is different. He has a gentle heart underneath.

After Ravi's confession, I liked him more than ever, and we resumed our walks to and from school.

Sudhir sneered at us, but since I had confessed to *Amma* about putting my arm around Ravi, he didn't have anything to hold over me.

I daydreamed of Ravi graduating Bible college, me finishing college, and *Appa* and *Amma* arranging our marriage. I knew what I had promised Nalayani, but I was sure *Appa* and *Amma* would approve now. I pictured myself in a wedding *sari* next to Ravi as *Appa* officiated. Ravi would start a new church, and I could start an orphanage, too.

Just like *Appa* and *Amma*.

After the service, I found Mother on the porch. It had been two months since her last visit, but that was a relief to me. I was sixteen now, and every time I saw Mother, I was filled with dread that she would bring up Vishnu.

"Your *appa* is not feeling well," Mother said solemnly. "He can barely work. He wants you to visit today."

Visit? Why would he want me to visit?

I panicked, trying to think up excuses but finding none.

"I can arrange for Dhiren to bring you home from here," *Amma* interrupted from behind me. "It's good for a sick *appa* to see his children."

I looked up at *Amma* apprehensively and hated myself for never telling her about Vishnu.

"If your husband can't work, you'll need food," *Amma* said to Mother, stepping over to grab a bag of rice from the collection table. "Here; take this."

Mother started to protest about stealing from God but finally took it with *Amma*'s insistence that this was God's exact purpose for the food.

"Thank you," Mother said, tears welling.

"Thank God," *Amma* replied. "If you need more, come back for more. We'll be praying for your husband."

Mother nodded thankfully, and we walked down to the *Qualis* with Dhiren and Sudhir and headed off for our village. I smiled weakly and waved up at Ravi, who watched us leaving from the porch above.

On the drive, I wondered what *Amma* would pray about my father. That Father would convert? That would never happen. That he'd get better? Deep down, I prayed he would die. My heart leapt at the thought of us being free from him—of Mother finally being free from him.

215

The feeling was fleeting, replaced by the dread of Mother becoming a widow; would that be even worse for her than living with Father? She would be avoided, shunned, alone. She may even be driven out of our village.

I tried to push away all thoughts of what lay ahead in our village; every possibility brought anxiety.

Suddenly, the Bible verse about God knowing the plans for me came to mind. *How did the words go? Something about God planning to give me a hopeful future?* I wondered if that hopeful future would be a marriage to Ravi.

We drove down the familiar cratered path, kicking up dust as we pulled up to our house.

Father sat on the doorstep, *beedi* in mouth. He looked terrible—swollen ankles, yellowed skin. Suspiciously, he wore a smirk as he watched me get out. He even waved. I saw concern crease Mother's face as she took in his appearance. My whole body felt unsettled.

Mother put her arm around me and led me inside.

"Come, Kashvi. I have something for you."

Father pushed himself up from the step, nodding as we passed.

"Nice to see you again, Kashvi."

The quiet warning bells in my head turned to clanging gongs. Father never acted like this. What was going on?

Once inside, all of Mother's concerns seemed to vanish, and a huge smile spread across her face as she held up a beautiful new sari—shimmering turquoise with a narrow red hem and intricate gold embroidery shining in the light. It reflected Mother's hope, but its radiance was in stark contrast to the dread I felt inside.

"It's for your engagement," she said, eyes glowing.

"My engagement?" I felt ready to vomit, unable to run from the reality I had been dreading for the last year and a half, ever since I had heard Father and Uncle talking.

216

I glanced at Kali glaring at me gleefully, her demented tongue wagging.

"Yes," Mother beamed. "*Appa* and I have arranged for you to marry Vishnu. Tonight, we're having the engagement ceremony."

She frowned at the look on my face. "I thought you'd be happy."

My lip quivered. I felt betrayed. "Happy? You said we were coming because Father is sick. Now you're saying I'm here to be engaged?"

"It was a surprise. Your *appa is* sick, and we want to be sure you're cared for if anything happens to him. Vishnu is working now; he's ready for a wife."

Years of bottled-up rage burst out like steam from a kettle. "No!"

Mother jumped back, the same terrified look in her eyes as when Father was about to hit her.

I shuddered, forcing my breathing to slow. "I'm not marrying him."

The door creaked, and Sudhir stepped in. I thought of all the times he'd joked about me marrying Vishnu. It wasn't a joke anymore.

"Kashvi, you can't deny this engagement," Mother's whisper trembled.

A shadow loomed from the doorway as Father stepped in behind Sudhir.

"Engagement?" Sudhir's voice broke the tension. "What engagement?"

Father hobbled up to me, his voice dropping to a menacing whisper as he rested a hand on my shoulder. "What was all that yelling I heard?"

The familiar sickly-sweet scent of alcohol surrounded me, making my stomach churn.

"Nothing." I shrank back from his touch, clenching my fists.

My eyes flickered to a knife on the shelf. A fleeting thought imagined the blade in my hand, driving it through Father's worn-out body. I bit my lip until I tasted blood, shaking away the violent image.

"You better get ready, then." Father's tone dripped with authority.

Or what? I scoffed in my head, wondering how he still possessed so much power over me.

"Wait," Sudhir spoke again, looking bewildered. "*Kashvi's* engagement?"

Mother's hopeful face returned. "Yes, she's to be engaged to Vishnu."

Sudhir's eyes widened as he glanced at me. He didn't know the conversation I had overheard over a year ago—all he knew were our childhood jokes.

No one knew, because I hadn't told anyone. I tried to figure out my problems on my own and now I had to face them alone, unprepared.

"What about Ravi?" Sudhir blurted out carelessly.

Fear flooded through me.

Sudhir, you fool.

Father's eyes darkened. "Who?"

"A friend… I mean…not really…" Sudhir stuttered.

"A boyfriend?!" Father snapped, eyes narrowing. He shifted towards me, his face twisted in anger.

My lips parted, but no words came.

Father's eyes were wild.

"Who is he?!"

Sudhir jumped between us defensively, but Father grabbed him by the collar and viciously barked, "Tell me who he is!"

"It—it was a joke! I was teasing her about a boy, but it was just for fun. She hates the boy, really…" Sudhir raised his hands, surrender in his voice.

Father's eyes blazed as his fingers tightened around Sudhir's throat, pinning him against the wall. "I don't know what they teach you at that Jesus place, but here, we don't make jokes like that," he spat, voice dripping with venom.

He released Sudhir when Dhiren appeared in the doorway.

"Hey, what's going on?" Dhiren demanded, taking in the scene as Father stumbled back, his frail body gasping for air along with Sudhir's.

Ignoring Dhiren, Father wheezed, "Do you want people thinking your *akka* is promiscuous? No more jokes!" He spat on the floor, a final, bitter end to the discussion.

He turned back to me, pointing at the sari. "Get yourself ready. Sudhir, help set up outside." Brushing past Dhiren, he stumbled outside.

Dhiren turned to Sudhir and me, full of confusion and concern. "What's happening here?"

"Nothing, *Anna*," I muttered, my voice empty. I wanted to flee, to run back to Karunai House. But I couldn't leave Mother. "We…we're fine now." I felt trapped.

Dhiren looked unconvinced and unsure of what to do. "I'll be right outside. Just say the word and I'll be here."

Sudhir looked as uncertain as I felt but walked slowly to the door. Our desperate eyes met, and I saw his deep care for me. I knew he had been trying to help with what he said, even if he didn't like what was happening between Ravi and me. He sighed and ushered a somber Dhiren out with him.

What would Father do if I refused? Dread gnawed at my insides. *Rejecting the engagement—an affront to tradition, an insult to* caste, family, and society—*it's unthinkable. And if he knew I didn't want to marry Vishnu because he is Hindu? Would Father take revenge on Karunai House and report them for forced conversions?*

Mother clung to my arm. "What could possibly make you think of refusing this engagement? Vishnu is a good boy…he doesn't drink, he—"

"How do you know he won't beat me?" I interrupted.

Mother blinked, stunned. "Vishnu is kind. What makes you say that?"

"Did you think *Appa* would beat you when you married him?" My words were coated in bitterness.

Mother's lips trembled, her eyes welling as she covered her face, her body shaking with quiet sobs.

"I don't want to get married at all," I lied, trying to buy time. "I want to go to college, live on my own."

"Do you have any idea the shame it will bring if you reject this engagement—not only for you, but for all of us?" Mother pleaded desperately. "We would be driven out of the village. Then what would your *appa* do to you?" Quietly, she added, "Or to me?"

Her words sent shivers through me. But through all my doubts, I knew I had to marry a Christian. I knew God required it of me; plus, I saw how women were treated better by Christian husbands.

Still, I feared telling Mother the truth. I couldn't risk everything: Karunai House, my life, her life.

Mother wiped her eyes and took a deep breath. "Kashvi, going outside tradition—the gods punish us for it. It brings sorrow, it brings… death."

Is that it? Is this engagement to appease the gods so they'll take Father's illness away? Or is she talking of her death…my death?

"I'm not old enough," I protested weakly.

"I was sixteen when I was married," Mother whispered. "Besides, this is just the engagement. The astrologers found an aligning *Muhoortam* date—a year from now, you and Vishnu will marry."

I'll still only be seventeen.

It was pointless to argue. No one would care.

I swallowed, my throat tight. Courage fled from me, leaving me empty and apathetic. The most impactful event in all my life, and I had no say in it. I was impossibly stuck. I couldn't put Karunai House, my life, and my mother's life in jeopardy all at the same time.

I'll accept the engagement. Buy myself some time. Push the problem down the road, like I always do.

I took a deep breath. "Help me put on the *sari*."

Mother's eyes lit up, and she helped me wrap the new *sari* around my trembling body. It was the first time I had ever worn one. She draped the loose end of the *sari* over my shoulder, then stepped back with a smile.

"You look beautiful, Kashvi."

I'd dreamt of my engagement as a little girl—wearing a stunning *sari*, my hair braided with fragrant flowers, my face painted with care. Gold earrings and bangles sparkling, their gentle clang a song of joy. Presenting myself and serving tea to my soon-to-be husband.

This wasn't that dream. This was a nightmare.

Mother began to work on my makeup. She applied black eyeliner under my eyes and dabbed talc powder over my face to give it a fair appearance. Lastly, she placed a red *bindi* in the middle of my forehead, right next to my scar.

Should I object? I hadn't worn a *bindi* since I arrived at Karunai House. *God is my source of knowledge and my protector, not some stupid dot. But why isn't he protecting me now?*

I had to come up with my own plan...I'd go along with the engage-ment for now.

As Mother applied beetroot balm to my lips, I wondered how long they had saved to buy the *sari*, makeup, and jewelry, and how bitter father was inside to have spent it on me. But it didn't really have any-thing to do with me. It was about him and his honor. He wouldn't present a "plain" daughter; that would bring shame.

What would he do if he knew I had other plans? And all his money bought nothing but a greater shame to come?

Voices grew louder outside. There was a knock on the door, and I jumped.

"Come in," Mother called.

Father stepped in, shutting the door behind him. His smile was unsettling.

"You look beautiful in that *sari* we got for you."

I forced a mocking smile back. Never in my life had Father said anything nice about my appearance.

"Vishnu is here," Father continued. "He'll take care of you if any-thing happens to me."

As he walked slowly out the door in his aged body, I hated him more than ever. He didn't care about me. He thought my turning from the Hindu gods was part of what brought his illness. He thought tying me to Vishnu would fix everything, that I'd submit to Vishnu and go back to my old way of life, my old gods and traditions.

Would Vishnu beat me if I refused to worship? Would God give me strength to refuse?

Mother stepped outside to make sure everything was ready. I stayed hidden inside, clutching my hands tight.

There was no way out.

When Mother returned, she set a dented serving tray down

and carefully arranged small steel cups of steaming milk tea. The sweet-smelling tea made me think of Mahiyu, and I wished for his simple, unwavering faith right now.

I grabbed the tray.

Let's get this over with.

Mother pushed the door wide open. Sunlight hit me like a slap. I stepped outside, blinking hard.

Family, neighbors, and villagers crowded around a large plastic woven mat spread on the bare earth. Men stood on one side, women on the other, bright *saris* and *lungis* blending in a riot of color. The air was heavy with the smells of sweat, sandalwood, and dust.

Father stood beside me, leaning heavily on a bamboo staff. His mouth was pulled tight in a smirk of satisfaction. Mother stood slightly behind Father, her eyes darting between him and me. She wore her nicest faded green silk *sari* with gold borders.

Among the sea of faces, I found Dhiren standing stiffly near the outer edge, one hand clamped protectively on Sudhir's shoulder. His usual easy grin was gone. His lips were pursed in anger. Sudhir leaned into him, looking lost and confused.

The chatter dimmed as people turned towards me expectantly.

The shimmering *sari* Mother had wrapped me in caught the sunlight—the red hem and heavy gold embroidery hinting at love and prosperity—but it was all just a mirage. I felt exposed, my midriff laid bare, everyone's eyes on me.

Vishnu sat cross-legged at the far end of the mat, stiff and proud in a new cream-colored *veshti* and shirt with a garland of fresh jasmine flowers slung loosely around his neck. His forehead was smeared with sandal paste. His hair was slicked back with coconut oil, making him look older.

His gaze crawled over me, then his eyes locked on mine. I shivered.

I forced myself forward, walking across the dusty mat to Vishnu. With trembling hands, I carefully offered the tea on the serving tray—first to Vishnu, then to my uncle and aunt who sat beside him.

Once the tea was offered, I set the empty tray aside and sat across from Vishnu on the mat, the way I'd been instructed. The formalities blurred together, and soon Uncle stood and placed a silver tray between us, its offerings gleaming: bananas, pomegranates, oranges, a pineapple, and, on top, a new folded *sari*.

As Uncle turned to sit again, the beady eyes of the Hindu priest caught my attention. In my nerves, I hadn't noticed him sitting there before. He was there to bless us.

It was the same priest who demanded Asha be brought into the temple to be healed, where she died instead.

My heart pounded as I stared at the old man with white ash smeared across his forehead, wearing nothing but a simple white *veshti* around his waist. Suddenly, I was back in the temple on that day banging my head on the floor, with Asha's parents' cries echoing in the shadowy candle-light. I watched all over again as Asha gasped in pain, near to death.

I fingered the hem of my *sari* and inhaled slowly through my nose, then out my mouth, reminding myself where I was.

Finally, I came back to reality…a reality no more comforting.

Sweat covered my body, and I wondered how long I'd been out of it. I looked around, and everyone was silent. They shifted closer in anticipation now. Custom demanded that I pick up the *sari* to show my acceptance of the engagement. I glanced back at my parents.

Father straightened; his face stretched into a rare, gleaming smile. I had never seen him look so satisfied. Mother looked the opposite, her hands clutched together, trying to hide her nervous trembling.

She was terrified I wouldn't go through with it. If I walked away right now, her life would be over and so would mine.

I reached out and lifted the *sari* with numb fingers. It weighed heavy in my hands.

I glanced up, desperate, and locked eyes with Dhiren. His jaw was tight, his fists clenched. Sudhir twisted under Dhiren's restraining hand and broke free, running off behind the house. Dhiren started to follow but stopped himself and turned back to me.

No one paid Sudhir any attention. Their attention stayed fixed on me.

Clutching the *sari*, I rose unsteadily and stumbled into the house. Mother followed behind me.

Inside, in the dim room, the smell of incense clung to the walls. I closed my eyes tightly and prayed.

Help me, God. Please. Show me a sign if you don't want me to do this.

I waited, heart hammering in my chest. No sign came. No sudden darkness, no talking animals, no transporting me far away.

Mother frowned at my hesitation, impatience flashing in her eyes.

I sighed, defeated, and wordlessly let her dress me in the *sari* Vishnu's family had gifted—it was crimson with heavy gold embroidery, a bolder façade than before. Stepping out in this new *sari* would symbolize my submission, my acceptance of this future.

Maybe, I told myself, *within the next year, before the wedding, I can find a way to undo this.*

When I stepped outside again, applause erupted. Vishnu rose from the mat, smiling as he stepped up beside me.

Men clapped and whistled, the noise jarring. Women shrieked and tossed turmeric and rice over Vishnu and me. Some ran forward to smear it into our hair.

Standing up from behind Uncle, the Hindu priest slithered up to us. The tip of his scraggly beard dipped itself in the brass plate he held, filled with a mix of powders, rice, and small flowers. He lifted his hand over us, sprinkling us with the mixture as he chanted "*Subham Bhavatu. Mangalam Bhavatu.* Let this union bring prosperity, long life, and many sons. May Lakshmi's blessings fall upon this house."

As he spoke, the crowd bowed their heads, murmuring "*Aum*" softly under their breaths.

I squeezed my eyes shut—not to receive a blessing, but to try to disappear. I tried to imagine Ravi standing beside me instead. But when I opened my eyes again, reality grinned back at me in the form of Vishnu's face.

Finished with my "duties," I turned sharply and fled into the house, bolting the door behind me. I tore at the *sari*, ripping the folds from my body, grinding the rich fabric under my feet. I clawed at my cheeks, desperate to scrub away the layers of powder Mother had painted on. Black streaks of eyeliner mixed with golden turmeric smeared across my hands.

Finally, I fell to my knees, shaking, helpless.

CHAPTER 24

My thoughts swirled like a cyclone as we drove away from the nightmare of my surprise engagement. The steady rumble of the vehicle's engine did nothing to ease the emptiness inside me.

I stared out the window of the *Qualis*, watching people going about their normal lives, hating them for it…hating everything.

What did I do? What was I supposed to do? How am I going to get out of this mess? Where are you, God? Why did you let that happen?

A verse from Karunai House popped into my head. *"When my father and my mother forsake me, then the* LORD *will take me up."*

Is this what taking me up looks like, God? You've taken away so much from me—Velu, Sarina, and Milo. Ammachi is sick and nearly died. I've already lost Asha, and now if I don't marry Vishnu, I'll lose my mother and Karunai House, too. But what will I lose if I do marry him?

Sudhir squeezed my hand. "What are you going to do?"

"I don't know," I said. "Before Karunai House, I would never have thought I had any other choice, and I would have been happy with the engagement." I sighed deeply. "That almost feels like it would have been easier."

"For now," Sudhir replied. "But we never would have learned about Jesus."

"Now I need to choose between Jesus and a dead *amma*," I whispered.

Sudhir winced at my harsh words. "God will protect us, right? That's

226

the truth we have to hold onto, *Akka*." He swallowed hard. "Is the suffering we experience now not worthy to be compared with the glory revealed later?"

My *thambi* looked at me apologetically, knowing the truth he spoke felt like daggers.

I was surprised again by how much Sudhir had changed since his accident. The little boy always trying to get out of work and antagonizing everyone was now giving me spiritual guidance.

"Do you believe that, Sudhir? Mother getting killed, Karunai House getting shut down—worth it for Jesus?"

Sudhir's eyes filled with tears. "*Akka*, Jesus saved my life. In more ways than one. I can't imagine how painful all of that would be, but I think that's what faith is for."

I mulled over his words, wishing he was the one with the dilemma if he had so much faith…wishing he would stop trying to sound so wise.

The *Qualis* pulled up to the big yellow gate of Karunai House. Ravi swung it open with a big smile on his face.

His smile faded as I got out and slammed the door. "What's wrong?"

"Nothing," I snapped, biting my lip to fight back tears.

Running to my room, I locked the door behind me and wept on my bed.

Bang!

The window rattled.

I got up and looked out the window. Ravi had tossed a volleyball at the glass.

Bang!

I unlatched the window and opened it.

"What's wrong?" Ravi asked.

I choked on the words, "I'm engaged."

Ravi laughed. "What's really—"

"I'm serious," I moaned. "I'm engaged to my cousin, Vishnu."

Ravi's face slumped, and he looked down in silence.

Say something! Tell me you love me and want to marry me!

A knock at the door behind me interrupted my thoughts.

"Kashvi," *Amma's* muffled voice called.

I slammed the window shut and wiped my face with my shawl. Stomping to the door, I unlocked it.

Amma wrapped me in her arms. "I heard what happened from Sudhir."

"I'm such a coward," I cried, words escaping between sobs. "I don't want to marry Vishnu. I want to marry a Christian. But I couldn't tell the truth. I just can't face the consequences."

Amma's touch brought on a mix of safety and anxiety as I wondered how long I would have her, too. She was quiet for a while as my sobs faded. I desperately wanted her to give me the simple solution that just hadn't crossed my mind yet.

Amma led me to the edge of the bed, and I sat beside her. "If you had said you wouldn't marry Vishnu because he's not a Christian, what do you think would have happened?"

"I don't know. My *appa* would hurt us all for the shame he would endure. He would try to get Karunai House shut down. He would beat me or Mother until I agreed. Now that I've accepted, it will be even worse for all of us if I break it off!" I began crying again.

"My dear, I understand what you did," *Amma* stroked my hair, "and I probably would have done the same in your shoes."

"But you stood up boldly to your parents," I said, thinking of *Amma-chi* turning her away from their home, *Amma* no longer welcome in her family. "I'm just weak. I can't do what I'm supposed to do!"

"It was difficult for me," *Amma* admitted, "but I was old enough to make my own decision. We don't know what will happen in your case. But you aren't responsible for your father's actions or anyone else's. It's up to you to do the right thing and trust God with whatever happens. If safety were placed above faith, Christianity would not exist in India. Every convert from Hinduism has to face some level of persecution."

"But who will marry a poor, low-*caste* girl with no *dowry?*" I asked, my voice trembling.

"Follow Jesus, despite the consequences, Kashvi. Even if this means you will never get married, it's still the right thing to do," she explained tenderly. "A true man of God will not care about your *caste*. *Appa* married me with no *dowry*. He wanted a Christian wife, not material possessions."

We sat in silence. I wondered if Ravi would care. I immediately felt shame, questioning my conviction about not marrying Vishnu. Was this even about Jesus?

If Ravi weren't in the picture, would you still feel the same way?

I wanted the answer to be yes. I truly wanted to marry a Christian and follow God's way. I only wondered if I would be able to muster up the boldness to choose him above all else.

"The actual marriage is a year away?" *Amma* asked.

I nodded.

"Well, that gives us time to pray about it," *Amma* said. "Let's ask God for wisdom, and we can talk after we've had some time to think."

"Okay," I said weakly, pleading with God in my heart that he would give me stronger faith.

Quick, heavy footsteps on the stairs drew our eyes to the door.

Mahiyu launched into the room. "Kashvi, quick, your *amma's* on the phone in the office."

Amma and I ran down, and I grabbed the phone.

"Kashvi!" Mother shouted on the other end. "*Appa's* collapsed at home, and he's not responding. I don't know what to do. The temple is closed, and I came to Pastor Kurumuni's to call you. Pastor Kurumuni says we should bring him to the hospital, but…"

My mouth hung open. I didn't know what to say.

If Father trusts in the gods to heal him, then let them heal him.

Amma grabbed the phone from me.

"Go back home to your husband. We are coming to pick you up!"

CHAPTER 25

The acrid scent of antiseptic dragged me back to those long nights spent in the hospital with Sudhir.

This time, it wasn't my *thambi* on the bed—it was my father, his skin a sickly yellow.

A sick patient groaned behind a thin curtain dividing the room. I stood behind Mother and Sudhir, who were sitting on chairs beside Father's hospital bed. Mother was attempting to muffle her sobs.

Why is she crying?

I rubbed my tired, wet eyes.

Why am I crying?

The swollen, discolored figure before us was the same man who had beaten us, the one whose death I often wished for. I couldn't understand the tears streaming down my face.

Amma stood behind my mother, her hand resting comfortingly on her shoulder. *Appa* leaned against the wall beside us, his eyes closed, lips moving in silent prayer. *Appa* brought me peace; I couldn't imagine losing him.

But my own father?

If karma *and reincarnation were real,* I wondered, *what would my father return as?*

A tingling sensation spread across the back of my neck.

Smack!

I slapped at the irritation and looked at my hand. Blood streaked across my palm, tiny legs protruding from the crushed body of a mosquito.

A mosquito. A parasite, feeding on others, draining them.

Fitting, I thought, wiping the remnants on the pant leg of my *chudidhar.*

My father lived a life of sin. Soon, he will pay for it. He deserves the torment of hell, the gnashing of teeth, the eternal fire that never dies.

Then my thoughts recoiled.

What about me? My lies, my wavering faith, my hatred? Don't I deserve the same fate?

Of course not! I argued silently with myself. *I'm not like him. I'm not a drunk…not violent…I never hurt anyone like he did. How could God look at me and my father as equals?*

A nurse poked her head into the room, checking the monitors. Her eyes narrowed. "Who let so many people in here? Are you all family?"

"No, we're—" *Amma* started to explain.

"Only family allowed," the nurse said, shaking her head.

Amma nodded respectfully. "We'll wait for you in the cafeteria," she whispered to my mother, then embraced Sudhir and me in a warmth that reminded me of a mother hen sheltering her chicks.

I clung to that safety and immediately missed it when she pulled away.

Appa and *Amma* slipped out of the room.

No one spoke; only the neighboring patient's grunts and the slow, constant beeps of machines filled the air.

After several minutes, Father's eyes snapped open, his body jerking, and he took in several feverish breaths as his hands latched onto the bed rails, knuckles white.

I gasped and pushed myself back, startled, nearly tipping Sudhir and me over.

"Nurse! Nurse!" Mother cried out the open door.

Father's eyes darted around wildly, his voice a rasp. "Where am I?"

"You're in a hospital," Mother whispered with a tremble. "You collapsed at home—"

"Is this that Christian hospital?" he asked.

"Y–yes," Mother stammered.

His gaze drifted to the IVs and monitors, the wires tangling around his fragile body. "Why did you bring me here?"

"The temple was closed," Mother's voice cracked. "You weren't responding, and I didn't know…"

"You nearly died," Sudhir declared. "They saved you."

Father shot Sudhir a glare. "What's wrong with me?"

"They said your liver is failing," Mother murmured. "They don't know how long you have left."

For a moment, Father stared at the ceiling, his eyes distant. He seemed to retreat inside himself, lost in thoughts I could only imagine.

He coughed violently, then after a few moments, he tried to speak, barely audible.

"Kashvi," he wheezed, gesturing weakly for me to approach.

I hesitated, then stepped slowly around Sudhir's chair up next to the bed. Father's frail hand reached out for mine. His fingers closed around my hand, trembling, his grip weaker than I'd ever known it could be.

"Kashvi," he rasped, "I want to see you married before I die. Vishnu can move in and take care of you."

My heart raced. "What…?" The word barely escaped my lips.

His pale face was so pitiable, his words seemingly genuine. For once, there was no hatred in his eyes, no stench of alcohol. He looked… human. Vulnerable.

An old memory surfaced. One of my earliest—before Grandfather died. As Father and I were walking to the temple, a man dressed as a demon charged at us. I remembered bursting into tears, and Father kneeling, gently grasping my wrist, telling me the demon was there to protect us, to scare away the evil.

That gentleness—was that the last time I'd seen it?

Tears stung my eyes. His dying wish was for me to marry Vishnu. Even after all the hatred, I found myself unwilling to deny him outright.

I opened my mouth, my voice faltering, "What about the *Muhoor-tam* day?"

"It's worse luck to marry after your *appa* dies." Father's entire body tensed, his face twisted in agony.

The nurse rushed in, pushing me aside. "Give me space."

I backed away, heart pounding, and slipped out of the room, collapsing against the wall in the hall. My heart betrayed my head and wished desperately for my father to actually care about me. A hollow feeling filled me.

Sudhir appeared in the doorway, wrapping his arms around me. "You don't have to do this, *Akka*."

I shook my head.

This is my punishment for not denying the engagement to begin with. My punishment for wishing Father was dead. I didn't buy myself any time at all.

Sudhir took my hand, leading me to the cafeteria.

On the way, I pleaded, "Please don't say anything about this, Sudhir. I need time to think without everyone telling me what to do."

He nodded slowly.

We found *Appa* and *Amma* sipping coffee, their presence a rock in the storm of my mind. I looked at *Amma*, her unwavering strength almost unbearable.

How can she always be so brave?

A few minutes later, Mother joined us, her eyes red-rimmed. "They gave him something for the pain," she said. "He's resting now. The doctors said…maybe weeks. Maybe months."

"We will pray," *Appa* said empathetically.

Pray for what? His recovery?

I want to pray for his death.

Amma rummaged in her purse, pulling out some *rupees* and offering them to my mother.

"Please, get something to eat."

Mother shook her head. "This is too much."

"You might be here a while," *Amma* said. "This is for more than one meal. Please, the money isn't ours—it's a gift from God."

Mother reluctantly took the *rupees*, standing up.

"Sit, actually," *Amma* urged. "You've had a long day. Let us get the food." She gave Mother's shoulder a reassuring squeeze and she and *Appa* joined the long, winding food line.

Mother looked at me, her face crumpling. "Your *appa* wants us to arrange the wedding with Vishnu next week."

I stared at *Amma*, standing in line, trying to find strength there.

"I can't do it," I whispered. "I can't marry him."

"You're engaged! You promised!" Desperation clung to every word. "You would deny your *appa*'s dying wish?"

"I—"

"He's doing this for your own good," she insisted. "Who will marry a low-*caste* daughter of a widow? I don't even know if Vishnu would go through with it if your *appa* was dead." She stared at me with wild eyes. "You must marry him. You have no choice."

"Listen, Mother, please..." I started, unable to look her in the eye.

I can do all things through Christ which strengtheneth me.

I thanked God for bringing the verse to mind. I could suffer. I could do it. I could do it with Jesus.

My voice came out barely above a whisper. "I love Jesus and can't marry someone who does not love him, too. As the only, true God."

"You care more about this Jesus than your own *amma*? More than your own life?" she shrieked hysterically. Her voice rose in anger. "You have no choice! What will your uncle do if you refuse? The village will stone us!"

The doctors and nurses in their scrubs at nearby tables glanced up at us with raised eyebrows for a second, then went back to their conversations. *Appa* and *Amma* were too far away to hear.

Sudhir rested his hand atop Mother's comfortingly. "*Amma*, please calm down. Listen to Kashvi."

"You've both turned against me!" Mother cried.

"You don't understand—" I stammered.

"No," she gritted her teeth, "I don't."

Sudhir pleaded with her, "What about the women's shelter *Amma* always mentions—"

"This is all her fault to begin with! Your Christianity has turned the gods against us," she sobbed, her head in her hands. "It's taken all sense from you and your love for your own *amma*."

"I just need time to think." I tried to hold Mother's hand too, but she pulled back from us both.

"There is no time," she cried. "Your *appa* is dying."

She thinks I don't love her? How can I do this to her?

"I'll make my decision by tomorrow."

I looked at her in silence, but she avoided my gaze. My heart tore in pieces as I saw my mother looking more broken than I had ever seen her at the hands of my father.

Appa and *Amma* returned with trays of food, oblivious to what had just taken place.

Mother stood, taking a food tray from *Appa*. "I'm going back to the room."

She stomped off without another word.

CHAPTER 26

I lay in bed, staring at the ceiling, each second stretching on forever. Father's bloodshot eyes, Mother's desperate pleas—it all played on a loop in my mind.

Guilt, shame, anger—how could I choose myself over my mother after all she had endured for me?

But it wasn't all about me. I had to choose Jesus. Vishnu wasn't a Christian.

Uncle's words echoed in my head: *"Once she's living with us, we'll drive all those Christian ideas out of her one way or another."*

If I refused, the consequences would be dire. Father's fury would fall on Mother, on me, on everyone connected to Karunai House. If he reported that Karunai House forced children to convert to Christianity, *Amma, Appa,* and everything they built could be destroyed.

Even if Father died, I would have to face Uncle. He could report Karunai House, too. And my mother would be a widow, an outcast. She would have nowhere to go, nothing to protect her. What would Uncle do to her, since she was the one who had sent us here in the first place? In his mind, she would be seen as the reason for his brother's death.

The thought twisted my heart. Obeying God would bring suffering on everyone I loved.

Run away, I thought. *Disappear. Escape the impossible choices. You could start over, serve Jesus far from here…but that would mean leaving Mother behind to endure the consequences alone.*

The moonlight filtered through the thin curtain, casting a pale glow across the walls.

But…if everyone believes I've been kidnapped, there will be no refusal, no shame for my mother, no retaliation from Father or Uncle. Maybe this nightmare can end without destroying everyone I love. Maybe this is God's answer.

I wrestled in prayer, asking God for wisdom. But deep down, I knew what was right. I had to deny the marriage.

But the voice in my head kept saying: *Run away.*

When the rooster crowed, I rolled out of bed, my mind still swimming with every possible outcome to the decisions I had to make.

Nalayani groaned in her bed, unwilling to wake.

I stared at my storage chest, the colorful outfits folded neatly inside. I quickly grabbed a couple of the outfits and dumped all the books, paper, and pens from my school bag into the chest. I stuffed the outfits into the bottom of the bag, then placed my Bible on top. Slipping into my school dress, I headed downstairs to start my chores.

I left my bag by the boys' bags on the porch outside the Common Hall and wandered around in a daze, collecting the eggs scattered by our hens until the drums sounded from the common room, signaling that devotions were about to begin. I left the basket of eggs I'd collected inside the kitchen and headed towards the music.

On my way to the common room, I noticed that Mahiyu had left the door to the storage room open, and I found myself walking towards it.

"Kashvi, devotions time," *Amma* called from behind me.

I jumped and spun around. "I…uh…need to get my Bible from my room," I lied.

"Go quickly."

I walked towards the girls' dorm with my eyes on *Amma*. As soon as she stepped into the common room, I turned around, grabbed my back-pack from the porch, and dashed into the storage room.

I shoved groundnuts, oranges, plantains, and bags of rice into my bag—anything that could sustain me. My heart pounded.

As I was leaving, I saw Mahiyu's clipboard lying on the shelf. I hesitated, then grabbed it, flipping through the inventory sheets until I found the wad of *rupees* I knew would be clipped behind them. I stared at the money, my conscience tugging at me.

"I'll put it back if I stay," I whispered. Rahab had lied to save the spies; I was doing this to save my mother, to save Karunai House, to save myself.

I glanced over my shoulder, then slid the clipboard into my back-pack. It would be less suspicious if the whole clipboard was missing and not just the money. Maybe Mahiyu would think he just misplaced it—though I knew he never misplaced anything. He was meticulous.

He would *never* stop looking for what was lost.

Pushing that thought aside, I peeked out of the room, checking for any other latecomers, but it seemed everyone was in the common room already. I slipped out, placed my backpack back on the porch, grabbed my Bible from it, and joined everyone else in the common room for devotions.

Amma's voice filled the air as she read from Psalm 27. "Though war should rise against me, in this will I be confident..."

I'd memorized this psalm, and I knew what the psalmist was confident in—that God was his light, salvation, and the strength of his life, so he didn't need to be afraid. The familiar words moved through me, pressing against my heart.

"In the time of trouble he shall hide me in his pavilion."

God, will you hide me? I can't handle this. You cared for me when my own parents forsook me—will you give me strength now?

Tears welled in my eyes, a few slipping down my cheeks. I wiped them away before anyone could see. Would this be my last devotions time here, surrounded by the people who loved me, who fought for me? The last time I would see Ravi, Nalayani, Sudhir...

No—I could be strong. I could refuse the marriage.

Amma's voice trailed off in my mind as she started to pray. Images of my mother flashed through my mind—her weary face, her desperate voice, her fear. My strength crumbled as quickly as it came. Tears trickled down, and I struggled to keep from sobbing.

If I ran, I would be doing it to protect them—all of them.

"Are you okay, Kashvi? You look sick," *Amma's* concerned voice startled me. She walked over, placing a hand on my forehead.

"I–I'm fine, *Amma*," I stuttered, just noticing devotions were over and everyone was filing out of the room.

"I don't think you have a fever, but you're sweating profusely." *Amma* handed me a bottle of water from her purse. "Drink this. You might be dehydrated."

Is this the last time I'll see you? The thought seized me, and I broke into tears again.

Amma wrapped her arms around me, her hand moving in slow circles along my back. "I'm here, my dear. I'm always here for you to talk to."

I pulled back, meeting *Amma's* warm eyes. "I love you."

"Oh, Kashvi, I love you, too."

I stared at her, tears blurring my vision. I wanted to tell her everything, to ask for help, for strength—but I couldn't risk it. She always did what was right; I wasn't that strong. I didn't want to disappoint her. The desire to run grew with every passing moment.

"I'm just…" I swallowed hard. "I'm just having a hard time understanding how I should feel about my *appa*."

I didn't admit to my immediate struggle and hated myself for it.

Amma sighed, her eyes searching mine.

"It's okay to feel conflicted, my dear. You've been through so much. Forgiveness doesn't mean excusing what was done to you. It means giving it to God, trusting him with justice."

I nodded, and *Amma* pulled me in for another hug.

"I'll be here, always."

Her words tore at my heart, and I wondered where my resolve had gone, wishing I could absorb some of *Amma*'s. We parted, and I fled to the bathroom.

I closed the door and turned, catching sight of my reflection—my face pale, my eyes red from crying. I remembered my first day at Karunai House, standing in front of this same mirror, staring at the stranger looking back at me. I had been so scared, so alone. Now, I felt the same fear, but this time it was laced with the pain of leaving behind those who had become my family. I felt completely paralyzed.

My stomach churned, and I doubled over, vomiting into the sink. I gripped the edge of the sink, the tears returning. There was no good answer. The weight of it all pressed down on me, and I felt like I was suffocating.

I needed to be away from it all. I gave up grasping for resolve and held tightly to my desire to disappear, escaping from the mess of my life. I rinsed my mouth, splashed water on my face, and forced myself to breathe.

I had to hold it together, at least until I was gone.

Walking through the courtyard, I said good morning to everyone, knowing it was actually a goodbye. Finally, I greeted Nalayani, Dhiren, and Mahiyu, trying to hold back tears.

When I hugged Sudhir, I lingered for a moment, whispering, "I love you, *Thambi*."

He looked up at me, confused. "Um…I love you, too…? Why are we saying this right now?"

I forced a smile, ruffling his hair. "Just…I'm proud of you."

Sudhir's eyes bored into me like *Amma*'s always did. I gave an unconvincing smile. He shook his head and turned towards the gate to leave for school.

I swallowed the lump in my throat as I looked around the place that was my only real home. Then someone tapped me on the shoulder, snapping me back to reality.

"Hey," Ravi said, "are you going to walk with me?"

"Yeah," I exhaled, and walked out of the gate beside him heading to school, my backpack weighing me down.

My heart pounded as my thoughts raced. My plan was to just slip away when no one could see me. Change into one of my other outfits, leave a torn piece of my school dress behind—maybe even smear a little blood on it to make it convincing that I had been kidnapped. After that, catch a bus to town. From there, I had no plan.

"Kashvi? Are you even listening?" Ravi's voice cut through my thoughts.

"Sorry, w–what?" I stammered, blinking up at him.

Ravi frowned, concern etched across his face. "I asked if you heard the new rhythm I was playing on the *dholak* this morning."

"Oh." I tried to smile. "I came in late. But I'm always amazed at how well you play."

Ravi chuckled. "I learned from the best."

His words made something click in my mind. Ravi knew how to survive—he had been on the streets before. He'd know where I could hide. He'd understand. He'd keep my secret.

Then another thought popped into my mind: *Would he run away with me?*

I imagined it—Ravi and me, starting over, away from all the weight and demands of tradition and *caste*. We could serve Jesus together, just us, and everything would work out. I knew he cared for me—it was obvious.

I breathed in his familiar scent. I felt warm and safe near Ravi. He could protect me, take care of me. He could be my escape.

Without thinking, I blurted out, "My *appa* wants me to marry Vishnu before he dies."

I waited for Ravi's response—for him to say I shouldn't do it, that he wanted me, that he cared about me…that he loved me.

But he said nothing.

I sniffed, wiping my nose on my shoulder. "I don't want to marry him. He's not a Christian. And I don't love him."

I paused again.

Still nothing.

"If I don't marry him, my *amma* will lose everything. She may even be killed. My *appa* or uncle could report Karunai House for leading me to reject the marriage. Karunai House could be shut down."

"Wow, Kashvi, I'm so sorry," Ravi finally spoke. "What did *Appa* and *Amma* say you should do?"

"They want me to refuse the marriage and trust God with whatever happens," I said, my voice trembling. "But I...can't do that. There's too much at stake."

Concern deepened in Ravi's eyes. "So, what are you going to do?"

My heart hammered in my chest. I looked at the road ahead. The other boys were far ahead of us.

"I can't deal with it...I can't hurt all the people I love. I'm going to run away. But...I need help."

Ravi stopped walking. "You want me to help you run away?"

"Y–yes, well..." I stammered, "I want you to run away with me."

Ravi's eyes spread wide in shock. "Kashvi, I...I don't know what to say. I can't just run away with you."

My stomach twisted, my heart pounding in my ears.

Why did I think he would want to run away with me?

"Are you okay?" Ravi asked. "You look like you're going to pass out."

"I just thought..." My voice cracked.

"You thought what?" Ravi asked.

It was now or never. I'd already said too much.

"I thought you loved me."

Ravi stammered, his hand running through his thick hair. He sighed.

"Kashvi, I care about you...but as a friend. As a sister. I can't run away with you. It's not right."

I didn't believe it. My voice rose, tinged with anger and pain.

"You mean you don't have any feelings for me? After all your flirting with me?"

Ravi shifted uncomfortably, eyes avoiding mine.

"I'm sorry, I thought you knew it was just...fun. We could never—I mean, my uncle would never allow…" He trailed off, his face filled with shame.

I stared at him in disbelief. "Is this because of *caste?*"

Ravi's gaze dropped, guilt written over his face.

"I'm sorry, Kashvi. I don't know what you expected."

"How many years has it been since you've even seen your uncle?" I spat. "He doesn't care about you.

"I…" Ravi stumbled over his words.

"Where was your uncle when you were on the streets, stealing to survive?"

Ravi's face flushed. "Kashvi, it's just the way things are." His voice sounded small, defeated—like my mother's when she spoke of fate.

"*Caste* shouldn't matter to Christians! You think you're better than a dirty *Dalit* like me." I fumed, bitterness boiling over. "I wasn't the one drinking in the woods, was I?"

Ravi's face hardened. "God changed my heart. Don't hold that over me."

"Well, he hasn't changed it enough," I snapped.

I stormed away, my chest tight with rage and heartbreak. I rounded the corner and hid behind the chapel next to my school, leaning over, ready to vomit again.

Ravi didn't follow.

*What a stupid, stupid plan. How could I have thought that Ravi—that anyone—would want a low-*caste *girl like me?*

I looked up, the cross atop the chapel catching my eye. For a moment, I considered praying—asking for help, for guidance. But I had lied, stolen, and planned to run away. God wouldn't hear my prayers now. It felt as though he had abandoned me, too.

"Are you okay?" Sudhir's voice startled me, and I turned around, wiping my eyes.

"I'm fine," I huffed.

"What are you doing back here?"

"I'm…praying." Another lie. "Why are you back here?"

Sudhir frowned in concern. "You were acting weird this morning. Then I heard you and Ravi arguing…"

"It was nothing," I said, my irritation rising. Why did he have to be checking on me now? My whole plan was falling apart.

"Are you sure?" he pressed. "It's been an awful few days for you, *Akka*. Are you still planning to refuse the marriage?"

"Yes." I sighed. It was a half-truth.

He nodded slowly, eyes searching mine. "So, are you coming in?"

"I need time to…finish my prayer," I said, trying to sound convincing.

Suspicion clouded his eyes. "Sure you're okay, *Akka*?"

"Why can't you just leave me alone?" I snapped. "Let me do what I need to do!"

Sudhir's concern dissipated. "Why don't you let others help you? You think you're smarter than everyone, that you always know best. Fine, I guess I'll stop caring about you." He turned and stomped away.

The bell rang. My plan was crumbling around me. I doubted anyone would believe I was kidnapped after what had just happened with Ravi and Sudhir, but I didn't care anymore. I only wanted out of this mess.

I quickly changed, then ripped a piece of fabric off my school dress with my teeth. I bit down hard on my lip. The pain seared and the familiar metallic taste filled my mouth. I smeared my torn dress piece across my bloody lip then threw it on the ground along with one of my earrings. I dumped out my school books and notebook onto the ground and stuffed what was left of my school dress into my bag.

Glancing over my crime scene, I found my notebook had fallen open to a sketch I'd drawn of Sarina, Velu, and me under the hugging tree. I wondered where Sarina was now, if she really was at that orphanage *Amma* found. Had she agreed to an adoption, or was she really going to come back some day like she said?

But it didn't matter for me anymore.

With the yard empty and everyone in class, I slipped away to the main road. I reached the bus stop just in time, climbing aboard the public bus without looking back.

CHAPTER 27

I stepped off the bus and into the chaos of a bustling market alleyway near the hospital. Motorcycles and cars forced themselves into the narrow passage, honking incessantly as they crept forward, people slapping their hoods and shouting at the drivers to turn around. Vendors crowded the sides, selling everything from snacks to cheap plastic toys. The air was thick with the competing smells of frying oil, incense, and sewage.

The area around the hospital seemed safer than anywhere else I could think of. There were many homeless people in this area—I remembered seeing their encampments when I came to visit Sudhir. I could learn from them how to survive.

It wouldn't take long before my absence was noticed at school, and Karunai House would be alerted.

Passing a booth selling shawls, I unzipped my bag and grabbed some *rupees* from Mahiyu's clipboard to buy a black shawl. I wrapped the shawl around my head, imitating the Muslim women I'd seen in the market when I was younger.

The money I have won't last long; I should have just stolen the shawl. I need to save the rupees *for things I can't easily steal.*

I felt like I was losing a part of myself—the thought of stealing came so quickly to my mind, and I didn't even feel shame over it. It didn't matter. Not anymore. Nothing mattered.

Or so I tried to tell myself.

I sat on the stairs outside a clothing shop, trying to think of what to do next, but my thoughts kept drifting back to everything I had left behind—all the people I loved.

The way I had yelled at Sudhir to leave me alone, when all he did was care…was that how he'd remember me? Tears spilled down my face. I tried to comfort myself with the thought that maybe I could come back someday, but shame pressed down like the black shawl over my head. I didn't know if I'd ever be able to show my face at Karunai House again.

Pull yourself together, Kashvi. You're on your own now. You need to take care of yourself.

I wiped away my tears, pushed myself to my feet, and walked into the first alleyway I found that wasn't crowded with people. Scooters and motorcycles zoomed past, loaded with crates, bags of vegetables, and stacks of inventory tied in precarious ways. A man on a scooter sped through a crossing alley, a mountain of burlap sacks somehow strapped to the back, and I leapt out of the way just in time.

I wandered, trying to familiarize myself with the streets and alleys. The city was a maze of sights, sounds, and smells—people shouting, vendors calling out their wares, stray dogs barking, temple music blaring through speakers. I turned into a quieter lane. Pastel-colored walls of old buildings cracked and peeled around me.

A boy ran by, laughing as he chased a worn bicycle tire. From an open window, I heard an argument—a man's angry voice, followed by the crying of a girl. I wondered if her life was like mine and if it would ever change. I wouldn't be the one to help her. My dream of going to college and helping hurting children—was that over? I was going to miss my entrance exams for next year.

Never mind that now, I scolded myself. *None of that matters. No time for dreams when I have to survive.*

Children played cricket in the alleyway, using a battered plastic chair as a wicket. A mother passed by, balancing her toddler on her arm and a bucket of vegetables on her head. A man pulled a cycle cart loaded with metal scraps. It felt strange to watch the world go on around me, unchanged, while everything in my life had fallen apart.

Coming out to a larger road, I found the sidewalk was crowded with makeshift stalls—people selling trinkets from blankets spread on the ground—between which were the beggars and drunks.

A woman with a gaping hole where her eye should have been rattled a tin can at me. I stopped in front of her and shuffled through my bag, grabbing a *rupee* from the clipboard. I dropped a *rupee* in her can, thinking to ask her of a safe place to stay, but I was interrupted by a crippled man who was rolling himself over from his back to his belly, over and over until he made it right up to us with pleading eyes. He must have found that the fastest way to move. I dug out another *rupee* and handed it to him so he would leave us.

Before I had the chance to ask the woman a question, I was swarmed by beggars, their hands outstretched, voices pleading.

A haggard man stepped up close to me, mumbling the word "please!" His breath smelled like Father's.

My heart raced and my vision blurred. I fled down the street before another flashback would incapacitate me. I finally slowed at a market square to catch my breath.

I can't do this! I screamed internally. *Soon my rupees will be gone, and I'll be just like them, begging…hopeless.*

My mind flashed back to Karunai House—to *Amma*, to the warmth and safety I had left behind.

Amma must have reported me missing by now. Shame washed over me.

I couldn't go back. *I'm not going back home to marry Vishnu, and I'm not going to reject the marriage and put everyone I love in danger.*

Looking around, I felt completely lost. I had no plan now. I was at the end of the road already.

What am I going to do? What can I do?

I thought of praying, but my soul felt so far from God that I couldn't even lift up my eyes. He wouldn't listen to me anymore, not after what I'd done.

Old carts lined the square, selling all sorts of goods. A garden cart carrying bottles of pesticides and fertilizers caught my eye. I stopped, staring at a bottle with a skull-and-crossbones symbol on the label.

My heart pounded as I thought about how I could really escape everything, and a cold sweat broke over me.

What hope is there left? I can't do this. I can't live on the streets, and I can't go back.

I set my backpack on the ground to count the *rupees* from the clipboard. My hand brushed my Bible, and guilt enveloped me. I looked back at the bottle on the cart and into my backpack again, grabbing the stack of *rupees*, then collapsed on the ground, tears streaming down my face.

"God, I just want to be done," I whimpered.

"Kashvi! Kashvi!" I heard my name, faintly cutting through the noise of the market.

Opening my eyes, I scanned the bustling square, vision blurred with tears.

I didn't hear my name anymore.

Am I hearing things? Has my mind broken completely? Am I going insane?

I looked at the poison bottle again.

Then, past the bottle, I saw him—Mahiyu, running towards me with an exaggerated limp, his face alight with relief.

"*Thangachi*, I found you!" he yelled, breathing heavily. "What are you doing out here?"

"*Anna*, I—" A mess of guilt and shame tangled in my throat as I dropped the *rupees* to the ground. I stared at the bottle on the garden cart, trembling.

"Oops!" Mahiyu gathered up the *rupees* and handed them back to me with innocent curiosity. "Did you want to buy some seeds, grow something new? We could ask *Amma*, you know."

His childlike sincerity broke me. I stared at my *anna* who stood before me, so full of joy and wonder. He wouldn't understand why I would run away—why anyone would run away from his wonderful home.

He made me wonder why I had run, too.

"How did you recognize me?" I pulled the black shawl from my head.

Mahiyu laughed. "That black thing can't hide you from me. You're my *thangachi*. I know you—the way you walk, the way your mouth moves when you talk, the way your face looks when you're scared or sad." He looked at me with concern. "Why are you hiding anyway?"

I swallowed hard, trying to form an answer. "I didn't know what to do, *Anna*. I've messed everything up, and I feel like God is angry at me. I think he's punishing me for not trusting him, and he's left me alone."

Mahiyu shook his head, stepping closer.

"*Thangachi*, Jesus isn't like that. He never leaves us alone. He loves us, no matter what."

His words warmed me, melting away some of the numbness. How simple his faith was.

"Why is it so hard to trust that sometimes?"

He shrugged, his eyes bright and genuine. "Because we're silly and we look at the wrong things."

The words sunk in. What had I been looking at? My fears, my pain, my hope in Ravi, my desire to take control of my life—they had become idols I fed until they grew bigger than God himself. My fears had paralyzed me as I obsessed over the pain of my past, basking in anger at my father instead of looking to Jesus.

I thought of my mother trying to appease every god, and I realized I hadn't really moved past my idolatry—I just had new idols. Tears filled my eyes again.

"How do you make yourself look at Jesus, *Anna*?" I asked, voice trembling.

Mahiyu paused, deep in thought, then smiled. "Jesus tells me to keep my eyes on him, so that's what I do," he said matter-of-factly. "I know he loves me with an everlasting love, because it says so in my

Bible, on page 627, Jeremiah 31:3." His smile widened. "He proved it by dying for me. That's how I know he'll make everything okay."

I couldn't help but smile, even through the tears. Mahiyu's confidence, his unwavering trust, was what I needed. Keeping my eyes on Jesus wasn't just an option that I could consider while weighing the costs and benefits. Obeying him was the only way. He was my Lord, and no one else. Following him meant going to the cross with him, crucifying my own desires.

"I've been trying to figure out my own life, my own way," I admitted. "I don't want to do that anymore."

Mahiyu nodded at me, oblivious to the turmoil of my day.

"How did you get here, anyway?" I asked.

"*Appa* and *Amma* brought me and the older boys to look for you. They said you never went to school, and *Amma* was worried." Mahiyu pulled a piece of paper from his pocket with a printed picture of me on it. "They found your things, but *Amma* said she was sure you had run away. She figured out the bus schedule and found the bus driver that would have driven by school, and he said you got off downtown."

"She tracked me down just like she did you when your uncle took you away." I smiled. "*Amma* would be a good detective, wouldn't she?"

"She would look funny in a police uniform!" Mahiyu laughed. Then he paused, looking around. "I was with Ravi, but I lost him when I saw you. I was so excited!"

Shame burned within me as I thought of what I had put everyone through.

"I sinned big, *Anna*. Do you think they'll let me come back?"

Mahiyu let out a loud, bewildered laugh. "Of course! You can always come home." He bounced on his feet, excitement bubbling up. "When we get back, I'll make you tea. It always makes you feel better."

I laughed, too, his words easing my fears.

I grabbed his clipboard from my bag nervously and clipped the loose *rupees* to it before handing it to him.

Mahiyu's eyes widened. "You found my clipboard!"

"It's…uh…missing some *rupees*." Shame curled in my stomach.

He blinked, processing my words. Understanding dawned his face, and with a soft smile, he said, "It's okay, Kashvi. I forgive you."

The lump in my throat grew, and I just nodded, unable to speak.

We stood up, and Mahiyu led me to where the *Qualis* was parked. Nervousness still lingered.

Would everyone be so forgiving as Mahiyu?

Noticing Mahiyu's limp again, I asked him about it.

"Oh, I'm okay. I twisted my ankle in my excitement to get you, but it was worth it."

CHAPTER 28

"Dhiren is waiting at the *Qualis*, and everyone is supposed to meet back there," Mahiyu explained, excited. "We're almost there now. Just two blocks, left turn, two blocks, right turn, one block."

I marveled at his memory and sense of direction, something I wished I had right now. How did he always manage to know exactly where he was?

Mahiyu gasped and limped ahead more quickly. His eyes seemed to catch something far down the alleyway. "Ameer! Sudhir!"

My heart skipped a beat, remembering my last words to my *thambi*. Mahiyu continued shouting, leaving confused faces and muttered scoffs in his wake. Finally, I spotted Sudhir—almost a block away, lost in the moving sea of people.

A sob broke out from my chest. Even from a distance, I could see Sudhir's flushed face and puffy eyes. He looked so hopeless, so devastated.

What have I done to him? How could I have just left him alone?

"*Akka, Akka!*" His call pierced the noise around us as he ran towards me. His strong arms wrapped around me, and I clung to him as we both cried, our bodies shaking.

"I'm sorry. I'm so sorry," I whispered between sobs.

Sudhir shoved me back suddenly, his eyes irritated. "Don't you ever do that again!" Then, just as quickly, he pulled me back into his arms.

"I just…didn't know what to do. Didn't know who to make suffer," I mumbled into his shoulder. "I couldn't deal with it."

"You made us *all* suffer this way." He pulled away again, holding me at arm's length so he could look at my face. "You don't have to do this alone, Kashvi. She's my *amma*, too. You're my *akka*. Let me help you."

I stared at the ground. "I'm too weak to trust Jesus, Sudhir. Why can't I trust him?"

Sudhir's eyes softened as he spoke. "You're weak, Kashvi. That's the whole point. You need to look to Jesus for the strength to trust him. And when you can't, that's what our family is for—to help each other come to Jesus when we can't do it on our own."

His eyes glistened, and for the first time, I saw my *thambi* not as a boy, but as a young man—a man of God. He was stronger than I ever gave him credit for. Gratitude welled up in my heart, and I silently thanked God for this *thambi* who wasn't just a better man than Father, but who was a *good* man.

Ameer and Mahiyu approached, joining the moment. "We need to find Dhiren." Mahiyu said.

Together, we followed Mahiyu through the twists and turns of the city until the familiar *Qualis* came into view with the towering, strong Dhiren leaning on the hood in prayer.

"Dhiren! Dhiren! We found her!" Mahiyu's joy was infectious.

Dhiren opened his eyes, his face breaking into a wide, joyful grin. "Thank you, Jesus!" he shouted before wrapping me in a massive hug.

I felt small in his arms, but safe. After a brief embrace, he pulled away, glowing with joy. "You all stay here in case anyone comes back. I'll drive around to find *Appa* and *Amma*."

Everyone's joy nearly made me forget my shame, but as we waited, I thought of seeing *Amma* and *Appa*, a deep apprehension settling in my stomach. Had they reported me missing to the government? What would happen then?

My heart clenched as I thought of the shame I carried for not trusting *Amma* and *Appa*, who had always done what was right, who had always tried to show me the same path. I put hope and trust in all the wrong places, and it had created a huge mess.

When Dhiren pulled up a while later, *Appa* and *Amma* trailed him on *Appa's* motorcycle. The joy and relief on their faces melted my fear into a deep sense of unworthiness. Despite everything I had put them through, they were elated to see me.

Amma leapt off the motorcycle and wept as she held me. "My dear, my child," she murmured between whispers of thankful prayers. Her tears soaked into my shoulder, and I could feel her heart pounding.

I felt *Appa's* steady hand rest on my shoulder. Surrounded by all this love, by these people who had risked so much for me, I broke down, unable to hold back the sobs that wracked my body.

"I'm so sorry," I wailed, wanting desperately to make amends. "I ran away, I stole…I…I'll make it up. I'll do anything—"

"We love you, Kashvi," *Amma* said softly, her voice breaking through my guilt. "You don't have to make anything up. You're here, and that's enough."

"I love you, *Amma*," I sobbed, the words escaping between shaky breaths. "Thank you for everything."

"Thank Jesus," *Appa* smiled. "He loves you more; remember that."

The weight of it all came crashing down on me, and I gasped for breath, my cries overwhelming me. Everything—the fear, the guilt, the shame—poured out of me as *Amma* held me tightly.

Appa turned to Dhiren. "We'll take Kashvi back to Karunai House and make some phone calls," *Appa* said. "You boys start gathering everyone back. And…" He leaned in to whisper something to Dhiren, handing him a small wad of *rupees*.

A pang of guilt stabbed at my heart as I remembered the money I'd stolen…and what I had almost used it for. But *Appa* turned back to me, his smile warm, overflowing with love and kindness. It calmed me, reminding me I was safe.

As the boys debated whether to start searching for everyone else or just wait for the rendezvous time, I climbed onto the back of *Appa's* motorcycle, clinging to *Amma*, who sat between us. The wind whipped against my face as we rode, the world rushing past in a blur. I laid my head against *Amma's* back, letting her peace wash over me.

I knew there would be much to confess, but I spent the ride home thankful that I no longer had to run or hide from anything. Whatever happened next, I would follow Jesus' way, and I had the best people by my side to help me do it.

When we approached the gate at Karunai House, *Appa* sounded his horn, and Nalayani opened the gate, her eyes swollen from crying. Her sadness shifted to joy as she realized it was me.

Nearly pulling me off the motorcycle, she hugged me tightly.

"You're okay, Kashvi! We were so worried about you." Her tears resumed. "I'm so glad you're back here."

"I'm so, so sorry," I said, my eyes cast downward. "I've made such a mess."

Amma cleared her throat gently. "Nalayani, why don't you go let the younger children know that Kashvi is back and that she's safe? We need to speak with her privately for a moment."

My heart pounded as *Amma* took my hand, guiding me towards her office with *Appa* following. Fear curled inside me, but I knew I had to face them. How could I even begin to make up for everything I had done today? I thought of all the chores, the cooking, cleaning, and bookkeeping—anything I could promise to do to make things right again.

Once inside the office, *Amma* rubbed my arm, her silence patient and gentle.

Finally, I found my voice. "My *appa* told me to marry Vishnu next week," I confessed. "He wants me to marry before he dies. It felt like no matter what I chose, someone I love would have to suffer. I wanted to protect my *amma*, to protect Karunai House, but I can't marry Vishnu, because he's not a Christian! I just wanted to escape it all."

My voice broke as I remembered the pesticide bottle and how close I had been to trying to escape everything for good.

Appa and *Amma* simply listened, their eyes filled with compassion. *Amma*'s hand resting on my arm provided a steady comfort.

I continued, my voice barely above a whisper. "I took the *rupees* from Mahiyu's clipboard—"

"We know," *Amma* said softly.

"You know?"

"I knew something was wrong this morning," *Amma* explained. "When you hugged me and said, 'I love you,' I could tell. Then Mahiyu mentioned the missing clipboard, and when the school called to say you hadn't arrived, I put the pieces together."

"You're not…angry?" I asked, my voice cracking.

Amma sniffed, her eyes brimming with tears. "Right now, I'm thanking God," she said. "Thanking him that you're safe and that you're here, confessing everything. That means more than anything you may have done."

"I bought a black shawl to hide, and I…" I thought of telling them what else I'd almost bought, but my shame held it back. "I'll make it up."

Amma cupped my face in her hands. "We forgive you, Kashvi. The money means nothing compared to having you back."

"Will you get in trouble?" I asked. "Because I ran away?"

Amma smiled. "They haven't shut us down after all these years. And they won't—unless that is God's will. I had to report you missing to the police and child welfare office as soon as the school called me. So there may be an investigation."

"What should I say?" I asked, my voice trembling.

Appa opened his Bible, paging through it, then he began to read, his voice steady: "We have made lies our refuge, and under falsehood have we hid ourselves: Therefore thus saith the Lord God, Behold, I lay in Zion for a foundation a stone, a tried stone, a precious corner stone, a sure foundation: he that believeth shall not make haste. Judgment also will I lay to the line, and righteousness to the plummet: and the hail shall sweep away the refuge of lies, and the waters shall overflow the hiding place. Isaiah 28."

He looked at me, his eyes piercing but kind. "Would you like to keep hiding under lies, Kashvi? Have they been a good shelter in the storms of your life?"

Amma added gently, "That cornerstone, that sure foundation, is Jesus. He is the way, the truth, and the life. We speak truth because God is truth, and in him, there is no darkness. When we run to the truth for refuge, we will never be disappointed."

I nodded, tears spilling down my cheeks again as I considered their words. Like Mahiyu said, we were often silly and looked at the wrong things. I didn't want to hide but live in the truth.

"Oh, I should call the hospital!" *Amma* exclaimed, picking up the phone to dial. "How could I forget about your *amma?*"

Mother... How did she *react to my disappearance? What did Father think?*

I couldn't worry about that anymore. I knew I had to let go of the fear and leave it with God.

No one answered in Father's hospital room, so *Amma* left a message for the receptionist to pass on, saying I had been found and for Mother to call back or come visit as soon as possible. *Amma* then moved on to call the police and child welfare officials.

I turned to *Appa.*

"*Appa,* how do I know that I'm truly a Christian?"

Appa's eyes softened as he looked at me. "Do you love Jesus and believe he paid for all your sins?"

"Yes."

"Do you hate your sin?"

"Yes."

"Then why are you doubting?"

Tears welled up in my eyes. "I can never seem to trust him enough. I ran away, I stole..."

"But you desire to serve and obey Jesus as your Lord?"

"I want to, but look at what I did today!"

Appa placed his hand on my shoulder, steady and firm. "Jesus paid for all sins, not just the 'little' ones."

"What about suicide?" I choked out, tears spilling over. "Could a Christian ever think about that?"

His eyes filled with tenderness. "Kashvi, someone who isn't a Christian wouldn't cry over her sins."

I broke down, my sobs echoing through the room.

Amma hung up the phone and rushed over, wrapping me in her arms.

"When Mahiyu found me," I cried, the words tumbling out in a confession, "I was counting out the *rupees* to buy pesticide."

Through *Amma's* eyes, I watched pain, fear, compassion, and gratitude mingling, and my heart sank, knowing how much I had added to the weight she bore night and day. She wiped my tears with her shawl— just like she had the first night I arrived at Karunai House, abandoned and scared. Back then, I had pushed her away. Today, I thanked God for leading me to the tenderest, most loving warden that ever lived.

Appa's voice broke through our crying. "Elijah and Jonah both asked God to take their lives. Job and Jeremiah wished they had never been born in their times of despair. Your concern about being a true Christian, your tears, and your confession—they all show the Spirit's work in you."

Amma nodded. "God's love is truly amazing, Kashvi. Sometimes it's hard to believe that he could love us, especially when we feel so unworthy. But there is no sin too great that he won't forgive when his children believe on him in faith."

Appa continued in a reassuring voice. "In Hosea, God says, 'I am God and not man.' Do you know what he uses as an example to show how different he is from us?"

I shook my head. "No."

"It wasn't his power or might, like we may imagine. It was that he wouldn't execute his anger on his people. We hold grudges, we get angry—but God isn't like us. Though we fail him time and again, he never forsakes us."

I burst into tears again, and *Amma* held me tight. All my life, before Karunai House, all I knew was my father's anger and punishment. Here,

I'd experienced what God was like. *Appa's* tender guidance, *Amma's* warm embrace; their free-flowing forgiveness gave me a little taste of God's attitude towards me. I had doubted whether *Appa* and *Amma* would accept me after what I'd done today, and I had doubted God the same way.

"What do I do from here?" I whispered, overwhelmed.

Amma looked upward thoughtfully. "Trust him. Give him your heart; ask him for the strength," she began. "Practically, concerning the marriage, we've talked about this before. I know it's incredibly hard, but you need to do what is right. When you do what is right, the consequences are in God's hands, not yours. And he is always good."

"It doesn't feel that way," I said.

Amma squeezed my hand. "I know, my dear."

I looked up at her. "How did you do it? How did you face your parents?"

"On my knees," *Amma* said softly. "That's where trust begins and ends—in prayer, asking for forgiveness, for strength, for everything."

"I think I need to spend some time with God now," I said, my heart longing for closeness with him again, needing to confess and to seek his love and forgiveness.

"Take all the time you need, my dear," *Amma* said. "When you're ready, come back to the common room. Everyone will be eager to see you."

I walked up to my room, closing the door behind me, and fell to my knees beside my bed.

I had asked *Appa* and *Amma* to forgive me, but I hadn't asked God. I had only asked him to make everything better, to take away the pain. Where would I even start?

Father, forgive me for not trusting you, for putting my hope in many others. I lied, I stole, and I nearly ended my life because I couldn't see any way out. I don't deserve your love, but you have shown it to me. You saved me—my body and my soul. Help me to stand up to my father. Help me to do what is right and to trust you with whatever comes. Give me the same trust and courage you gave Amma. Help me to live in obedience to you alone, keeping my eyes fixed on you.

A peace unlike anything I had ever felt encompassed me as tears ran down my face. I remembered the words of the Heidelberg Catechism that *Appa* had taught me.

I, with body and soul, both in life and death, am not my own, but belong unto my faithful Savior Jesus Christ.

My future wasn't in my father's, uncle's, or the government's hands. It rested securely in the loving hands of my heavenly Father.

I kept praying as I made my way up to the roof. The air was crisp, and the sky stretched endlessly above me. I thought of everything God had done for me, of all the ways he had carried me. The stars sparkled against the velvet sky, and I felt so small, so humbled.

He calls every star by name, yet he cares for me—a little Dalit *girl from a tiny village.*

A surge of gratitude overwhelmed me as I looked up at the heavens.

Just then, the quiet night filled with the roars of engines and honking, and I looked over the edge of the roof to see a stream of cars and motorcycles pulling into Karunai House. The *Qualis* pulled into the courtyard with Mahiyu hanging out of the window.

"She's up there," Mahiyu shouted, pointing up at me and waving with a huge smile.

The courtyard filled with the joyful shouts of my family as they poured out of the SUV. I smiled and ran down to meet them.

Dozens of motorcycles pulled in, carrying church members and the rest of the boys who couldn't fit in the *Qualis.*

I watched Ravi slide out of the *Qualis.* Our eyes met, and I saw shame cloud his expression. I wasn't sure how to feel or how to react. I felt embarrassed for asking him to run away with me. How would our relationship change on campus now?

After a moment, he broke eye contact and turned towards the boys' dorm, leaving me feeling hollow.

The other boys crowded around me, giving me hugs and peppering me with questions. Time seemed to slow down as I stood there, surrounded by joy and love. I took in each of their smiling faces, thinking of all the wonderful memories I had with them.

How could I have even considered leaving this family?

The church members gathered around, waiting their turn to welcome me back. I noticed Dhiren and Mahiyu at the back of the *Qualis*, fiddling with something. They heaved down a giant pot of *biryani*. A couple of men from the church rushed over to help carry the enormous pot over to the kitchen patio. Ameer scrambled into the back and emerged with a cake. He beamed at me, holding the cake up proudly before running it to the kitchen.

My favorite meal and a cake—they were planning on serving everyone. I felt so unworthy. This was grace. I didn't deserve any of this. I deserved the opposite.

Appa gathered everyone over by the kitchen and opened in thanksgiving and praise to God for bringing me home, then everyone went up for the *biryani* served by Nalayani, Mahiyu, and Dhiren.

Appa, *Amma*, and Sudhir sat by me as we devoured the delicious food. Mahiyu walked over by us with a heaping plate when he was done serving and started eating before he even sat down.

Between furious bites of *biryani*, Mahiyu announced loudly, "*Thangachi*, I'll remember this date as the day you were lost and found!"

I smiled. "I'm sure you will, *Anna*."

He nodded eagerly, swallowing his food. "The day you came to us was May 21st, one day before your birthday. I served you tea in the upstairs living room. You looked so scared."

"I was." I smiled softly at the memory. I had been so terrified then; I couldn't possibly have imagined the care I would get here.

"Your hair was tangled and full of lice, so *Amma* shaved it off," he added straightforwardly.

I winced at that less-than-fond memory.

"And your clothes were dirty, so Sarina gave you one of her dresses and cleaned you up," Mahiyu continued. He paused for a moment, his smile fading a moment as he looked deep in thought, surely thinking of Sarina.

Mahiyu went on, his face lighting up again. "You were so skinny. I remember how quickly you ate that night."

I laughed. "Did I eat faster than you?"

He shook his head, his eyes wide with mock seriousness. "No, no one eats faster than me. That's my talent." He shoved a handful of food into his mouth to prove it.

We all laughed, the joy washing over us. And for a while, I forgot about everything else—the doubts, the fears, the burdens. As I served cake to everyone, I felt a lightness in my heart that I hadn't felt in a long time. The love and laughter surrounding me in that moment melted away my fear.

After the church members left for the night, I sat with *Amma* and *Appa* on the steps of the Common Hall, feeling the coolness of the stone beneath me.

Sudhir walked up and sat beside me, resting his head on my arm, like he used to do with our mother. "I'm glad you're back, *Akka*. I would have been lost without you."

I swallowed, trying to find words.

"And I'm glad you came back because we got cake," he added with a glint in his eye.

I swatted at him playfully, and we shared a familiar smile.

Amma chuckled but then frowned, as if remembering something. "I'm surprised your *amma* hasn't called back. I'll have to try calling the hospital again after devotions."

"What happened when you told my *amma* I was gone?" I asked hesitantly.

Amma sighed. "Before we began the search, *Appa* and I went to the hospital to see her. She was devastated, weeping. She kept blaming herself."

My chest tightened, picturing my mother—alone, guilt-ridden.

Amma continued, "She went in to tell your *appa*, and he asked to speak to *Appa* alone. *Appa* was bracing for the worst, expecting anger, blame—but instead, your *appa* asked who Jesus really was."

"What?" I blinked, taken aback.

"*Appa* shared the gospel with him—how we are all sinners, worthy of death, and that Jesus Christ is our only hope of salvation."

My heart pounded. Was she about to say my father believed? I wasn't sure I wanted to know the answer. I didn't want my father to believe; I wanted him to experience God's wrath for what he did to us.

"What..." I asked, my voice barely audible, "what did he say?"

"He said nothing. He just stared ahead, deep in thought. *Appa* prayed for him and left."

I let out a breath I hadn't realized I'd been holding, relieved.

"I'm not trying to give you hope, Kashvi," *Amma* said quietly. "I just thought you should know. He was willing to hear, and now it's in God's hands."

Hope? It wasn't hope to my ears. I didn't want to spend eternity with my father. How could heaven be perfect if he was there?

I remembered Jesus' words—if we do not forgive others, God will not forgive us. A lump formed in my throat. The injustice of it gnawed at me. "How would I ever forgive him?"

"Holding onto hatred and bitterness is just another false refuge, like we talked about earlier." *Amma* spoke gently. "It can't protect you—it only hurts you. True healing comes in Jesus, under his shelter and in his way."

I nodded, though the thought still seemed impossible. *How could I not hate him?*

Dhiren's voice shouted out from across the courtyard urgently. "*Amma!* Have you seen Ravi?"

Hearing his name, I shivered. I had forgotten Ravi amidst everything, and I hadn't seen him since he arrived.

Amma frowned, shouting back. "No, I haven't."

Dhiren jogged up, worry etched on his face. "None of the boys have seen him since we got back. I just checked every room in the dorm, and he's not there. I checked our room and...his clothes are gone, too."

The faint ring of the office phone interrupted us. We all rushed to the office, hoping for news about Ravi.

Amma snatched the receiver, her knuckles white around it. "Hello, this is Karunai House, Vasantha speaking."

Her face stiffened. I could hear the faint, trembling voice on the other end—familiar.

Amma turned towards me, her expression a mix of sorrow and compassion. She held the phone out to me. "It's your *amma*. Your *appa*... he's gone."

CHAPTER 29

I watched as Sudhir finished wrapping a white cloth around Father's corpse, which was laid out on a bamboo bier in front of our house. He spread bright orange and red marigolds over the body and sprinkled sandalwood oil onto Father's head, the fragrances mingling together with the smell of death.

Sudhir stood, his face solemn, and walked over to me. He wore a white button-up and a white *lungi* wrapped around his waist. The harsh sunlight reflected off his freshly shaven head, a traditional mark of the eldest son mourning his father's death. He looked more like a man today than ever before. The scars over his bald head were a testimony to God's miraculous act of saving his life.

Our house seemed smaller than I remembered. Everything seemed smaller. The little Kali idol inside was just a tiny hunk of metal, the cursed tree behind the house was just a tree now. My father, my *caste*, my fate—all of them had once loomed over me, but they were nothing now.

Dhiren stood behind us, yawning. None of us had slept all night. While Sudhir and I made funeral arrangements with Mother, Dhiren had organized a search party for Ravi, looking for him well into the early hours. A pang of guilt twisted inside me. Ravi had left in shame—perhaps from feeling responsible for my running away, perhaps from rejecting me over my *caste*—whatever the reason, he was gone.

Villagers began arriving, gathering in a circle around the body. My heart dropped when I saw Vishnu approach and stand beside Sudhir. Chills ran down my spine.

He still thinks we're getting married.

I felt guilt sting deep within me. Vishnu wasn't to blame for any of this, yet soon he'd carry the heavy burden of rejection—a shame too great for many to bear—simply because I had lacked the courage to stand up to Father.

Heavenly Father, help me to trust in you. Help me to trust that you will work all these things for good.

Father's death meant the marriage would be postponed for at least a year, but that didn't change the fact that I was still engaged. I knew I had to break it off soon, but it wasn't appropriate today. I wished I could just get it over with.

My uncle and Vishnu stood together, with my aunt standing in their shadows. Uncle was uncharacteristically silent, no smiles or light-hearted banter. With Father gone, Uncle was the one I had to worry about. He would be just as much of a threat as Father would ever have been when he learned the engagement was off.

Mother emerged from the house in a plain white sari, and all eyes turned to her. Her face crumpled as she fell to her knees, a guttural wail escaping her lips. She crawled towards Father's body, her cries growing louder, her grief raw and untethered. Sudhir moved to help her up, but she pushed him away.

When she reached the bier, she began beating the ground with her fists as if she could somehow bring Father back to life through the vibrations. My heart clenched as I watched her—was she shattered over the loss of a man who had treated her so cruelly, the same man she had sent us away from to protect?

I stepped forward with the other women, placing my hand gently on Mother's shoulder. The women around us burst into weeping, sharing in her grief. Tears rolled down my cheeks too, though I didn't cry with the same intensity.

Anger and sadness mixed with the relief in my heart. I couldn't believe he was really gone. I remembered *Amma* telling me of *Appa* sharing the gospel with him.

Could he have changed at the last moment? Like the thief on the cross?

The idea made me sick, but guilt pierced my heart. I tried to justify my feelings to myself like I always did. *It's right for me to want God's justice for Father.* But guilt for my thoughts remained.

Uncle stepped over to Sudhir, handing him an unlit torch and placing an arm around his shoulders. They walked together towards Father's body. Sudhir's eyes were wide, uncertain. Uncle took out a matchbox, struck a match, and lit the torch, guiding Sudhir through the ritual.

Uncle began chanting a mantra.

"We meditate on the divine light of the Supreme Being, the Creator of the earth, the atmosphere, and the heavens. May that divine light inspire and illuminate our intellects."

The first recitation was quiet, with only a few joining in. By the second time, more voices chimed in, filling the air with the familiar rhythm. Sudhir held his lips tight. Uncle noticed, frowned, and gestured at Sudhir to join in. Sudhir hesitated, glancing nervously at the onlookers, and began mouthing the words softly.

I wondered if chanting this was wrong if Sudhir was speaking from his heart about the true and living God—or was I making justifications like I had for myself at the temple so long ago? I prayed God would forgive Sudhir if it was a sin.

Uncle nodded at Vishnu and another man from our village. They stepped forward to the back corners of the bier while Uncle and Sudhir took their places at the front. The wailing stilled for a moment. Together, the men and boys lifted the bier, and Uncle began a new chant.

"The name of Ram is the truth! Truth alone is the path to liberation!"

The other men echoed his words, their voices rising in unison. I strained to see whether Sudhir joined in as they began the slow procession towards the cremation site, but I couldn't tell. The lamenting cries of the women started again, piercing through the air.

All the men followed the bier, continuing the chant, but Dhiren stayed back by me. I began to follow, but Auntie grabbed my arm, her grip firm.

"Only men," she said. "You know that. It's a bad omen for women to be there."

I watched as the procession disappeared in the distance. Auntie joined the huddle of women surrounding Mother, all of them weeping, grieving, except for me. I stood beside Dhiren, feeling alone in the strange form of grief I experienced, wondering if there was something wrong with me.

Should I be grieving like them?

After a few moments, Mother got up and walked towards the house, picking up a cake of cow dung as she went. She used her hand to mix it with water in a pot and began flicking the mixture along the walls, the sacred act supposedly purifying the house from any lingering negative energy.

All I wanted was to be with Sudhir right now. He was the only one who could really understand the conflicting emotions tearing at me. I needed him.

I began to walk behind the house, catching Dhiren's questioning gaze.

"I'm going to the women's field," I said.

He nodded, looking down at the ground, kicking a stone, unsure of what to do with himself.

I walked down to the women's field, glancing over my shoulder to make sure no one was watching, then broke into a run behind the neighboring houses, following the procession path at a distance.

As I approached the cremation site, I hid behind a thick patch of bushes. Peering through the leaves, I saw the men set Father's body on the pedestal. They gathered wood, stacking it around the bier along with cow dung cakes, all while chanting, "The name of Ram is the truth! Truth alone is the path to liberation!"

I could see that Sudhir remained silent this time, his lips once again pressed tight, but no one else seemed to have noticed.

When the wood was finally set, Uncle motioned for Sudhir to circle the pyre. Holding the torch in one hand, Sudhir dipped his other hand in a clay pot Uncle was holding and sprinkled the water from the pot around the pyre.

Uncle finally noticed Sudhir's tight lips and shouted, "Why aren't you chanting?"

Sudhir's reply was too soft for me to hear.

"Ram is not truth?" Uncle bellowed, snatching the torch from Sudhir's hand. His voice rose with rage, "This is all your fault! Get away before you corrupt his next life, too!" Sudhir froze, wide-eyed, until Uncle thrust the torch towards him. "I said, get away!"

Sudhir turned and ran. I followed him along my parallel route behind the houses. Once we were out of view of the cremation site, I cut over and intercepted him.

"What are you doing here?" Sudhir gasped, breathless.

I wrapped my arms around him, tears streaming down my face. "I just wanted to be with you."

"I couldn't say 'Ram is truth,'" Sudhir rubbed his bald head, "so Uncle drove me away."

"I know. I saw it all from the bushes," I whispered. "I'm proud of you."

Sudhir looked at me, a mix of disbelief and relief in his eyes. "You were watching?"

"Yeah," I nodded.

"Well…what do we do now?" Sudhir wiped the sweat dripping from his brows. "What's Uncle going to do when he comes back?"

I grabbed Sudhir's arm and stopped. "I want to go back. I want to see it through to the end."

"But I was kicked out, and you're not supposed to be there in the first place."

"No one will know we're there," I said.

Sudhir nodded hesitantly, and we made our way back to the bushes near the cremation site.

Uncle held the torch, a bottle of liquor in his other hand. He took a swig, then handed it to Vishnu, who did the same.

So much for Vishnu not drinking, I thought. If God hadn't brought us to Karunai House, I'm sure I would have ended up in a marriage just like Mother's. Vishnu would have become just like Father. Sudhir… he'd have become just like Father, too.

When the bottle made its way back to Uncle, he put the liquor bottle to Father's mouth, then he poured the rest over the wood. Uncle touched Father's lips with the torch and the alcohol ignited instantly, flames dancing around Father's head, then spreading to the wood surrounding him until everything was engulfed. The liquor that wrecked Father's body from inside now helped to destroy his body from the outside, too.

This ritual was meant to bring purity and peace, but in those flames, I saw screaming and torment. That was his reality now—God's judgment.

Unless he changed, I considered bitterly before convincing myself it wasn't possible.

My thoughts shifted to Asha, to her body burning along with her parents in their home. She hadn't known Jesus either. Was she now in the same place as Father? My legs wobbled, a wave of dizziness hitting me as I sat abruptly, feeling bile rise in my throat.

There is none righteous, no, not one. The scripture echoed in my head.

Asha was no better in God's eyes than Father, I thought, just as bitterly. *How is this fair, God?*

Sudhir's quiet sniffle pulled me from my thoughts, and I turned to see tears sliding down his cheeks.

"Kashvi," he whispered, his voice quivering, "Is it wrong for me to feel…relieved that he's gone?"

I hugged him tight, tears streaming down my own face. "I don't know, Sudhir. I don't know how we're supposed to feel. But I'm relieved, too."

"God saw everything he did," Sudhir murmured. "He'll be judged, right?"

I prayed for this. I wanted him to die and be judged by God.
"Yes, he will…" I answered slowly. "God is just."

I wiped Sudhir's face gently as he sat down beside me. I drew a cross in the dirt with my finger.

But…what if Father did change? The possibility would not leave my mind.

"Sudhir, what if Father believed before he died?" I asked. "*Appa* shared the gospel with him, and we know God can change anyone. What if he's in heaven now? How would that make you feel?"

Sudhir stared at the ground for a long time.

"I don't know if I'd ever be able to forgive God for forgiving him!" I said, reaching for something—validation, or maybe truth.

Finally, Sudhir looked up and stared at me. "It feels unjust because we aren't looking at the cross. We don't think Jesus' sacrifice was big enough."

We sat silently for a while, thoughts about justice and forgiveness ruminating in our heads.

Finally, I laid my head on his shoulder. "I think for me, it feels unjust because I think I'm so much better than him…"

Though I stopped bowing to pagan idols, I was no different. I made an idol of myself. I was an idolator just like Father…like Asha…like everyone, rebelling against my creator with the body he gave to me. I wept, trying to see myself as God saw me, a worshipper of myself and my own desires. I ran away, stole, nearly ended my life, and I did all that despite knowing Jesus and his great sacrifice for me. My sins were worse than my father's, because I knew more deeply the one who I sinned against and what he requires of me.

Everyone deserves eternal flames…especially me.

Sudhir finished my thought. "The only difference is grace." He wiped his eyes and folded his hands in a silent prayer. I followed after him, asking God to forgive me for not understanding how great my sins were and for thinking I was somehow more worthy of grace than others.

Uncle began another chant that echoed through the clearing. "Lead me from falsehood to truth, from darkness to light, from death to immortality."

Immortality—they wouldn't want that if they knew what that eternity entailed.

I thought of Mother, still refusing to accept God as the only true God, as I stared at the flames consuming Father's body. I remembered the stories *Appa* had shared about William Carey, the missionary who fought to end Sati—the practice of burning widows alive on their husbands' pyres. That was the "light" Hinduism offered. If we had lived two hundred years earlier, Mother would be on that pyre with Father.

Heavenly Father, thank you for leading me from falsehood to truth, from darkness to light. Please lead my amma, too. And my uncle, Vishnu...everyone in my village. I had never wanted to pray that before.

Sudhir broke the silence. "How are you going to explain where you've been all this time?"

"I'll tell them the truth," I said, determined. Then my stomach sank. Dhiren. He probably thought I'd run away again. We had to get back.

We watched as Uncle and the others added more wood to the pyre, preparing to leave.

"Let's get back before they do." I stood.

Once no one was looking in our direction, we sprinted all the way home.

All the women had gathered in a circle around a fire outside our home, black smoke curling up from Father's clothes that Mother was burning. I scanned the crowd for Dhiren but didn't see him anywhere. The moment the women noticed Sudhir and me, every head turned towards us.

Mother shuffled up, her face puzzled. "Sudhir, where are the other men?"

"They're still at the pyre," Sudhir replied, uneasily.

Mother frowned, confused. "Then why aren't you..." She trailed off, her gaze shifting past us to the approaching figures. The men were returning.

Mother turned her focus to me, her face hardening. "And where have you been?"

"With Sudhir," I admitted.

"Kashvi!" she gasped. "It is forbidden for women to be there."

Her voice drew the attention of the other women, who surrounded us, murmuring questions, voices overlapping in a flurry of confusion.

Uncle stepped forward, the rest of the men trailing behind. "What is going on here?"

"Kashvi says she was at the cremation site," Auntie blurted.

"What?!" Uncle demanded, his eyes locked on mine.

"I was behind the bushes," I said. "I just wanted to see it myself."

Uncle's eyes narrowed, fury twisting his features. "A woman there!" His eyes shot to Sudhir. "And a son who refuses to bless his *appa*'s soul into the next life!"

I glanced around for Dhiren, praying he'd intervene. Where was he? *He's probably searching for me.*

Uncle stomped up to Sudhir and me. "You're the reason my brother died!" Spittle spewed from his mouth. "You brought this curse of the gods!"

"Fake gods can't curse anyone," I shot back, meeting his gaze with the same defiance I had once showed my father—the same defiance that had earned me the scar on my forehead.

A collective gasp rippled through the crowd.

Smack!

My head snapped to the side as Uncle's hand connected with my cheek. My skin stung, and the shock froze me in place.

Sudhir leapt between us.

Stepping back, I groaned at myself for letting my anger control me. This wasn't the way to show what following Christ was about. Nothing Uncle did could change who I was in Christ. I swallowed the anger that had been bubbling inside me. If God hadn't led me to Karunai House, I would be just like him—believing the same lies, worshipping the same idols.

"We're all under a curse, but it's a curse from the living God," I said, my voice timid. "Jesus is the only way to be free from it."

"Blasphemy!" Uncle shouted. "And you expect to marry my son?"

He said it as if it were a threat, but I took it as sign from God that this was the proper time to end the engagement, despite the circumstances.

"No," I said, and with that one word, a boulder of weight fell off my back and I felt an incredible peace.

I glanced at Vishnu, who stood just behind Uncle, confusion swarming his face. He must have been sure he misheard me. I felt sorry for him—he didn't know the truth like Sudhir and I did. And I had never told him.

"I agreed to the engagement because I was a coward, scared of my *appa*," I said, answering the confused faces and drooping jaws all staring at me. "But I'll only marry someone who loves Jesus. I'm sorry for agreeing to it. I'm sorry for deceiving you."

Uncle's lips pulled back in a snarl, veins standing out on his forehead. "You liar!" He lunged at me, but Sudhir pushed him back.

"You cursed little demon!" Uncle roared, wrestling with Sudhir. Uncle easily threw him to the ground and jumped over his body after me.

I took off running, Uncle's footsteps pounded behind me. I didn't make it far before a shove sent me sprawling across the gravel, scraping my knees and hands.

Uncle loomed above me, his face twisted in rage. "You Christians think you're better than us," he hissed. "You want to destroy our traditions, our way of life."

"It's not about being better; I'm not better." I held my hands up, shielding myself as I looked up at him. "It's about what's true."

"The truth is you need to understand your place in society!" Uncle growled. "If you won't honor our gods, you're a traitor, wishing their curses upon us."

He meant to break me, to make me fear him. He wanted me to become like Mother—accepting everything as a part of my *karma*.

"I won't worship a false god," I declared.

"Then leave!" Uncle shouted, kicking up gravel at me. "Run!"

I stumbled to my feet and headed towards the house, watching Uncle over my shoulder

"I said leave!" He grabbed a stone and threw it at me. I flinched as it struck my back. He threw another, and it whizzed past my head.

Suddenly, Dhiren ran up from behind the house. He sprinted towards me just as I reached the crowd in front of the house, confusion etched across his face.

Sudhir was being held back by Vishnu and another man. Dhiren rushed towards them, and they let go as the towering figure approached.

"What's going on?" Dhiren demanded.

A stone bounced past his feet, and I turned to see Uncle, rage contorting his features. "Chase those curse-bringing blasphemers away!" he yelled. "They brought this death, and they will bring death to us all!"

Shouts erupted as the men scooped up stones. Fear clenched my chest and my legs froze.

Dhiren didn't hesitate. He seized Sudhir's wrist with one hand and mine with the other. "Run!"

We bolted towards the *Qualis*. Stones flew—one thudded into the dirt beside me, another cracked against the car ahead of us. A sharp pain burst across my scalp. I stumbled, dizzy, clutching the side of my head, but Dhiren yanked me forward.

Just as we reached the vehicle, a scream cut through the chaos—Mother!

I spun around, my heart seizing. Uncle stood over Mother, who lay on the ground curled up in a ball.

"She sent them to that Christian home! It's her fault, too!" Uncle raged, and he kicked Mother in the side. "Leave!"

Mother didn't move, her face crumpled in pain. I stood frozen in shock. Dhiren and Sudhir ran back for her, shielding their faces from the stones. They each took hold of an arm, lifted her up, and carried her back towards the *Qualis*, shielding her as stones and angry shouts pelted their backs.

I looked over the faces I had known all my life—uncles, aunts, cousins, neighbors—their eyes full of vengeance.

I opened the *Qualis* door as Dhiren and Sudhir staggered up with Mother. They pushed her in, then Sudhir and I clambered in after her, breathless, hearts pounding. Dhiren jumped in the driver's seat and twisted the key in the ignition, but the engine ground uselessly. Stones peppered the vehicle, shattering the rear window. We crouched on the floor behind the back seat as glass rained down.

"Come on, come on," Dhiren muttered, pounding on the steering wheel before turning the key again.

This time, the engine roared to life. Dhiren shouted a relieved, "Thank you, Jesus!" and slammed it into gear, speeding away from the volley of rocks.

I clung to Mother, both of us sobbing as the distance grew between us and our village. Every attachment to our old life was shattered like the glass around us.

Thank you, Father, I prayed, trembling. *It's over.*

Rejected from my home, there was only one place I would ever call home again, and I couldn't wait to get there.

EPILOGUE

With tears in his eyes, *Appa* dipped his hand into a bowl of water, then sprinkled it over my head.

"I baptize you in the name of the Father, and of the Son, and of the Holy Spirit."

As the water dripped down, I glanced around at the faces in the congregation. *Amma* sat in the front row, her eyes glistening, her smile possibly the biggest I'd ever seen it. Beside her sat my mother, tears filling her own eyes as well.

Mother had come a long way. A man from church helped her get a job at a shoe factory, and she lived at a Christian women's shelter. She came to church every week. Though she had stopped visiting temples, she still feared the superstitions of her past. Every day, I prayed that she would let go of that fear and truly bow the knee to Jesus. But I knew from experience how hard that was.

Mother sat in a chair at the front, and Sudhir sat on the floor beside her, his face serene. We had grown so close through everything that had happened, the bitterness of childhood bickering long gone. He was focused on his studies, determined to find a good IT job to help support our mother.

In a chair on *Amma*'s other side was Sarina, my best friend. We exchanged tearful smiles. Sarina had refused adoption for two years, telling the child welfare workers she already had a family at Karunai

House, though they insisted she would be better off in accepting adoption. The day she aged out of her orphanage, she showed up at the gate of Karunai House. Sarina now worked as a part-time staff member, handling the bookkeeping and helping with cooking when she wasn't busy with her college classes. We were her family, just as she was ours.

Six young foster girls sat on the ground around *Amma* and Sarina. By some miracle, a Christian judge began to mandate girls from traumatic backgrounds specifically to Karunai House, because she believed this was the only place they would find healing. These mandates bypassed other government agencies that had prevented us from taking in more girls in the past. God had answered our prayers—Karunai House was once again a refuge for hurting, forsaken girls.

In the back, I noticed Velu, sitting beside his former sorcerer uncle. He had grown into an energetic, outgoing boy—a far cry from the speechless child I had met him as.

Behind him, Mahiyu stood in the doorway, waiting to welcome anyone who came late. He was ever the servant-hearted caretaker; after all, he was the one who had found me when I most needed it. Beside him stood Dhiren, my protector and the one who always brightened my day.

I spotted Nalayani swaying with her newborn. She'd been waiting for this baby ever since losing her first so many years ago. *Appa* and *Amma* had arranged a marriage for her to young man who had aged out of Karunai House before my time.

In fact, all around me were the familiar faces of young men who had aged out of Karunai House. Many were now living independently, some married, some with children of their own.

When Nalayani moved off campus, I became the warden of the girls' dormitory. Now I was pursuing a degree in social work, hoping one day to open a foster home myself. I wanted to share my story, to give broken girls like me the same hope—the hope found only in Jesus Christ.

After *Appa* finished the prayer, I sat down next to Sarina. *Appa* preached on Jeremiah 29:11: "For I know the thoughts that I think toward you, saith the LORD, thoughts of peace, and not of evil, to give you an expected end."

As he spoke, I reflected on my life: the years of my father's abuse, the constant fear for my mother, the friends taken from me, the engagement to Vishnu—all the times I had questioned why God allowed me to suffer. I realized now that I had been asking the wrong question. I should have been asking why God allowed his own Son to suffer on the cross for me. He had worked every painful moment of my life together for my salvation.

After the service, I was surrounded by joyful friends and church members congratulating and encouraging me. Eventually, I made my way to the porch, where Mahiyu and Dhiren were serving lunch in celebration. Mahiyu handed me a plate of food, and I sat on the porch ledge, looking down at the street.

A familiar face caught my eye—Ravi, riding on the back of a motorcycle. I waved in disbelief, and he waved back before disappearing around a corner.

My heart raced. I hadn't seen Ravi since the day he had run away—the day *I* had run away. I wanted to ask for his forgiveness. I felt a burden of guilt for driving him away from Karunai House, the home that had become his family as much as it was mine.

Appa found Ravi one night, months ago, outside the church after Bible study when he was locking up. Ravi had gone back to living on the streets, drinking, but he wanted to return to us. *Appa* took him to a Christian rehab center and continued visiting with him regularly.

I tapped *Amma* on the shoulder as she walked by.

"I just saw Ravi."

Amma smiled. "*Appa* told him about your baptism. He got special leave from the rehab center to come here, accompanied of course. He wanted to be here."

"Really?" I asked. "He doesn't hate me?"

"No, child," *Amma* said.

"Then why did he leave so quickly?"

"I think he's still ashamed of running away and going back to drinking," *Amma* said. "It's hard to face others when you've sinned greatly, even when you know they will forgive you."

I'd told *Amma* about asking Ravi to run away with me and his hurtful response. She had reminded me how difficult it was to not think about *caste*, even for Christians. We talked about God's good plan for my life and the need to trust him as a faithful father.

I had hoped and prayed that Ravi would truly change and never go back to his old ways again. I wanted to ask forgiveness for sinfully pressuring him to run away with me. I missed his friendship, but I no longer thought of us marrying, even if he did change.

Ammachi shuffled over and took my hand, wishing God's blessings upon me with all the excitement her frail body could muster.

"Did I ever tell you how Jesus saved me?" her wise voice crackled.

She had told me many times, but it never grew old. Her passion never dimmed. *Appa* brought a chair over so *Ammachi* could sit, and I called my mother over so she could hear her story.

As *Ammachi* spoke with her familiar joy and conviction, I remembered God's words: *For my thoughts are not your thoughts, neither are your ways my ways.* I looked around at the smiling faces of my brothers and sisters that were gathered to listen. God's ways truly were higher than mine.

Varali, the first traumatized little girl to come to Karunai House after me, cuddled up beside me and wiped away a tear from my cheek.

"Why are you sad?" she asked, her little voice filled with concern.

"I'm not." I smiled. "These are tears of joy."

I lifted her onto my lap, remembering my early days at Karunai House—how I had wondered at *Amma's* tender care, how she had wiped away my tears. Now I saw clearly—it wasn't merely a motherly touch I had felt; it was the love of my Savior, reaching down to catch every tear.

When *Ammachi* finished, I looked up at *Amma*, and my eyes filled with tears once more. She smiled knowingly and engulfed me in her strong arms, an embrace joined by all those around us—those God brought into my life to care for me, and those for whom I could care.

Forsaken by my father and mother, the Lord took me in, and he provided abundantly.

This, I concluded with a heart overflowing, *this is my family. This is God's family.*

CULTURAL NOTE

Throughout this book, I tried to portray Hindu beliefs and Indian culture accurately. However, given the complexity and diversity of both Hinduism and Indian traditions, I acknowledge that my perspective—through western eyes—is limited, and any inaccuracies are unintentional.

Here is a brief overview of several key issues addressed in this story, and how Christianity brings hope in the face of them.

Caste System

The reality and impact of the *caste* system is often downplayed in India today. However, it still deeply shapes Indian society. Though the treatment of those in the lowest castes has improved, discrimination based on caste is still a common issue.

Caste is woven into the very fabric of Indian society. A person's *caste* is unchangeable; it is inherited from their parents and printed on identification documents. *Caste* dictates occupation, social status, who one marries, and where and how one lives. Indians will often accept their place in society (or *caste*) as their lot in life, which means they will not expect or even hope for any sort of pity, compassion, or social mobility. Rather, the only hope is future reincarnation that will reward them for the good they do in their present life.

Women & Widows

Some ancient Hindu sages taught that a soul with poor *karma* would become a female, born to serve males. In India, women are often treated as objects. High rates of rape, abduction, abuse, and aided suicide reflect this grim reality. Abandonment and beating of wives is common—and often considered justified by those who witness it or know about it.

Worse than abuse from a husband is the death of one. Widows are treated as walking curses, believed to bring bad luck wherever they go. Widows identify themselves by wearing white or dull-colored *saris* with no makeup or jewelry. They are expected to be silent and stay out of sight, especially during religious events, festivals, or weddings. They may lose their property or jobs. Because widows supposedly bring bad luck, many are rejected even by their own families.

Orphans & Abandoned Children

India has an estimated 20 million orphaned or foster children, in part due to the mistreatment of women. If a father leaves, the mother often must abandon her children to survive. Most government-run orphanages are overcrowded and underfunded, marked by abuse, poor hygiene, lack of nutrition, and emotional neglect. Because of this, many children run away, preferring life on the streets to the conditions inside.

Suicide

Teen suicides rates in India are alarmingly high—especially among girls, with ingesting poison being the most common method. *Dowry*-related shame is a frequent cause of suicide among adults.

Dowry

A *dowry* is property, money, or other gifts expected to be given by the bride's family to the groom's family as part of a marriage arrangement. Often a greedy groom's family will demand a *dowry* so costly that it can bankrupt and ruin a bride's family. The practice of *dowry* results in thousands of deaths each year in India. A bride and her family may be killed or commit suicide because of *dowry* disputes. The pressure begins before a girl is even born, as many poor families will abort girls to avoid future *dowry* burdens. Marriages between family members often involve a lower *dowry*, so cousin marriages are common (especially among poor families).

Child Marriage

Though child marriage has declined in recent years, it is still widespread. About 25% of women in India are married before turning eighteen, despite laws that forbid the practice. Parents may even remove their daughters from school, robbing them of basic education, just to teach them how to care for a home and then marry them off.

Christianity's Transformation

Missionaries to India brought not only the gospel, but also education, medicine, and social transformation. A man named William Carey is remembered for his translation work and his campaign to end *sati*, the ritual burning of widows with their dead husbands. Others, like the Scudder family, founded hospitals and schools that served people regardless of sex or *caste*. While Indian life in general has benefited greatly from these contributions, the root of the problems still exists. Thus, a true and lasting transformation will only come when hearts are changed by the gospel.

Christianity changes how we see people's worth. It teaches that everyone has dignity, no matter what *caste* they're born into. That promise brings hope and purpose to lives trapped by a system that says their future is already fixed. In Christian churches in India, all *castes* are meant to be equal. Yet even there, old *caste* ideas sometimes slip in— some congregations choose leaders only from higher *castes* and frown on marriages between people of different *castes*.

Christianity has also reshaped how women, widows, *dowry*, and life in general are viewed. Churches in India often have more women than men because they are safe, loving, and caring places for women that have been rejected by family and society. Christianity's rejection of materialism and value for all human life prevent issues related to *dowry* and abortion.

The majority of orphanages in India are run by Christian organizations because of the clear calling in scripture to care for orphans. These homes often offer much better care than government-run shelters, but in recent years, tens of thousands of Christian organizations have been forced to shut down. The most notable was Compassion International, which served foster children in India for 48 years before being shut down in 2017. It had provided nearly $45 million per year in aid.

With so many foster children in India, the potential for societal change is enormous. The Indian government has targeted Christian organizations because children raised in Christian homes often grow up to reject Hindu tradition and refuse to support radical Hindu politicians. Today, Christian organizations that still receive foreign funding are heavily monitored, and even minor infractions can lead to shutdowns.

Religion & the Reformed Church

India has over 1.4 billion people: about 80% are Hindu, 14% Muslim, 3% Christian, and a small percent follow other religions like Sikhism and Buddhism. Of the Christians, around 60% are Protestant, 33% Catholic, and 7% Orthodox.

In the mid-20th century, most of the Anglican, Methodist, Presbyterian, and Reformed churches merged into two denominations: the Church of North India (CNI), and the Church of South India (CSI). In the process, they lost their unique beliefs and practices, and Reformed theology faded significantly in India.

My hope is that this story doesn't simply shine a light on social ills in India, but that the light and hope of the gospel of peace in Jesus Christ alone shines through these pages. May God preserve his church in India and cause it to flourish, bringing those in the darkness of paganism into his marvelous light.

Soli Deo Gloria!

GLOSSARY

Akka – Elder sister

Amma – Mother

Ammachi – Grandmother

Anna – Elder brother

Appa – Father

Banyan – An Indian native tree whose branches droop down as roots that grow into new trunks, creating its own small interconnected forest.

Beedi – A cheap cigarette alternative made from tobacco hand-rolled in a leaf.

Bindi – A small mark or dot worn on the forehead between the eyebrows representing the "third eye"—the center of spiritual awareness and wisdom beyond the senses.

Biryani – A rice dish layered with spices and slow-cooked so all the flavors blend together.

Carrom – A tabletop game of Indian origin where players flick small wooden discs into corner pockets on a smooth board.

Caste – A social hierarchy in India that assigns people to groups. *Caste* is believed to be assigned from the gods based on *karma* from your previous lives. *Caste* is inherited from parents at birth and dictates occupation, social status, who one marries, and where and how one lives.

Chapati – A soft, round flatbread made from whole wheat flour, cooked on a hot griddle.

Chudidhar – A three-piece outfit worn by women, consisting of a long tunic, fitted pants, and a shawl.

Dalit – A member of the lowest class in the Indian Caste System.

Dholak – A traditional Indian wooden hand drum in a barrel shape with a head on each end. One head is pitched for bass and the other for treble.

Dowry – Property, money, or other gifts given by the bride's family to the groom's family as part of a marriage arrangement.

Karma – A belief that one's actions, good or bad, influence future outcomes, either in this life or in future *reincarnations*.

Karunai – Compassion, mercy, or grace

Lungi – A casual cloth, patterned or colored, wrapped around the waste by men during hot weather or relaxing at home.

Muhoortam – "auspicious," divinely chosen days determined by astrology for special events like weddings, engagements, and other ceremonies.

Pacheta – A game that involves throwing one stone in the air and picking up the others before catching the falling stone again.

Puri – A small, round, Indian bread made from wheat flour, rolled thin and deep-fried until it puffs up.

Qualis – The model name of a Toyota-made SUV with a boxy shape and 10 seats (which means it fits over 20 people in India).

Reincarnation – the belief that after death, a person's soul is reborn into a new body—human, animal, or other spiritual being—based on their *karma* from previous lives.

Rupees – Indian money

Sagotharan – Brother in faith

Sagothari – Sister in faith

Sari – A long, unstitched piece of cloth draped around the body and over the shoulder, worn by women across India as traditional dress.

Thaipoosam – A Hindu festival in which people often carry heavy burdens and pierce their bodies while seeking forgiveness and purification.

Thambi – Little brother

Thangachi – Little sister

Tuk-tuk – A three-wheeled motor vehicle with open sides, used as taxis in India to carry people short distances. They are also referred to as an auto or rickshaw.

Veshti – A long piece of unstitched white cloth worn by men around the waist and legs for formal or religious occasions.

Our Mission

To glorify God by making accessible to the broadest possible audience material that testifies to the truth of Scripture as understood and developed in the Reformed tradition.

Reformed Free Publishing Association
1894 Georgetown Center Drive, Jenison, MI 49428-7137
Website: rfpa.org
E-mail: mail@rfpa.org
Phone: 616-457-5970

www.ingramcontent.com/pod-product-compliance
Lightning Source LLC
Chambersburg PA
CBHW020433030726
47495CB00006B/1777